RANDOM HOUSE

LARGE PRINT

Praise for Dave Eggers's
THE EVERY

"At once sharply satirical and bighearted, darkly comic and profoundly serious, **The Every** is a novel for our time."   —Elizabeth Kolbert,
author of **Under a White Sky**

"[A] great-grandchild of Zamyatin's **We,** but now the 'perfect society' is Silicon Valley. Be careful what you wish for!"   —Margaret Atwood,
author of **The Handmaid's Tale,** via Twitter

"**The Every** is a brilliant exploration of the American obsession with efficiency that will also make you laugh until you cry. With a unique eye for the absurd, Eggers ultimately illuminates how human beings cannot be reduced to algorithms unless we allow ourselves to be. Dazzling and essential."
—Allison Stanger, Leng Professor of International Politics and Economics, Middlebury College;
External Professor, Santa Fe Institute

"Unforgettable. With brilliant humor and enormous suspense, **The Every** examines how technology is indelibly redefining what it means to be human, and how it already has."   —Van Jones,
author of **Beyond the Messy Truth**

"Eggers proposes an uncanny world on the border between the impossible to imagine and the already in play. Every reader is implicated. We are all members of that passive army willing to trade freedom for convenience. As digital culture blossomed, people wondered if machines could be made to think like people. The more compelling question is the one Eggers poses in **The Every:** Are people content to become machines?" —Sherry Turkle, author of **The Empathy Diaries**

"I don't know what's more frightening: Dave Eggers's relentlessly inventive worldbuilding of a pseudo-virtuous surveillance economy run monopolistically amok or that his near-future dystopian satire may be a more naturalistic rendering of our present than we'd like to admit. Novels like **The Every**—equal parts comic entertainment and ominous explication—are one of our best means of resisting the dehumanizing seductions all around us and imagining a better world." —Teddy Wayne, author of **Apartment**

"Goddamn, it's real good." —Emerson Whitney, author of **Heaven**

THE
EVERY

THE
EVERY

or

AT LAST
A SENSE
OF ORDER

or

THE FINAL DAYS
OF FREE WILL

or

LIMITLESS
CHOICE
IS KILLING
THE WORLD

DAVE EGGERS

R A N D O M   H O U S E
L A R G E   P R I N T

Cover design by Eve Weinsheimer
The secretly disturbing Every logo was designed by Jessica Hische.

The Library of Congress has established a Cataloging-in-Publication record for this title.

ISBN: 978-0-593-50134-4

www.penguinrandomhouse.com/large-print-format-books

FIRST LARGE PRINT EDITION

Printed in the United States of America

1st Printing

This Large Print edition published in accord with the standards of the N.A.V.H.

For V

"Give the people a new word, and they think
they have a new fact."
—Willa Cather

"If at first the idea is not absurd,
then there is no hope for it."
—Albert Einstein

"Is there not also, perhaps, besides the innate desire
for freedom, an instinctive wish for submission?"
—Erich Fromm

CHAPTERS
WITH READING TIME (APPROX), MATCH % (EXACT), AND AGGREGATE READER SCORE

I	12 min read	88% match	Score: 86.67
II	11 min read	81% match	Score: 82.18
III	14 min read	67% match	Score: 89.22
IV	66 min read	97% match	Score: 61.34
V	81 min read	91% match	Score: 71.45
VI	09 min read	34% match	Score: 78.91
VII	23 min read	55% match	Score: 98.33
VIII	45 min read	28% match	Score: 90.12
IX	78 min read	13% match	Score: 76.89
X	91 min read	76% match	Score: 45.87
XI	10 min read	92% match	Score: 41.45
XII	10 min read	83% match	Score: 09.18

XIII	10 min read	89% match	Score: 14.66
XIV	13 min read	44% match	Score: 56.86
XV	32 min read	67% match	Score: 42.81
XVI	23 min read	33% match	Score: 93.87
XVII	92 min read	39% match	Score: 91.65
XVIII	64 min read	46% match	Score: 84.02
XIX	32 min read	53% match	Score: 86.43
XX	11 min read	94% match	Score: 88.12
XXI	07 min read	63% match	Score: 90.22
XXII	01 min read	78% match	Score: 81.33
XXIII	88 min read	75% match	Score: 44.63
XXIV	76 min read	84% match	Score: 58.04
XXV	07 min	18% match	Score: 01.54
XXVI	12 min	23% match	Score: 34.87
XXVII	09 min	98% match	Score: 81.77
XXVIII	11 min	91% match	Score: 86.08
XXIX	41 min	67% match	Score: 45.68
XXX	34 min	34% match	Score: 90.67
XXXI	23 min	37% match	Score: 45.67
XXXII	07 min	66% match	Score: 76.01
XXXIII	08 min	61% match	Score: 26.17
XXXIV	76 min	74% match	Score: 88.60
XXXV	44 min	71% match	Score: 81.41
XXXVI	22 min	80% match	Score: 99.67
XXXVII	18 min	76% match	Score: 82.27
XXXVIII	12 min	23% match	Score: 80.98
XXXIX	56 min	11% match	Score: 76.01
XL	12 min	65% match	Score: 86.67
XLI	09 min	88% match	Score: 67.02
XLII	22 min	91% match	Score: 81.98
XLIII	17 min	02% match	Score: 34.92
XLIV	23 min	76% match	Score: 90.02
XLV	11 min	81% match	Score: 88.91
Acks	14 min	76% match	Score: 75.81
Note A	10 min	51% match	Score: N/A
Note B	88 min	67% match	Score: 100.91

NOTE: This story takes place in the near future. Don't try to work out when. Any anachronisms of time and physics occur on purpose. All errors pertaining to technology, chronology or judgment are intentional and exist to serve you better.

THE
EVERY

I.

DELANEY EMERGED from the dim subway and into a world of sterling light. The day was clear, and the sun struck the Bay's numberless waves and threw golden sparks everywhere. Delaney turned away from the water and walked the hundred feet to the Every campus. This alone—taking the subway, making her way to the gate unaccompanied, without a vehicle—made her an anomaly and confused the gate's two guards standing in their booth. Their domain was glass, pyramidal, like the tip of a crystalline obelisk.

"You **walked** here?" asked one of the guards. ROWENA, by her badge, was maybe thirty, raven-haired and dressed in a crisp yellow top, snug like a bicycle bib. She smiled, revealing an endearing gap between her two front teeth.

Delaney provided her name, and said that she had an interview with Dan Faraday.

"Finger, please?" Rowena asked.

Delaney put her thumb on the scanner and a grid of photos, videos and data appeared on Rowena's screen. There were pictures of Delaney she hadn't seen herself—was that a gas station in Montana? In the full-body shots, she was slouching, the burden of her too-tall teenhood. Standing by the booth, Delaney straightened her posture as her eyes wandered over images of her in her Park Ranger uniform, at a mall in Palo Alto, riding a bus in what looked to be Twin Peaks.

"You grew your hair out," Rowena said. "Still short, though."

Delaney reflexively ran her fingers through her thick black bob.

"Says your eyes are green," Rowena said. "They look brown. Can you get closer?" Delaney got closer. "Ah! Pretty," Rowena said. "I'll call Dan."

While Rowena was contacting Faraday, another snafu occupied the second guard, a gaunt and sullen man of about fifty. A white van had pulled up, and the driver, a red-bearded man sitting high above the guards' window, explained that he had a delivery.

"Delivery of what?" the gaunt guard asked.

The driver briefly turned his head toward the back of the van, as if to be sure of his impending description. "It's a bunch of baskets. Gift baskets. Stuffed animals, chocolate, that kind of thing," he said.

Now Rowena, whom Delaney assumed was the

alpha of the glass obelisk, took over. "How many baskets?" she asked.

"I don't know. About twenty," the driver said.

"And is anyone expecting these?" Rowena asked.

"I don't know. I think it's for potential clients maybe?" the driver said, a sudden exhaustion in his voice. This was evidently a conversation already far longer than what he was accustomed to. "I think these are just gifts for some people that work here," he said, and reached to the passenger seat, where he found a tablet and tapped it a few times. "It says these are for Regina Martinez and the Initiative K Team."

"And who is the sender?" Rowena asked. Her tone, now, was almost amused. It was clear, to Delaney at least, that this particular delivery would not be consummated.

Again the driver consulted his tablet. "It says the sender is something called MDS. Just M-D-S." Now the driver's voice had, too, taken on a fatalistic tone. Would it matter, he seemed to wonder, if he even knew what MDS stood for?

Rowena's face softened. She murmured into a microphone, apparently speaking to a different security phalanx within the Every. "Never mind. I've got it. It's a turnaround." She tilted her head sympathetically to the driver. "You can turn around just up here." She pointed to a cul-de-sac fifteen yards ahead.

"So I drop the baskets there?" the driver asked.

Rowena smiled again. "Oh no. We won't be accepting your . . ."—the pause seemed meant to allow sufficient venom to accumulate for the next, heretofore benign, word—"baskets."

The driver raised his hands to heaven. "I've been delivering for twenty-two years and no one's ever refused delivery." He looked to Delaney, who was still standing next to the booth, as if he might find in her a potential ally. She averted her eyes, resting them upon the campus's tallest building, an aluminum-clad corkscrew tower that housed Algo Mas, the company's algorithm thinktank.

"First of all," Rowena explained, clearly uninterested in the driver's history of successful delivery, "your cargo doesn't meet security thresholds. We'd have to X-ray every one of your . . ."—again she hissed the word—"**baskets,** and we aren't prepared to do that. Secondly, the company has a policy whereby we don't bring unsustainable or improperly sourced goods onto campus. My guess is that those **baskets**"—somehow she'd made it an epithet—"contain extensive plastic packaging? And processed foods? And factory-farmed fruit without organic or fair-trade certification, all of it no doubt covered with pesticides? Are there nuts in these"—still more venom—"**baskets**? I'm assuming so, and this campus is nut-free. And you said something about stuffed animals? There's no way I could let you bring cheap non-biodegradable toys onto campus."

"You don't accept **non-biodegradable toys**?" the driver asked. He had his meaty palm against the dashboard now, as if bracing himself against collapse.

Rowena exhaled loudly. "Sir, I've got a few cars behind you now. You can turn around just past the booth." She pointed to the roundabout that was no doubt busy all day with people, trucks and goods, unwanted by the Every, returning to the unexamined world. The driver stared long at Rowena, and finally put his van into gear and rolled toward the turnaround.

The scene was odd in so many ways, Delaney thought. A non-Every delivery driver in the first place. Five years earlier, the Circle had bought an ecommerce behemoth named after a South American jungle, and the acquisition created the richest company the world had ever known. The subsummation necessitated the Circle changing its name to the Every, which seemed to its founders definitive and inevitable, hinting as it did at ubiquity and equality. The ecommerce giant, too, was happy for a new start. The once-rational, once-dependable online marketplace had been allowed to devolve into a chaotic wasteland of shady vendors, product knockoffs and outright fraud. The company had ceded all control and responsibility, and customers began to peel off; no one loved being cheated or deceived. By the time the site course-corrected, they'd lost the trust of a fickle public. The Circle engineered a stock takeover, and the site's founder, increasingly distracted by divorces and lawsuits, was only too happy to cash out and devote his time to space exploration with his fourth spouse. They were planning to retire on the Moon.

After the acquisition, a new logo was conjured. Essentially it was three waves crashing around a perfect circle, and hinted at the flow of water, the bursting of new ideas, of interconnectivity, at infinity. Successful or not, it improved upon the Circle's previous logo, which implied a manhole cover, and easily beat the longtime logo of the ecommerce behemoth, which was an insincere smirk. Because the negotiations had been fraught and finally unfriendly, now that the merger was complete, it was unwise to use the ecommerce company's previous name on campus; if it was mentioned at all, it was referred to as **the jungle,** lowercase j intentional.

The Circle had been in nearby San Vincenzo since its inception, but a fortuitous confluence of events brought them to Treasure Island, largely manmade, in the middle of San Francisco Bay—extending from a real island called Yerba Buena. This new landmass was built in 1938, the intended home of a new airport. When WWII broke out, it was converted to a military base, and in the decades since, its patchwork of airplane hangars were slowly converted to maker spaces, wineries, and affordable housing—all with breathtaking views of the Bay, the bridges, the East Bay hills. No developers would touch it, though, given the unknown military (and presumed toxic) waste buried under its abundant concrete. But in the 2010s, speculators finally worked out the mitigation, and glorious plans were drawn up. A new waterport was built, a new subway stop was added, and a four-foot wall was erected around the perimeter for the next few decades' expected sea-level rise. Then the pandemics struck, capital dried up, and the island was there for the taking. The only catch was California law dictated that access to the waterfront be public. The Every fought this quietly, then publicly, but ultimately lost, and a shoreline perimeter path around the island remained available to anyone who could get there.

"Delaney Wells?"

Delaney spun left to find a man in his early forties standing before her. His head was shaved, and his large brown eyes were magnified by rimless glasses. The collar of his black, zippered shirt was positioned upward, his legs smothered in snug green denim.

"Dan?" she asked.

After the pandemics, handshakes were medically fraught—and, many thought, aggressive—but no one substitute-greeting had been agreed upon. Dan chose to tip an imaginary top hat in Delaney's direction. Delaney offered a brief bow.

"Should we walk?" he asked, and slipped past her, through the gate. He strolled not into campus but out into the island's perimeter sidewalk.

Delaney followed. She had heard this was the way of most first interviews at the Every. With humans as with non-biodegradable toys, the Every did not want the unscreened, the unchosen, risking the infection of the campus. Each new person presented a security risk of one kind or another, and given that interviewees like Delaney had no clearances and had not been vetted in any thorough way—not beyond nine or so cursory AI screenings—it was best to conduct the first interview off-campus. But this was not what Dan said.

"I need to get my steps in," he said instead, pointing to his oval, a ubiquitous bracelet able to track myriad health metrics, made by the Every and required by all insurers and most governments.

"Me too," Delaney said, and pointed to her own oval, which she loathed with molten fury but which was integral to her disguise.

Dan Faraday smiled. Every candidate, Delaney was sure, came wearing all possible Every products. It was not pandering. It was an obligatory ante before the game began. Dan motioned Delaney to cross the street, entering the public promenade.

Forgive me, Delaney thought. **Everything from here on out is lies.**

II.

For now, Delaney's task was to charm Dan Faraday so outrageously that he recommended her for a second, more thorough interview. There would be at least three after that. Some Every employees, she'd heard, had been interviewed twelve times over six months before being hired.

"We can talk and look around," Dan said, his eyes amiable, reasonable, seeming incapable of anything but calm deliberation. "If you see some food or beverage you want along the way, we can stop and sit."

The tiny neighborhood around the Every campus, a string of ostensibly private-sector businesses catering to tourists there for the view, had the look of a hastily assembled film set. There was a dimly lit architectural firm devoid of people, and brightly decorated but depopulated pastry shops and vegan ice cream parlors. The streets were largely empty but for the occasional pair of people looking precisely like Delaney and Dan: actual staff member—or Everyone—interviewing potential employee, or Everyoneabee.

Delaney, rarely nervous, was rattled. She'd spent years assiduously building her profile, her digital self, with meticulous care, but there were so many things she couldn't know if they knew. More pressingly, on the way to the campus, Delaney had been shammed. On the subway platform, she'd dropped a wrapper, and before she could pick it up, an older woman with a phone had filmed the crime. Like a growing majority of tech innovations, the invention and proliferation of Samaritan, an app standard on Everyphones, was driven by a mixture of benign utopianism and pseudofascist behavioral compliance. A million shams—a bastard mash of **Samaritan** and **shame**—were posted each day, exposing swervy drivers, loud gym grunters, Louvre line-cutters, single-use-plastic-users, and blithe allowers of infants-crying-in-public. Getting shammed was not the problem. The problem was if you got ID'd and tagged, and if the video got widely shared, commented on, and tipped your Shame Aggregate to unacceptable levels. Then it could follow you for life.

"First of all, congratulations on being here," Dan said. "Only three percent of applicants make it this far. As you can imagine, the AI screenings are very rigorous."

"Absolutely," Delaney said, and winced. **Absolutely?**

"I was impressed by your résumé, and personally appreciate that you were a libarts major," Dan said. **Libarts.** Dan had either invented this or was trying to popularize it. As if unsure how it was going over, he pinched the end of his shirt-zipper. "As you know, we hire just as many libarts majors as we do engineers. Anything to propagate new ideas." He let go of his shirt-zipper. It seemed to be his way of holding his breath. As he formed and uttered a sentence, he held the zipper; if it came out okay, he relaxed and let it go.

Delaney knew about the Every's openness to non-engineers, and relied upon it. Still, she'd gone to great lengths to make herself uniquely appealing even among that math-weak category.

Two years ago, Delaney had moved to California and had worked for a startup—Ol Factory, it was called—whose mission was to bring smells into gaming. Their most successful release, **Stench of War!,** brought the smells of diesel, dust and decaying flesh into the homes of teen boys worldwide. She assumed that Ol Factory was plumping itself for Every acquisition, and she was proved correct when that deal was finalized, eighteen months after she joined. The founders, Vijay and Martin, were brought to the Every and given nothing to do. Delaney, being relatively new to Ol Factory, was not automatically brought with the acquisition, but Vijay and Martin were determined to get Every interviews for anyone at Ol Factory who wanted one.

"Your background and point of view, actually, are just what we look for," Dan said. "You're disobedient, and we strive to be, too." **Disobedient** was a recently favored word, replacing **mutinous,** which had replaced **insurgent,** which had replaced **disruption/disruptor.** Dan had the zipper in his fingers again. It was as if he wanted to unzip it completely, to break out of this shirt, like a child chafing at an itchy sweater. The sentence having cleared his internal censor, he let it go.

They passed a shop that purported to sell hardware, and was full of hardware, beautifully arranged, but free of customers or staff.

"I've always admired that about the Every," Delaney said. "You planted your flag on Titan while everyone else was contemplating the Moon."

Dan turned his head to her and Delaney knew the combination had landed. His eyes were warm and admiring, and then they narrowed, signaling a transition to more serious terrain.

"We read your paper," he said.

Delaney's face burned for a moment. Though her thesis was the centerpiece to her candidacy, and, she was sure, much of the reason she'd been granted an interview, she hadn't expected to get into it so quickly. She'd assumed this first interview was simply a sanity check.

She'd written her college thesis on the folly of antitrust actions against the Circle, given whether or not it was a monopoly was immaterial if that's what the people wanted. She coined the term **Benevolent Market Mastery** for the seamless symbiosis between company and customer, a consumer's perfect state of being, where all desires were served efficiently and at the lowest price. Fighting such a thing was against the will of the people, and if regulators were at odds with what the people wanted, what was the point? She posited that if a company knows all and knows best, shouldn't they be allowed to improve our lives, unimpeded? She made sure the paper was disseminated online. It had been mentioned, she came to know, on various internal Every staff threads and had been referred to, briefly but significantly, in a rare EU ruling that went the Every's way.

"The salient points in what you wrote were discussed a lot around here," Dan said. He'd stopped walking. Delaney marveled at how quickly her armpits could become dank swamps. "You articulated things that of course we believed to be true, but we'd been unable to get the ideas across effectively."

Delaney smiled. The Every was the company most crucial to the dissemination of the world's ideas—in the form of words and audio and video and memes—and yet the company had absolutely no clue how to explain itself to governments, regulators and critics. The Every's leadership, especially since the forced semi-retirement of Eamon Bailey, erstwhile barker and evangelist, was perpetually tone-deaf, arrogant, and occasionally outright offensive. They had never seemed sorry for any regulatory crime, nor chastened by any misery-causing use of their products. The Circle had disseminated hate a million times a day, causing untold suffering and death; they had facilitated the degradation of democracy worldwide. In response, they formed committees to discuss the problem. They tweaked algorithms. They banned a few high-profile hatemongers and added poorly paid moderators in Bangladesh.

"The way you framed the antitrust struggles we've had," Dan continued, "through the lens of history—it was very enlightening, even for someone like me, and I've been here since the beginning." His voice had gone wistful. "You have a very fine mind, and that's what we solve for here."

"Thank you," Delaney said, and smiled to herself. **Solve for.**

"How was it received by your thesis advisor?" Dan asked.

She thought of her professor, Meena Agarwal, with a stab of regret. Delaney had taken Agarwal's course, "Free Things > Free Will," her sophomore year, and had fallen boundlessly under Agarwal's influence, coming to believe that the Circle was not only a monopoly but also the most reckless and dangerous corporate entity ever conjured—and an existential threat to all that was untamed and interesting about the human species.

Two years later, when Delaney asked Agarwal to advise her thesis, she readily agreed, but was shocked when Delaney turned in a 77-page treatise on the anti-entrepreneurial folly of regulating the Circle. Agarwal had given Delaney an A. "I grant you this grade for the rigor of the argument and research here," Agarwal wrote, "but with profound moral reservations about your conclusions."

"I did well," Delaney said.

Dan smiled. "Good. There's still **some** respect for intellectual independence in academia."

Delaney and Dan turned a corner and almost ran into another first interview in progress. A stylish young Everyone was walking with a man who appeared to be at least fifty but was trying frantically to look more vibrant and necessary than his age might imply. His glasses were orange-framed, his button-down black and shiny, his sneakers new and electric green. His interviewer was a lean young woman in silver leggings, and Delaney was sure she saw the woman's eyes meet Dan's and open wide for a microsecond in mocking distress. Dan gave her a tip of his imaginary top hat.

"We're committed to hiring without regard to age," Dan said, and Delaney wondered if he saw her, at thirty-two, as fulfilling a kind of anti-ageist

quota. "Older candidates have so much life experience to draw from," he said, and swept his
eyes across Delaney's shoulders, as if she kept her
wisdom there.

"Shall we?" he said, and guided Delaney toward
a playground, designed by Yayoi Kusama and paid
for by the Every. **Adults welcome!** a sign said, and
then, below and in parentheses: **If accompanied by
a child.** Delaney glanced at the small print, which
emphasized the importance of Play (always capitalized) in the creative life of adults.

Capital-P Play was last year's management theory,
following multitasking, singletasking, grit, learning-
from-failure, napping, cardioworking, saying no,
saying yes, the wisdom of the crowd > trusting one's
gut, trusting one's gut > the wisdom of the crowd,
Viking management theory, Commissioner Gordon
workflow theory, X-teams, B-teams, embracing simplicity, pursuing complexity, seeking zemblanity,
creativity through radical individualism, creativity
through groupthink, creativity through the rejection
of groupthink, organizational mindfulness, organizational blindness, microwork, macrosloth, fear-
based camaraderie, love-based terror, working while
standing, working while ambulatory, learning while
sleeping, and, most recently, limes.

"How were things at Ol Factory?" Dan asked, sitting on an enormous rubber mushroom. Delaney
sat opposite him, on a llama made of recycled
plastic fibers.

Delaney knew that the easiest mistake she could make now would be to criticize her former bosses. "It was outstanding," she said. **Outstanding,** she'd heard, was a word beloved at the Every. "They treated me well. I learned a world every day." **Learned a world.** She'd never uttered this phrase before. But when she glanced at Dan, he seemed to approve.

"I liked that acquisition," Dan said. "The numbers were big but the talent was . . ." Delaney was sure he normally would have said **outstanding,** but she'd stolen the word. He found an alternative: ". . . stellar. What did you think of the acquisition price?"

"Talent is expensive," she said, and he smiled. It was the only right answer, because there was no logic to the numbers. The Every had bought Ol Factory, a three-year-old company with twenty-two full-time employees and no profit, for just shy of two billion dollars.

"Well put," Dan said.

There did not seem to be a point in any purchase, for any tech buyer or seller, unless the price was a billion dollars. Delaney had paid attention to Ol Factory's revenues, and was unaware of any incoming funds that exceeded $23 million in the totality of the company's existence. And yet the price the Every paid to purchase the company was $1.9 billion. This was much like the unprofitable headphone company that went for $1 billion, and the unprofitable VR firm that went for $2.8 billion, and the unprofitable nonviolent gaming firm that went for $3.4. The numbers seemed based on little more than the roundness of the figure and a wonderful logic loop: if you paid a billion, it was worth a billion—a bold notion unburdened by a thousand years of business accounting.

"I haven't met Vijay and Martin," Dan said. He was swaying now, and Delaney realized that his mushroom had a flexible stalk. She wondered if her llama might be similarly malleable. She tried. It wasn't.

"I believe they're in the Romantic Period," he said, waving a hand in the general direction of the campus. Somewhere in there, Vijay and Martin were installed. She liked them a great deal, and assumed they were now miserable, as were every team of founders-who'd-sold-out, and would be for the five years they'd agreed to stay while vesting, after which they would peel off and start family foundations.

But the billion-dollar acquisitions kept the world of tech alive and dreaming, and the smartest entrepreneurs were those who recognized that preparing oneself for Every acquisition was far easier, and far more logical, than either staying private and trying to make a profit—Sisyphean madness—or going the treacherous and unpredictable route of an IPO.

"I know your title changed a few times, so can you talk about your role at Ol Factory? Doesn't have to be linear," Dan asked. "Can I?" He stood up and

indicated he wanted to switch to Delaney's llama.
Delaney left her llama and took his mushroom-seat.

"It was amorphous," she said, and saw a flash
of admiration animate Dan's eyes. Another word
he liked. He was easy, she realized. For years, the
Every, through its auto-fill algorithms, had squeezed
out thousands of words, favoring the most-likely
over the lesser-used, and this had had the unexpected effect of rendering wide swaths of the
English language nearly obsolete. When a word like
amorphous was used, the ear of an Everyone was
surprised, as if hearing an almost-familiar song from
a largely lost time.

Delaney laid out her employment history at
Ol Factory. She'd come in as an executive assistant,
more or less, and for a while after that was called
Office Manager, though the job was always the same
in that it encompassed everything. She arranged for
the snacks and lunches. She arranged for the maintenance of the offices, kept everyone fed, hired and
directed the gardeners. She put on every event, from
brown-bag office meetings to Presidio retreats to
Martin's wedding on the peak of Mt. Tamalpais (for
which she'd had to hire a team of paragliders willing to fly in tuxedos). She explained all this to Dan,
with total honesty but hoping to impress upon him
that she did not want to plan parties and handle catering at the Every.

"I did do some of the interviews for new staff,"
she noted. "Just the initial sanity checks." She

smiled knowingly at Dan, hoping he would appreciate this attempt at connecting tasks common to them both.

He smiled back, but perfunctorily. She'd hit a nerve. And she'd hit nerves before. The Everyones she'd met, six or seven of them at bars or dinners, were invariably normal humans, every one of them idealistic and very often brilliant in some way, and most of them capable of candor about their work and lives. But there was, with each of them, a line that was not crossed. She would be chatting amiably with them for twenty minutes about the many questionable or ridiculous aspects of life within the Every, or its occasionally positive but usually disastrous impact on the world, and just when Delaney felt that this Everyone was free to say and think as they pleased, some subject, some sentence, would go too far, and this new Every-friend would retreat to a more formal, defensive posture. The word **monopoly** was not spoken. **Kool-Aid** was not said. Any comparison, even in drunken jest, between Jim Jones, or David Koresh, or Keith Raniere, and Eamon Bailey—the Circle's co-founder—was considered in poor taste and not remotely apt. The mention of Stenton, another of the company's Three Wise Men, who had left the Every to form an unholy alliance with a public-private company in China, soured any conversation beyond repair. Knowing what to say about Mae Holland, now the Every's CEO, was hard to know.

Mae had begun, ten years ago, in the Circle's customer service department, soon becoming one of the company's first fully transparent staffers, streaming her days and nights, and because she was utterly loyal to the company, and also young and attractive and reasonably charismatic, she rose through the ranks with startling speed. Her detractors found her dull and exasperatingly careful. Her fans—far greater in number—considered her mindful, respectfully ambitious, inclusive. Both sides, though, agreed on one thing: she hadn't brought a significant new idea to the company in all her years there. Even after the merger with the jungle, she seemed perplexed with what it all meant and how the companies might be threaded together for maximum benefit.

"Ol Factory was how many people?" Dan asked.

Delaney knew Dan knew this number, and that if she herself didn't know the exact number of employees, it would paint her as either someone who didn't care about her fellow staffers, or as someone who couldn't count.

"Twenty-two and a half," she said. "There was one new dad who was working part-time when we were acquired."

"They had a good life-balance there, do you think?" Dan asked. He was pulling on his shirt-zipper again.

Delaney told him about the many days they took lunches outside, the thrice-yearly retreats (which she planned), the one warm Friday in June when Vijay and Martin sent everyone to the beach in Pacifica.

"I like that," Dan said. "But given you started at such a small place, do you think you'd like working at a much larger company like the Every? We're looking for a certain degree of absorbability."

"I do," she said. **Absorbability.**

There had been nineteen suicides on this Every campus in the last three years, mirroring a global uptick, and no one wanted to talk about them—chiefly because no one at the Every seemed to know why, or how to stop them. Even the number nineteen was debatable, for there was no local news, there were no journalists—all of that wiped out by social media, the advertising apocalypse and, more than anything else, the war on subjectivity—so any knowledge of the deaths at all was pieced together from rumor and quickly muffled accounts by those on the Bay who'd seen a body here or there washed ashore. That was one of the ways Everyones often chose—they threw themselves to the sea rising all around them.

"I have to admit," Delaney said, "I had a feeling that Ol Factory might be acquired sooner or later, so I've had time to think about coming here. Not that I would presume to be hired. But I have had time to ponder it, and savor the prospect."

Delaney's purpose in joining the Every was to kill it. She'd waited years for the chance to work at the company, to enter the system with the intent of

destroying it. Her college paper had been the beginning of her on-again, off-again subterfuge. Even
then she knew she'd need to appear to them an ally,
a confrere they could welcome inside the gates.
Once inside, Delaney planned to examine the machine, test for weaknesses, and blow the place up.
She would Snowden it, Manning it. She would feel
it out and Felt it. She did not care if she did it in the
civilized, covert, information-dump sort of way her
predecessors practiced, or through a more frontal assault. She intended to harm no one, never to graze
a physical hair on a physical head, but somehow
she would end the Every, finish its malignant reign
on earth.

Dan dismounted his llama and checked his oval
again. He began to jog in place, picking up the
pace until he was a blurry mess of knees and fists.
This went on for two minutes, no more, at which
point a celebratory sound came from his oval, and
he stopped.

"Sorry," he said to Delaney, panting. "It's a promise I made to my wife. It's why I went vegan, and
why I have to do cardio when the oval says it's opti-
mal. She died last year."

"Oh God. I'm so sorry," Delaney said.

"Have you gotten an MRI recently?" Dan
asked her.

She hadn't. Dan had pulled up his sleeve, revealing his phone, attached to his forearm, a popular
new style. He scrolled through what seemed to be

thousands of videos of the same woman in a home with blond floors, in a hammock on a verdant slope, kneeling in a rose garden. She looked far too young to be gone.

"This is Adira," he said, as the thumbnails sped by. He seemed to be trying to decide which one to show Delaney, a person whom he had just met. "She was already Stage 4 when they found the tumor," he said, and looked up at the Bay Bridge, at a tiny car catching the light as it sped silently westward. "Anyway. She made me promise I'd stay ahead of things, health-wise. I urge you to do so, too."

"I will," Delaney said, utterly blindsided. Dan, she was certain, actually cared about her and her health, and this felt like a cruel trick.

He continued scrolling. Delaney prayed he would not choose a video, that he would not ask her to watch it. But he did.

"She was a big runner," he said, and Adira came alive on the screen. She had just finished a race, and was standing with her arms folded over her head, pacing, smiling, with the number 544 pinned to her tanktop. Delaney hoped she wouldn't have to hear Adira's voice.

"Sorry," Dan said, and turned up the volume.

"Did I just do that?" Adira asked, heaving, smiling.

"You did," an offscreen voice said. It was Dan's. He sounded so proud. "You did it, my sweet," and the footage ended.

Dan's finger tapped the screen and scrolled again, looking for more moments in Adira's life to show. He seemed to have everything there, all of Adira, in the phone strapped to his arm, and Delaney stood next to him, watching him search and search for more.

III.

"I CAN'T DO IT," Delaney said.

"Why?" Wes said. "Because his wife died?"

"Yes. Among other things."

"Did he ask if you rowed crew?"

People did this often. It was something about her height, her shoulders. People asked about crew, volleyball, sometimes basketball. She was at least four inches taller than Wes, a fact that didn't seem to bother him, or even cross his mind. He'd never mentioned it.

"No," Delaney said. "It's just that he was normal. A normal person. I didn't see that coming."

"We talked about that eventuality. That you might like people there," Wes said. "Are you dressed?"

Wes Makazian stood at the door, wiry and angular and bow-legged, and with his dust-colored hair—really a tumbleweed—he brought to mind a nineteenth-century cattle rustler. His eyes were small and bright, his mouth and teeth comically oversized; when he smiled, he looked like a small but happy whale.

"See me?" he said. "I'm dressed."

In life generally, Wes preferred not to wear long pants, or shoes, and spent most days—weeks—in drawstring shorts celebrating the Utah Jazz, a team for which he had no allegiance. He'd found a T-shirt he liked, too, bearing the face of Olof Palme, assassinated leader of Sweden, and because the dead man's face obscured Wes's toddler-tummy, he bought eight of them, and was rarely seen in anything else.

"Is it cold out?" Delaney asked.

"Is it cold out," Wes repeated. He had a hoodie on under his Palme shirt. Wes, and Olof, turned to the dog. "She lives by Ocean Beach and she asked if it's cold out."

Hurricane, Wes's middle-aged dog, looked up at Delaney, his eyes pleading. Delaney could get ready in minutes, but Wes and Hurricane were never not ready. Delaney grabbed a sweater and pushed her head through.

"Please don't put on the sneakers," Wes said.

Watching her lace up her shoes filled Wes, and even more so Hurricane, with spiraling woe. As she began, Wes turned away and Hurricane danced in circles, his claws clicking like tap shoes on the whitewashed floors.

"What about sandals?" he asked. "Or velcro?"

Delaney skipped the double knot she usually applied to each shoe.

"Happy?" she asked.

They pulled the door closed and passed the window of the main house. Wes's mother, Gwen, was in the kitchen, doing someone's taxes. She didn't look up.

Wes and Delaney lived by the Pacific in a tiny backyard unit they called the Sea Shed. The Bay Area had become a comically unaffordable place, with landlords throwing ludicrous rent numbers into the air, each ask a call almost always answered by new and naive money. But here and there, vestiges of the old San Francisco could still be found—odd attic units, converted garages, windswept cottages in the backyards of aging hippies refusing to gouge young tenants. Delaney had found such a place deep in the Outer Sunset. Near the Doelger Fish Co and smelling profoundly of it, the cottage came complete with furniture, a washer-dryer, and a thirty-six-year-old man named Wes. The main house was owned by Wes's mother and her wife Ursula. "I live with my moms," he told her before she moved in—a line she'd heard him deliver a hundred times since.

As the driveway met the street, Gwen hailed them from the front door. "Lemonade, please," she yelled. A homemade lemonade vendor had recently set up near the beach. He would be chased out by

health officials soon enough, but until then the
moms always asked Wes to bring some back. Gwen
waved to Delaney.

"Don't," Wes said.

"Hi Gwen!" Delaney said.

"Keep walking," he said. "We'll be here for an
hour. Hi Mom!"

Delaney got along brilliantly with Gwen and
Ursula, but they didn't know what to make of her.
They were awake to unseen narratives, so they were
disinclined to believe her relationship with Wes was
chaste. They nodded gamely when told she and Wes
were only friends, but they believed something else.
They trusted few people and fewer systems. That's
why they lived in a trog house, and why Gwen saw
her work as a tax accountant as a form of social protest; her clients all paid their fair share.

Rose, the mail carrier, appeared. Delaney said
hello and moved on; she knew Rose and Gwen
would forget entirely about the mail and talk about
their gardens. This, this needless chatting while on
duty, was the kind of thing—there were so many
things—that drove anti-trogs over the edge. The
inefficiency, the opacity, the waste. Nothing was as
wasteful and nonsensical to them as the post office.
All that paper. All that money lost, so many tens
of thousands of unnecessary jobs, trucks, planes,
dead trees, carbon. After she killed the use of cash
currency, and all paper and paper products (she'd
bought a dozen paper mills so far, just to shut them

down), it was Mae Holland's mission to end the post office, the sacred cow of all things trog.

Trog was a term with subjective connotations. Originally considered a slur against tech skeptics, those same skeptics reclaimed the word and wore it proudly, and soon it was applied by all sides to anything resistant to tech takeover. The Sea Shed contained no smart devices; nothing was permanently (or easily) connected to the internet. They could choose to get online via satellite but only with a maniacal attention to security and anonymity. Such living had become exceedingly rare and far more expensive. Insurance rates for trog homes were always higher, and the fight to outlaw trog housing altogether was entering its second decade. Citing a litany of dangers, Every lobbyists had successfully made it illegal to house children in trog homes; the law was soon expected to encompass all people and all dwellings. The neighbors, most of them anyway, were suspicious—a frame of mind supported by the Every. The company had acquired a series of apps where neighbors could share gossip and fear, and the apps' algorithms elevated all posts that questioned just what might be going on in these unconnected homes. In most cities, there were neighborhoods holding out, though; San Francisco's was called TrogTown, and the Every made sure it was perceived as a den of filth, crime and bad plumbing.

Delaney and Wes were on 41st Avenue now, the

road bending down toward the sea. Hurricane was straining against his leash.

"I don't know what I was thinking. I'm not a spy," Delaney said. "I have no training for this kind of thing."

"Training?" Wes said. "What training would prepare you?"

Wes was that rare but not unprecedented thing, a talented coder who lived off the grid—a tech trog. And because he had separated himself socially for much of his life, his worldview had remained that of a high-minded teenager: bad was bad, good was good, rebellion inherently noble. It took Delaney seven months before she trusted Wes enough to tell him of her plans, but he immediately understood and urged her on.

"I can't do it," Delaney said. "Thought I could, but I can't."

Wes stopped. Hurricane pulled more determinedly against his tether. He was seven in human years, his muzzle showing gray, but he was a runner, always had been, and tearing across the hard wet sand near the ocean was his joy. He was a mutt, but Wes—and anyone who saw him run—was certain he had greyhound in his blood.

"Maybe we can destroy it from the outside," she said.

Wes grinned. His eyes bulged with inspiration. "We can!" he said. "I'll send a strongly worded letter. And you can stand beyond the gates with a picket. Maybe one of us writes a novel."

"Stop," she said. "I can't go back. The problem is guile. The people who work there are guileless."

"But they collectively do harm," Wes said.

"But my existence there would be founded on deceit."

"While you intend to save the world," Wes said. Pleased with himself, he began walking again, much to the relief of Hurricane, who was on the verge of self-asphyxiation. At the beach, Wes unleashed Hurricane and the dog took off, spitting sand in his wake. He ran for an hour solid, every day, and any day without a run he was agitated, restless, erratic even. He chewed on wires and ate Delaney's shoes and looked achingly through the blinds.

"They already set up the second interview," Wes said. "You're halfway in."

This was not true and they both knew it. Delaney looked at the sea. The surf was coming in like an army of merry mops.

"I was thinking about learning how to sail," she said. "And how to use a lathe. We had two pandemics and I never learned to use a lathe. I could run a movie theater! The Alexandria's still closed. Or tapestries. I'd love to weave a tapestry."

"Tapestries," Wes said, looking to the sea. "I can see you doing tapestries."

When Hurricane finally tired he loped back to

Wes and dropped theatrically at his feet—his way of saying he was ready to go home.

At the stairs from the beach to the concrete promenade, they encountered a woman in a black windbreaker, reflective stripes on her arms, a kind of bumblebee assistant.

"Hey folks," she said. "Just making sure you're aware of the changes to the beach policy in regards to pets. Is your dog chipped?" She craned her head left and right, assessing Hurricane from above. "We're asking everyone," she added.

"He's not," Wes said, attempting to control his annoyance.

The woman chewed her lower lip. "Well, starting next week, all dogs within city limits must be chipped. For your safety and theirs. In case he gets lost?"

"He won't get lost," Wes said.

The woman rolled her eyes. "The portion of the beach available to chipped pets will be between the two markers you see here." She swung her arm toward the beach, where an area about as big as a two-car garage had been set aside. "And leashes will be required."

"Chips and leashes," Wes repeated.

"For your safety and the rest of those who want to enjoy the beach," the woman said.

Wes glared at her briefly, then looked away. She was wearing a high-res cam around her neck, so any scowl or foul word would be caught and noted. "Thank you," he said, and they walked on.

Once out of earshot, Wes exploded. "Fucking Christ!"

Ocean Beach had been the last place in the city, the last place for fifty miles, where dogs were allowed to run off-leash. He glanced at Hurricane, who seemed worried at Wes's tone of voice.

"When I was growing up, you could have bonfires here," he roared. "You could surf or fish without a permit. You could run, swim, screw, do whatever. Why? Because this place is vast! It's like five miles long. There's room for anything. Fuck!"

Far offshore, ocean rain blurred the sky above the Farallon Islands.

"You have to kill this company," he said. "Ultimately it all comes back to them. Kill the Every and we have a chance."

Delaney didn't know what to say.

"I need distraction," Wes said.

They dropped Hurricane off at home and went to Free Gold Watch. It was a retro arcade on Waller, a block from Haight and a stone's throw from the panhandle that ended Golden Gate Park. No Cams read the sign on the door. HERE BE TROGS. Inside, a half-dozen people played pinball and **Centipede.** Delaney had never been able to figure out who worked at the place. There never seemed to be anyone in charge, and yet the space was always functioning and clean. Wes put a quarter into an undersized **Galaga.**

"You want in?" he asked. Delaney shrugged. He put in a second quarter. Delaney leaned against the wall and, through a mirror, watched a man in a Damned T-shirt play an Old West target-shooting game.

Wes died quickly and made room for Delaney.

"How's Pia?" she asked.

Pia was Wes's ladyfriend. His word—ladyfriend. She'd lived with Wes when Delaney had moved in, and for their first week together, Delaney had found Pia brilliant and witty. As a child, Delaney and every girl she'd grown up with had wanted to be a marine biologist, and Pia was an actual marine biologist—always slingshotting herself around the world following fellowships (was currently in Chile). Eventually, though, it became clear to Delaney that both Wes and Pia were under the impression that Pia was the world's most alluring woman. Delaney heard the tales daily, the implication being that no human could meet Pia Minsky-Newton without loving Pia Minsky-Newton. Pia was fine looking but to Pia and Wes the blinding glory of her face was a constant burden. Her hair, which was on the stringy side, was, in Pia's eyes and Wes's, Kennedian, and her bust, which seemed average to Delaney, was, in their view, a continental shelf that inspired the relentless leering of the world.

"She's good," Wes said, "but there's this guy Karl

in her program who's been basically throwing himself at her. He wrote her a song—"

"Is she coming back for Christmas?"

"I think so. For a week. Your turn." Wes ceded
the machine to Delaney and she promptly got
herself killed.

"You have to go back. Do one more interview,"
he said.

"I can't be the one. I can't be a spy. I don't even
dress up for Halloween."

"Don't you have an ex-boyfriend who went
undercover? The fish and game guy in the neon
wraparound sunglasses? Dirk?"

"Derek. You know his name was Derek."

Derek, sartorially indifferent but deeply sincere,
had become an undercover agent for Montana
Fish and Game. He posed as a buyer of bear
and moose and out-of-season elk; the work was
surprisingly dangerous.

"You know what he said the key was to lying
under pressure?" Delaney said. "If they ask you a
question that will necessitate a lie, they'll be able to
tell if you answer that exact question—they'll read
the lie immediately. But if you answer a different
question, one you form in your mind, all the things
that give away the lie, your eyes, mouth, facial muscles, won't be addressing the lie. They'll be in service
to this different question you're answering—which
you'll be able to answer truthfully."

"Thank you for that disgusting word salad," Wes said. "I understood nothing. But I'm happy for you. Sounds like you have it figured out. You have a lying strategy, so you're golden."

"But I have nothing to offer them. You're the coder. Why don't you do it? I'd be your assistant."

Wes let his ship drift into a missile. He looked at Delaney while the explosion rumbled onscreen. "This was your plan, Del. You've been plan-ning it for years now. You can't just give me your dream. Plans for subterfuge and overthrow are not transferable."

"But it would be so easy for you. You get in there, write some . . . What do you call it?"

"Code."

"Really? Just code? Okay. You write some code, blow the place up from within."

"There is no code that will blow the place up," Wes said. "You know this. That's because it's not about the code, or the software, or even the people who work there. The way you end that place will be something we haven't thought of yet, something you'll only realize once you get inside."

Wes's eyes went distant again. "Damn, I'm hungry."

They ate at a nameless noodle place on Haight, another trog haunt. They sat at the bar, eating and watching Stever, the proprietor, clean the

stove under a sign that said WE ARE OBLIGATED
TO TELL CUSTOMERS THAT THIS ESTABLISHMENT
HAS NO CAMERAS. EAT HERE AT YOUR OWN RISK.
Stever's real name was Steven Han, but a decade
earlier, a grizzled Haight-Ashbury denizen with a
ragged-velvet pageboy cap had begun to call him
Stever, and he adopted it, thinking its insouciance
blunted the pain of his dreams deferred. Stever had
a degree in Russian literature from Berkeley, and
couldn't believe he was running his Chinese parents'
noodle shop. He took out his frustrations on the
oven and stove; he cleaned them hourly and with
great prejudice.

"Stever, you should take it easy," Wes said. "It's
been what? A month since the hernia?"

Stever burrowed his eyes into Wes.

Wes's mouth dropped open. "Oh shit. Was that a
private thing?"

Stever moved his tongue around his mouth;
it was something he did when he was too angry
to speak.

"Sorry, man," Wes said. "Jesus. My brain. It
doesn't—it lets me down. But Delaney doesn't care.
Delaney, do you care about Stever's hernia?" He
turned to Delaney, who was trying to remember
what a hernia was. "She probably doesn't know what
a hernia is. Stever, where are you going?"

He'd disappeared into the back room.

"You're right," Delaney said. "You can't be
the one. You can't keep a secret. Mainly because

you can't remember what you're supposed to keep secret."

Wes seemed content with this assessment, given it had absolved him of becoming a spy.

"Now I'm thinking if I can just kill emojis, that would be enough," Delaney said.

"You see the Secretary of State use a few today?" Wes asked. "He was celebrating the anniversary of **glasnost,** and he used a dancing rainbow. On the official state account. Our species has no dignity. No **path** to dignity."

"That reminds me," Delaney said.

"No," Wes said.

For years Delaney had been cultivating a social media persona that would make her candidacy for an Every job seem probable. Even to get the first interview, she knew they'd probed every post she'd made since grade school. Her years off-grid as a park ranger necessitated she develop and maintain a hyperactive digital self. She registered hundreds of frowns and smiles each day. She commented, rated and, for the last year or so, she'd thrown herself into taking selfies while posing as Popeye the Sailor Man.

"You're not doing Popeye again," Wes said.

"People post at least twenty a day," she said. "I've done eleven."

Wes let his head drop to the counter.

Delaney couldn't have Wes in the photo, and Stever didn't allow Popeyes inside. So she walked out of the restaurant and removed a tiny corn-cob pipe from her pocket. She put it between her teeth, tilted it up and leftward, and took a selfie. She sent it to her 3,209 followers and returned to the bar.

"How many of those have you sent, total?" Wes asked.

"Since the beginning? Like six months ago?" Delaney looked at her phone. "Four thousand, two hundred and ninety. They tell you when you've missed a day."

The popularity of Popeyes had lasted longer than Delaney had thought possible, far outstripping its predecessors—planking, ice-bucketing, elbow-earing, top-hatting, tongue-depressing. Each day for six months now, Delaney had sent her friends and relatives twenty or so Popeye pics and they reciprocated. The Every had begun the trend, had engineered it to gather location data and examine sundry data points about human behavior, and a billion people had been only too happy to comply, because the fun of taking pictures with a corncob pipe between one's teeth was impossible to resist and, in its own small way, united the world's people.

"Done?" Wes asked.

When it was time to pay, Stever made up a number. He had no fixed prices, no calculator, kept no track of sales tax. They paid in cash—Stever only took cash—and left.

"Let's walk," Wes said. "Phones off."

They turned off their phones, removed the

batteries, and Wes produced a magnetic bag he'd engineered himself. It blocked all signals going in or out. They tossed their phones inside.

"We taking the dark route?" Delaney asked.

"We should," Wes said, and they passed under a large sign. **You are entering a path without surveillance cameras. Citizens choosing this path assume associated risks. SFPD.** The city had a patchwork of such sidewalks and roads and trails, making it possible to walk more or less across the city free of the camera's gaze. It was one of the few cities with such areas, given they invited crime, and suspicion of crime.

They walked in silence until they were in a deeply wooded part of the park, all around them the smell of wet pine and puddles.

"I know it must be strange and intense," Wes said. He leaped to touch an overhead bough— something he did. He was a child, and was rewarded by a small shower of dew and pine needles. "But you're not infiltrating the mob," he said, shaking his shoulders like a dog. "The worst thing that can happen is they fire you, right?"

The path ended at the Great Highway, where they turned their phones back on. They walked along the oceanfront, and noted a nickel-bright necklace of stars over the sea.

"Those stars," Wes said. "I wish I knew what those were called." He waited a moment. "You don't know them, either."

"I do not," Delaney said.

"One of us should," he said. "Right?"

Delaney lay in her bed that night, looking through her tiny window at a half-hearted cloud. Wes slept in the next room, their two mattresses separated by little more than drywall. She could hear him arranging himself around Hurricane—the swirl of bedsheet, the whoop of his comforter given air and settling down upon man and dog.

"Night," Wes said from the other side of the wall.

"Night," Delaney said, and knew his next words.

"Love you," Wes said.

It had seemed strange, so unreasonable, the first time he'd said this, a year and a half ago. At that point they'd only known each other six months. His was a brotherly love, she knew—he'd never hinted at more—but why have it be love at all? She'd been gobsmacked the first time he said the words through their paperthin wall. She'd reflexively answered, "I thank you," and then was up half the night trying to make sense of it.

The next morning, unprompted, he explained it. His moms, he said, were loving, were devoted, but never said the words, but he **liked** the words, especially in the dark, before sleep. He liked to say them and hear them, he said, so as a boy he'd begun to say them to himself, turning his head one way then the other: **Love you/You too.**

"And I do love you," he'd said to Delaney, "so I

say it." He'd assured her that she didn't need to say it back, given how unusual it was in her world (she was from Idaho) for two friends, roommates, to say such things to each other. But she found she wanted it, too. She so coveted the words, counted on them, thought during the day of these unacceptable words he'd say to her through the wall at night.

"I love you," he said that first night.

"I thank you," she said that night and every night thereafter.

IV.

"I LIKED YOUR POPEYES," Jenny Butler said. "Can I see your pipe?"

Delaney had fallen in love with this woman, her second interviewer, in minutes. First the accent; she was from Mississippi and Delaney had never known such a person, such a musical manner of speaking, the way **pipe** became **pahhhp.** And her face, fleshy and dimpled, and her eyes, always wide, always amazed. She was known by all as Jenny Butler.

"So many Jennys here," Jenny Butler explained. "You'd be surprised. Especially among us"—here she whispered conspiratorially, cupcake frosting on her teeth—"the over-forties. The Julies are the same way. Have you met Julie Zlosa? Probably not. We just call her Zlosa. And the Michelles! There are far too many Michelles."

Jenny Butler was gregarious and unfiltered and instantly Delaney knew she would sail past this second interview without incident. Delaney had hoped this one would be inside the Every gates, but again she found herself at the base of Yerba Buena, this time with a SpaceBridge scientist, sitting at a cupcake shop that, like every other storefront on the island, seemed to have been erected moments before, and only for the purposes of some Everyones' momentary presence.

"Should we do a Popeye together?" Jenny Butler asked.

They inserted their pipes between their teeth, pressed their temples together and took the picture. As they checked the result—very cute, they both agreed, dignified even—a black motorcade sped past, en route to the Every gates.

"I think that's the UN Secretary-General," Jenny Butler said. "What day is it? Wait, don't tell me." She snuck a glance at her oval. "Yup, that would be her. She's asking for money. They always are. Not that Mae Holland is Ted Turner."

Jenny Butler winked at Delaney, then her face fell. "You might not know who that is. Ted Turner? He gave a hundred million to the UN. Or was it five hundred?"

When Delaney told her she did know who Ted Turner was, Jenny Butler's face opened again into a toothy smile.

"Relief!" Jenny Butler said, stretching the word into a long and beautiful shape. "You never know.

The weird gaps in people's knowledge now. No ten people know the same ten things. I bet you were young when the Release went down."

The Release had happened only ten years earlier. In a hack presumed to be orchestrated by Russia, the complete email histories of over four billion people had been made public. Just as with the hack of Sony by North Korea, jobs were lost, reputations ruined, marriages crushed and friendships shattered. The emails were passed around gleefully by tens of millions, and the media—its last, lost patrols—printed and discussed those emails that revealed hypocrisy or corruption by the powerful, the wealthy, the famous, and many others who were none of those things.

And after six months of handwringing, recrimination, a few thousand murders and perhaps a half-million suicides, the world forgot about the Release, and what it said about our means of communication and who stored and controlled it, and simply accommodated it, kneeling before new masters. From then on, every message written by every human was assumed to be subject to exposure—to be permanently searchable and public.

"You know," Delaney said, bullshitting in a way she suspected Jenny Butler would know and appreciate, "I was already careful with my way of expressing my feelings, my thoughts. The Release, I think, just made everyone more aware of the power of their words."

Jenny Butler sat back and squinted at Delaney. "Well said. Okay, speaking of releases, now that we're Popeye pals, what did you think of the movie?"

Delaney took a bite of her cupcake, hoping it would allow her to nod in agreement with Jenny Butler and be absolved of expressing a more developed opinion. There had been a movie made about the Circle—when it was still called that name—by a talented director and starring actors of consummate skill and renown, and yet the movie, despite its pedigree, was considered unsuccessful and was seen by few. The company, like an autocrat who survives an assassination attempt, emerged only stronger.

"What did **you** think of it?" Delaney parried. She and Wes had practiced this: whenever possible and especially when a question might send her into dangerous territory, she turned the questions back to the questioner. It flattered, it deflected.

Jenny Butler held up her forefinger as she chewed. Her nails were painted but chipped, like the outer tiles of a space capsule damaged upon re-entry. "Are you kidding? I **loved** the movie," she said. "I mean, I know not everyone around here was thrilled about it, but still, it's a movie **about the place where I work**! I'm from Mississippi, so that's still a big deal. It was the first time my mom was actually impressed."

This second interview was a staple of Every culture. Colloquially known as Random Meets

48

Random, it was an idea borrowed by Mae
Holland, and was a notion Delaney actually
admired—perhaps the one notion put forth by
Mae that Delaney did not consider the work of
a kind of soulless, conscienceless, world-ending
secular antichrist.

Random Meets Random meant that everyone at
the Every, from engineer to founder to sous chef,
had to participate, even if only once a year, in an
interview for an entry-level candidate who had
passed the first screening. Thus a random Everyone
would interview a random candidate, regardless of
their fields of expertise. A PR manager might interview a coder, a data scientist might meet an aspiring
art director. In this case, Jenny Butler was an astrophysicist and Delaney was a libarts generalist who
was happy, she told Jenny Butler, to bloom wherever
she was planted.

"So you worked on the last Mars driller?"
Delaney asked, and Jenny Butler stopped chewing
to stare incredulously at her.

"How did you **know** that?" she asked. "You
couldn't have presearched me, because they don't tell
you who your Random might be. And you didn't do
the thing where you pretend to go to the bathroom
to look me up on your phone." Delaney smiled,
then Jenny Butler seemed to doubt her version
of recent events. "You **didn't** go to the bathroom,
did you?"

"I just know who you are," Delaney said. Jenny Butler's division, SpaceBridge, was founded by Eamon Bailey but was not, it was assumed, beloved by Mae Holland. SpaceBridge was not entirely practical and not at all profitable. Bailey had used discretionary Every billions to send rovers to the Moon and Io, to mine passing asteroids, to capture and return ice from Saturn's rings—a few dozen highly unnecessary missions that Delaney had found magical and which caused her some moments of conflict. If she brought down the Every, these space-exploration projects would quickly end, for there was no company with the Every's cash—and certainly no company with a Bailey willing to spend it simply to know the galactic unknown. Mae Holland had expressed superficial fealty to these endeavors and the philosophy behind them, but no one pretended these sorts of things would happen were it up to her alone. Her interests were earthbound.

"But I don't know what you're doing now," Delaney said. "Are you allowed to say?"

Delaney knew that a candidate could only fail this second interview by failing to show interest in the interviewer's work. That was the twist, the only twist, of Random Meets Random. Though it was, ostensibly, about the Everyone getting to better know the candidate, it was more a test of that candidate's curiosity about the Every and its people. A poor candidate would ask the Everyone no questions. A very poor candidate would ask about money, or benefits, or vacation, or some reductive, mercenary concern.

"Well, there are two things, very different," Jenny Butler said. "They're not secrets, really, so I can tell you. The first is just a side thing—an app that calculates the month and year of your death. It's outside my usual field, but I had the idea one day and everyone was very supportive. Have you heard of this already?"

Delaney had ceased breathing. She shook her head, no.

"It's 91 percent effective," Jenny Butler said, "but we'll be able to get that number up a bit. This doesn't cover people dying of freak accidents, things like that. But based on lifestyle, diet, habits, genetics, geography, and a few hundred other inputs, we can zero in pretty well. The **month,** for sure—and we're getting closer to knowing the day. I found it a great comfort when I did mine. We could do yours."

"To find out when I'll die?" Delaney said.

"What are you doing for the rest of the day?" Jenny Butler asked.

"Don't you already know?" Delaney said.

"Ah, good one," Jenny Butler said. "But seriously. We'd only need a few hours." Before Delaney could answer, Jenny Butler sent and received a flurry of texts, only to find that between scheduling squeezes and Delaney's lack of security clearance, it was not to be.

"Well, another day," Jenny Butler said, and then rolled directly into a long soliloquy about a Mars rover team she was on, how superior it was to the Japanese and European versions, and to the twice-failed Chinese models. It took Delaney fifteen minutes to recover from the thought that this bright-eyed astrophysicist with the charming accent could blithely create, as a side project, an app—an app!—that would remove much of the mystery from human life, and was now talking about the next Mars launch.

Eventually Delaney steadied herself enough to ask questions, to seem fascinated and admiring. At the end of their allotted hour, Jenny Butler was so taken with Delaney, and so convinced of Delaney's genuine interest in the work of SpaceBridge and launch trajectories and landing velocity, that she invited Delaney to the launch, two months hence, of a new explorer headed for Mercury.

"Whether you're working here or not," Jenny Butler said, grabbing Delaney's hand and gripping it tight, "you **will** come as my guest."

V.

"JENNY BUTLER IS A LOVER OF ALL MANKIND," Carlo said, and quickly corrected himself. "**Human**kind." He blushed desperately. Delaney was careful not to react but nevertheless was astonished: an error like that was almost unheard of among public-facing Everyones.

Next to Carlo was a green-eyed, unblinking woman named Shireen who did not seem to notice or care about his error.

"Jenny Butler's the absolute **best,**" Shireen said. Her eyes were not only open wide but her pupils seemed to be trembling.

"And!" Carlo went on, grinning, clearly overjoyed that his error was forgotten or at least forgiven, "what Jenny Butler said about you was just **ridiculous.**" He looked at Delaney and she noted the same thing: his pupils were trembling. They conveyed something between total engagement and low-level terror.

"Ridiculous!" Shireen said. Her mouth stayed open long after the word had evaporated from the room.

It was a week later and Delaney was finally on campus. Not in any of the main buildings, but she had entered the Every gate, and had been led to a low-slung timber-clad building covered with vines and succulents. Inside, the structure was a white box, a kind of utility space to be used for times and people like this.

Delaney's appointment had been for 3:00, but she had been asked to arrive at 2:30. She had gone through a fascinating security process that had taken fully twenty-eight of those thirty minutes. She had emptied her pockets and had her bag scanned, then was made to walk through a ten-foot pink tunnel, utterly silent. Her phone had been placed in a device that resembled a very snug microwave in which, she assumed, it was being scraped of all its secrets. The soles of her shoes had been wiped, and the wiping cloth had been put into a small silver box which eventually sang an approving song. After briefly reading legal language indicating that she could not reveal what was said in the interview, anyone she met or anything she saw, and that anything she said was theirs to keep, she signed three documents via finger-on-tablet.

"All your feeds are very interesting," Carlo said.

"Very thought provoking!" Shireen added. "You scored high on word variety. Top two percent!"

"Listen," Carlo said. "**All** your numbers are great. Socials, PrefCom, and of course the culture index is super-high for our candidates. But you knew that. For this interview, though, we like to get to know a bit more about the future you see. You were at a startup, and you've put an extraordinary amount of time into examining the Every from the outside. We read your paper."

"Your paper was so interesting!" Shireen said.

Carlo turned to Shireen with a smile of terrifying insincerity, then pivoted back to Delaney. "Delaney, what do you think the Every should do next?"

Delaney paused. She and Wes had a proposal ready, but she hadn't expected to unveil it so soon.

"I know ideas are hard," Shireen said.

"I actually do have an idea," Delaney said.

Carlo and Shireen looked far more surprised than Delaney expected. Shireen's surprise approached revulsion.

"Can I dim the lights and use the screen?" Delaney asked.

Their postures straightened.

"Sure," Carlo said. "Are we being treated to an actual **presentation**?"

Shireen looked panicked. "Something you **prepared**?"

On one level this was madness. Intellectual property was guarded with maniacal fervor here and in every related industry. The Every did not expect most candidates to simply give up a million- or

billion-dollar notion in an interview. But Delaney
had heard more than a few stories of candidates
doing so anyway, presenting good ideas with no
strings, and therefore being readily hired, not just
for the quality of their ideas but for their trust in the
Every and—more importantly—for their willing-
ness to sublimate their own gain to the overall
well-being and growth of the company where they
hoped to work. Giving up an idea or two in an interview spoke, most importantly, to confidence, a
confidence that the candidate had no scarcity of
ideas—that these ideas came with enough frequency
that giving up one or two in an interview was no
great sacrifice. Conversely, went the logic, those who
guard their ideas jealously likely have few.

Carlo rose to turn off the lights. "I should remind
you of the agreement you signed—"

"Of course," Delaney said.

Everything said in the room was being recorded,
she assumed, and besides, the agreement had
pounded home, chances are that any notion given
breath in the interview was already in development
on campus.

She and Wes had spent a week working up a
rough prototype; Wes, usually listless and without
self-direction, was relentless and untiring when
given a task. Delaney had told him to be ready
today for its unveiling.

Delaney stood and took a meaningful breath.
"I've been thinking about friendship," she said, and

let the sentence land. Carlo and Shireen were smiling like children who had snuck into a matinee.

"Scientists again and again find," Delaney continued, "that people with long-term, authentic friends are healthier, happier, and live longer."

Shireen nodded slowly, as if this was new and fascinating information. Her fingers, which seemed to want to write this down, tapped absently on the tablet in front of her. Delaney had the spontaneous idea to include Shireen in the presentation.

"Shireen, you seem like someone who has a lot of friends."

Shireen nodded cheerfully, then, responding to Carlo's urgent glance, decided she should articulate this aloud. "Yes I do," she said.

"But are there times when you're unsure about them?" Delaney said. "Some moments when you're not one hundred percent sure where you stand?" Before she was finished, Shireen was nodding vigorously, then remembered to speak her approval, too. "Yes. For sure."

"Tell me about that," Delaney said, and Shireen lit up.

"Well, sometimes I'll text a friend—just something like a rainbow emoji followed by a two-way arrow and a question mark. You know, to let them know I'm happy and hope they're happy."

"And then you wait," Delaney said.

"Right!" Shireen said. "And while I'm waiting . . ."

"You wonder if they hate you and are plotting against you and will spread lies about you and ruin your life and you'll want to die?" Delaney said. She expected a laugh, but the faces of Shireen and Carlo had gone gray.

"I wouldn't use those words, exactly," Shireen said, "but—"

"We wouldn't put things in such graphic terms . . ." Carlo added.

Delaney backtracked. "Of course not," she said. "I'm sorry. I'm a backwoods gal, as you know. I have some refining to do." Their faces were still worried, borderline anxious. She needed to plunge ahead.

"What Shireen described is something we all live with," she said. "It's uncertainty in the one place where we need it most. With our personal relationships. Our friendships."

Now Shireen's face relaxed, and Carlo, who had gone briefly crosseyed, returned his expression to calm interest.

"For years now, we've counted our friends here at the Every . . ." Delaney paused momentarily to see if her use of **we** had registered and had met with approval—it had. "But is that really the most important measurement? If scientists tell us that the depth of our friendships is the most important thing, shouldn't we be measuring not the **quantity** of friends, but the **quality** of those friendships?"

Carlo and Shireen were listening with mouths

slightly agape. Delaney assumed she was hired. Now she only had to get through the presentation without unforced error.

"So I was sketching out an app," she said, "that brings some certainty to what's always been vague and frankly a bit chaotic. Can I show you? I'm assuming this is ready?" She pointed to the wallscreen, which she tapped to activate. "Guest," she said. "Seven-Oh-Eight-Eight-Nine." A small box appeared on the screen and Delaney pressed her thumb to it. Her fingerprint connected her to her account, and soon the screen came alive with the life-size face of Wes, his closed-mouth smile seeming, Delaney thought, a bit too amused. Wes's resting face appeared mocking, and he knew this, so he tried, always, to pepper his speech with words of unmistakable gratitude and sincerity.

Delaney turned to Carlo and Shireen. "I hope you don't mind, but I asked Wes, an old friend of mine, to be ready today."

Shireen looked doubtful and Carlo flashed an unhappy grimace. "It's fine," he said finally. "Hi Wes. How are you?"

Delaney turned back to Wes. Until this moment, she'd assumed he was in their kitchen, but now she saw the distinct outline of a toilet tank. He was sitting on the can. This was his idea of a gag.

"Wes, can you hear us?" Delaney asked.

"I can!" he said, and added, "I'm so grateful to be with you!"

"Do you think you might be more comfortable elsewhere?" Delaney said. "I have a sense the connection would be stronger in another room."

"No, it's super-strong here. Potent, actually," he said. "How is **every**one?" he asked. **Idiot,** Delaney thought. He'd specifically promised not to make this joke.

A few more pleasantries were exchanged before Delaney tapped a code on her tablet and a digital frame, embedded with icons, surrounded Wes's face.

"Tell me about your day, Wes," Delaney said.

Wes began talking, telling the tale of a day filled with average social calamity and embarrassment, while Delaney made sympathetic sounds and asked well-timed follow-up questions. As she spoke, the icons, sixteen of them, appeared in the frame, just below Wes's chin, and began flickering with activity.

"As you can see," Delaney noted, "as we talk, our AI is analyzing Wes's facial expression, eye contact, and vocal intonations. I know emotion detection is a big interest for the Every now. Obviously the tech exists and will only get better." Nine of the sixteen indicators below Wes's chin were green, seven red.

"Looks like Wes is being truthful, as you can see here," Delaney said, pointing to the first green indicator. "Over here, though, this facial sensor is red, indicating that he's tense. If he were relaxed, this indicator would be green. The rest of the sensors are tracking things like candor, humor, sincerity and warmth. Wes has always been very funny, so you can see that the humor sensor reflects that."

"Whoa," Shireen said.

"Meanwhile," Delaney continued, "our conversation is being transcribed and algorithms are analyzing the text, looking at the actual words spoken for keywords and phrases that are commonly used between authentic friends. So we have the facial rec analyzing surface indicators, the text being examined, and these two measurements are collated with Wes's vitals, heart-rate, blood pressure and glucose levels, which are being monitored of course through his oval."

Shireen and Carlo nodded earnestly. The best thing to do, Delaney knew, was to include Every tech in her own, implying she was not replacing theirs, but was simply adding on.

"Here you can see some of the aggregate numbers at the bottom. The conversation so far is rated 86.2, which is decent, and I think reflects the fact that Wes and I have an easy friendship. Anything over 80 is genuine. Over 90, though, is extraordinary."

"And Wes is seeing the same numbers on his screen?" Carlo asked.

"For this demonstration, yes," Delaney said. "But there would be times you'd want the data traveling just one way. For example, if I was unsure if Wes was being truthful on a specific topic, or if I wasn't certain he was an authentic friend generally, I could set the tech up to deliver the metrics only to me."

"I love this," Shireen said, her eyes wide.

"In this case," Delaney continued, "at the end of the conversation, we each get a score and a general assessment of the quality of the interaction. This one interaction of course goes into a larger folder of all the one-on-ones with Wes, and all our interactions are then aggregated and assessed as a whole. Sociologists who study friendship," Delaney said, making up the statistic—"determined that a person will spend about 92 to 98 quality hours a fiscal quarter with a genuine friend, so that baseline is factored in. Users, of course, can choose to see where they're at with overall quality hours."

"Amazing," Shireen said.

"And this is an actual functioning app?" Carlo asked.

"No, no," Delaney said. "None of this is real yet. All the numbers you see on the screen are just made-up for now. But most of this tech already exists. It's all available, off the shelf, really. It just hasn't been put in one place. I'm not an engineer, as you know. And frankly I'd love to see it happen here at the Every."

"Incredible," Carlo said. "So who helped you with the coding?"

"Well, it's not exactly coding, but Wes helped, yes."

"Wes, are you still there?" Carlo asked.

"I am," Wes said.

"Well done," Carlo said. "It's elegant."

"Elegant?" Wes said, seeming genuinely moved by the word. He'd rested his palm on his chest. "Thank you."

"Thank **you**," Carlo and Shireen said in unison, then exchanged looks of confusion and embarrassment and, Delaney thought, maybe some latent sexual tension? There was a lot happening between them.

"You're welcome," Wes said, and with that, logged off.

Carlo turned the lights on and checked the time.

"I hate to be the wet blanket here," Shireen said, "but some years ago, a company tried to launch an app, I think it was called People, maybe spelled with two e's, and its purpose was to rate other humans, the same way you might rate a hotel or rideshare driver. For whatever reason, that seemed to cross a line with many users and pundits. The app's founders became not-so-popular and it never launched. I wonder how you would navigate those . . ." She paused, finding the most neutral word. She settled on "sensitivities."

Carlo shot an imploring look Shireen's way, as if aghast that she might be jeopardizing what had otherwise been a dream interview with a candidate who was giving the company a gilded new prize.

"It's a good question," Delaney answered. "And one I've thought about quite a bit. The first thing is that we've accepted the rating of all kinds of people. We rate drivers, cops, judges, contractors, doctors, plumbers, professors, chefs, waiters, neighbors, of course government officials—what occupation doesn't have some rating system?"

Carlo and Shireen shrugged in vigorous agreement, though Carlo was refusing, for the moment, to look at Shireen.

"Early in this century," Delaney said, "people accepted the rightness of measuring each other numerically. Why? Because numbers are inherently fair, while humans are inherently not fair. I think we all recognize that the only thing worse than being measured is **not** being measured, right?"

Shireen laughed out loud, almost a shriek. Carlo's head seemed to vibrate with aggravation. Delaney smiled at them both, papering over their interpersonal tension with a sense that they were all of one mind.

"With Peeple—you're right, that was its name, two e's—they were asking for an evaluation that was both public and static," Delaney said. "The public part was an issue, of course. It reduced a human being to a number, which is something I know you would never stand for here at the Every."

Carlo nodded slowly, closing his eyes briefly to emphasize just how much he appreciated Delaney's gracious explanation to Shireen of what was, to him, so obvious.

"With my app," Delaney continued, "this is a fluid system, constantly malleable, ultra-responsive to input and effort. It can change every day, provided the user is attentive to it. The second, and more important distinction, is that whereas that previous, misguided, app sought to rate **strangers,** this is exclusively between **friends.**"

"Ah!" Shireen said, feeling vindicated. Her probity had yielded an essential clarification.

Delaney was building toward the final line, her favorite line—she'd planned to end the presentation with a statement so perverse it almost caused her internal bleeding. She placed her palms on the table and tried in vain to conjure some wetness in her eyes.

"For something so important in our lives, friendship is woefully unexamined and under-studied. I think we deserve better. If we value friendship as much as we say we do, then let's get serious. Think of how much more genuine and authentic our friendships could be," she said, "if we just apply the right metrics to them."

Carlo said nothing. Shireen said nothing, but seemed ready to explode. Delaney wondered if it was all too much. Too silly? Any reasonable person would have her arrested.

After the longest and most dramatic of pauses, Shireen's inner light went bright again. "I would use this **daily,**" she said. The veins of her neck tightened. "**Day**-ley."

"Do you have a name for it?" Carlo asked.

"Well, I'm toggling between GenuPal and AuthentiFriend," Delaney said, and immediately knew that the right thing to do would be to ask them to weigh in. "What do you two think?"

"GenuPal is more positive," Shireen noted.

"But AuthentiFriend is more pro-active, right?" Carlo mused, looking thoughtfully over at Shireen, who he had evidently forgiven. "It feels like an action to perform. As in, **I need to authenticate a friend.**"

"Right, right," Shireen said. Carlo beamed, apparently believing he'd come up with the name, and perhaps the app, too.

Shireen was looking out the window, where a stray pelican was visible, flying low over the water, as steady as a bomber.

"I still like GenuPal," she said.

VI.

THE STORY THAT LATER PROLIFERATED at the Every was that Delaney had grown up in a log cabin. This was not quite true but not quite false. Her parents had raised her in a house made of logs, but the home could not be called a cabin. It was spacious and built in 1988, by one of the uncountable construction firms in Idaho that specialized in modern log homes. With seven rooms and 2,200 square feet, it would not qualify as a cabin, but it was not showy, and it was indeed located in the woods, in a small town called Ghost Canyon, next to a winding meltwater stream at the base of the Pioneer Mountains. Though her family had phones and computers and televisions and every other modern amenity, she remembered her early years as taking place outdoors to the soundtrack of rushing water.

Her family's house stood on four acres, the land divided equally between two sides of the bending river. Behind the house her parents had built a covered pedestrian bridge that spanned the stream, and on the bridge they'd installed a swinging bench, which they covered with pillows and blankets, and there Delaney would sit and swing with her dogs while the water rushed like frantic glass below.

Their neighbors across the river kept horses, and from her bench Delaney watched the horses nodding and trotting and swatting; between the mad sparkling river and the ponderous movements of the horses, she could spend hours in passive distraction. When she learned to read, she brought her books to her bench, and with her dogs next to her, occasionally coming and going to investigate squirrels and mice, Delaney could spend whole afternoons.

But when she started school, her parents began to worry. They ran an organic grocery in town and were at the store most days. After school, it was much easier for Delaney to simply bike home, and when her parents closed up the shop, they usually found Delaney home and alone—not playing sports, not with friends in town. Delaney spent a great deal of time by herself, they noticed, and when she didn't bring classmates home for playdates, they fretted. She seemed so content to read, or stare into the fire, or sit on her bench over the rushing river, that they undertook a haphazard series of interventions and countermeasures. They had her tested. They had her socialized. They filled her afternoons with extracurricular activities at school and at their church. They filled her weekends with playdates at friends' houses and at hers, and Delaney had no objections to any of these things. She enjoyed the pottery classes, the Spanish and guitar lessons. She made friends relatively easily and liked nothing better than to show these friends her dogs and her river and the horses on the other side of the bridge.

But she still spent what they considered an inordinate amount of time alone, and out of love and concern for her well-being, and thinking that she needed to connect easily with friends in the medium of her generation, when she turned twelve years old, they bought her a phone. It cost $1,000, an expense they considered outrageous but necessary for her connection to her friends when not physically among them. She did not resist it.

The device was so many things: it was a television, a telephone, a research tool, a limitless archive, a stereo, an arcade, an extraordinary still camera, a competent video camera, a portal to political movements, pornography and pederasts. Her parents later said—and they were not prone to exaggeration—that in the first month, Delaney spent eighty hours a week using it. Delaney explored only a fraction of its capabilities, first watching the entirety—thirty-three hours—of a vintage show called **Riverdale.** She watched six seasons of another, even older, show, called **The Office.** She finished **Friends, Outer Banks, iCarly** and **All American.** She discovered music, curating a playlist that soon grew to 1,130 songs. Her friends were not frequent texters yet, so the phone did not have any immediate effect on her social life. But instead of spending time on her bridge over the river, Delaney spent those hours in her room, rarely sleeping but never quite awake.

After four months of observing her behavior, her parents instituted a regulatory system, whereby she could only use the phone three hours a day. She obeyed this while they were awake, but easily found secret hours after they fell asleep. She watched her shows from ten-thirty p.m. to one or two in the morning, and woke up at seven every day, fitting in another entertainment hour before school. She fell asleep in class frequently and was reprimanded. She finished her sixth-grade year far behind where she'd begun, with a baffled note from her homeroom teacher—"I've never seen such a sudden drop-off. Did someone die?"—and her parents spent the summer pondering radical solutions.

The next few years were full of predictable skirmishes. Her parents devised restrictions and she found ways around them. They installed filters and she easily flouted them. They went to support groups and watched grave documentaries and came back with new restrictions, filters and strategies, none of which had any effect at all. And all this preceded Delaney's entry to social media. The Circle's endless and overlapping platforms tripled her engagement and deepened her addiction. By the time she was thirteen she was sending approximately 540 messages a day—most of them blurry pictures of herself in the corner of a screen; it was a thing. And texts. And brief dance videos. And, for a six-month period when an app called Fingrnls reigned, sending close-up photos of her fingernails bearing five-letter acronymic missives.

Her parents, finally, intervened again, this time sending her to a detox camp in Montana, not far from her grandmother, JuJu—a former airline pilot, onetime bass fishing champion, and serial dater of far younger men. Delaney was supposed to spend a month there, without phones, with no connections at all beyond the eighteen other girls, generally her age. Their days were structured but not militant. It was not a boot camp. They worked the farm. They hiked. They rode horses, milked cows, birthed calves, fed goats. They rose with the sun and slept through the night, and after a month Delaney asked to stay through the year. She did so, visiting JuJu every weekend, loving the simplicity of it, the very few things in her life. In eighth grade, she rejoined her Idaho school, feeling happy and balanced and strong.

Then something odd happened. Her school, which had been warning parents, since kindergarten, about the dangers of screentime and the atomization of the adolescent attention span, began an inexorable march toward full digital immersion. Her teachers did not assign her homework during school; instead, they posted the homework after school, online, and required students to complete it on CircleClass, an online platform known to collect all-encompassing data on every user. Her social studies teacher assigned videos that had to be watched online, while her English teachers required her to type her papers and submit them through CircleWrites, using that app's semifunctional AI grammar and spellcheck functions.

Delaney's parents, who had given up wifi to keep their daughter offline, were squeezed. For a time, they took her to the library each night, to use the internet connection there, but the drive was thirty minutes each way, and finally they were forced to restart their wifi, and to dance again with the very addiction they'd successfully snuffed out. It was like curing their child of a meth dependency only to have her school require that its students maintain, at all times, a low-level high.

Meanwhile, the school continued to warn about social media and the black hole of screentime. They prohibited phones in the classroom while allowing laptops, which the students easily jerry-rigged to show porn and pet videos. The educators lamented the diminishing attention span of their students and the obsessive digital contact from parents, while requiring that students have internet access to complete even the most basic tasks, and issuing every parental permission slip and directive through digital-only conduits. On Tuesday her parents would attend a school-sponsored evening devoted to teen tech addictions and how to break them, and on Wednesday her algebra teacher would assign two hours of homework that had to be done online. At an all-school assembly on Friday, a guest speaker would exhort the students to spend the weekend offline and away from all devices, and throughout the day, Delaney's instructors would each assign weekend homework that could not be completed or turned in without looking at a screen.

Delaney was irritable, always on edge, dinged eighteen hours a day by classmates wanting to compare notes, and innumerable representatives of her school following up, revising, amending, rescheduling, clarifying. She was sleeping less than five hours a night. Finally, after she was found slumbering midday in the school's utility closet, they decided as a family that home-schooling was the only viable option. Back at home, Delaney slowly retrained her mind. In a few weeks, she could think for an hour straight. After a month, she could concentrate enough to read books, could form original thoughts that were not just slight variations or reactions to ephemeral text fragments. After three months, she retook her spot on the bridge over the river and reclaimed her mind.

But no one expected the ecommerce site named after the South American jungle to get into the food business. Especially not the organic food sector. But they hit the grocery world like a mile-wide meteor, causing an extinction event for any small store that had the misfortune of existing where they had designs. The jungle's organic grocery—FolkFoods—moved into town, and within eighteen months Delaney's parents had sold their store and were working, whipped and ashamed and wearing green aprons, for the chain.

Delaney was ashamed, too, and filled with rage. Her parents had given up. They justified their new existence as a holding pattern. They had seven years of mortgage payments left, at which point they had unlimited options. They could sell the home and live out any whim—relocation to an Amsterdam houseboat, a year in Yelapa, the Peace Corps in Uzbekistan. They talked rationally and even defiantly about their employer, and were determined to win the battle against their rapacious corporate invader, even if simply by taking their money, leaving and living well.

But something happened along the way. Year by year they became less feisty, less critical of their new overlords. More than a few times, they referred to the store in the first-person-plural. Delaney watched them lose their fight, their spark. They worked ten-hour days and were underpaid. They were required to have devices on their persons at all times, so their work hours could be tracked to the minute and where they could be reached day and night for the most minor but relentless questions

and updates and schedule changes. They were de-
feated, exhausted and, worse, they were less interesting. Because their devices dinged them a few times
a minute, their minds were reshaped to the jittery,
needy psyche that ruled the digital realm.

Delaney was happy to leave. She went to college
at Reed, doing her best to choose classes where she
could maintain some real-world balance. Each semester, Professor Agarwal posted, Luther-like with
paper and rough-hewn nail, a list of tech-resistant
classes offered on campus—known as Agarwal's
Analogs—and Delaney threw herself at those, no
matter the subject. She finished with a liberal arts
degree and a plan to kill the company that had stolen her childhood and the will of her parents. But
then she'd lost her nerve. She paled at the thought
of giving more of her life to fighting a way of life
preferred by her fellow humans.

So she became a forest ranger, rotating annually
through the Rockies, the Sierras, New Mexico and
Oregon. In the trees and on the mountains, it was
an entirely different world, utterly apart from tech
takeover, until she arrived at her station one day to
find that phones were mandatory for all hikers.
FOR YOUR SAFETY, the refrain went, for it was far
easier to count and control numbers, and to facili-
tate rescues, if all humans in any park or preserve
were trackable and reachable. The new rules were
not unexpected and the resistance was scant. Most
people entering any park were bringing phones

already; the only new twist was the enforcement and registry. After a few weeks, when no opposition was offered, Mae Holland made a gleeful announcement that her company had spearheaded—and would fund—the saturation of the campaign, which she called **Find Me in the Natural World,** complete with a series of digital posters made to look like the classic 1940s National Park Service advertisements. The Every would provide phones to any park visitors who didn't have them, and their tracking apps would be added, free, to all hikers who had phones. Which was everyone.

The day of this announcement, this call for surveillance in the woods, Delaney was at her station, halfway up Mt. Lassen, an expired volcano in northeast California. It was then that Delaney was re-radicalized. She stared down at the alpine lakes strewn around the base of the mountain, and she chose war. She pictured a conflagration, a revolution, a burning-down. What these companies had done was nothing less than radical speciation. In a few short decades they'd transformed proud and free animals—humans—and made them into endlessly acquiescent dots on screens. Citizens in cities had given up their liberties early in the twenty-first century, but the natural world had remained wild, and people could stay hidden, could move freely. But the last vestige of freedom—the ability to move through the natural world unobserved—fell away on a Friday, and no one noticed.

Mae became Delaney's enemy, the enemy of all that made humans vital. She needed to be toppled and Delaney had the vainglorious belief that she could be the one to do it. But she had no power screaming from the woods. She'd have to get inside and start cutting wires. She quit the forest service and moved to San Francisco. She took the entry-level job at Ol Factory—like Dan Faraday, Vijay and Martin were tickled by her exotic background. And though she liked her coworkers, liked them a great deal, in fact, there was an apocalyptic obedience at play there that she didn't know if she could reverse. She and all staff had to acquiesce to trackers that counted their hours, their minutes, their keystrokes and measured their productivity (merits were **daisies,** demerits **durians**). Day to day, the consequences were minimal and seldom spoken. It was only when there was an assessment or dismissal that the data was awakened; then everything the under-performing employee had ever said or done was unearthed and examined and compared to averages, aggregates, standards and expectations. Vijay or Martin would see the data and shrug, would smile apologetically, helplessly. It was not, they were keen to emphasize, their decision.

While at Ol Factory, while planning her side-assault on the Every, the final straw for Delaney was nothing involving the consolidation of wealth and power made possible through mass surveillance and the numerification of lives. It was a message from her father. "Sad news, Del. Grandma JuJu died last night." This was followed by a tiny yellow face, looking like a Pac-Man in frontal view, with water-falls of tears flowing from its wee eyes. Seconds later, her mother seconded the message. "So sad," she wrote, and punctuated this with a slight variation on the first emoji—this yellow face was crying, too, but had little arms extended from its round body, and these hands were formed into fists that were try-ing to stem the tears. Her mother followed this face with the words, "She was a sweetie," and this state-ment was helped by another tiny animated emoji, a cartoon grandmother tilting back and forth in a motion meant to be either rocking or dancing.

Delaney's devastation was many layered. She would never be able to correct this moment, the news of her JuJu's passing not delivered by tear-ful phone call, or in person, or in any way fitting of thousands of years of human evolution toward increasing refinement. The news of her grand-mother's death was delivered by weeping Pac-Man. When Delaney confronted her parents, they couldn't recognize the transgression. They pointed out—correctly, Delaney had to admit—that JuJu loved emojis, too.

VII.

"NOT TOO MANY PEOPLE START THIS WAY," Kiki said. Kiki was Delaney's acclimator, assigned to show Delaney the campus and get her settled into her first rotation. Kiki was no more than five feet tall, with hair the color of Neptune and the build of a woodland fairy.

"I don't take it for granted," Delaney said. "I'm so grateful." She was nauseous. Through three interviews and an orientation, Delaney still hadn't been allowed onto the main campus. Instead she had been relegated to outer buildings and, for the orientation, the auditorium, with about a hundred other new hires.

"I like your outfit, by the way," Kiki said, "very retro! Hi!"

Delaney had the sense that Kiki was no longer talking to her. She glanced at Kiki to find she was talking to her screen strapped to her forearm.

"That is so good, honey! So good!" Kiki sang. On

the screen, Delaney caught a glimpse of a small boy with a mop of black hair. They were in the shadow of Algo Mas, and Delaney reached out to touch its aluminum cladding just before it began its upward revolutions. There was chatter, almost impossible to confirm, that the first wave of suicides happened here, Everyones throwing themselves from the balcony of its penthouse, called the Aviary. It had since been closed.

"Yes, you tell Ms. Jasmine how much I love that," Kiki said.

Delaney could hear nothing of the boy's voice coming through Kiki's earpiece, could only watch Kiki's eyes dart back and forth, taking in her son's face and surroundings.

"Okay, hon-hon," Kiki said, "I'll check back in with you in a few." She paused. "Just a couple minutes. I know the other parents are still there." Another pause. "I'll be back in ten. Okay. Bye-bye."

Now Kiki refocused on Delaney, and they began walking.

"My son Nino. He's five. He goes to the Every Schoolhouse. Have you seen it? Probably not—you just got here! It's on the other side of campus, near the beach. It's really a fantastic school, the scores off the charts . . ." Kiki trailed off and stopped walking. She tapped her ear. "Yes," she said. "Thank you so much, Ms. Jolene."

And now she was back.

"They really encourage parental participation,

which I love. I **love** it. The parents each volunteer
ten hours a week, which is pretty standard, but here
they go above and beyond by inviting parents to sit
in on the schoolday as often as they can. It gives the
kids such comfort." She focused on Delaney, then
looked at the screen, then back to Delaney. "Where
was I?"

In the distance, Delaney could see a wide flower-
shaped expanse of buffalo grass that she felt sure
was the Daisy—she'd heard of the Daisy. The grass
was an incandescent green, and was dotted with a
menagerie of Everyones in bright clothing, but now
Kiki had stopped.

"Are you on OwnSelf?" Kiki asked.

"No, not yet. I'm on HelpMe," Delaney said.

"Oh, I have to move you over to OwnSelf.
I'm actually beta-testing a new iteration. It's
really extraordinary."

In anticipation of coming to the Every, Delaney
had been using HelpMe for a few years; it was a relatively basic app that consolidated all your reminders, calendars, birthdays, appointments and even
dietary goals into one place. Advertisers loved it.
A user programmed in their desire to eat a protein
salad once a day, and that desire would be sold to
those selling protein salads. It was caveman-simple,
worked for everyone, and was worth billions for the
Every. It had been invented by two Manitoba teens
in a weekend.

"OwnSelf is so much more comprehensive,

though," Kiki said. "I think HelpMe has, what, twenty-five data points?"

"Something like that," Delaney said. Hers had twenty-two.

"OwnSelf has five hundred, baseline," Kiki said. "Mine's got six hundred and seventy-seven, and one of my goals is to get to eight hundred by next month. And OwnSelf will actually get me there, right?" Kiki laughed, and looked at her screen and frowned. "I mean, that's the point. It's all about helping you attain your own goals." Her oval dinged. "Oh wait."

She spent another half-minute on FaceMe with her son. Delaney stood in the shadows watching the activity on the lawn's gently undulating topography. There seemed to be some kind of modern dance being performed—a group of figures in lycra bodysuits.

"See," Kiki continued, "I set my goal to FaceMe with Nino twelve times during his schoolday, and OwnSelf pro-rates the day and keeps me on track to achieve that—collating with his teachers' own OwnSelfs. All the OwnSelfs can talk to each other, which is so key. That way there's no excuses. If you have the time, the OwnSelfs coordinate, put whatever it is that needs to get done on your schedule, and it gets done." Kiki squinted toward the Daisy. "I fought it for a week or two, altering the OwnSelf itineraries. But I always made it worse. The one thing humans are not good at is scheduling, right?"

"That's just science," Delaney said.

Kiki rolled her eyes in relieved approval.

"OwnSelf just helps you get there. It pre-divides the day, but it also allows for variances. Like this walk with you . . ." She looked at her screen. "It's taken three and half minutes longer than expected, and we haven't even started yet. So other things will be moved around. But it's relentlessly focused on helping you get done in a given day what you planned to get done. I can't tell you what a difference that makes when you lay your head to sleep. I mean, total peace."

"Right!" Delaney said.

"Speaking of which, we should walk."

They left the shadows, and Delaney's stomach cinched. Up ahead, she saw dozens of people in the full sun of the wide lawn. They seemed to be doing some kind of exercise, or were for some reason all in tight and colorful exercise clothes. Among so many people, she'd be discovered immediately. She was so obviously a spy.

"That's the Duomo," Kiki said, pointing to what seemed to be an Italian church. "Bailey went to Siena, loved this building, the stripes mainly, so he brought it here. Or made a copy of it?" She stared at the building, as if it might answer. "I think it's actually the original and now the copy is in Siena. Does that sound right? Anyway, some of the space exploration people work there."

They were almost at the main lawn. Delaney

had to remind herself how to walk. How could she not be found out? She couldn't remember if people move their arms. Did they move them up and down, or just swing them? Swinging seemed silly. She decided against swinging, instead moving them in small circles near her hips.

"Over there are the pods," Kiki said. "On-campus living. There are about 5,000 Everyones living here now. Makes it so easy. No commute! Would you want to do that, do you think? Hold on."

Kiki's oval had dinged. She stretched her arms upward and let them drop slowly, as if swimming the length of a pool underwater.

"Have to be mindful," she said, and lifted her arm to show Delaney her screen. "My first goal was fitness and wellness. I want to exercise, but I don't want to decide when to do it. Or what kind is best, what day is arms day, which day is legs and abs. OwnSelf just lays it out, and shows where you are on a minute-to-minute basis. There's no guess-work. Like right now"—she tapped her oval—"it's showing me I'm at 3,401 steps for the day, which is 11 percent ahead of where I usually am at this time. So I can probably slack off for the next hour, right?"

Delaney had the sense Kiki might be making a joke.

"As if!" Kiki said, and laughed theatrically.

Delaney pretended to laugh, too. Kiki stopped abruptly.

"You know how laughter is so good for your

health?" she said. "Minimum is twenty-two minutes a day—Morris proved that last year—so," she said, reading her screen again, "OwnSelf's telling me I have a ways to go on that metric today. I'm at two and a half minutes, but they're having an open-mic tonight, so I'm thinking that should cover it."

"Wow, you really have it down," Delaney said.

"I know. But listen," Kiki said, "I can hook you up with OwnSelf, too. It's . . ." Kiki searched for a long word. "It's spectacular." She looked at her wrist and smiled. "I've never felt more in control."

Another ding prompted her to pull a tube from beyond her left shoulder. Up till then, Delaney had assumed that Kiki's small burgundy backpack was decorative.

"Water," Kiki said. "Otherwise I don't drink enough." She took a long pull on the tube and it retreated into the pack. They started walking toward the light again. "Okay, here's the main gathering area, if you will. Some call it the Daisy, which makes sense, because of its shape."

They entered the densely populated expanse of winding walkways lined with wildflowers. Now Delaney took in Kiki's clothing, which had come alive in full sun. She was wearing a catsuit with a camouflage pattern of green and pink sequins bisected by a single zipper, which extended from her left ankle to her right shoulder.

Next to spritely Kiki, Delaney felt lumbering and leaden. When she'd chosen her clothes that morning, jeans and a cornflower cotton blouse, she had not thought she was dressing in any consciously antiquated way. But compared to the Everyones around her, she felt like an extra in **The Crucible.** They were all in lycra and they weren't exercising. She'd seen people dressed this way in the city, but the concentrated effect of so much lycra in one place, every curve and bulge articulated, was new. A man overtook them and Delaney realized he, too, was wearing leggings, which hugged and amplified his manhood. She made an involuntary sound, something between **Excuse me** and **Oh sweet Jesus.**

"Did you say something?" Kiki asked.

Delaney couldn't elaborate. Everywhere around her were men in form-fitting bodysuits, their penises in stark relief, and this she had not expected. The third decade of the twenty-first century had been accompanied by a gradual but unstoppable transition to ever-tighter clothing for body celebration and the fanciful implication that the wearer might be a superhero. The last bastion of the demure was the area of male crotch, but Delaney realized that, in the spirit of equity, it had to fall away. A workplace like the Every couldn't plausibly say breasts could be wrapped in tight lycra but penises could not.

"No," Delaney mumbled. Then, tragically, she looked at a section of ice plants and added, "Lots of succulents." She was trying to form a sentence unrelated to phalluses.

"We're encouraged to get our Vitamin D when we can," Kiki said, and pointed to the sun. "Doesn't the campus look gorgeous on a clear day like this?" She continued to point out the buildings, the services, the eateries, the vegetable garden, the ecstatic dance studio, a large gulag-looking building dedicated to the study of creativity—and all the while Delaney's whole physical form was awake and tingling, her eyes darting toward and away from every curve and bulge, a riotous battle of leering and shame.

"Are these parrot tulips?" Delaney asked, desperate to focus on something wholesome. She squatted down to touch the fringe of a flower. As she held a tender petal she looked up at Kiki just as a male crotch passed her at eye level, fully and fragrantly.

"I think so," Kiki said. "But **you** should know—you were the forest ranger!"

Delaney cackled idiotically and thought she'd choke. She tried to breathe.

"Almost forgot," Kiki said, seeming alarmed. "Can you download something? I'm sending you an update for your phone."

Delaney found the update and downloaded it. "Got it."

"You've been using TruVoice, I take it?"

"Always," Delaney said.

TruVoice had governed much of online communication since Delaney had been in high school. It started simply as a filter. A person would type or dictate a text, and TruVoice would scan the message for any of the Os—offensive, offputting, outrageous, off-color, off-base, out-of-date. O-language would be excised or substituted, and the message would be sent in a manner fit for posterity. **Sound like yourself,** TruVoice promised, and the vast majority of its users, some 2+ billion in 130 languages, saw it as a godsend.

"The update just builds on that," Kiki said, "but for verbal communication. Obviously we can't change your words in real time, but now TruVoice analyzes what you say, gives you a summary of your word usage at the end of each day, and shows you where you can improve."

"Wonderful!" Delaney said.

"It really **is** wonderful," Kiki said. "I've learned so much about my own communication. Wait. You have kids? No, right?"

"Not yet!" Delaney sang.

"I have a son," Kiki said. "He's five. He's at the school here. Did I already tell you that?"

Delaney had the feeling she was talking to some-one on speed or cocaine. Was it really water in that burgundy backpack? She'd rarely seen this kind of mania.

"And research says kids need to hear a hun-dred thousand words by the time they're three. Something like that. So TruVoice helps me with the overall number and also word variation. I'm still at 65 percent in terms of variation and difficulty—I'm a verbal dummy, it turns out—but now I know what I need to work on."

"Wonderful!" Delaney said again, louder than before.

"See, they'll note that repetition at the end of the day," Kiki said. "You won't get penalized or anything. It's just to help us do better."

Delaney almost said **Wonderful** again, just for her own amusement. Instead she said, "Of course."

"And it's almost eliminated my cursing," Kiki said, "which used to be a problem. Same with focus and length. I had a tendency to ramble, and TruVoice identifies off-track . . ." Kiki stopped. "What's the word? This is so funny."

"Verbiage? Meandering? Blather?" Delaney suggested.

"Yes, thanks," Kiki said. "It helps me get to the point. Early on, my directness scores were in the forties, but now they're high fifties."

"Kudos," Delaney said.

"Excuse me?" Kiki said.

"Oh. I just said **kudos.**"

Kiki tapped her screen. "Ah. Kudos. Like 'congratulations.' Got it. That's a Level-3 word, too. I'll get extra points for that one. Kudos. Kudos. Take a look."

Kiki showed her phone to Delaney. A man passed between them, wearing what seemed to be the outfit of an Olympic swimmer, his phallus pointing from his crotch to his left knee.

"Sorry!" Kiki said, and tapped her screen. "See, here's my word total for the day so far: 3,691. That's not counting every contraction and conjunction, of course. On the second line, you can see it's broken down by level. Today I've spoken 2,928 Level-1 words, 678 Level-2, seventy-six Level-3, and nine Level-4 words. Which isn't great, in terms of Level-4. But, that's the basic self-improvement part of the app. I can build on that. Growth mindset, right?"

"That's my motto," Delaney said.

"Good motto!" Kiki said. "Kudos!"

They shared a laugh. Delaney felt sick. She liked Kiki, felt for Kiki, wanted to save Kiki, and she was lying to Kiki. How long could she lie to this guileless, frenzied face? She pitied her own soul. Out of the corner of her eye, Delaney saw a pair of men in slalom ski outfits, decorated with faux-flames, having a conversation while squatting.

"Squatting is, like, way better than regular standing," Kiki noted. Her phone emitted the sound of a sad trombone. "See, that's a reminder. I'm trying to cut down on saying 'like.' I get the trombone when I do. And look." Kiki pointed to a string of words and phrases on her phone. "Here are things I said that AI flagged as problematic." She indicated a string of words in a red box: **screw, nasty, Cosby, Oriental.** "These are all words I've said today. Isn't it funny what was flagged? My mom is Chinese, so I could apply for a Permission to Say, but the AI is just noting the word **Oriental** is on the O-list. So I just need to explain I was referring to a rug. Then I get those points back."

"Wonderful," Delaney said.

"The other aspect is HR-oriented," Kiki continued. "So if TruVoice hears one of the Os, it makes a note. End of every week, you get a summary, and it goes to HR. It's not a big thing, but it protects you and everyone you encounter in case you say something considered problematic. That way, if you think **you're** in the right, it's recorded. If **they** think **you're** in error, same thing—there's a recording to reference. So you'll get the initial ComAnon—you'll get them every day, they're anonymous, they matter if they add up, but you shouldn't worry if they don't. Anyway, you can get them erased if you check the transcript and you're right."

"Super-convenient," Delaney said. "And this goes into PartiRank?"

Kiki looked taken aback. "Oh, we don't have PartiRank! That was phased out, like, **months** ago." Another sad trombone; Kiki grimaced. "A lot of people thought the rankings were a bit too competitive and stress-inducing."

"So these numbers aren't aggregated?"

"Well, they're collected, of course. For your own reference. They wouldn't be too useful if they weren't collected!" She threw a breezy laugh over her shoulder. "And of course combined with other metrics. Like PrefCom and AnonCom. You'll read

about that in your onboarding docs. AnonCom
allows coworkers to register complaints—well,
not complaints, really, but suggestions for your
improvement—anonymously. Those go into your
folder, with all the performance measurements,
participation points, smiles, ComAnons, shams,
step count, sleep hours, frowns, etcetera. All your
numbers are available to you and all Everyones,
and then are merged to create one aggregate number, and then Everyones' numbers are listed in
ascending order."

"But it's not a ranking," Delaney said.

"Definitely not," Kiki laughed. "That's why it's
called Everything in Order. You can see the difference between that and PartiRank, which was a lot
more hierarchical."

"Sure, sure," Delaney said.

"The EiO number—get it? EiO? The song?"

Delaney smiled weakly. Kiki hummed a few notes
and continued. "The EiO helps with the quarterly
deëmployment moment. Obviously who's subject
to deëmployment is too important and subjective to
have people do it, so it's the bottom 10 percent, department by department. That way it's fair."

"That's who's let go?" Delaney asked.

"Deëmployed, yes." Kiki smiled. "But the number of course isn't the only determinant."

"But there's no human factor."

"Well, no. Of course not. That would open it up
to bias."

A pair of men, built like dancers, walked by wearing sheer bodysuits. One wore a yellow water-carrier like Kiki's, its tube dangling provocatively. Delaney felt light-headed.

"Is there a restroom close?" she asked.

Kiki directed her to a nearby railing, just above the grassline, leading down a spiraling staircase to a single, underground bathroom. Delaney rushed down its rubbery steps and opened the door with a shush.

"Hello Delaney!" a voice said. She looked up to find a cartoon skunk on the wallscreen. Delaney's name appeared in an animated bubble extending from the skunk's mouth. "Let me know if I can help!"

Delaney entered the stall and locked the door and sat, clothed, on the toilet. She wanted badly to call Wes, to try to describe what she'd just heard, and what she'd seen, all the lycra and body parts, but she didn't trust the bathrooms on campus, knew she shouldn't let down her guard anywhere on the grounds. She only needed a moment to strategize, to control the movement of her irises, to think this through.

She stood up. "Are you finished?" the cartoon skunk asked. It was now on the door, looking politely away.

"No," she said.

"Don't let me rush you!" the skunk said, and then hid behind an animated tree.

Delaney sat down again. She had to think about how she'd speak from then on. She knew she was on camera, that she'd be on camera, multiple cameras, at all times on campus. Between this and the dicks she didn't think she'd make it.

"Can I sing you a song?" the skunk asked.

"No thanks," Delaney said. She tried to slow her breathing. She closed her eyes, and all she saw were the members suffocating in shiny stretchy fabric.

"Need more time?" the skunk asked.

"Yes please," Delaney said.

Delaney stood and flushed the toilet. Nothing happened, but the cartoon skunk appeared on the wallscreen behind the toilet. "No deposit made. No flush necessary!" the skunk sang. A quick sparkle flashed from its breezy grin.

Delaney left the stall, pulled at the bathroom door but found it was locked.

"Hold up, partner!" the skunk said, and the same words, **Hold up partner!** appeared in the cartoon-dialogue bubble. "Not till you wash up! Remember, twenty seconds minimum. Doctor's orders!" On the screen, the skunk began washing, too, while singing the Happy Birthday song.

Delaney stepped to the sink, minimal and rectangular and carved from obsidian. The soap dispenser dropped a dollop into her hands and the water was briefly activated. In the mirror, a digital timer appeared and began to count down from twenty. The skunk was still washing its own little hands, directly opposite, now singing the song a second time in Italian.

Delaney watched the timer. The birthday song had begun again. She still had fourteen seconds of washing to do. It was interminable. Eight seconds left. Delaney thought she'd rub her skin off.

"Looks like we're almost done!" the cartoon skunk announced, and did a backflip. After landing, the skunk dried its hands by doing a kind of woodland jazz-hands maneuver. "Go forth and stay human!" the skunk said, and when Delaney tried the door this time, it opened to the light. A corresponding ding sang from Delaney's phone.

"All set?" Kiki asked.

Another man passed wearing a wrestler's one-piece. This one covered half of his torso and stopped mid-thigh. His manhood was encased, it seemed, under a dome, a cup or jockstrap, Delaney didn't know which. Codpiece? She looked away, only to find two people, a man and a woman, standing face-to-face, each wearing form-fitting black bodysuits interrupted by no pocket or stitch. The woman was chesty, the man powerfully built, the curves of his thighs yearning for the curves of hers.

"Time for the onboarding doc. Let's head over here," Kiki said, and brought Delaney to a small building, ivy-covered, a twin to the one where she'd met Shireen and Carlo.

Inside, the room was empty, and Delaney exhaled elaborately.

"Last bit of housekeeping," Kiki said, and handed her a tablet. "The final onboarding doc, which we ask that you read carefully. Obviously the eye tracking knows what you've read, so . . ."

Kiki made for the door. "Initial every page and sign at the end. I'll come back in thirty minutes," she said, and left.

Delaney woke the tablet and Mae Holland's face appeared, filling the screen. "You made it," she said, and her eyes widened, as if she was both proud and a bit surprised. "You're joining us, and we couldn't be happier." It was a recording, but still, Delaney found herself briefly star-struck. Mae still looked like a newbie herself—those bright dark eyes, that olive skin, as smooth as a river stone. "We are so grateful you chose us, and I can't wait to see you on campus. If you see me, stop me and say hello!" She smiled, and Delaney took her in—the high cheekbones, just short of severe, that nearly lipless mouth. The lights upon her were perfect, setting her skin aglow, her eyes elated. Then she was gone, replaced by the onboarding document.

The sentences were fascinating, written with the strangely florid and willfully capitalized style common to the industry. "You are invited to bring your most Joyful Self to campus each day." "Your personal Fulfillment is our goal." "You are Seen Here." "You are Valued here." "Touching, including shaking of hands or Hugging, is de-approved unless between signers of Mutual Contact Agreements."

"This is a plastic-free campus." "This is a fragrance-free campus." "This is an almond-free campus." "Paper is Strongly discouraged." "Smiling is encouraged but not mandatory." "Empathy is mandatory." "Guests must be announced 48 hours in advance." "Vehicles that burn fossil fuels require an Exemption." "This is a Collaboration zone." "This is a Sacred place." "Everyones with children under five are encouraged to bring them to Raise Every Voice." "Non-company hardware is de-approved." "Downloading of non-vetted Software is de-approved." "All correspondence on company-provided devices is subject to screening." "Attendance at Dream Fridays is required Because They Are Awesome." "Attendance at Thursday Exuberant Dance is not required but urged because it is **next level.**" "This is a beef-free campus." "This is a pork-free campus." "Until further notice, this is a salmon-free campus."

The second Delaney was finished, Kiki's face appeared in the doorway. "Your medical intake!" she gasped. "You should have had it done by now. What time is it? We can get you in."

She hustled Delaney out and into the light.

"We're going to the Overlook?" Delaney asked. She'd read about the Overlook, and could see it, like a white spiral exoskeleton, on the hills above Treasure Island. What she'd read painted it as a mecca of tranquility—a place where Everyones could get **unparalleled healthcare in a spa-like setting with astounding 360-degree water views.**

"No, no," Kiki said, and looked briefly up at the array of white buildings in the distance. "The Overlook is for . . . It's not for basic intake, it's for . . . Wait. What time is it? Hi honey!"

She was with Nino again. "I'm sorry, hon-hon, Mama's working. And you have your own assessment today, so you stay till four." Kiki's eyes welled. "This helps Jolene know how you're doing. It helps Mama, too. Nino?" She tapped her ear and turned to Delaney apologetically. "Just a sec."

"Oh, hi Gabriel. I didn't realize you'd cut in. How are you?" Kiki was looking assiduously at the cement underfoot. "Yes. Got it. Of course." She tapped her ear again and smiled at Delaney.

"I'm assuming you had your DNA sequenced?" Kiki asked.

"For college, yes," Delaney said. It had been required at most schools, first state then private—insurers had forced the issue.

"Good, so just have to get the vitals, blood, X-rays, things like that," Kiki said, and they walked briskly to the clinic. Kiki's rubbery legs carried her ahead of Delaney and, finding Delaney falling behind, periodically she stretched her hand back, her fingers open like a star, her rings twinkling in the sun.

When they stepped inside the clinic, Delaney saw no humans. There was no reception desk, there were no doctors. The medical professions had been decimated by doubt and litigation, with the vast majority of patients preferring AI diagnoses over those of humans, which they considered recklessly subjective.

"Okay, it says you're scheduled for Bay 11," Kiki said, and took a moment to reconcile the map on her armscreen with her physical environs.

Delaney looked down the hallway and saw the numbers ascending toward 11. "I think it's this way?" she said.

Kiki looked up and, after a painfully long time examining the hall, its numbered rooms, smiled with relief. "Great. You go on and I'll come back when you're done."

Delaney walked down the hall, past the other bays, most of them containing a human lying on a medbed, the rooms dim but for the bright reflections of the patients' interiors on the wallscreens.

When she entered Bay 11, the room was empty but the wallscreen was alive with a series of neon pictures—three-dimensional visualizations of an embryo in a womb. The detail was astonishing, far beyond anything Delaney had seen before. This must be proprietary software, she assumed, something being tested on campus. The embryo was larger than life, perhaps three feet high, its eyes enormous, covered with a pink vellum, its tiny watery heart fluttering like a kite in high winds. The image was left over from whomever was last here, Delaney assumed, and before she could stop herself, she was scanning the screen for the name, and the moment before the screen went dark, she found it. Maebelline Holland.

Stunned, Delaney held her breath. She listened for anyone outside the door, anyone nearby. There was no one. She stepped into the hallway, stupidly looking for Mae Holland herself. The hallway was empty, and Delaney returned to the medbed. She thought about leaving. Seeing what she saw put her in some jeopardy, she was sure. Would she be expected to tell someone what she saw? Would the room's many cameras already know? To reveal it was an invasion of privacy—medical information like this being still unpublic—but to not reveal it: wasn't that a problematic elision?

The screen came alive again. It was a recording of a woman in a white coat, a stethoscope around her neck and a clipboard pressed to her torso. "Hello Delaney," she said. "I'm Dr. Villalobos."

The rest of the intake was unsurprising. Because Delaney's medical history was digitized, the Every simply had to add her data to their own database and update a few metrics. As the medbed scanned her, Delaney cycled through the possibilities. It seemed highly improbable that there was another Maebelline Holland on this campus. But it also seemed unlikely that the CEO of the Every would have used this nondescript medbed, let alone leave this most personal information onscreen for the next visitor to find. Above all, it was impossible that Mae Holland was pregnant. Her life was lived with unrivaled transparency; she was still fully Seen. To be true to those principles of the Seen, she would have broadcast her first visit to any doctor, her first knowledge of her pregnancy; anything less would breed suspicion, would perpetuate corrosive secrecy. And beyond that was the issue of carbon impact. Population growth activists had become more vocal and their questions—must you? should you? have you any right?—were seeping into the mainstream. If anyone would debate these questions openly, and seek a kind of customer consensus about her own babymaking, it would be the face of the Every.

So she could not be pregnant. That embryo being truly inside Mae Holland was not possible. But Delaney had no way to find out. It was one of the few pieces of medical data still outside Right to Know laws. During the second pandemic, new laws were rushed through all over the world, giving all citizens the right to know who had a virus and where they likely got it. It only seemed right, and contributed to the general well-being and slowing of the spread. And what about lice and mono? HIV and herpes? No one had a right to spread these afflictions—pinkeye!—and everyone had a right to know who was afflicted. Public registries became the norm, and the idea of keeping medical information private became indefensible. It put others at risk and thwarted scientific progress.

But pregnancies were still secret, or the law treated them as such. Delaney couldn't even search "Mae Holland pregnant," because the typer of those words would immediately be known. The second wave of the Right to Know laws had codified a person's right to know, in real time, who was searching for them and what information they sought. The searcher, to be sure, also had the right to know who was watching their searches, creating a two-way mirror effect, which occurred a billion times a day, of a searcher searching while the searched watched the searcher searching.

Could Wes do the search? Delaney wondered. And if this was indeed the truth—that Mae was carrying a child—she had concealed it. And if the head of the Every had purposely hidden this information, how could Wes access it? If anyone could find a way, he could. He had all the necessary tools of a hacker, but his brain was strange, too—his was a nonlinear mind that found back doors and side doors and crevices and cracks that wouldn't occur to anyone else.

"Okay, all set," Dr. Villalobos's recorded self said.

Delaney got dressed, and while buttoning her shirt, had a series of thoughts, none of them more rational than any other. She thought this could be a set-up, a test of how she would handle such sensitive information. But if so, there was no right response. Such a private matter should have been private in the first place. This was the unnecessarily awkward position Mae herself had sought to eliminate—the keeping of secrets, the sowing of distrust and fostering of conspiracies. Delaney had no choice, really, but to wait. As unorthodox as it was, perhaps Mae was simply waiting for the right time to reveal that she was bringing another human into the world.

VIII.

The moment Delaney entered the foyer, Kiki's face appeared. "All set? We're heading for the Reformation," she said. Delaney, still dazed, followed her out of the clinic and into the light.

"This is a more retro part of campus," Kiki said as they walked through a corridor of hangars and warehouses. "The building we're going to used to be airplane storage for the Navy, but was strategic for us because it abutted the old unused subway line. So we repurposed the tunnels for our trains. Follow me."

They entered a vast open-plan steel building that resembled nothing so much as a nineteenth-century factory. Delaney almost expected to see vacant-eyed children fixing rusting machinery.

"After it was a plane hangar this was actually a steelworking . . ." Kiki said, then was unable to think of the noun—plant? factory?—that might properly end the sentence. She pretended that the

word was implicit or unnecessary, though, and
distracted herself and Delaney by taking in the
cavernous space. It had room for three commer-
cial airliners and a fleet of buses, too. Bright bolts
of fabric had been strung from the steel beams, in
an effort, no doubt, to bring a festive mood to the
grim industrial space, but because the undulating
fabric had already absorbed whatever black dust still
dropped from the building's ancient ceiling, it made
the scene look somehow more tragic.

"Are you on right now?" Kiki asked, gesturing to
Delaney's cam.

"Oh no," Delaney said, "I was told to turn it off
for the med-eval . . ."

"Right, good," Kiki said. "You can go on again, if
you want."

Years ago, Delaney had bought and began to wear
a cam, in anticipation of her Every infiltration, and
to her surprise, the experience had been distinctly
underwhelming. She realized her life was generally
unremarkable and unwatchable. And when it was
approaching interesting, she found, true to Mae's
insistence, the camera on her chest forced her to behave better. The catty comment she wanted to make
did not make it past her self-censor. The double-dip
she contemplated with her celery stick at the baby
shower (client of Gwen)—this was thwarted by
the expectation that it would be caught, examined
by strangers with mouths agape, made part of her

permanent history. So she modeled the behavior she wanted from herself. She was less interesting, surely, and less funny—for humor does not easily survive the intense filtering that the twenty-first century made mandatory—but she was also kinder, more positive, more generous and civil.

"Delaney?"

A thin pink man stood before her, with a yellow flame of hair extending diagonally from his forehead. Delaney smiled and in greeting he placed his hand on his chest, a hand as pale and delicate as a capuchin monkey's. She glanced downward, just beyond the hand, fearing another penis, but was happy to find the pink man was wearing a sarong.

"Delaney. Welcome," he said, closing his eyes and smiling beatifically. "Taavi," he said, and pointed to a badge that verified his claim. "You know something about our work?"

"I do," Delaney said.

A shadow of irritation passed over the pale eyes of the pink man.

"Well, too bad," he said. "I'm required to give you the whole spiel, to make sure the record shows you got it." He pointed to the cam hung from his neck.

"That's my cue," Kiki said. "I'll check in with you EOD." She took Delaney's wrist, squeezed briefly and meaningfully, then sheered off with alarming speed. "Hello Nino!" she sang as she disappeared.

* * *

"Between 1990 and 2025," Taavi said, and began to walk, "the personal storage industry in this country grew from about 2,200 locations nationwide to over 520,000. These storage campuses occupy, on average, three acres, which means about a million acres are being used for ugly boxes containing useless boxes. This of course constitutes an environmental catastrophe. The land on which these ugly boxes stood had previously been open land, farms, pasture, backyards, public parks. And every time a storage unit popped up and got noticed, more people got the idea they needed to save every last piece of plastic or lint they'd ever possessed."

Taavi stopped at a screen, where a map of the United States throbbed with red dots. "So people rented these storage units, and the storage unit developers built more to serve skyrocketing demand. Soon enough every town had one, two, ten of these storage complexes."

The dots on the screen doubled, tripled.

"We became a nation of hoarders. And just when we might have gained some self-awareness and even shame about our hoarding, the television shows about storage units appeared, and that grew the market again. It was ludicrous. I mean, a TV show about storage units?"

Delaney laughed, and Taavi paused and closed

his eyes to absorb her laughter, as one would the warmth of the sun.

"This was, for a time at least," he continued, "primarily an American phenomenon. But like so many crass and insufferable trends, they start here and proliferate elsewhere. Canada was next, and within a decade they had a million acres of storage boxes, too. Then Australia. Then an odd smattering of other countries—Croatia, Turkey, South Africa. In Brazil they clear-cut rainforests for this nonsense," he said. They had arrived at an empty workstation.

"Anyway, we had to turn back the tide," Taavi said. "That's the origin story for Thoughts Not Things. Have you used it?"

All around them were carts full of photo albums of varying age and condition.

"For my mom and dad, yes," Delaney said. Her parents had tried to send their albums here, but Delaney had thwarted the plan. She scanned the photos herself and saved the albums in a storage unit halfway to Boise.

"You read and signed the onboarding docs," Taavi said, "so you know this. But now that we're at the workstation I'll just point out the obvious. Let's have you sit."

Delaney sat. The chair was perfect.

"You'll see that there are pedals under the desk, with adjustable resistance. You can pedal like a bike or use it like a stairmaster. The equipment of course knows when it's being used, and that data is yours. You know the health guidelines. You shouldn't sit more than sixteen minutes at a time, so you'll get reminders to stand, stretch, walk around."

"Wonderful," Delaney said. "I'd totally forget otherwise."

"It's been so lovely to meet you." Taavi turned to a woman sitting in the next workstation. "You're Winnie?" he asked, looking only briefly in her direction.

"Yes, Winnie," the woman said, standing and waving to Taavi and Delaney. "Welcome, welcome," she said.

Winnie was in her mid-forties and dressed much like Delaney, in jeans and a cotton blouse. And with the baton passed, like Kiki before him, Taavi peeled off and with remarkable alacrity returned to whence he came.

Winnie was a stout woman with deep dimples and dark, shining eyes. She smiled brightly at Delaney. Her hair was black and curly, pulled back into a wooly ponytail. A tiny Texas flag had been taped to her monitor, and next to her desk was a small plastic aquarium containing a pimply and bulbous lizard.

"That's Ricky," Winnie said. "He's a leopard gecko."

Her eyes searched Delaney's torso until she saw the cam. Her cheerful face fell just enough to seem utterly drained of joy.

"So you're Delaney!" she said, performatively.

"I am," Delaney said.

Winnie touched her ear. "From Idaho!"

They went this way for a time, with Winnie receiving information about Delaney via her earpiece, and Delaney confirming it.

"Well then," Winnie said finally, and cracked her knuckles. "It's probably best just to watch what I do, right?"

Delaney rolled her chair into Winnie's workstation and sat behind her. Her breath was shallow and quick.

"I've actually never trained anyone," Winnie said. "I'm only seven months into the job myself. I was doing graphic design for restaurants, basically. Menus and websites, right? Then my cousin sent me a listing for something here, something about scanning, and it paid about three times what I was making, so . . ."

Winnie looked judgmentally at her feet.

"That's awesome. I'm so excited," Delaney said.

Winnie brightened. "Well, obviously this place is incredible. The benefits are insane. I have three kids. You have kids?"

"Not yet!" Delaney said.

"Well, they have all these early-college programs here, these savings plans . . ." Again Winnie seemed to be having an argument with some part of her that struggled with her existence at the Every. Delaney decided she'd been some kind of counterculture type

at some point—maybe before the kids? Her forearms were dotted with tiny tattoos that looked like a
swarm of bees or beetles.

"So where should we start?" Winnie asked,
wholly adrift.

"You know," Delaney said, "just pretend I'm not
here. I can pick up on things pretty quickly, and if I
have a question I can stop you."

Winnie let out a happy sigh. "Thanks. Thanks.
The woman who trained me was so organized and
methodical, and I honestly couldn't do what she
did. She's actually head of the department now,
but isn't down here a lot anymore. Did you meet
her? Aneet?"

Delaney said she had not met Aneet, and again
urged Winnie to go ahead with her work; she didn't
want her to fall behind on whatever quotas she
was supposed to meet. Somehow the word **quota**
seemed appropriate in a place like this, which
seemed designed for the manufacture of steel stools
or the riveting of wings to jets.

"Okay, here's where I'm at," Winnie said. She
stood, and lifted the cream-white lid on a low-slung
device, revealing what appeared to be an enormous
piece of glass, easily three feet by four.

"Scanner?" Delaney asked, looking at the familiar
lights and oddly old-fashioned machinery under the
glass pane.

"It is," Winnie said. "The hope is to scan as
many pictures as you can at once. I mean, obviously

there'll come a point where robots can do this, but right now the work is still confusing to them, I guess, and sometimes too delicate. Look."

She pulled a photo album from the cart next to her desk. The cover depicted Ft. Lauderdale in the 1960s. Its plastic pages crackled as she opened it.

"First you have to see what you're up against, right?" She flipped through the book, the photos mostly small color pictures of a 1970s Christmas populated by a family of large-haired persons. The photos had rounded edges, and like most of the snapshots from the era, all of the action was taking place in the bottom third of each frame.

One by one, Winnie carefully transferred the photos from the album, peeling them slowly, the mild adhesive leaving trails of yellow, and placed them face-down onto the scanner bed.

"You know that game Memory?" Winnie asked. She stared at Delaney and seemed very interested in the answer.

"We called it Concentration, I think," Delaney said. "Where you have all the cards face-down and you turn them over one by one?"

"And try to get matches, right," Winnie said. She looked wistfully at the scanner. How Winnie had not been fired—this was perplexing. She had no sense of urgency, and seemed to lose her train of thought after every third word. "So then you drop the cover," Winnie said suddenly, and closed the lid clumsily.

An urgent ding sounded from Winnie's computer, followed by another from her oval.

Winnie's eyebrows bounced. "Sixteen minutes. Time to move around," she said, and then began marching in place, her knees as high as she could manage while wearing snug denim. With every fourth step, Winnie did a kind of twisting motion at the waist, with her elbows high. Then she returned to marching. Delaney had not been invited to join, so she simply sat and looked into the rafters.

Finally Winnie sat down and directed her attention to her screen, where perfect digital representations of all eighty pictures appeared. With some screentapping from Winnie, the photos were individuated, oriented, and laid out in a grid. Winnie told the program to scan for faces, and the people in the pictures were identified and a sidebar appeared, showing all of the photos, 1–83, in which each of the people were represented.

"The client gave us a list of people," Winnie explained, "and now the AI is finding each." Names appeared below each photo—Dad, Mom, Grandpa, Eloise, Barky.

Another ding came from Winnie's wrist. Winnie glanced down and laughed. "Can't believe I forgot." She reached for a thermos and drank from it. "Water," she explained. "Four liters a day. I used to wear the waterpacks, but it was upsetting my posture." She swallowed for a troubling amount of time, and finally her oval dinged with satisfaction. Winnie put the thermos back.

"Okay, now the pictures are in the system," she continued, "so you can do a thousand things with them. I can send all this to the client now, and let them go hog wild with genealogy or more detailed labels. With PastPerfect, the computer can figure out when each shot was taken, and that's important to a lot of people. The AI can do captions, and that's surprisingly popular. 'Grandpa at Christmas.' 'Uncle Phil at Christmas.' That's a free service and basically everyone opts for that. After we send them back, the clients can alter or improve the captions, but most people don't bother."

Winnie had lifted the scanner's lid and was absent-mindedly gathering the photos again—without the care she'd put into their arrangement on glass. Once she'd gathered them all into a sticky pagoda of curled paper, she dropped them into a large bin resting on the conveyor behind Winnie's desk. The bin contained thousands of photos of all sizes and ages, weddings and christenings and holidays, presumably, everyone now mixed together, humbled and democratized and destined for pulp.

"You can fit ten thousand in here," Winnie said. "You'd be surprised." Winnie tossed the puffy-covered album, with its lurid Florida sunset, into a different bin. "The albums you can't recycle," she said defensively. "We would if we could. But we can't. They get incinerated. Whoa. It's lunch. You hungry?"

On the way to the cafeteria, they passed a labyrinth of conveyors, murmuring and clicking, winding through workstations. Mae Holland had bought the company that designed and built most of the world's airport conveyors—a strange purchase, everyone agreed, but for the past five years she'd been buying a dizzying array of real-world companies, companies that grew food and built cars and planes, and so this purchase, at $44 million, tiny by Every standards, did not attract undue attention.

Now Delaney could see the bins moving, stuffed high with photo albums but other things, too—summer dresses, wicker baskets, 1980s-era stereos and soiled baby blankets, all moving through the building before leaving through a rubber-flapped door.

"I'll teach you that part, too," Winnie said. "It's basically the same thing we're doing, but with larger objects, the kinds of things that created the need for this storage-unit craze in the first place. The objects get a 3-D scan so thorough that the object could be easily re-created if need be. But face it, most of this stuff is junk. And if we can somehow convince people to let go of it by giving them a 3-D scan of their childhood bed or their dead son's trophies, then we can get rid of the objects, and end the hoarding that will end the world."

"So the conveyors take the stuff back to the client?" Delaney asked.

"God no," Winnie said. "Aren't you listening? That's why we're on the subway line. The stuff gets on train cars and heads east, then downstate for incineration. Danish style."

Outside Copenhagen, two sisters, whose father had been an industrial-waste management exec, had invented a carbon-neutral incinerator that reduced almost anything to a durable black paste that was mixed into certain kinds of concrete. It had become especially popular with California prison-construction firms.

"People don't know how to decide what to keep or not to keep," Winnie said. "So they keep everything. But we try to give them a better choice. We take a picture, and the stuff goes away. One less thing in the world."

IX.

"AND THE AFTERNOON?" WES ASKED. He was
sanding down a wart on the inner side of his big
left toe. It was a weekly ritual, and a reason he
wore only sandals. He could not wear standard,
roofed shoes.

"And in the afternoon," Delaney said, "I scanned
the photographic memories of thirty-eight people,
had an algorithm caption these photos, making
them somehow more anonymous, and then I tossed
these hundreds of original and irreplaceable photos
into a large bin to be recycled by another machine
and turned into prison paste. And Winnie did this,
too, but slower."

Wes nodded, assessed his work, and began sanding again. "Tell me," he said, "of this Winnie."

Winnie was not, Delaney noted, the kind of
world-beating uberhuman one would expect within
Every walls, but instead a married mother of three,
for whom an Every salary and health plan, and four

weeks of vacation, and maternity leave, paternity leave, bereavement leave, and a college-savings plan, and two-week all-ages kids' summer camp—also free—was utterly unattainable anywhere else.

"Eventually we had to coordinate our movements," Delaney said.

"I don't understand," Wes said, and then stared at the wall for a long second. "Oh wait. I know. The company's using motion sensors to gauge how fast you're working. Do you have any kind of foreman in the department? A supervisor?"

Delaney hadn't thought about it, but now she realized there was no such person in Thoughts Not Things.

"That means the AI is handling the supervising," Wes said. "And I'm guessing the staff prefers it that way. It's objective and can be gamed. They know where they stand at all times. So Winnie asked you to slow down?"

"She said things like **Be careful,** and **Make sure you get it right.** But I didn't catch on. Finally she wrote the words **Slow down please** on the inside of an old wedding dress heading for the fire."

"Is anyone going faster than you in the department?"

"No one. When I figured out Winnie's note, I looked around and saw that basically everyone was moving at the same pace."

"Right. That's the only way it works for them. The AI is comparing everyone against each other. A fast outlier would set new expectations and throw off the system. But if everyone's in the same general range, then no one's noticed."

"We work so slow," Delaney said. "It's unreal."

"At least they gamed the tech. Have to respect that. So you very slowly turn the world's beloved pictures and objects into paste?"

"That's the photos. With the other objects, we do a 3-D scan and then they go onto these conveyors, and the conveyors dump them onto these train-cars, and those go to the incinerator. Which is out in Fremont apparently, in the former Tesla factory."

"So you scanned what, exactly?" Wes asked.

Delaney tried to remember the other objects she'd scanned and sent to their doom. A pair of cowboy hats. An antique medical bag made of alligator skin. An intricate box kite clad in striped silk. The collected work of Nat King Cole on vinyl. Maybe a hundred letters, most of them handwritten and in their original envelopes. For the first handful of objects, Delaney had felt some sadness, knowing she would be the last person to touch these once-precious things. After an hour, though, she felt nothing. There were too many things in the world—too many to care about any one of them in particular.

"Can we look at your dashboard for the day?" Wes asked.

"No," Delaney said.

Wes grabbed her work tablet. "Too late. Okay, Overall, an 86," he said. "Is that good?"

Delaney didn't want to care, but she cared.

"Eighty-six seems low," he said.

She stared at the ceiling. Occasionally there were lizards on their ceiling. None tonight.

"Six AnonComs," he said. "Those are anonymous complaints from coworkers, I assume? How can you already have six complaints? What did you do?"

Delaney had no idea.

"Most of them are given codes," he said. "You got three 11s. What's an 11? Oh, here it is. 'Lack of interpersonal awareness.' You got an 8, too, which means you caused discomfort for a coworker. Wait. You got two 8s. Those are 'mini-discos.' Is that mini-discomforts? I bet it is. It also says you're late in filling out Personal Encounter Satisfaction Surveys for a bunch of people. PESSes. You should pick up the pace on those. Looks like Kiki needs one. And Taavi, Winnie . . . Delaney? Are you listening? You're churning?"

Delaney was churning. Churning was an obligation at home, too—the Sisyphean task of posting, smiling, winking, frowning, rainbowing, sending and receiving Popeyes, shopping and pretending to shop, and watching microvideos of people slipping on wet grass or falling off mountains. To seem normal to the Every, she had to churn. A college friend living in Bali sent her a Popeye; she was in a white bikini, surrounded by a cerulean sea. Delaney sent a smile. A cousin in Seattle sent a request for micro-funding; she was starting what she called a digital winery. Delaney directed $20 to her and got a pulsating star in return. Her mother sent a sham of a neighbor leaving her recycling bin on the curb all week; Delaney sent a double-sham accompanied by a stern-faced emoji.

"Go on," she said. "I can hear you."

"This dashboard has at least a hundred health metrics," Wes said. "Did you know your heart-rate peaked at 10:32 a.m.?"

"I remember that," Delaney said.

"You want to hear about your minute ventilation?"

"Absolutely I do," she said.

"You know what minute ventilation is?"

"Well, **yes,**" she said. "I've been thinking about it all day."

"You don't know what it is. It's how much you breathe in a 60-second period. Ideally you move around six or seven liters of air a minute. Want to know how much you averaged today?"

"No. Yes. Fifty?"

"Six-point-one. I don't know if that's good."

"I bet it's good," she said. "It sounds ideal."

Delaney was asked to frown at the recent imprisoning of a Tunisian dissident, so she sent a frown. Nike was having a sale on leggings; she sent a smile. Another Popeye came through, this one from her mom in Idaho. Delaney found a Lisa Simpson emoji with bulging eyes and sent it to her. In return, her mom sent her a gif of fireworks exploding into a rainbow. Delaney had long ago subscribed to a Russian car-accident video service; a new video came through of a multi-vehicle collision outside of Minsk. She watched it at double time and sent both a smile and a frown. A friend in Chicago regularly sent short videos of her cats projectile-defecating; Delaney watched the newest—this cat seemed to be very happy after release. Delaney sent the friend the same firework-rainbow her mother had sent her.

"Did you know you can watch your day at work?" Wes said. "Look." He'd already called the footage up. Delaney was viewable from twelve angles arranged in a grid.

"Ah, look at you and Winnie exercising. Are you pretending to pass a medicine ball between you? That's fun. And now you're marching in place. Look at you! That knee elevation!"

Delaney reached over and closed the window. Wes called up another spreadsheet.

"They have everything here," he said. "They have all the companies the Every bought this week. 'We welcome new family members!' it says. You know how Apple used to buy one company a week? The Every's doubled that. Says here they just bought a Canadian paper mill. Wonder why."

"To shut it down," Delaney said.

"Oh right. That must be the same for Carter Plastics. They took on a blimp maker, too. I like that. That must be Bailey. Whoa, they bought Maersk—the shipping company. And did you get this text from your parents? They cc'd me. 'Welcome to the Every! Now the whole family's in the family!' What does that mean?"

"They work for FolkFoods."

"Oh god. You all **do** work for the same company! That is really depraved. How did I not put that all together?"

Delaney had no idea. The gaps in what was obvious and what Wes saw were often baffling.

"When did they buy Nestlé?" he asked. "I must have missed that. You heard about Pillo, the mail-order prescription company? That went for twenty-two billion. You're not listening."

"I am listening."

"This is weird. They also bought a company that teaches AI to read lips. That actually happened. In real life. So do you want to hear more about your day and how you fell short?"

"You know I do."

"They have minutes sitting, minutes standing, words spoken. Wait, minutes of laughter? It says you're under-average for Laughter minutes. They capitalize the L but not the M."

"That reminds me," Delaney said. She went to the feed of a college acquaintance, once a comedian, who had just announced he was making a short film about the spread of online disinformation. In the announcement, he misspelled **disinformation,** the

FCC, and his own name. Delaney sent him a smile and $20.

"You also got a ToT. Terseness of Tone," Wes said. "At 3:32 p.m. Who were you terse to at 3:32?"

It had to be Winnie. She hadn't talked to anyone else in the afternoon. Winnie had asked Delaney to watch a video of her son—was it Fabian?—catching a football during gym class. Delaney had been lifting a marble bust to scan it before incineration, and had grunted "In a sec" while heaving it onto the glass.

Winnie had said nothing to Delaney about it, and when Delaney was finished sending the bust to its doom, she'd watched the football video and had expressed amazement at young Fabian's catch. But Winnie had still registered the complaint.

Wes squinted at the screen. "It says, 'I understand she was under stress that moment but my feelings were de-elevated.' Did you know you were de-elevating Winnie at 3:32?"

Delaney hit herself with a pillow, then yelled into it.

"I'm assuming these complaints are mandatory," Wes said. "AI identifies what should be the average, so Winnie's just hitting her quota. Otherwise she'd be flagged for an anomaly. Yep, I just checked your own AnonComs. You're below average on those. Did you do any AnonComs today?"

"I didn't know I had to," Delaney said.

"Looks like twelve is what they expect. Find

twelve things that upset you about your coworkers each day and you're fine."

Delaney was exhausted. She stood, walked two steps to the doorway that separated her bedroom from Wes's, and turned back to him. "So what do you think, will I find a way to take down this company while incinerating strangers' pictures and wedding dresses?"

"I think you're on your way," he said.

She closed the door and fell into bed, dizzy from the day. She could hear him tapping on the other side of the drywall.

"You got another AnonCom," he said. "At 11:03 p.m. Your score went down to 84.6. But I think it'll hold there for tonight."

"Now please stop," she said.

He stopped. "You going to sleep?" he asked.

"Trying," she said.

Delaney heard him arrange himself with Hurricane, the two of them scratching and thumping, and finally there was the whoosh of his comforter taking to the air and settling upon dog and man.

"Night," he said.

"Night," she said.

"I love you," he said.

Totally unreasonable, she thought. Just unneccesary and odd.

"I thank you," she said.

X.

A WEEK WENT BY AND DELANEY had sent a thousand irreplaceable possessions to the fire, issued the requisite number of specific and inconsequential AnonComs, and otherwise adopted Winnie's cheerful affect toward their work of destruction. It was banal, routine, accompanied by Winnie's chatter about her kids and husband, and her husband's friend, Luke, who Winnie insisted was a stone-cold fox and, even better, didn't know it. At regular intervals, she and Winnie got up to exercise in place, high-stepping and desk-pedaling, and then went back to scanning and incinerating.

After work each day, Delaney went home and she and Wes left their devices at home and walked to the waterfront, Hurricane's leash taut. He yearned to leap to the sand and couldn't understand why they were walking on the concrete when, just beyond the wall, the limitless beach beckoned.

"You think I should chip him?" Wes asked.

Delaney shrugged. A permanent chip in Hurricane's tibia in exchange for the right to run leashed in a circle on the sand? There were no good choices.

"So I take it you haven't seen the right wires to cut?" Wes said. "I notice that the Every is still standing."

"I'm establishing trust," Delaney said. "False sense of complacency. Playing the part. Establishing a—"

"Got it," Wes said. "So: no plan."

"I will feel bad when the Every dies," Delaney said. "People like Winnie losing their jobs."

"There are other jobs," Wes said. "Less incineratey jobs."

"But for a mother of three like Winnie, the benefits are phenomenal. And she clocks out at five on the dot. All her machines stop working the moment she puts in eight hours."

"Right. A million lawsuits citing unpaid overtime died the second that software was invented. And she gets paid handsomely."

"How would you know?" Delaney asked, but of course he knew.

"Give me some credit," Wes said. "Did you even read your onboarding docs? Everyone's salary at the Every is accessible to any other Everyone. Radical transparency. Did you know she got a DUI when she was eighteen?"

"Wes, stop."

"It's all there. You didn't look? Every address she's

ever had. Anyway, when the Every dies, something will replace it," he said.

Delaney thought about this. The Every, or its component parts, had aggregated power over twenty-two years, and with the seemingly once-in-a-lifetime blending of minds, the Three Wise Men, two of whom, now, were rarely spoken of. Could it be replicated? After Delaney freed the world from the Every's death-clench, would some other tech python simply take its place? It seemed unlikely. But with Tom Stenton gone, they were more vulnerable; he was a dead-eyed shark that never tired—and had been key to the company's relentless consolidation of power. Ty Gospodinov was a fragile idealist, a sometime critic of what the Every had become, and no one had seen him in years; he'd been given an unlimited budget to pursue his hope of living for-ever. Bailey, a self-described **autodidact dilettante,** was actually interested in other people, in know-ing them, connecting them, improving them. But his side interests, like space travel and searches for famed shipwrecks, were all costly and impractical. Mae had somehow synthesized the most potent of all their traits, and had an unflagging focus they all lacked. She rarely left campus, didn't dabble in phi-lanthropy or politics; she had no family ties; she was always public but never showy, embodying, with startling consistency, a life lived online and utterly open to view.

"You see Bailey?" Wes asked.

"He's not there. They say semi-retired, but he's not there, period."

"Mae? Any sign of her?" Wes asked.

"I saw her feed. She was on campus today, but nowhere near my department. Thoughts Not Things is sort of the Allentown of campus. She doesn't visit, doesn't call."

"She's embarrassed," Wes said. "She hasn't had an idea in ages. I think she's ashamed to be too out there until she does. She hasn't done a Dream Friday in years."

Delaney had almost forgotten the 3-D ultrasound. "And she's pregnant, apparently."

"But—" Wes went mute.

Delaney explained what she'd seen her first day, and together they replayed Delaney's thoughts on the matter. Wes stared at the dunes to the south, trying to figure it out.

"She uses the same medbeds as everyone else?" he asked. "Actually, that makes sense. She would use the same facilities. That's her." His index finger was extended, as if he intended to begin counting the facts, but then abandoned it. "But the rest of it—leaving the screen up wouldn't happen. She would have personally refreshed it before leaving. Which means it would have had to be re-activated by accident. Some glitch. Which is so unlikely."

"So someone did it on purpose," Delaney said.

"Which is a thousand times less likely," he said.

"So now I'm thinking it **was** intentional. Something someone meant you to see. A test of some kind."

"On my first day."

"When else? You know how fucking weird they are."

Delaney walked a few steps with that notion. A gust from the Pacific sent a jittery spray of sand their way. Hurricane sneezed.

"It's the kind of thing Stenton was into, apparently," Wes said. "Does anyone mention him?"

"Not yet," Delaney said. "He's still in China."

"I know he's in China!" Wes said. "He can't stop failing over there. No one has ever failed so loudly and often."

By all accounts, when Stenton left the Every for Huawei, it constituted the most galling betrayal in the history of the industry, and immediately rang the bells of a dozen regulatory and anti-espionage agencies. Mae and Bailey had felt well-covered in terms of patents—and oddly, Stenton was never quite on the inside when it came to the most prized products in the pipeline. Still, fears abounded that Stenton had taken some unknown patchwork of Every IP to China—and not just to China but to Huawei, the Every's largest competitor in the making and marketing of phones. The only seeming upshot of this was that since his arrival, Huawei's fortunes had slumped. Following his advice, Huawei had slashed the features and price for their phones, hoping to harvest, or create, a bargain-minded market that did not care for, or need, the Every's $2,100 phone. Stenton had, though, been proven wrong so far. Huawei's phones were less expensive but were considered flimsy toys. They broke. Their fit and finish was cretinous and crude.

"Their phones are too light," Wes said.

Everyone thought their phones were too light, and this was Stenton's doing entirely. He'd been hellbent on making Huawei's phones featherweight, spending hundreds of millions on lighter batteries, lighter plastic, lighter semiconductors—but as it turned out, people did not want their phones light. They wanted to sense their heft, to know they were there.

And they certainly did not want them cake-cone fragile. Stenton's Huawei phones broke when dropped, broke when sat on, broke when exposed to cold and heat. They felt cheap and they were cheap, and ultimately they were not wantable objects. When Stenton's three-year Huawei phone calamity played out and was proven disastrous, the schadenfreude in the Every, and in California generally, for such a traitor of the values of quality—for there really was pride in the objects designed (not made) in the Bay Area—was extreme and unhidden. Each Huawei stock-price tumble, each rebuke of Stenton in the Chinese press was wonderfully satisfying and poetically just, and any fears that Stenton was a brilliant Prometheus bringing Every-fire to Beijing—or at least Guangzhou—were unfounded.

Stenton's mercenary life choices stood in stark contrast to those of Eamon Bailey, who became only more likeable the further he was nudged aside by Mae. The less he was involved in the day-to-day, the more obvious it became that his primary interest had been in knowing and sharing for its own sake. Making the systems work elegantly had been Ty's purview, and the monetization had been Stenton's. Bailey was the mouthpiece, the trustable uncle who actually thought, on balance, Every tech was improving lives, connecting far-flung families, was democratizing all of humanity's ac-cumulated learning, was making billions feel less bewildered, less oppressed and less alone. His side projects, like the asteroid-walkers, the solar blimps, the cross-country hyperloop, continued, though Mae had reportedly shortened the leash on all non-core endeavors.

"Is Bailey's crazy library still there?" Wes asked. "The one with the fireman pole? What about the tank with the transparent shark?"

Delaney did not know about the state of the shark, or Bailey's library, and this frustrated her. She'd read a few books on being undercover, in-cluding Donnie Brasco's, and most of the narrators warned against complacency—becoming too ac-customed to the surroundings, too sympathetic to the players. She'd spent more time thinking about Winnie and Winnie's kids, and their health plan and college options, than she had studying and dismantling the company's intricate machinery of doom. She was going to fail.

Meanwhile, Wes had stopped walking. Hurricane was again caught between them, straining at the leash.

"Okay, shit," Wes said, as if he'd just concluded a strenuous dialogue with his conscience. "I can't keep secrets. They asked me to come in and interview."

"What? Who did?"

"Your workplace. The Every."

"You?" Delaney said.

"I know. I'm a fucking idiot, but yes, me."

"I didn't mean it that way," she said, though she had meant it exactly that way. "But you didn't apply, did you?"

Immediately Delaney knew what happened. Wes had helped with her AuthentiFriend presentation. He'd done most of the actual programming and design. Shireen and Carlo had liked the app, and it had been discussed in elevated quarters—maybe even at the Gang of 40, among the company's top minds. The Every did not hesitate to hire anyone exhibiting both talent and initiative, given the two were rarely found in the same person. The ambitious rarely had ideas, and the talented were often lazy or impossible to be near. How could she bring in an accomplice and name him, show him, announce him, and then expect the Every to forget his existence? Of course they called him.

"I don't have to go in," he said.

"Do you really want to?" she asked.

"Even if just to see the place," he said.

Delaney was suddenly furious. "You're planning to take the money of a company that represents the most obvious monopoly the world has ever known?"

"I'd be taking a little bit of their money. Actually, a lot of their money. It wipes out all my college—"

"The company that stole childhood from you and me and a billion other children?"

"My moms would resent that, I think. You forget I grew up in a trog—"

"The company that's coddled dictators around the world, which sells surveillance software to every autocracy? That's enriched its founders and stockholders on the backs of unpaid billions who are studied and—"

"I see this as a way to get that unpaid labor back," Wes said. "At least for me."

"The company that made possible the end of American democracy and the rise of illiberalism here and abroad. Putin and Bolsonaro, who have been in office, what, a hundred years now—"

"Charismatic men with some good ideas," Wes said.

"Don't joke. Every country has their own digital secret police. Any dissent is squashed before it can begin."

They continued on, a swirling wind at their back. Hurricane rushed to chase a pair of crows from an overflowing garbage can.

"Listen," Wes said. "I can help. Gather intel."

"I don't want your intel. You're not good at this. **I'm** not good at this, but you'll be terrible. You can't lie and you can't keep secrets. If you take a job there, then **I** have no chance at pulling this off. You'll be the worst spy, and I'll be compromised within a week."

"Compromised?" Wes said. "You're not an actual spy, you know. You can't be compromised when you're just, you know, you. And I haven't gotten the job yet."

Delaney saw the potential for Greek tragedy. He would be hired, would endear himself, would find his loyalties split. Though at first he'd remain neutral, letting Delaney do her thing so long as he was not an accomplice, eventually he'd see Delaney as not a whistleblower but as a sociopath trying to take away the livelihoods, security, pensions and happiness of tens of thousands of Every employees, many of whom he liked very much as humans.

"This is so wrong, Wes," she said. She wanted to run and scream.

"Delaney. One year at that place kills all my debt."

"A week ago you were planning to be on the outside, remember that? You were setting up triple satellite firewalls so you could work from out here, and help blow all this up . . ."

"I still want that," Wes said.

"Do you hear yourself? You want the company to be taken down, but you're going to accept a job there and develop an app we both know is species-ending?"

"Okay. I know how that sounds, but I also had a different idea. Which was, hear me out: would you consider waiting a few years?"

Delaney couldn't speak.

"Don't look like that," he said. "You know it's logical. It's just more methodical. You want revenge now, but the better way is slower and more thorough. We both work there a few years, sock away some money, and then, once we know the workings of the place, together we kill it from the inside. Or outside. Whatever you think."

Delaney knew what he was saying was perfectly rational. It might even improve their odds of success—to work there unnoticed, gaining trust and access while also together saving a few hundred thousand dollars for the inevitably lean times when, after their takedown, they would be unemployable.

"No," she said. "Just because you're suddenly soft and mercenary, it doesn't mean I wait."

In the dimming light, they stood and stared at each other. Delaney was wrecked. Her closest friend was sabotaging her sabotage.

"I'm hungry," Wes said, "and it's getting dark."

"You go home," she said. "I need to walk."

Wes and Hurricane headed back, and Delaney found the next set of steps down to the sand. The wind had picked up and she needed its resistance. She'd walk all the way to the Cliff House, she thought. Or dare to go barefoot in the shallow surf. It couldn't be over 50 degrees this time of year, but she wanted the shock of it.

"Hello," a voice said. A figure in a dark jacket stood at the concrete stairway. Another sort of beach monitor. Without Hurricane, Delaney felt no need to slow down. As she took the first step toward the sand, though, the man went into action.

"I'll need to see your phone or oval," he said.

When she asked why, a white beam shone in her face. The man was holding his phone up to her, filming her, its light an assault.

"New city ordinance," the man said. "There have been drownings on this beach and a string of thefts. To enter the beach you need to register with either your phone or oval. This protects you and others."

He spoke the words in a practiced monotone, filming all the while. Delaney had no tracking devices with her, so wouldn't be allowed on the beach. She also knew every second she was on camera was a risk; she'd be shammed and the Every would know. As he filmed, she kept her chin down and her face in motion, hoping this might thwart easy facial recognition. This encounter, she knew, would certainly be flagged by AI. Her only vague hope was that it wouldn't be linked to her name.

Delaney quickly turned away and hustled to the sidewalk.

"Thanks for your compliance!" the man sang to the back of her head.

As she walked home, Delaney fumed. This was the Every's doing—another public space brought within their field of surveillance. She was angry, too, that she knew nothing about this new restriction. But how could she have? There was no longer local news. Starved of advertising and attacked as inherently exploitive and predatory—people no longer trusted filters, curators, observers and intermediaries—journalism had died quietly and alone.

When Delaney got home, she found Hurricane in the bathtub, Wes kneeling over the edge with tweezers and gauze.

"Glass," he said. "Just after we left you."

Hurricane took his paw back and when he put weight on it, he squealed. He'd pushed the shard in further.

"Goddamnit," Wes said. "See? Do you see?"

Delaney paced through the living room, hearing Wes through the half-open door. "Fucking beach monitors!" he yelled. "Tell me to chip a dog!" The causal relation was tenuous, but Wes's version, Delaney knew, was forming. Hurricane couldn't run on the beach, so he was forced to walk the glass-strewn pavement, where a lime-green sliver cut him to the bone.

In an effort to release some of the tension in the Shed, Delaney went to open the window, and, on the sill, amid Wes's crude clay sculptures, there was a perfect black globe, a plastic orb dotted with a hundred pinprick holes.

"What is this?" she yelled. She knew what it was. It was a smart speaker—one of the Every's, a HereMe. She brought it into the bathroom. Hurricane looked up, deeply confused, his bloody paw in Wes's hand.

"Is this what I think it is?" she asked. "When did you get this?"

"It's not **on,**" Wes said, with exhausted condescension. "I knew you wouldn't approve. They sent me one yesterday. I thought you'd seen it."

Delaney was dizzy and sick. She picked it up, shook it, having no idea why. "How do you know it's not on?" she said.

"Because among the two of us, only one knows anything about these devices. Can I help my dog? Do you care? It's not even charged. It has no batteries and hasn't been plugged in. I just liked the way it looks. Don't shake it. And—"

Delaney went to the window over the toilet, opened it, and threw the globe over the neighbor's fence. It shattered on the driveway.

"Jesus, Delaney!" Wes yelled.

She'd never done anything so rash in her life. But the prospect that the device had been recording everything they'd been saying, that her work would be undone before it even began, because her moron-accomplice had brought an actual spying device into their home—it took her to desperate places. She retreated to her room.

Delaney's phone dinged. It was a survey from Everything Outside, which she took to be the privatized version of the Department of Parks and Recreation. She hadn't heard of this entity. "Please rate your recent interaction with us!" There were five options, starting with a happy yellow face and descending to a red-faced one with eyes clenched in fury. She sent a happy face; she had no choice.

Later, Wes appeared in her doorway, the white stem of a lollipop extending from his mouth.

"Sorry," he said, the stem bobbing, "you're a lunatic, but I can see why you'd be upset. Not to the point where you'd destroy something like that, but I should have told you."

"Can you at least take that out when you talk?" she asked.

He removed the lollipop and regarded it, as if apologizing to it for removing it from its cozy residence. "I should have told you as soon as they contacted me. I know this. And I can see how it could be a wrench in your plan. But I should at least see what they have in mind. That much is just common sense, right?"

"You can't work high," she said.

He put the lollipop back in his mouth. "Delaney. I know that." With his mouth full, he sounded high.

"No edibles, no sprays. Nothing," she said.

"I know. I know they do drug tests and—"

"No," she said, "they don't do **tests.** They know every aspect of your entire physiology at all times. Haven't you read about this? It's how you get their healthcare."

"They allow pets, though," he noted, holding the now-naked lollipop stem in the air like a baby scepter. "I'm bringing Hurricane. He'll sleep at my feet."

"I can't stop you," Delaney said, while thinking of ways she might be able to stop him.

"I have to say, Pia's pretty excited, too," Wes said. "She said she was proud of me. I don't know if she ever said that before."

"I can't believe this," Delaney said.

Wes chomped on the hard remains of his lollipop. Delaney had never seen him so pleased with himself.

"Who knows," he said. "They might not hit me back."

Delaney knew this was not true and could not be true. The Every did not leave loose ends.

XI.

BUT THEY DID NOT CONTACT WES on Wednesday
or Thursday. Delaney went about her work these
two days, digitizing and turning to paste hundreds
of heirlooms, oil paintings, middle-school science
projects, about twelve thousand photos, then sending their digital versions to clients from around the
world with rudimentary and often incorrect captions made by an insentient system. The work was
repetitive but just varied enough to induce a kind of
hypnosis that Delaney found soothing. And Winnie
rarely stopped talking.

On her desktop screen there was a grid of camera
feeds—at least thirty-two by Delaney's casual count.
Each of Winnie's children wore a cam, and their
feeds each occupied one box, their schoolrooms
another ten or so, her husband's cam and workplace another six, with at least a dozen monitoring
her home, her parents' home, and what seemed to
be an elderly relative in an assisted living center.

There were no moments in any day that Winnie didn't know where each of her children was, where her husband and parents were and what they were doing. If anyone did something out of the ordinary, AI would flag it and she could play it back to see if it merited her attention or correction.

"You have your parents on cams, I hope?" Winnie asked her. "They must be getting older . . ."

Delaney was so startled to be asked a question that it took her a moment to answer. "I do," she said. It seemed noncommittal and banal enough to discourage any follow-up.

"You know, I've been meaning to tell you that you can keep in touch with them here. Have you done any participating today?"

"Not yet," Delaney said.

"Let's get ten minutes in," Winnie said, and lunged for her phone. Delaney got hers.

"We do anything we want?" Delaney asked.

"Company stuff, personal stuff, anything," Winnie said. "It's important to keep up with your personal relationships. They really emphasize that here."

Winnie had turned her back to her and was gone, her face unusually close to her phone, thumbs flying. Delaney churned through her feeds and accounts. Her mom sent her a picture of a neighbor's new car; she sent back a smile. Rose, their mail carrier, sent a photo of her son's new girlfriend holding a baby; Delaney sent a rainbow. Ads for tampons appeared, and for guns and gum and a heat-saving kind of double-paned glass. A college friend sent a minivid of a volcano currently erupting in Chile. Unsure if a smile or frown was appropriate, Delaney found and sent an emoji of a worried-looking unicorn. On her Every feed there were 311 notices from that day alone. She sent them into Wes's auto-churn app and moved into her news feed. A minivid of a couple being carjacked and shot to death in Ukraine appeared and thereafter was part of Delaney's mind. It was followed by a survey: **Would you like to see more like this?**

"Oh look," Winnie said, and she pointed to one of the boxes on her screen. A handsome man was speaking in front of a phalanx of American flags. "Have you watched him? Tom Goleta?"

Delaney had been following him closely for months. Goleta was a presidential candidate who posed—as much as any political entity could—an existential threat to the Every. Word was he'd be coming to campus in a few weeks.

"He's very tough on this place," Winnie said, as she sent a bin of porcelain cups and plates to the fire. "I can't figure out why Mae invited him here. Doesn't that seem unwise?"

It was no longer exotic to have a gay presidential candidate. In fact, since the advent of the Indiana mayor—never president but now a senator—no presidential election had been without one. Though, to be sure, every gay candidate had been in a certain mold—mild, married, Midwestern. Tom Goleta was all of these things, and added a fourth M—Methodist. His résumé seemed precision-sculpted to create the ultimate Every foe. He had been a formidable trial attorney, then a consultant, then a deputy head of the FCC, then on the anti-trust task force that had exposed collusion between the world's six remaining oil conglomerates. He ran for Senate with no prior election experience and won by eight points against an admittedly aging and error-prone Republican opponent who could not pronounce **quinoa.**

Goleta was one of the few politicians who had not succumbed to going Seen. For ten years it had been the norm, whether the constituents wanted it or not. To broadcast one's days, one's meetings and hearings and campaign events spoke of transparency: **I have nothing to hide, so watch me.** Only a smattering of leaders were still dark, and most were anti-tech crusaders. Goleta insisted his interest in the Every was not that of a crusader, and that his frequent allusions to monopolies and the near-certain applicability of anti-trust legislation was not a crusade. But when he decided to run for president, the Every emerged as a central focus of his platform; his attacks, even if rhetorically mild, had a populist flavor and played particularly well in the thousands of towns that had acre-sized data centers in their midst that employed few or no locals in their construction and staffing or maintenance, and somehow found a way to avoid all taxes.

Delaney craned her head to look at Winnie's screen. Goleta's parents hailed from two of the hemisphere's calmest places—father from Belize, mother from Davenport, Iowa—and his demeanor was preternaturally at ease. He seemed never nervous, never unloved. His jaw was strong, his eyes sensitive, all-seeing. He was always noticing someone in the crowds around him, someone who might need a moment of connection with him, a few seconds they would not forget. In the video Winnie wanted Delaney to see, he was standing in front of a hundred young voters outside the latest iteration of Antioch College.

"My people have been in the U.S. since 1847," he began. "My great-great-grandfather, a white man, was a typesetter for an abolitionist newspaper in Alton, Illinois. Because he would not leave his post, would not leave that press, he was killed by a pro-slavery mob. I have his diary, and it says some interesting things about the standards he lived by as a typesetter. He actually refused to typeset pro-slavery sentiments—that goes without saying—but he also refused to typeset lies. It's in his diary. 'To typeset a lie is a crime. It's taking a back-alley whisper and making it a national scream.'"

Winnie paused the video and turned to Delaney, her jaw slack. "And his husband is hotter than he is." Delaney was unsure if Winnie had missed the central message of the video, or had simply moved on to more prurient interests. Winnie spent a minute finding a few choice photos of his husband Rob, a city planner, whose Nordic masculinity somehow made Goleta, who looked like he could lift a car, seem anemic by comparison. Winnie unpaused the video.

"Now we have the Every," Goleta continued, "which has no problem disseminating any lie you pay them to. They've distributed countless lies about me and Rob, about our families, about Rob's military service, about my religion. I think that's wrong, and I think my great-great-grandfather would find that wrong, too. The idea that the Every is like a phone company, and is only carrying messages on wires with no obligation to the truth, is so dishonest it does not warrant a retort. They are publishers, for two reasons: one, the messages they send are seen by masses of people—sometimes billions—and two, they disseminate the printed word in a way that is permanent. Period. That is radically and inarguably different than carrying private spoken messages from one person to another, as the phone company once did. It's the difference between a note passed between two kids in class, and a kind of skywriting that can be seen instantly by everyone in the world, and that's everlasting. And if you disseminate untruths, you are liable for any and all damage that lie does. This is such a simple application of libel law that it's flummoxed lawmakers and regulators for decades now. But it's time to act. I don't care if it's social media or some wiki. If you provide the platform to spread these lies, you are accountable. I will hold you accountable."

Again Winnie paused and turned to Delaney, her eyes agog.

"How do we counter that?" she asked.

Delaney had no answer. Over the years, members of Congress, and governors, and presidential candidates long before Goleta, had tried and failed—had immolated in towering fireballs—while attempting to take on the Every. Invariably that candidate would find themselves on the wrong end of scandal. Invariably there would be mountains of evidence made conveniently available to social media and attorneys general. Digital messages would emerge containing unpardonable beliefs, statements, photos, searches. Invariably a digital mob would come for them and amplify these flaws and transgressions. With a hundred other battles to wage, more approachable dragons to slay, it had been years since any politician had suited up to fight the Every.

Just as Delaney was contemplating Goleta, and how he might do the job she intended to do—but far more effectively, publicly, and permanently—Winnie extinguished the screen.

"Dream Friday!" she said. "Your first one!"

XII.

DELANEY AND WINNIE were among the last to find
seats in the auditorium, and the moment they sat
down, Winnie commenced knitting—she had
brought her knitting—what appeared to be a shirt
for a miniature person with an extraordinarily short
torso. Delaney was tempted to ask just what Winnie
was making, or who in her life would fit into this
garment, but the silence the knitting had engen-
dered was welcome. There was the occasional tick of
the needles, but otherwise her movements had the
silent agility of a praying mantis.

The room was full, with thousands of Everyones
in attendance, most carrying on murmured conversations while attending to one or another personal
screens. Delaney scanned the audience and quickly
recognized two men shuffling from the aisle into
middle seats, wearing matching Every-issued waterpacks. It was Vijay and Martin, her bosses at
Ol Factory. Delaney had heard nothing of their

work since the company had been acquired, and now they looked defanged, dazed, made useless. The Every was full of founders who had been bought, only to have their creations killed or buried, forgotten. Delaney stared at them as they took their seats. Someone leaned over to say hi to them, and they smiled faintly. They seemed utterly at peace, no longer ambitious, free from work and the responsibility to create.

A petite woman strode onto the stage. She wore a crimson bodysuit, with an enormous copper necklace, seeming to be a kind of sunsplash, covering her chest.

"Hello Everyone," she said, throwing her rubbery arms up, her hands spinning at the wrist like plates atop narrow poles. There was modest applause, with pairs of Every heads meeting, whispering variations on "Who is that?"

A voice behind Delaney answered, a bit too loudly, "Victoria de Nord, I think. You remember her?"

Victoria de Nord was taking in the muted applause like it was a ten-minute ovation at Cannes. Finally she arrived at center stage and, with hands behind her back, she spun slowly left and right, as if overwhelmed by the applause, which had tapered quickly from polite to muted to a few confused taps of palm to knee.

"I'm Victoria de Nord, but you probably knew that," she said. She smiled and spun left and right again. She seemed wholly unaware that no one knew who she was.

"How are we all doing today?" Again she paused for an uncomfortably long time, scanning the crowd, as if her question might actually yield actionable answers. Delaney had grown fond of Winnie, in her way, and had found Jenny Butler and Dan Faraday and even Kiki and Carlo and Shireen likeable to varying degrees, but witnessing Victoria de Nord, Delaney remembered how unctuous the leaders of this company could be, and vowed to remind herself of this ridiculous person if ever her commitment to revolution flagged.

"Welcome to Dream Friday!" Victoria said, and again looked left and right for what seemed like hours. Murmuring among the audience began, as Everyones, accustomed to more stimulating and time-conscious presentations, began to wonder if this were some sort of test. It should have been Mae Holland on this stage, making this introduction, but she was noticeably absent. She was unquestionably the face of the Every, and it was assumed that she made the most consequential decisions. And yet, with the exit of Stenton, the sidelining of Bailey and the wholesale disappearance of Ty Gospodinov, the Every lacked a visible and vocal leader, and seeing this—someone like Victoria who could be nudged onto the stage, a mistake acknowledged by all involved—proved Wes's point, that Mae was shy about, ashamed even, to appear in a forum like this without a new idea.

"Today we're delighted to have with us Ramona Ortiz," Victoria said, and the audience, knowing Victoria would soon leave the stage, exhaled collectively and loudly.

"We all know Ramona from her groundbreaking startup, Enlightened Traveler," Victoria said, "which the Every brought in-house three years ago. She's got some big ideas for the future of travel, and . . ."

The rest of Victoria's introduction was painfully long and pointless, but eventually she ceded the stage to a woman wearing black tights, a black skirt and a cream top. Her name appeared in large sanserif white letters on the screen behind her: Ramona Ortiz. Her thick straight hair was cut short, almost Beatlesque in its rounded volume, and had been dyed a neon red. The look, almost impossible to pull off, Delaney thought, worked effortlessly on her. She strode onto the stage with a busy, almost distracted confidence, as if she were stopping by for a moment on her way somewhere more pressing.

"So I'm here to talk about—what else—travel," she said. "As you know, travel has been my life. Six years ago I started Enlightened Traveler . . ." She waited for applause. At first it was muted, but the manners of the audience kicked in and the clapping filled out to a respectable ovation.

"Thank you," she said and then said it again,

"thank you"—unnecessarily, for the applause had evaporated. "Enlightened Traveler was meant to encourage environmentally responsible travel, and facilitated users making better travel choices by curating the most eco-friendly airlines, accommodations and outfitters. Three years ago, my company was acquired by the Every, where it's made over 2.2 million ecologically progressive trips possible."

Now the applause came on stronger, though Delaney felt a collective ignorance pervading the room. Delaney had done her homework on the Every, but this company, this acquisition, had escaped her, and, it seemed, had escaped the notice of most Everyones. Given the fact that the Every acquired at least three companies a week, it stood to reason that many would go unnoticed.

"But lately," she said, "my take on the utility and morality of travel as we know it has changed. Let me back up. I was born in Nosara, Costa Rica, in 1995." Footage of a small town emerging from a lush seaside jungle appeared on the screen behind her. Scattered applause and a few whoops emerged from the audience.

"Yes, some of you know this place," Ortiz said, her voice lowering. "And the fact that you know this place is a problem. Perhaps even **the** problem. Let me tell you why. This film you're seeing was taken in the 1990s, before Nosara was discovered by Americans and Europeans. This is the town now."

A montage of crowded streets, gaudy with T-shirt

and tourist-oriented shops, overtook the screen. A
tour bus waddled through the narrow streets. Dazed
visitors in cargo shorts ambled down the sidewalk
in front of a Best Western. A shot of an Avis rental
car office. A Little Caesars pizza outlet. A mound of
tin cans and plastic bottles dumped in the jungle.
A series of For Sale signs, all of them presented by
multinationals like Sotheby's and Chavez-Millstein.
In one shot, a man in a lizard-print shirt was pointing and yelling at a local woman selling jewelry
from a streetside folding table.

"I saw my country," Ortiz continued, "and especially my little town, overrun and fundamentally
changed by tourism. I saw the land grabs. I saw my
family and neighbors priced out and pushed away.
We moved again and again, as foreign multimillion-
aires and developers bought every hectare anywhere
near the sea or possessing any view. We went ever-
inland until we were living on the third ring of San
José—that's the Costa Rican capital, not the city in
the South Bay—next to the Pepsi bottler.

"If you've been to Costa Rica in the last twenty
years, you've seen that it is essentially Florida—
a playground for the American middle class. Every
beach is wrecked with cheap trinket shops and
pizza places. Any pristine valley they could stretch a
zipline across, they did. The country has lost much
of its identity, and my fellow Ticos and Ticas run
around like obsequious little capitalists, chasing the
tourist dollar. My people have, in my opinion, lost

their dignity. No offense if you've been to Costa Rica," she added, to a few chuckles. "I don't blame you individually. But I blame us all, collectively, for our avaricious pursuit of cheap experiences abroad."

The offensive scenes of a ruined Costa Rica were replaced by a succession of aspirational shots of travelers alone and in pairs, trekking with seeming respect and humility, through Nepalese and Peruvian scenery.

"I started Enlightened Traveler," Ortiz said, "to foster a better way of seeing the world. We booked travelers in small groups. Long before the pandemics, we discouraged cruises—surely the death of the oceans and the very antithesis of meaningful travel or sustainable tourism. We singled out responsible outfitters and guides and encouraged everything from homestays to ecotourism to trips that combined sightseeing with service. I thought we were helping. And maybe we were. Surely the kind of travel we were fostering was better than tour buses and cruise ships. But then I started doing the math. I know many of you are good at math, so chances are you'll get ahead of me here."

Onscreen, a flattened global map appeared, and on it white dots began to sprout. They popped up in hundreds of places, from the Cook Islands to Newfoundland.

"These are the places I've personally been. In twenty years, I've seen eighty-eight countries. I've been to every continent. I've met so many phenomenal people and I feel like my perspective broadened every time I landed in a new place.

"But it came at a cost. A pretty monumental cost. A few years ago, I realized that as a frequent traveler, an obsessive traveler, really, I'd been responsible for over two hundred and seventy tons of carbon dioxide in my lifetime of globetrotting—and that was from the flights alone. No amount of carbon offsets could reverse the damage I'd done."

Delaney had the feeling she would soon see an image of an animal in existential crisis, and she was correct. The screen showed an emaciated penguin wandering into a convenience store in Tierra del Fuego, startling the customers, before collapsing.

"As you know, they have yet to make a solar-powered airplane built from hemp," Ortiz said, to polite laughter. "Absolutely all air travel is enormously harmful to the planet, and yet we continue to fly. Why? Because we want to. We want, we want, we **want.** And even the most enlightened environmentalists close their eyes to the damage they do when they fly around the planet, often in private jets, to warn the public about the dangers of fossil fuels. It is beyond hypocrisy. And I was guilty of it, too. So I had an idea. I had a revelation. It's called Stop and Look."

For a moment, Delaney wondered how the words would be butchered. The "and" would inevitably be a +, but what else?

Onscreen, the name of the program was rendered as Stop+Lük.

Sweet lord God, Delaney thought. She hadn't seen the umlaut coming. Any second, she knew, Ramona Ortiz would be positing that her new initiative would have a hand in saving the planet.

"This will, I believe, revolutionize the way we see the world," Ortiz said, "and it might even have a hand in saving the world."

Delaney's mouth opened to laugh. She looked around her. No one was laughing. She sat on her hands.

"Last year, there were 1.8 billion leisure arrivals worldwide, as the post-pandemic travel orgy continues—and continues to kill the most popular destinations. Let's start with one of the most tourist-choked places on the planet: Venice. Last year, thirty-four million people came to Venice, a city roughly the size of Manhattan. That itself is madness. Now let's think about the two to three tons of carbon it took for each of those tourists to get there. That's about seventy-five, eighty million tons of carbon emissions expended just to send tourists to a tourist-choked city. Add to these costs the sheer misery experienced by the residents of the city, and by the tourists themselves. Last year, there were seven-hour waits just to walk in Piazza San Marco plaza. It's lunacy. And it has to stop."

Hundreds of Every heads were nodding in

agreement. It was always good to stop things that needed to be stopped.

"There's a better way," Ortiz said. "You can still see Venice. You can see Venice, and probably even see it more authentically, without ever leaving your house. The future of travel relies on you using your head."

Now Victoria de Nord reappeared, waving and smiling effusively, as if the crowd had demanded an encore. She handed Ortiz a standard virtual reality headset, and strode offstage in a fugue state, as if clutching an Oscar she'd just won.

"Here's how it works," Ortiz said, and a grid appeared on the screen behind her, showing dozens of desirable destinations, Capri and Dubai and Vegas and what seemed to be the Swiss Alps.

"Because we were just talking about Venice, let's take a tour of that gorgeous city. But this will be a tour with zero carbon emissions." On the grid she singled out the Venice thumbnail and it grew to overtake half the screen. The other half morphed into a grid of smiling faces with names below.

"Here's a sampling of your tour guide choices, each of them certified by the Italian and the Venetian tourism board. They are historians, teachers, even a few gondoliers. And they're all residents of Venice—most of them born there. Because he's ready to go, I'm going to choose Paolo Marchessi."

One of the smiling faces in the grid overtook the

screen, his still photo becoming a live feed of his grinning face. He was a round-faced man of about fifty, with salt-and-pepper hair and small wire-rimmed glasses. "Ciao, Paolo!" Ortiz said.

"Hello, Ramona!" he said.

"Ready for a customized tour?" she asked him.

"I am," he said.

She turned from the screen to the auditorium. "Paolo is outfitted with a rotatable camera, much like we've been using here for our other VR projects. Let's get the view from that camera."

On the screen, a hyper-crisp view of the Grand Canal, aglow at sunset, emerged. "This is a live feed," Ortiz said, "so while we do this demonstration, you'll be able to see the sun setting over the water." The feed was gorgeous.

"From the comfort of your home," she said, "you put on any VR headset, and instantly you see what your guide sees, with a 360-degree range. You want to go see the old Armory district? Tell Paolo to walk you there. He takes you wherever you ask, and all the while he's introducing you to people and places only locals would know. Guide or be guided, up to you. You control the experience. You pay by the hour or by the day, and you save money and maybe the planet, too."

Applause filled the room, and Delaney joined in the noise. Despite herself, she knew she would take one of these tours. A half-dozen places she'd wanted to see occurred to her instantly as prospects. Schools would use this. Retirement homes. And yet somehow this would, Delaney was certain, make things worse. She pondered the unintended consequences of Ramona's clearly well-intentioned notion. On the one hand, it would mean the collapse of much of the world's tourism industry and a few hundred million lost jobs. On the other hand, it would be fantastic for agoraphobes, germaphobes, those afraid to fly or leave the house.

"Let's talk cost," Ortiz continued. "Stop+Lük's costs are so miniscule compared to traditional travel that it makes most of that seem absurd. If I were to fly to Venice from San Francisco tomorrow, between flights and accommodations for a week, it would run me about $6,500. But through Stop+Lük, the cost per day is only what we pay Paolo per hour, which is about $100. You can get a thorough tour of Venice in half a day, which would be about $500. And everyone benefits. Paolo might give two tours a day, so that's $1,000 for a local historian. Not bad, right, Paolo?"

There was no answer. He seemed to have left the scene.

"Paolo?"

"Yes, Ramona?" Now he was back.

"I was saying that if you gave two tours a day, that might be $1,000. Not bad, right?"

"Not bad," he agreed. "If I get the two tours,

yes. Much depends on scheduling. The catch is, do I need a regular job, or is this my regular job? And there is the issue of benefits and pensions, two things we rely on here in Italy."

A momentary half-smile of amusement flickered across Ramona's face. "All good points that we will be working out as we go," she said, and with a button she muted Paolo, who was not heard from again.

She turned back to the Every audience.

"So, as you see, Venice is relieved of a massive chunk of its excess tourist burden. Money goes to locals, not to cruise ships. And best of all, the planet breathes a bit easier. You don't drive to the airport. You don't get on that plane. That plane doesn't fly. The cruise ships don't sail, polluting the oceans as they go. Planes and ships don't unload thousands of tourists who all get in separate taxis. All this stops. That's the 'Stop' part of the Stop+Lük name. I should have said that before, I guess." She laughed charmingly at her omission.

"Here's the best part of it all," she said, and the Grand Canal was replaced by another grid of desirable locations around the world. Now each one had a smaller grid below it, each box featuring a smiling face.

"We have thirty-two locations ready to go at launch," she said. "We've focused on some of the world's most overburdened sites—Paris, London,

Shanghai, Annapurna, Machu Picchu, Angkor Wat, Gizeh. Right now we have an average of eleven guides per location, depending on the size of the city or attraction of course. We foresee this all multiplying rapidly and organically, much in the way rideshare did back in the day."

Delaney looked at Winnie's hands, which had not stopped working throughout the presentation. The result was a sweater for a dog-sized human or poorly shaped dog. It was squat and ragged and the color of burnt butter. Winnie, Delaney was delighted to know, could not knit.

From the stage, Ramona Ortiz was taking questions. A portly man noted that there would be no risk of malaria, food-borne illness, seasickness and what he called "a host of other travel-related ailments." A tall woman with Newtonian eyeglasses suggested spreading the zone a bit, adding less-known locations to Stop+Lük's offerings, perhaps at a discount, and Ramona winked and said that was among their Stage 2 notions. The last question was, like the first, more of a suggestion.

"I hope we're incentivizing good travel choices," the woman added. "Travelers who reduce their carbon footprint are given discounts on other products and experiences, for example."

Ramona agreed that that would make a lot of sense, and then laughed about how time had gotten away from them while they were Stopping +

Lükking, and with that, the lights came up on Delaney's first Dream Friday. When they left the auditorium they were greeted by a twenty-foot-wide sign, carved from salvaged timber, that said: IF YOU LOVE THE WORLD, LEAVE IT ALONE.

XIII.

"I'D USE THAT," WES SAID. "I'd use it today. I hate planes."

It was Saturday and they were sitting in two rickety folding chairs in the small yard between the moms' house and the Shed. It was one of few outdoor spaces in the neighborhood not seen by any neighbors' surveillance cams. The smell tumbling from the Doelger Fish Co was strongest Saturday mornings. After an hour in the yard, Delaney felt like she'd gorged on a seafood buffet.

"I always catch something on planes," Wes continued. "On the buses **to** planes. Even before the viruses, I'd get sick every time. Then I'm sick the whole time I'm on vacation and after I get back, too."

For a while Delaney debated with him but she realized, with a low-level kind of alarm, that Wes was both her accomplice and the Every's perfect customer. He was forever trying to find ways to stay inside and avoid engagement with humans in real space. And though he carried a low-intensity outrage about privacy issues, he prized convenience above all, and readily used dozens of Every tools without any security protections—especially if that tool was new. He had tried everything and was both easily delighted and quickly bored.

Hurricane limped down from the Shed and arranged himself into a furry bundle at Wes's feet. His wounded paw was raw and swollen.

"He chews off every bandage," Wes noted. He'd brought him to Kathy the Vet three times and three times she'd bandaged his wound, only to have Hurricane gnaw it off. "She said we could put him on dog drugs. Anti-depressants."

Delaney reached down to stroke his snout. It was cold, clammy.

"He can't run," Wes said. "So he's stuck here, and he chews on the bandage. You see his back paws? He's gnawing those, too."

Through the moms' kitchen window Delaney could see Gwen. She waved. Ursula appeared next to Gwen and the two of them stared at Delaney and Wes for an uncomfortably long time.

"You got a letter today, by the way," Wes said. "A paper letter." He jogged inside the Shed to get it. Delaney opened it to find a neat blue sea of undulating cursive. It was unmistakably Professor Agarwal's. After college, they'd written each other occasionally, and Delaney had sent her a note when she'd moved to California to start with Ol Factory, but it had been at least a year since Delaney had gotten anything back from her.

"That from your professor?" Wes asked. Delaney had waxed on about Agarwal. Her theories, and just as crucially, her indignation, were the basis of much of what Delaney and Wes talked about—the foundation of all their plans.

"Don't mind me," Wes said, and closed his eyes to the sun.

> Dear Delaney,
> I received some kind of auto-update announcing your job at the Every. I decided to mail you a letter so they don't read this and put it in some permanent record they surely have on you.
> Delaney, I must say I'm a bit flabbergasted. Not that I'm surprised that someone from my class would have gone to work there—seems like half the people I've taught now work there. But not you. You might have been the most technoskeptical student I've ever taught. Before your thesis, that is, which, as you know, surprised me a great deal.
> And I admired that about you. You thought about things. You seemed in touch with the ways that humanity was being fundamentally changed—how we were moving from an idiosyncratic species that coveted our

independence to one that wanted, more than anything, to shrink and to obey in exchange for free stuff.

Now you work there—at the factory that manufactures conformity. I'm an old person now so I will speak my mind. I think you're better than this. My heart hurts to picture you there, to think they've swallowed another rebel soul.

Please leave.

Yours,

Agarwal

Delaney refolded the letter, a raw ache in her throat. Her sadness always lived there, a dry hollow pull that stole her voice. She knew she couldn't tell Professor Agarwal anything. She couldn't even write her a paper letter back; the risk was too great.

Agarwal was a radical, after all, unpredictable and even rash. Delaney remembered Agarwal leading a one-person protest on campus against surveillance. She stood just a hair over five feet tall, and was speaking evenly, with barely controlled venom, into a megaphone almost as big as herself. The demonstration questioned the college's use of cameras in virtually every public space on campus. Delaney stopped to listen to the diminutive woman, who enlightened her thirty or so listeners that there were eighteen hundred cameras on campus; that the Circle had provided these cameras at

a steep discount; that their footage was accessible
by local police and owned by the Circle; that it was
stored off-campus and was presumably being used
in untold ways; that it was coordinated with their
on-campus purchases (cash was not permitted) to
ensure that at least 23.2 hours of every student's
day could be tracked and recorded. Their grades,
scores and attendance were all aggregated into
one highly digestible digital dossier, and this dossier was accessible by a startlingly broad swath of
university staffers.

"If you are being surveilled," Agarwal was roar-
ing through her megaphone, "you are not free! A
human being watched cannot be free!" Students
hustled past, earbuds installed.

"There is no safe amount of asbestos or surveillance," Agarwal yelled. A graduate student, studying
anthropology, began filming her.

"This college has no right to film you, anywhere
or anytime!" Agarwal implored. Now students were
making a wide berth around her. "Students, I beg
you to wake up."

No one woke up. The vast majority of her fellow college students had been subject to cameras in every classroom since preschool. Their
parents had known their whereabouts every
moment of their lives, and they had never
thought it cumbersome—had never known an
unsurveilled life.

Now, holding Agarwal's letter, Delaney wanted

badly to go to her, tell her of her plans, to conspire
with her. But she knew Agarwal would try to talk
her out of it, favoring protest, the writing of papers,
the supporting of reformers like Goleta. She would
find Delaney's gambit insane and impossible.

Delaney looked over to Wes's chair and found
him gone. She opened the door to the Shed and
the wind whipped it against the wall with a bang.
"Sorry!" she yelled. She found Wes sitting on his
bed, staring at his screen with mouth agape.

"What are you watching?" Delaney asked.

He turned his tablet to her. The screen held
a watery image. It seemed to come from a head-
mounted digital camera, showing someone surfing
or paddleboarding.

"So?" Delaney said.

"So this is Bailey."

Delaney scanned the screen and found a description below the video feed. "Come surf with Gunnar
and me!" the text said. "In Nicaragua."

"Did you know he was in Nicaragua?" Wes asked.

"No," Delaney said. "I don't know if anyone has
been thinking about his whereabouts at all."

"On Saturday afternoon," Bailey's caption continued, "I'll be trying out some radical new sensory-
transference software. As many of you know, we
implanted a device in my thalamus designed to
allow others to feel what I feel. In this case, of
course, it'll be my son Gunnar. Gunnar suffers
from cerebral palsy, so surfing in Nicaragua is not a

possibility for him. He'll be at home in California, but he and I will be connected, via satellite, such that he will feel the sensations I feel: the volume of the waves under me, my speed as I descend a swell, possibly even the smells and sounds I experience. This could be a major breakthrough for all. It'll certainly be interesting for Gunnar and me. Join us. —Bailey."

Delaney looked for the viewer-counter, and saw that it was <1000. The Every had, a few years before, given those posting videos the option of using rounded numbers, to diminish the watcher-chasing that had plagued the format from the start. The less-than symbol, though, had a tragic effect, making every watcher-count somehow a disappointment, forever less-than.

"There's a comments section," Wes said, "and that's almost empty. I think there's only a few dozen people watching. If that."

"Do you have the audio on?" Delaney asked.

"Sorry. No," Wes said, and activated the volume.

Immediately Bailey's distinctive voice blasted through. "Here we go, my friends. What a day on the water!"

The view from Bailey's camera was unsteady. He seemed to be paddling on his knees through choppy waters, about two hundred yards from shore. A khaki-colored beach was visible in front of a stripe of green forest and, far beyond, the black slope of a primeval volcano.

"For those of you just joining, I've been out here for about twenty minutes now," Bailey said, his breathing loud, "trying to beat the crowds." Here he panned from the water to the beach, where there were no humans whatsoever. He let out the slightest chuckle. "And I think I've found a nice little break. I've caught a few decent waves, and did my customary shredding of said waves, much to the entertainment of the vast audience at the beach."

Above the beach, Delaney could now see a troubled sky, with darkness at the corners of the frame.

"The weather, as you can see, will soon be unfavorable," Bailey said, "and thus there are no spectators, intentional or not. No bystanders, no dogwalkers, no beach combers, nothing. But we don't care, do we, viewers? No, we do not. We are breaking new ground here, and I can't wait to see what Gunnar thought of all this."

"Still only a few people watching," Wes said. "It's bizarre."

"If any of you have been watching from the start," Bailey continued, "forgive me for repeating myself. But what we're trying to do is test some new tech that allows two people, very far away from each other, to feel the same things. In this case, as I rise and fall on the ocean, waiting for the right wave, my son Gunnar is at home, and the sensors he's wearing will trigger the same feelings in him, primarily by manipulating his own thalamus—he'll feel like he's rising and falling on the sea, too. I've gotten some help from our muscle precision optimizing group, so I want to give a shout out to them. With their help, along with that of our experience transference team, Gunnar's brain and body should be able to make sense of the different inputs and should be able to create a facsimile experience. It'll be the first time we can share this sport, a calling, really, one that's given me immeasurable joy in my life."

"Did he mention MPOs?" Delaney asked. "I thought they banned that." Muscle precision optimization was a catch-all term for nanotechnology that improved—perfected, really—eye-brain-muscle coordination. A tennis player using it could place a ball in the exact same spot a hundred times out of a hundred. Errors were virtually impossible.

"Professional sports banned it," Wes said, "but Bailey's in Nicaragua. Now I'm guessing this is **why** he chose to do this demo down there. The thalamus-implant, too—not legal here."

"Not yet," Delaney said.

"Now, just as an FYI," Bailey said onscreen, "I should say that though we've tested this many times on the Every campus, this is the first field test where the sensors are under open-ocean conditions. That's all I can say. I feel like I'm buzzing from head to toe with a strange vibration that's new to me, and I find it very exciting."

The camera's point of view changed a bit then, and went lower, closer to the water. "As you can see, I'm resting for a second, because I've been out here a while, and I am, after all, a fifty-seven-year-old man. There's a bit of a drift here, with the wind coming from the south and taking me down the beach pretty quickly. I think if I paddle in a little, I'll move a bit out of the current that's currently— get that? Currently? The current that's currently taking me . . ."

Now the camera's view was shaky, the frame jumping a bit from side to side and up and down, water periodically soaking the lens and then washing down its surface.

"He's really far from the beach," Wes said.

"Is that bad?" Delaney did not know how to surf, and didn't know how far was too far.

"Well, maybe not so far for a young guy, but he's pretty damned far out. A current like that can take him a half a mile in seconds."

And as they watched, they heard Bailey paddling, but saw the shore grow smaller with every moment. Quickly it became a thin yellow rope, then the faintest gray thread.

"Nadia, can you see if you—" Bailey said. His breath was labored, his words clipped. "Maybe adjust the sensors? I need the battery—"

A wave seemed to swamp Bailey and his camera. For a few long seconds the lens was underwater. Then it emerged again.

"Turned off—" Bailey managed to say. "I've got the craziest migraine coming on. Nadia?"

Now the camera was very close to the water, and at an angle.

"I think he's lying on his board," Wes said.

"Stevie, my head feels like it's imploding," Bailey said. "I'm thinking the sensors are having some bad reaction to the salt water. Stevie, can you just shut it off? Better do that and I can get into—"

His voice broke off.

"The microphone died," Delaney said.

"No, listen," Wes said, and turned up the volume as high as it would go. They heard the waves tapping at the hollow board. Another moment of silence passed.

"We should call someone," Delaney said.

"Us?" Wes asked.

The microphone roared alive again. "Nadia!" Bailey grunted. "Call an SOS. Something's wrong. Call—"

The camera angle tilted and then plunged underwater. A second later it was up again, showing the white sky, the jagged waves. Then underwater again.

"Jesus Christ!" Wes said. "They won't turn it off, will they?"

"No," Delaney said, and she knew it was true. The Every never stopped broadcasting, never took any video down. It was their interpretation of the First Amendment, and their status not as a publisher but as mere conduit. If you turned on your camera, that was your prerogative. If you watched,

that was also your prerogative. If you chose to stop
watching, up to you. Never did the Every interfere.

For years, there had been pitched battles between the Every and various governments around
the world, who had weakly protested when bullies
broadcast their conquests, when murderers streamed
their killings, when terrorists beheaded and incinerated soldiers and innocents. Other companies
caved and tried to keep ahead of the abuses, hired
thousands to monitor and delete, but soon these
companies realized that every horrific video was immediately copied dozens of times and disseminated
in hundreds of different ways, the most wretched
examples copied so many times they could never
be removed.

When Mae Holland assumed power she put an
end to the belief that the Every could or should be
the censor to the world. The era was new, and violence and death would be broadcast, period. The
next step—and the Every was certainly at work on
it, on a hundred fronts—was ending crime and tam-
ing our id and choking off the desire to see these
horrors in the first place. The key was not in supply,
she said, but in demand. You couldn't, after all, turn
off the spigot, lest you stanch the flow of all that was
good. The same cameras that were occasionally used
to broadcast evil were used, a million times a day,
for preventing it, reporting it, holding perpetrators
accountable. Purse-snatchings, red-light runnings,
cop shootings, racial profilings—every violation of

human rights was liable to be caught on camera, and the perpetrators brought quickly to justice. The occasional misuse of the technology was an unfortunate byproduct of the new paradigm, but it was, Mae thought—and most thought—an acceptable tradeoff for the increased safety felt among most of the planet's people. The observed world, the filmed world, the recorded world, was a safer world.

But then there was something like this, a live-streamed death. Around the world, people had died on camera tens of thousands of times—hundreds of times a day. Many times it was planned, as family members gathered virtually around ceremonial deathbeds. Usually, though, these deaths were caught by accident—car crashes, freak occurrences, people carried away by mudslides or shot in drive-bys. But something quite like this had never happened—the excruciatingly slow-motion death of a peaceful and prominent citizen.

Eamon Bailey's camera remained on and broadcasting for the 32 minutes he continued to breathe, and for the seven hours and eleven minutes he floated in rough seas. Wearing a wetsuit designed to float, he'd been separated from his surfboard and had drifted west, then north. Though his position was known—his sensors could pinpoint his location—a series of squalls had prevented anyone from mounting an effective search.

When his body washed ashore, his camera continued to broadcast video from the beach, the horizon crooked, the sand a volcanic black, while gulls occasionally came to inspect Bailey's face. The foamy surf overtook the lens occasionally, one time sending a fleet-footed crab across the frame, the auto-focus doing an admirable job of sharpening on the crab's right pincer and inquisitive antennae before another wave came to take the curious creature away again.

Bailey was finally found by a pair of Nicaraguan teenagers who'd been watching the broadcast, had recognized the beach as near their homes, and had, on a bet, walked down to see if the dead man on the screen was a dead man in real life.

XIV.

BAILEY WAS GONE, and Delaney knew she and every Everyone would be expected on campus on Monday. She arrived at 8 a.m. to find, under a bright cloudless sky, hundreds of bouquets and wreaths set against the outer gate of campus, with about fifty people wandering up and down the candy-colored memorial. A pair of Every staffers were photographing the bouquets and wreaths and gifts, and soon after, they were removing anything plastic or non-biodegradable for speedy incineration. Delaney heard Everyones and civilians talk about Bailey's age, and the likelihood of aneurysms. A dog grabbed a purple octopus someone had left—Bailey's spirit animal, he'd once noted—and ran down the sidewalk with it. When he thought he had time and opportunity, the dog tore it open and spilled its white stuffing all over the street.

On campus, Everyones sat in small groups on the lawn, all of them wearing slightly more demure bodysuits. One older man even wore a suit and tie. They leaned against one another and peered down at phones and tablets; amateur memorial videos had begun to pop up. Those who had known Bailey in childhood sent adorable photos of him on a banana-seat bicycle.

Social media chirped about Gunnar, his thoughts and feelings, but it did not seem likely that Gunnar would be issuing his own statement, which many zingers and posters felt not fair for someone so central to this drama. If the idea was to let Gunnar feel what Bailey was feeling, did Gunnar experience death, too? At least in some secondary but still horrifying way?

Delaney found Jenny Butler, her Random, sitting alone under a lemon tree planted high on an artificial berm, and approached her slowly. When Jenny Butler heard her footsteps, she turned suddenly, and her face lit up. In a flailing series of gestures, she got up, embraced Delaney, and begged her to sit with her.

"Bailey hired me," Jenny Butler said. "He was my Random, just like I was yours. Can you imagine?" Her Mississippi lilt was intensified in grief; she stretched **imagine** into a gorgeous arc. "He loved being the Random, he told me. He genuinely loved people—you know this, right? It wasn't an act. Everything he did, he did because he was fascinated by every single person. It was almost a curse. Every person he met, he thought was just indescribably

interesting and unfathomable and full of possibility and . . ." She was overtaken by sobs. Delaney
squeezed her shoulder.

"That's why he did that stupid thalamus implant," Jenny Butler said. "He didn't want any
boundaries between any two people." She looked
up, collecting herself, and finally sighed.

"But I think there could be a limit," she said. "To
the interpersonal connections. To our . . . porosity.
Maybe we do need boundaries. Secrets. Even physi-
ological secrets. I mean, the man is dead because he
couldn't keep anything to himself."

Delaney almost said **Sharing is caring,** but decided against it.

"Anyway, thank you. I'll miss you," Jenny
Butler said.

"What do you mean?" Delaney pictured her
throwing herself into the sea as some kind of suicide
tribute to Bailey.

"My department's dead," she said. "All the space
projects are dead, or will be soon."

Delaney hadn't thought about it, but knew she
was right. Mae did not buy personal submarines or
get enthused about orbiters and space-mining and
the colonization of Mars and Io.

"But whatever," Jenny Butler said. "I wouldn't
have done any of this without him. I applied for a
job in marketing, right? But he saw on my résumé
that I'd studied aeronautical engineering years before, and so we talked about that for the whole

hour. Then he brought me back the next day to talk to his SpaceBridge team, and a week later he'd made room for me there. I mean, who **does** that?"

Mae had returned from ForwardRetreat—an annual summer-camp-style gathering of artists and influencers she organized and sometimes attended—and was broadcasting her day. In a black bodysuit and gray pashmina, she walked along the flowered fence outside campus, keeping her hands folded in front of her in a vaguely ministerial configuration. She nodded silently, eyes closing in agreement, as mourners told her all that Bailey meant to them.

Inside, she led informal gatherings in different departments where the only task was to add to Bailey's legend, to celebrate him, and to that end, there were endless stories that mirrored or exceeded Jenny Butler's. It seemed that Bailey had personally hired hundreds, had paid down countless college loans, had sent flowers to the grandparents of junior staffers and helicopters to find lost pets.

As the day went on, there were tributes from the current president and two predecessors, a hundred or so CEOs and dozens of heads of state—with a special eulogy given by the Every's custodial staff, who Bailey had made the best-paid in North America. Bailey, it appeared, had never made an enemy. That was Stenton's role; he shadowed the memorial silently, trying to stay out of the way, but his spectral presence, his furtive glances, had the opposite effect: people were unnerved and hoped he would soon leave. Meanwhile, online, the footage of Bailey's death had been condensed into ever-shorter versions for various news purveyors. Humorists and trolls had then repurposed the footage into a music video, set to early-era Beach Boys, and a fake promo for the Nicaraguan Tourism Board.

The next few days were unstructured for most, certainly for Delaney. Kiki, her guide, told her the week would be "unusually loose," and it was. Delaney was free to wander the campus on Monday and Tuesday, attending grief-groups and participating in a half-dozen vaguely sporty activities Bailey had enjoyed, from lawn bowling to jarts (safety jarts) and nonviolent larping. It wasn't until late Wednesday that Delaney received an apologetic, even sheepish, text from Kiki, asking if she was feeling up to continuing the conversation about the app she'd mentioned in her interview.

Shireen and Carlo would love to introduce you to some of the developers who want to be involved, she'd said in her message.

When Delaney entered the room, eleven people stood up and looked at her with tilted heads and sad eyes. There seemed to be some implication that Delaney was close to Bailey, or was particularly devoted to him.

"You holding up okay?" a voice said. Delaney turned to find Shireen standing more or less on top of her. Delaney caught sight of Carlo, who had his hands clasped in front of his stomach.

"Tough week for us all," he said.

"I'm sorry for your loss," Delaney said, and scanned the eyes in the room in a flailing effort to see who among them knew Bailey well. To the last person they seemed to be suffering. A few had the haggard looks of mourners who had been up late talking. One woman was nodding to herself, seeming to be engaged in an internal conversation of affirmation and resolve.

"Sit, sit," Carlo said, indicating an empty chair with a tablet set on the table before it. "We're using Sozeb, which I guess is obvious."

Delaney looked down to find a diagram of the table, with thumbnail cartoon versions of each person at the meeting, each positioned as they were in real life. This was a kind of meeting software that she thought had become passé or obsolete. But the Every was like this, she knew—at once avant-garde and hopelessly square—devoted above all to using its own products and acquisitions far beyond their expiration date.

As Delaney was introduced to each of the nine new people, their thumbnail would glow for a moment on the tablet, with their title— Blue-Sky Developer (BSD), Experience Engineer (EE), Design Devotee (DD)—appearing below their animated avatars. As Carlo and Shireen spoke,

their words were transcribed on the tablet with dif-
ferentiated attributions. The few words Delaney had
said since she'd sat down—"So happy to be here"—
had appeared perfectly on the transcription immediately after they'd left her mouth. Because this
meeting involved IP there could be no doubt about
who said what.

Delaney looked at the attendees, searching for the
attorney, but was struck by the intense look she was
getting from a woman about her age, whose avatar
was a fierce Scottish warrior but whose name was
the comparatively peace-loving Heather. Heather
had fixed her with as close to a death-stare as might
be acceptable at the Every, which meant she was
smiling brightly while something about her corneas
was vibrating with suspicion and limitless rage.

"Heather was actually working on something a bit similar to your GenuPal—" Shireen
said, and then laughed. "Wait. Did we decide on
AuthentiFriend or GenuPal?"

Carlo smiled stiffly. "I still think AuthentiFriend
has the kind of authority and action-orientation
that implies it's based on science," he said, and
then glanced at Shireen, who quickly looked away.
"GenuPal has an unfortunate echo of MySpace,
no?" he added.

Delaney took Heather to be a junior staffer who
did not seem to carry great weight in the room. The
person who did, and who took over the meeting

after Carlo and Shireen's introductions and their brief summation of their interview-cum-pitch session with Delaney, was named Holstein.

On Delaney's tablet, Holstein was the only attendee who went by one name, and whose avatar was simply her actual picture, a no-nonsense photo presenting her exactly as she was in real life. She appeared to be at least fifty, with gorgeous white hair that swept around her head like a hurricane seen from space. Behind blue-framed glasses her eyes seemed to be black, her eyebrows painted on with severity. And as striking as her face was—every part of her head demanded fixation and fealty—the most mesmerizing part of her were her arms. Exposed from fingertips to shoulder and unsullied by jewelry, they appeared to be sculpted from bronze. Their musculature was just short of obscene, their coloring a good four shades darker than her face, as if she'd been using them, for decades, to shield her face from the sun, or in the construction of ships.

"I like AuthentiFriend," Holstein said, and with this resolution, Carlo and Shireen both seemed to collapse with relief. Someone had made a decision.

Holstein looked at Delaney and Delaney tried not to blink.

"Delaney," Holstein said, in a steady, flutish voice, "I first want to say how impressed I was that you presented this idea during your third interview. That shows great courage and self-belief and it makes me confident that this is not the first or last

idea you have had or will have." Delaney opened
her mouth to say **thank you** and **no, it isn't,** but
Holstein continued, and Delaney knew instantly
that they were on the clock, and Holstein and her
magnificent arms would leave the room within minutes. "We'd like to develop your app. Would you
want to be part of the core group?"

"I think—" Delaney started.

"It's not mandated," Holstein added. And
Delaney understood. She was not being invited to
this stage of the development.

"Because I just started here," Delaney said, "and
I'm a roamer, still exploring and learning as much
as I can, I think I'd prefer that you take it and run
with it." She directed the last few words to the in-
furiated staffer whose name she glanced down to
find again. Heather. "Especially if Heather's got a
head start and would like to incorporate anything
of AuthentiFriend into her project." And with that,
whatever volcanic antipathy was sputtering inside
Heather cooled.

"Well said," Holstein replied. "Anything else?"

She looked around and put her palms on the
table. Now engaged in the realization of purpose,
her arms seemed to double in potency and magnifi-
cence. As if emboldened by the arms, Delaney had a
thought. It was not yet fully formed, but she could
hear it whistling toward her, like a happy train.

"One thing," Delaney said, buying time. And
then it arrived. She would see how far this idea

could be taken. How far they'd allow it. She saw no risk in the gambit, and the reward might be great—to see if there existed any ethical line the Every would not cross.

"Well, especially given the loss of Bailey, and the risk of deep trauma and depression on campus," Delaney said, "I think we need to consider the initial application of AuthentiFriend as really just a stepping off point for the tech."

Holstein's eyes were fixed on Delaney. Rattled, Delaney turned away. She considered simply shutting up, but the words had already arrived, and she needed to see what effect they'd have on the room.

"You all are probably working on this already, but I was thinking how crucial this tech would be for detecting depression. As you know, it goes undiagnosed over twenty-two million times a year," Delaney said, pulling the number from the air and finding only agreement among her audience. "That's in North America **alone**," she added, in a last-second addition that made her stat seem at once more inflated and more credible. "And this rate is highest among young people. I believe that AuthentiFriend could be made to look for symptoms of depression, and could assess them immediately and objectively. No months-long delays in getting help. The tech is already built into the app. Right now it's there to detect, for example, truthfulness in voice and facial expression, but it could be programmed to look for tonalities and speech patterns that hallmark depression."

The assembled Everyones were nodding, shaking their heads, trying to look both solemn and outraged by the very fact of depression and its being overlooked, while still encouraging Delaney.

"And think of kids in rural communities without mental-health professionals," said a balding man with spectacular sideburns. Delaney's screen informed her that his name was Louis.

"Or in countries where mental illness is stigmatized," said another man, this one with a long blond beard and named Jens.

"Right, **right,**" Delaney said, and plunged forward with the coup de grace. "And it's really important to note that the app needs time to properly assess the user. It could give a quick judgment, and that could alert the user whether there's any sign of trouble. But to do the work thoroughly, a wider data set would be needed. My estimate is that the user would need to spend six to seven hours a day on the phone, for at least three to six months—that would be the minimum to really get it right. The user could do anything on the phone, of course, use any social media or games or apps. All the while the tech would be collecting visual and oral cues. By reading facial indications, recording speech patterns, key words and phrases—and by analyzing the users' searches and exactly what the users read and watch, and for how long—we could absolutely predict the signs of depression and even, I would expect, see early signs of suicidal ideation."

"Didn't I tell you?" Shireen said, tapping both temples with her index fingers. "This lady's incredible. Think about how many Overlook admissions we could avoid."

Carlo shot her an outraged look, and Shireen took in a quick, sharp breath. "I mean . . ." She was trying to read Carlo's eyes, as if to limn what he wanted her to say. "I just—"

He turned to Delaney. "This is groundbreaking. Vital."

Delaney smiled in a way she thought both humble and solemn, then turned her hand into a determined fist. "But for it to be most effective, we need to have **access.**"

"Access is so key," Shireen whispered, her eyes suddenly wet.

"We need data, as much of it as we can get," Delaney said. "So if we're going to really address depression among young people, we absolutely must keep them on their phones as much as humanly possible."

XV.

"I HAVE IT," Delaney said.

"You have it," Wes said. "I'm glad. What do you have?"

"I know how to kill this thing," she said.

They were in the Shed, cutting cucumbers, pretending that they could cook and would cook. The cucumbers were to be the beginning of a salad. Pad thai was to follow, but would not follow. They would give up and order out.

"Of course you do," Wes said. "And it's about time. How?"

"We push it too far," Delaney said. "We push it over the cliff. We feed bad ideas into the system. Like AuthentiFriend. I gave this well-armed person named Holstein such terrible ideas today, and I wasn't even sure why. Now I know. It's the only way."

"We make it all worse," Wes said.

"Yes! We inject the place with poisonous ideas,

the Every adopts them, promotes them, and pushes them into the collective bloodstream of the world's people."

"And they overdose," Wes said.

"I was thinking get sick, but sure, okay, overdose."

"And they finally say Enough," Wes said, and held his knife high like a sword. He looked out to the back window, his other hand shielding his eyes, though it was night.

"Right," Delaney said. "We make everything more diabolical and ridiculous. And finally someone will say, 'At long last, have you no shame?' Or whatever they said to Joseph McCarthy."

"Have you no shame, **sir,**" Wes corrected.

"Right! I like the **sir.**"

"But with Mae, it'd be, 'At long last, have you no shame, **miss?**'"

"Maybe ma'am?"

Hurricane was on the kitchen floor, awaiting fallen scraps.

"How about **Ms. Holland?**" Wes said. "It's somehow respectful and condescending at the same time."

"'At long last, have you no shame, **Ms. Holland?**'"

"That's good," Wes said. "And you'll be the one to say it?"

"No, no. The world at large," Delaney said. "The people!"

"Oh right. The people! Which people?"

"All the people!" Delaney said, her voice rising. "The citizenry!"

"Ah, the citizenry," Wes said. "I like them. They always do the right thing." His voice sounded both hopeful and doubting.

"Humanity will finally turn away from the endless violations of decency, privacy, monopoly, the consolidation of wealth and power and control," Delaney said.

Wes examined Delaney's face. "You're serious. Oh, okay. That's good. And you're starting with AuthentiFriend?"

"It's terrible but it's silly," she said. "That one alone—if they roll it out on a large scale, people will be outraged. They'll leave in droves. They'll smash their screens, run to the hills. There'll be a global pause, a reckoning, a re-calibration."

"That sounds good," Wes said. "Re-calibration. Got it. It might even provoke regulation. Are we for regulation?"

"Of course we are," Delaney said. "We'll push it so far they'll be forced to step in. The FCC. The EU. The UN."

"The WWF. The WNBA."

"Stop."

"FIFA. ZZ Top. Can you imagine the combined power of the FIFA and ZZ Top? Those guys would raise a ruckus."

"I'm serious," Delaney said.

"No, I know," Wes said. "I'm serious, too. I think

it could work. You're supposed to rotate through a bunch of departments. So whenever you go at the Every, you seed that division with bad ideas." He crouched down to stroke Hurricane's snout. "Look what they did to this animal." Hurricane whimpered weakly, his paws reaching out, galloping vainly in mid-air. "He used to be a paragon. They took away everything wild and good about this animal."

XVI.

"Impressive presentation," a man said to
Delaney. She was on campus, surrounded by
men, and was doing her best to keep her eyes from
wandering below the belt. "I'm Fuad," this man
said, and did the same tip-of-the-top-hat gesture
that Delaney had hoped would be limited to Dan
Faraday. If this proliferated she wouldn't survive.

"Thank you," Delaney said, and looked for wine.
They were at an eatery, at what she'd been told was a
celebration, but there was no wine, no hint of wine.

Delaney's presentation had been recorded and replayed hourly since she'd made it two days ago, and
now she was at a new eatery on the edge of campus, four stories up, with a commanding view of
the steel-gray Bay. Technically this was a mandated
gathering called Mix-a-Lot, wherein Everyones
from far-flung departments were sent to cross-
pollinate, but it had been repurposed to celebrate
AuthentiFriend and the AuthentiFriend team.

Delaney was desperate to dull her mind, certain that her ploy was obvious to all. She cursed herself; she'd gone too far. What she'd said to Holstein et al. was so gaspingly stupid that every person in that room, and now this mixer, would know. With every rerun of the show, it was more likely they'd see through her nonsense. They might be devout but they were not dumb.

"Very impressive," Fuad repeated, "but I believe it can go much further."

Delaney coughed into her hand. If the subterfuge didn't kill her, these sincere and deranged people would. She needed wine. Where was the wine? She looked around her like a mother who'd lost a child in a mall.

"What can I get you?" Fuad asked.

"Oh, just—" she said, still flinging her eyes about.

On three long tables, food had been laid out on enormous platters, and Everyones were standing around, talking and eating food with their hands. There was no packaging, no utensils, no glasses or plates. And there was no wine.

Fuad said he was in youth outreach. He nodded with his hands occupied—his left held sashimi and his right encircled a sparkling, jiggling globe. It was the size of a golf ball, with the liquid inside held so by the thinnest membrane.

"I asked to be added to the AuthentiFriend team," he said. "I hope you don't mind." He popped the globe into his mouth and, with the slightest pressure from his jaw, it burst, and he swallowed it. He managed to make the action seem effortless.

"Not at all," Delaney said.

He was the first Everyone she'd met thus far who could reasonably be called suave. Though he wore an unmarked red T-shirt and black pants—not leggings—his affect was that of a man in an ascot, holding a cane and drinking brandy from a snifter.

"I'll try to be of service," he said, and with his palm on his sternum, bowed slightly with eyes closed.

Fuad put another jiggling globe into his mouth. When Delaney had entered the eatery, she'd thought they were water balloons for after-mixer merriment. His jaws clenched briefly, causing a distant shush to sound from his throat. A purple droplet emerged from the left corner of his lips.

"Have you had one of these?" he asked, and reached toward a pyramid of similar orbs. He took another, this one pink.

She picked up a yellow one. "Probably lemon-ade," he said. She put it in her mouth, which it filled, gelatinously, still full and round. She tried not to make a disapproving face, tried not to gag.

"Now push down and it'll pop," he said.

She applied pressure and nothing happened.

"A bit more maybe?" Fuad said, smiling sympathetically.

She pushed her tongue against it and it broke.

The juice, liberated, shot into the backs of her teeth, her throat, the roof of her mouth. She choked, spit, coughed. A rivulet spilled from her mouth and onto her shirt.

"They take some getting used to," he said.

She hacked and gasped.

"You okay?" he asked.

"I'm fine," she said. She looked for a glass of water but realized her mistake. She recovered and eyed the pyramid of tiny balloons as she would an ancient enemy. Finally she stood up straight again, and smiled. "That was wonderful," she said.

"The idea," Fuad explained, "is changing habits. You know the campus doesn't accept any single-use products or packaging."

Delaney rolled her eyes. "Of course."

"Well, Tamara Gupta took it further. You know her?"

Delaney had actually read about Gupta. She was a water usage expert, and had taken a strong stand first against the use of potable water to wash dishes, then against dishes altogether.

"I thought her book was provocative," Fuad said. "Mae brought her in to do an assessment, and she calculated that just here on the main campus, we were using about half a million liters of water a year just to wash our plates and glasses. That shocked me. Shocked everyone. So we're seeing how well we get by without plates and cutlery."

"I like it," said a new man, reaching across them

for a celery stalk. His features were sharp, birdlike, his eyes restless. He wore a gunmetal gray catsuit with multiple zippers and pockets, under which various devices and antennae sprouted and bulged. Carrying a banana in one hand and his new stalk of celery in the other, he made their duo a trio with agonized nonchalance.

"Francis," he said, lifting his chin to Delaney. Delaney took in his outfit, sweeping her eyes over his pocketed torso while careful to stop at the waist.

"How are you, Francis?" Fuad said with the faintest hint of wariness. "This is Delaney."

Francis ate his banana in two bites and threw the peel into a large compost pile situated meaningfully in the middle of the eatery. Delaney caught his bony posterior, celebrated in gray lycra, and looked away.

"Very well, thank you," Francis said. He opened a zipper on his right forearm, exposing a sleek phone, a model Delaney hadn't seen. "You're new, I assume," he said. "Your last name is?"

"Wells," Delaney said.

His fingers busied themselves on his phone. She and Fuad had no choice but to wait for Francis to complete the operation, the two of them engaged in the tragic everyday byproduct of the time—watching a fellow human tap on a screen, waiting for the result. While they waited, Delaney had a quick tingle of recognition. Hadn't there been a sexual liaison between a Francis and Mae Holland? The Francis in front of her looked at least forty. Mae must be in her mid-thirties by now, so yes, this could be him. It might have been the light, but Delaney saw a few feathers of gray hair near his temples.

Now Delaney's face appeared on his little screen. "Delaney Wells? I love it. It says you're a roamer." With Delaney standing in front of him, he read about her for a full thirty seconds before finally looking up. "Very interesting. Log cabin."

"Francis is with PrefCom," Fuad explained.

"Oh," Delaney said, a bit too enthusiastically. She'd wanted to meet someone from Preference Compliance—the darker, stricter, more punitive side of Are You Sure? PrefCom enforced brand loyalty and consistent consumer behavior through an array of punishments and disincentives. PrefCom was the fastest-growing division on campus and, Delaney thought, one of the key vehicles she could steer off a cliff.

She looked at Francis again and knew it was him. He'd filmed a sexual encounter with Mae, years ago. It had happened on campus, when Mae was new to the company. It had sparked a debate about who owned such footage, and ultimately Mae had had to live with it; once in the world, all video, all photographs, all documents, **belonged** to the world. How could Mae, a proponent of radical transparency, object to the posting of a moment meaningful to this man? Delaney was sure this video was still up, accessible to all.

"Your presentation was very provocative," a new voice said. Yet another man joined their group, this one much older, almost sixty, with an accent Delaney took to be German.

"Thank you," she said. He introduced himself as Hans-Georg. He wore frameless glasses over his small pale eyes, which seemed both amused and disappointed. His hair was long and dark, streaked with gray, falling mythically to his shoulders. He wore a simple flannel shirt, loose-fitting jeans and immaculate white tennis shoes. He seemed in all ways to be in the wrong place, in the wrong decade.

"I, too, am a roamer," he said. "Rotater? Which is correct?" He looked to Fuad for help.

"Either," Fuad said. "You both are rarities here. I'm almost envious, in that you get to see every corner of this place. Few do."

"Perhaps because I came so far, I am given these privileges," Hans-Georg said. "I know there are other Germans here, but I think I'm the only one from Weimar. I know Bailey is a Goethe enthusiast. I'm sorry, **was** a Goethe enthusiast. That was terrible. Ugh."

Delaney had been prepared to meet the Germans. The campus, she'd read, was recently flooded with them. She assumed it was an effort to appease German regulators; if the Every employed thousands of Germans here and abroad, perhaps their government would ease up on their neverending regulatory war.

"Excuse me, though, Delaney, but I have to ask," Hans-Georg said, "do you worry that encouraging young people to stay on their phones even longer each day will provoke more scrutiny for the Every?"

"The unmeasured life is not worth living," Francis said. "Pascal."

Delaney smiled at Francis. He was gloating. The quote, or misquote, seemed to be something he was ready to insert into any conversation. Hans-Georg appeared to know the mistake, too, and chose to smile and return to his question for Delaney.

"So soon after VRotTot, it seems like poking the bear, no?" he asked.

VRotTot had been a very expensive pilot project, years in the works, that had sought to acclimate children to the disorienting effects of virtual reality by equipping them at infancy with helmets to be worn while awake and asleep. Parents had been promised higher IQs and probable admission to elite universities, but pediatricians had raised a holy rancor and the program was abandoned, billions lost.

"Interesting," Delaney said, stalling. She needed to pivot back to the food, and then escape.

"Have you had these?" she said, indicating the pyramid of drinkable balloons. "So good."

"I have," Hans-Georg said, and sighed while looking at the feast.

"Too much?" Francis asked him. Hans-Georg shrugged amiably.

"Hans-Georg grew up in East Germany," Fuad noted. "They didn't have such choices back then."

"Yes," Hans-Georg said. "I remember going to Berlin with my aunt. This is after the wall fell. I'd never been in the West. I remember standing in front of a bakery, looking in. There were so many beautiful things! Fifty types of cookies, dozens of different cakes. Every sort of croissant and muffin, and every kind of bread. Pretzels! Chocolate-covered pretzels, pretzels with raisins, with cinnamon, with salt. And marzipan! I had never seen marzipan, though I'd heard about it from the ballet, with the rat with many heads . . . how do you say it in English?"

"The Nutcracker," Francis said.

"Yes!" Hans-Georg said. His eyes were merry. "So we stood outside the bakery, too nervous to go inside. And I looked up at my aunt, and she was crying."

Francis nodded, his mouth set in a satisfied smirk. "That's why the wall came down. People wanted choices. They wanted a free market."

"I'm sorry," Hans-Georg said, smiling politely while his eyes turned wistful. "You misunderstand. She was crying because of the waste. It was evening when we stood outside that bakery window, and she knew all of that wonderful food would be thrown away. To her, it was shattering." Hans-Georg looked at the buffet as if it, too, contained unimaginable gluttony.

"Too much choice," a new man said. He was sturdily built, dressed in a short-sleeved bodysuit. His arms, roped with muscles, were crossed in front of him like blades.

"Too much," Hans-Georg said. "This is what my aunt said. 'Why do we need so many things?'"

The new man was listening to Hans-Georg but was staring at Delaney.

"She saw it as a kind of Western corruption," Hans-Georg continued, "a symptom of excess and folly. She had been a member of the Party, sure, but she had a point. There was too much then and there's too much now. I'm sorry Gabriel. I'm monopolizing Delaney."

"Gabriel," the new man said, and nodded.

"What do **you** think?" Gabriel asked Delaney, and the intensity of his stare caused her to look away.

"About choice?" she asked. Francis drifted from the conversation, and Fuad left, too, though in a decidedly different direction from Francis. Gabriel's eyes never left Delaney. He took no notice of their exit.

"Yes, choice," Gabriel said.

"It's the burden of our time and the root of most planetary malaise," Delaney said.

Gabriel's head tilted back and forth like a pendulum, as if to say, **Maybe, maybe not, but well said.**

"Yes, yes!" Hans-Georg said. "Exactly. Gabriel's research has found much the same thing."

Hans-Georg provided room for Gabriel to elaborate, but Gabriel said nothing; he continued to stare at Delaney as if she were someone he'd known long ago and was trying to place.

"Gabriel's main finding," Hans-Georg said, "was that choice is one of the primary stressors for the last three or four generations. Millennials, Gen Y and Z—it's not just fear of missing out. It's the paralysis of unlimited options. Am I correct, Mr. Chu?"

Now Delaney placed this new man. He had seemed familiar to her from the start, but Delaney had been unsure why. Now she knew that the unflinching man standing near her was Gabriel Chu. His reputation was global. He'd founded U4U.

"You're Gabriel **Chu**," Delaney said, and he shrugged. This was, she assumed, a bit of a game he played—humbly introducing himself as Gabriel, and letting the realization come slowly.

This man, Delaney knew, was one of the truly dangerous people at the Every. Ramona Ortiz could make all travel a crime against the planet, but Gabriel Chu seemed capable of turning a billion minds into paste. He'd obliterated all personality tests, made a mockery of Myers-Briggs, laughed heartily at Walter Clarke and Wilhelm Wundt. About Freud, he'd said, "His work has the intellectual heft of a streetside astrologer." In a widely

seen meme, to Freud's followers he'd said, "You keep
your dream diaries and lewd little stories. I already
know the future of humankind." Other than that,
he seemed like a down-to-earth guy.

"Have you ever done one of his surveys?"
Hans-Georg asked Delaney.

Now Gabriel's mouth tensed; he seemed interested in knowing the answer.

"Of course," Delaney said, and Gabriel's face
softened. "All the time. They're addictive."

For years, Delaney had eyed U4U with a mixture of respect and horror. Their personality quizzes, all of them titled innocuously and positioned as
fun and frivolous, were wildly popular. What kind
of co-worker are you? Are you a closet authoritarian? Could you be more productive as a Buddhist?
What does your moisturizer say about your ability to seek true happiness? The quizzes varied from
short and whimsical to intricately involved and
purportedly scientific. U4U, originally a standalone
app, was a hit, and their surveys, some branded
and some anonymous, were shared widely, and
Gabriel Chu, the founder—with a PhD in clinical
psychology—became a kind of public intellectual.
His short talks on personality and its fluidity were
watched by millions and led more users to his surveys. With each, the user's score would be tabulated,
proving they were a culinary connoisseur or com-
mendable parent or recommendable lover.

When U4U was bought by the Every for $2.1 billion, much of the world was shocked, given the surveys had seemed middlebrow and innocuous, but Delaney assumed the worst and was eventually proven right: the surveys were extracting the kind of behavioral information that otherwise the Every and its clients could only infer or guess at. Because they were done for fun, and because they asked dozens or hundreds of deeply personal questions, the surveys revealed the users, who were consumers, at their most unguarded. Information that many people wouldn't offer in a clinical setting they willingly provided in a survey they filled out for entertainment.

"When I did my clinical internship," Gabriel said now, "I worked with students in their teens and twenties. Mostly college students. And the vast majority of the people we saw in the clinic complained about the same thing: the stress and paralysis of unlimited options."

"Imagine," Hans-Georg said, his voice an awed whisper. "Under the Soviets, all people wanted was more than one kind of bread. But now that we have choices, we are oppressed by them."

"People want three choices, not sixty," Gabriel said. "And for a vast array of categories, they want no choices at all. For example, we found that of 1,000 respondents, only 77 wanted to choose their mattress. The rest just wanted one that was comfortable and affordable and well-sourced. The stress comes in thinking you'll get yours home and realize it's inferior, or you paid too much, or it was made by sweatshop children."

Kiki appeared. "There you are!" she said, pointing at Delaney. Kiki always knew where Delaney was, and yet was always surprised to find her. She nodded to Gabriel and Hans-Georg. "I need to talk to this one. She hasn't done a Welcome2Me! Yours was fun, Hans-Georg. Didn't it involve classical music?"

"It did," he said. "Debussy, yes."

The word Debussy did not register with Kiki. She tapped her oval. "Right," she said finally, pulled Delaney toward the exit.

"I hope we can talk again," Gabriel said. "Maybe, during your roamings, you can roam into U4U. Both of you." He looked to Hans-Georg and did an admirable job of conveying that the invitation was being extended to both of them. But his eyes lingered on Delaney as she retreated.

As they took the stairs to the ground level, Delaney took in Kiki's outfit. She wore a form-fitting red top with a feathered pattern. Her leggings were made to look like a mermaid's lower half—scaled, sea-green, almost phosphorescent. Her waterpack had been adorned with a dorsal fin, which bounced menacingly as she galloped down the steps.

"Fish and feather?" Kiki said. "This is one of

AYS's new faves. I love it. Made in Greece, by ex-felons. Follow me."

Delaney made a mental note to find out what AYS was, then realized Kiki was talking about Are You Sure? She knew Are You Sure?—the sunnier, more stylish counterpart to PrefCom. Are You Sure? was ubiquitous, an all-powerful consumer conscience. When you were about to purchase an environmentally unfriendly jacket, for example, you'd get a dialogue box. "Are you sure?" it would ask, and list a better alternative.

They walked, and Delaney's peripheral vision tried to make sense of the half-fish, half-bird slinking along next to her.

"So, Welcome2Me. It's time," Kiki said. "We like new Everyones to think of a way we can better get to know you. We've found that usually there's this incredibly slow trickle of interpersonal contact that occurs over a year or two, which is just too long and not quite right. We've discovered through the work of Dr. Chanapai . . . Do you know her?"

Delaney thought Kiki would appreciate being, between the two of them, the sole knower of the work of Dr. Chanapai, so she said she did not.

"Well, she explains that newcomers to any culture should immediately celebrate their arrival, and celebrate the culture they're bringing to this new, second culture. So we ask newcomers to celebrate themselves. Maybe you share a culturally significant dish, or if you have a talent, you might sing or play a mini-concert. People have done karaoke, all kinds of things. A guy from Indiana made a mini–corn maze, though there were some complaints after that one. You're from Idaho. Do they have corn mazes?"

Delaney's oval vibrated, though she had not set it to vibrate. She looked down. **Greetings,** the message read. It was from Francis. **In order to improve my interactions with Everyones,** he wrote, **I'm asking new acquaintances to answer a few questions to rate my interpersonal skills.** Delaney scrolled down. There were thirty-two questions. **1. Did you find me approachable? 2. Did I maintain adequate eye-contact?** For each question, there were five emojis to choose between, from a fanged devil to a grinning angel.

"Delaney?" Kiki said.

Delaney looked up. "I'm sorry. Corn mazes? Not that I know of."

Now Kiki was looking at her phone too. Her face fell with every line of text. Finally she looked up.

"You okay?" Delaney asked.

"It's fine," Kiki said, her lip quivering. "Just got a major sham. I was in an old photo near a guy who was just convicted of assault—a bunch of assaults. And I guess this went up yesterday and I didn't know. I have no idea how I didn't know. I should have known. So twenty-four hours go by and I haven't denounced him and explained why I was in the photo."

Another ding came from her phone. "They found a text from me to him. I can't remember this guy! It was eighteen years ago. Why was I texting him?"

"What does it say?"

" 'Hi Paul. Kiki here.' "

"I don't think you should worry about that," Delaney said.

"I'm not. Well, I mean, it's just coming at a bad time. My Shame Aggregate just isn't where it should be. I try to be a good person but then these things pop up and . . ." She sniffed and ran her hands over her face.

Delaney looked at Kiki, feeling that the best thing she could possibly do would be to tuck her under her arm and flee.

"I'm sorry," Kiki said, straightening herself and dabbing her eyes. "We need to get your things straight. Welcome2Me. No corn mazes."

"No, I don't think so," Delaney said.

Kiki's oval dinged. "Hi Nino! No. Mama's not crying . . ."

Delaney looked away, trying to give Kiki some privacy, and her eyes alighted on a pair of men in ankle-to-shoulder lycra. Theirs, though, was somehow thinner than any she'd seen before; it was nearly sheer. On one of the men, she could see the dark swaths where hair proliferated underneath.

Now Kiki was back. "Good, so maybe something else," she said. "Maybe something forest ranger-y. Something outdoorsy but not scary like corn mazes?" she asked. Her face tensed for a moment, as if picturing the filth and chaos of the natural world. "Or maybe **at** the Every but **about** the outdoors? You can show pictures. Someone once showed **Moana.** I think that person was from Fiji, so—"

"I'll think about it," Delaney said.

"And it doesn't have to be huge. Maybe just forty people. That's a nice sampling. And those forty people can spread the word of all you're bringing to campus."

"I'll come up with something," Delaney said.

"We're just so happy you're here," Kiki said. "**I** am especially. You're a good listener, and you don't judge."

Delaney felt awful. All she'd been doing was judging—especially Kiki, who she was certain was on the verge of a nervous breakdown.

"Anything you do will be perfect," Kiki said.

Delaney smiled, knowing this could not possibly be true.

XVII.

"WE SHOULDN'T GO IN TOGETHER," Delaney said.

"Why?" Wes said. He was pulling his arm through the sleeve of a baggy flannel shirt. "They must know we live together. It would be weirder if we arrived separately."

Wes working at the Every was both horrifying and oddly comforting. Delaney felt the risk of her nefarious intention being discovered was increased tenfold with Wes on campus; he was at once guileless and forgetful. It seemed quite possible he would mention her subterfuge just as casually as he'd order a poke bowl.

"Should I wear a cam?" he asked.

"No. Don't do anything you normally don't do. They know your history already. They'll ask you about being trog, and you should just be honest. But you can withhold your most private thoughts."

Delaney began with her shoelaces.

"I can't watch," Wes said, and actually left the room.

When he was sure she was finished—she was—he returned. "How should we get to campus? After Stop+Lük, is there a right way? We could sail! Wait." He tapped his shirt pockets, as if in one of them he might find a boat.

They debated for a time what means of transportation would seem most logical and Everypropriate. In the end, they ordered a rideshare car purportedly powered by the sun. They waited on the couch; Hurricane limped over and draped himself on Wes's feet. Delaney still couldn't believe he'd been hired after one interview. They wanted him to work on AuthentiFriend, the joke app they'd made up to get her a job she didn't want.

"Did they tell you who would be acclimating you?" Delaney asked.

"They might have."

"You don't remember," she said, and despaired. "Maybe that's good. Just continue to be spacey. And forget my name, too."

"Your what?"

"Really. It's better if you never mention me."

"I don't even like you, Anastasia."

"The separation should be significant."

"Significant separation, got it," Wes said. "Now tell me, Olivia, do I get to meet Jenny Butler, the astrophysicist who knows the time and date of her death?"

"She's gone," Delaney said. "When Bailey died, all the space programs were killed."

"Huh. I guess she didn't see **that** coming," Wes said, and waited for a laugh. Hurricane let out a whimper.

"They acquire an average of three companies a week," Delaney said. "They kill programs just as quickly. Everything off-Earth is dead."

"Ah," Wes said. He noticed something on his toe. He found a file and began an artistic sort of sanding. He said something Delaney couldn't understand, talking as he was between his knees.

"Sorry," he said. "I was saying that the company just became far less interesting. I know I wasn't bound to work on lunar landers, but I would have liked to be near the people who were."

Delaney thought and hoped briefly he might actually choose to quit on day one. It would make everything so much simpler.

"But I guess I have to at least see what it's like," he said. "Especially given I can bring Hurricane."

"Not today," Delaney noted.

"I know. But there are probably a thousand pets on campus," he said. "Most of them came with the jungle. They were big on pets. They have their own vet, daycare, playgroups. There's a rabbit area, apparently. A warren."

"I don't think it's a warren," Delaney said. "I think it's a fenced-in area where they put the rabbits."

"That's a warren. Rabbits live in a warren."

"It's not a warren. Warrens are underg—"

The tinkling ring of Wes's flip phone sounded. He opened it and read a text. Delaney's body tensed. In seconds, she was sure that Wes would tell her of another suitor seized by the allure of Pia Minsky-Newton. Wes tapped an answer and clapped closed his black clamshell. Delaney waited for some new complaint about the burdens of her looks, but it did not come.

Delaney's phone notified her the car had arrived. They said goodbye to Hurricane, walked outside to find a man in a helmet driving a violet-colored shuttle.

"Before we get in," Delaney said, "you know everything in these cars is recorded."

"Of course," Wes said.

"I know you know," she said. "But up to this point it's just been academic. Now it matters. From here on out, until you return here tonight, assume everything you say will be heard, can be searched in seconds. It's a historical record available to anyone."

"Right," he said.

"My personal strategy is to slow down. Talk slower. Pause before speaking. You'll see that a lot on campus. People talk slowly, cautiously. Everything you say is permanent there, so people are exceedingly careful. I told you about TruVoice."

"You did. Got it," he said as they climbed into the car.

"Can I do an iris?" the driver asked. His voice, breathy and stressed, came through an overhead speaker.

Delaney leaned into his scanner. A happy ding confirmed she was the person who had ordered the car.

The driver looked at Wes. "And you?" he asked.

"I'm just a passenger. And not in the database," Wes said.

"You haven't had an iris done?" the driver said. He looked at the house from which they'd emerged. "You aren't trogs?"

"No. Just glaucomic," Wes said.

This didn't satisfy the driver. He spoke of safety, of having a right to know who was in his car.

"Wes," Delaney said, "can't you just bump his phone?"

Wes had a smartphone that he used in such situations, and thought wise to bring to work. Bumping, the quick exchange of dossiers via phones, was a cruder form of identification, but after examining Wes's file, looking for felonies or poor ratings from other drivers or service workers, the driver accepted him and they were off.

"Poor Pia," Wes said.

Delaney felt a stabbing pain somewhere behind her eyeballs.

"Apparently there's this prince," Wes said. "Did you know they still had princes in Norway? Pia met him at a climate conference and he wouldn't leave her alone. Then he introduced her to his dad."

Delaney took a stab. "The king?"

"Right, the king! And then the king was flirting with her for twenty minutes, in front of everyone. She's thinking she might have to wear a disguise."

Delaney had never before lent any oxygen to this fire of delusion, but she felt plucky. "But could anything hide her beauty?"

Wes sighed. "You're right. I should tell her that."

Every person has his blind spot, Delaney thought. She looked out the window, at the piers extending from the Embarcadero like a porcupine's quills. But if I don't know my own blind spot, she wondered, what does that mean? Being blind to one's blind spot: it did not portend well.

When they were on the Bay Bridge and the Every campus was laid out below in all its manic geometry, Wes sighed.

"I've never had a job before," he said.

"Sure you have," she said. She tried to assess whether he needed to self-censor more, but decided—on the 50-50 chance they were being heard by Every AI, and eventually HR—his candor and vulnerability would be considered endearing.

"Actually, I haven't," he said. "Not a job where you go in for a set amount of time. Where your hours are accounted for. Where you eat when other people eat."

Delaney's phone rang an unfamiliar ring. She saw a text from Francis. She'd been getting them since meeting him but now he'd found a way to change her ring tone. **Remember to fill out my questionnaire!** it said. **Looking forward to your feedback!** This was punctuated by an emoji face which looked both happy and anxious.

"Francis?" Wes asked.

Delaney smiled tensely, silently, reminding Wes to mind his words.

"Check it out," the driver said. He slowed before the offramp to Treasure Island. There was a line of a dozen cars ahead of them; Delaney craned her head to see what was happening.

Wes pointed to a man standing on the steel barrier of the bridge, just before the exit. He was about sixty, with a short white beard, wearing jeans and a tan sportcoat. Over his head he held a sign.

"I can't read it," Wes said.

Delaney leaned across Wes. "My wife's murder is watchable on all your platforms. Why? I ask you to remove my wife's murder from your platforms."

The line of cars ahead of them all seemed to be slowing to read the sign, or to be sure that the man didn't intend to jump in front of traffic.

"The Widower," their rideshare driver said.

"What's that?" Wes asked.

"They call him that, the Widower," the driver said. "He's been out there for weeks."

As their car passed the man, he looked through their window, his small blue eyes landing fully on Delaney and Wes. He knew they were Everypeople. He shook his sign at their car and yelled, "See me!"

Delaney took Wes's hand and squeezed it, reminding him not to say more. He looked away and let go of her hand.

"See me!" the man yelled again. He seemed ready to jump on their car. Delaney had not heard of this man, his sign. But it was not a novel concept. This man's wife was killed, by a stranger, by police—it didn't matter. Once it was filmed, it was posted, and once it was posted, it was eternal. This man's wish would not be granted.

"Do something!" he yelled. "I know you work there!"

Delaney looked into his eyes. He was no more than ten feet away, his eyes wild. She mouthed the words, **I'm trying.**

"What?" he yelled. "What did you say?"

Wes turned to Delaney, shocked. Had she really said something, or made some gesture, to this man on the bridge with the sign? Wouldn't that jeopardize everything they planned to do?

She held her hands in surrender, and finally the traffic eased. As her heart hammered, they got off on the Treasure Island exit and began the winding descent to the Every.

There had been brief and briefly effective campaigns against the company's amplification of hate, disinformation, gore and misery, but none had lasting effect. Outrage was rare and thus action impossible. And the one time the Every attempted to address the issue proved that their culpability was shared with a few billion willing collaborators. In an effort to appease the EU, the Every's braintrust invented a new social media platform, Blech, which was designed as a home for all things ugly and anti-social. The hope was that the trolls and sociopaths would go there, would self-select and be contained in a festering netherworld of misspelled insults and cancellation-lust. One or two percent of users, Bailey theorized, were spoiling the web for everyone else. But when Blech went live, seeded by a host of the web's worst offenders, millions, then billions, of seemingly normal humans followed. It became more popular than the rest of the Every's platforms combined. People wanted the bile and blood and fireworks, so Blech was quietly merged into the mainstream Every platforms, then subsumed. The heaven of the Every could contain hell, too.

Delaney and Wes approached the front gate, the sun shining on the campus in hazy shafts. She looked at her watch. They were thirty minutes early.

"I'll take you to breakfast," she said.

Breakfast was held in an enormous light-filled atrium, where forty long granite tables radiated from a grand round buffet. The space was more festive and participatory than any of the other eating areas Delaney had seen, with one end of the room dominated by a large screen, the sides curved forward like a vast parenthesis. **Inspiration? Advice?** the screen asked. **Speak freely to the Living Wall of Inspiration, Gratitude and Good Feeling!** Silent images of smiling Everyones faded in and out onscreen. A stagey picture of Mae Holland shaking hands with a police officer appeared. "We are proud to partner with local police departments in making neighborhoods safer," the text below read. "Through our DeputEyes program, our communities are more engaged than ever in promoting safety on every block through mutual observation . . ."

"I see," Wes said, "that this eatery is called Noshville."

The look on his face was great anguish.

"There are so many interesting names for things here!" Delaney said brightly and carefully.

They circled the buffet, an explosion of wet color. Every fruit was available whole or cut into dazzling shapes. Chefs stood behind silver tins of latkes and veggie sausage and a kind of faux bacon made of seaweed. After realizing there were no plates, Wes filled his hands with pineapple cubes and gluten-free oatmeal spheres.

"My eyes," Wes muttered. "I feel bad for my eyes."

He had not blinked since they arrived. He sighed

and looked at the buffet table, where two dozen men and women were eating, hand to mouth, in multicolored lycra. He nodded to a group of men in their early forties, every flat plane of their buttocks visible, accentuated and shimmering in the morning sun.

"I want this to not be happening," he said. "It's not right."

Delaney implored him to be silent. He popped a jittery globe into his mouth and squeezed his jaws shut. His eyes clenched and opened, tearing up just a bit, before he swallowed and grinned. She had a feeling he might like the drink-globes. They were silly, and without fail he liked silly.

"These I like," he said.

"The screen," Delaney said. "Look."

He turned to see it. **Secrets Are Lies,** it said, in a flowery font. **Sharing Is Caring.** These were default messages. **The World Wants to Be Watched** was offered calligraphically. Notices of upcoming classes appeared. A seminar called **Creativity: Can It Be Bought? And How Much Should It Cost?** would be happening later that day, online, led by a visiting statistician.

Diners were invited to send new statements to the screen—anonymously if desired—which would then be displayed, in four-foot type. Those contributions deemed good were given smiles, and if those smiles added up, that statement would stay onscreen and grow. The hope was that the wall would become a sort of kinetic digital salon, though the result, as far as Delaney had seen, had fallen short of the Algonquin Round Table. **Celebrate yourself!** said the first new message. **Thank you!** said the second.

"I didn't expect all that fruit," Wes said. "Not the fruit in general, but the tropical fruit. The stuff that's not in season in North America. Look at that mountain of bananas."

Delaney had a thought. With widened eyes she tried to convey to Wes that something was beginning and that he needed to pay attention. "What?" he said, looking around. "What's happening? Is something happening?"

She fixed her mouth into a terrible smile. He took the hint. She assumed their words were being recorded and screened, in real time, by TruVoice. "How can we be eating bananas in California," she said, "when they're picked by underpaid workers in Guatemala, three thousand miles away?"

Wes nodded. Finally he caught on. Or caught on that he should try to catch on. "This is actually a valid question," he said. "Do bananas really come from Guatemala? I thought it was closer than that. Don't we grow bananas in Florida?"

"We should send these thoughts to the screen," Delaney said, and tried to remember what unforgivable name the screen had been given. "To the . . ." She looked around and found the name carved into the wall. "To the Living Wall of Inspiration,

Gratitude and Good Feeling." She had no plan beyond seeing how pliable this system was.

"Let's ask the **community**," she said, "how they feel about the carbon cost of these bananas coming so far." She nodded to Wes's flip phone, which lay dormant and face-down on the stone table.

"I wish I could," he said. "It's such a valid concern!"

He pointed to her own phone.

She shook her head and pointed to his.

"Blamed. Get. I'll," he said.

This was a theory of his, largely borne out: AI got confused when words were out of sequence. These three words, somewhat suspicious in logical order, were innocuous out of sequence, and wouldn't register. "Credit," she said. "Get. You will."

He sat back and crossed his arms and sat that way for a full minute.

"Job. Got. For. You. I did," Delaney said.

Finally he lifted his phone and typed, using T1 predictive text and a complicated relay-system he'd invented to get messages from his ancient phone to modern recipients.

"I'm concerned about the presence of bananas here," he typed. "What's the carbon cost? We're three thousand miles from Guatemala. Must we have bananas today?" He hovered his finger over the send button.

"Really?" he asked Delaney. She nodded and he sent.

They waited. The sentences appeared, but only for a moment in the corner of the screen, soon pushed out by someone promoting their podcast, called Ideal Starts with I. **It's about how we love ourselves more,** they noted.

"Bananaskam," Delaney said.

Wes looked confused.

"Banana**skam**," Delaney repeated.

Wes shook his head again. Some years before, the word **flygskam** had been invented in Sweden, meaning **flight shame.** It was used to drench social opprobrium on those who flew places where they could take trains. (Its more morally desirable twin was **tagskryt,** or **train pride.**)

Wes typed the word **Bananaskam** and sent it to the screen. It appeared and then disappeared. Instead, the word "Greenland!" appeared and spun and was showered in digital confetti. Long a hold-out, Greenland had finally adopted Demoxie, the Every's voting software, bringing the total number of countries using it to one hundred and twenty-two. It was free, after all, and only required that all citizens have Every accounts. Voting in most countries was now done through the Demoxie, which made elections far more secure, with voters' personal information and political choices completely private, unless a government or Every strategic partner wanted that information, in which case it was readily sold. The word "Greenland!" glowed once more, and all around the cafeteria, Everyones nodded, smiled, and went back to churning. Delaney gestured to Wes to try again. He did.

Bananaskam appeared on the screen, larger this time.

I had that album, someone wrote in response. **Cruel Summer!**

Wes, suddenly competitive, tapped quickly on his phone. "How is it okay to be eating bananas now, in Northern California? At what cost, human and carbon? #Bananaskam!" He sent it, and now, because it was the third mention, the word **bananaskam** appeared in large pulsing letters. Delaney saw the heads of a few diners turn and tilt. Phone and tablet-tapping ensued, and the word **bananaskam** grew larger and morphed into a fiery red font.

Now a new message appeared onscreen: "Guatemalan banana plantation workers are paid $6 a day. They put the bananas on container ships—some of the worst ocean polluters. Gas and oil leaking all over the Pacific. Then to Long Beach. Then up Highway 5 on gas-burning trucks. All so we can have bananas where and when we have no right to them. #Bananaskam!"

"Is that you?" Delaney asked.

Wes shook his head, showing his idle hands.

"Now send it home," Delaney said. "Bananaskam = banana shame."

"Joke," Wes said. "Obvious. They'll know."

"Know?" Delaney said. "Never. Here. Jokes. None."

"BANANASKAM = BANANA SHAME," he typed, and pushed send. Thirty heads read the phrase and nodded.

Soon the entire screen was anti-banana, and an enterprising kitchen staffer had gotten the message. He removed the twenty or so remaining bananas, secreting them out of view.

In the course of breakfast, **bananaskam** begat **pineappleskam** and **papayaskam.** Any fruit not grown in California was accused and found guilty. The kitchen workers stayed busy, removing each newly demonized fruit, and by the end of lunch, the consensus was that anything eaten on campus had to be grown within 100 miles and transported to campus without use of fossil fuels. Even that was considered a holding position, to be improved upon—the perimeter shrunk and carbon load made negative. Onscreen debates were held about what, beyond the campus's heretofore recreational and decorative tomato and lemon and lime gardens, could be grown on campus, or brought there by sail. Studies were planned, nearby farmland was bought, and a sign hung over the eatery from that day on: WE HAVE NO BANANAS, it said, and that made everyone very proud.

XVIII.

"THERE YOU ARE!" The words were sung by a voice behind Delaney.

It was Kiki, her eyes exultant. Again, though she knew Delaney's whereabouts always, each time she saw her, she was overcome with delight to find her where she knew she was. At the moment, they were outside the lobby of Algo Mas.

Today Kiki's jewelry was bulbous and wooden but just short of bizarre, her bodysuit white and legs covered by knee-high boots equal parts Barbarella and Condoleezza. But Kiki's face seemed to have aged years in a week. Delaney couldn't say this. She couldn't even say she looked tired. That would be flagged by TruVoice, and AnonCom, and probably ComAnon, too.

"You okay?" she asked instead.

"Me? Yes!" Kiki said. Then, as if realizing she'd sounded overly defensive, she started over, first with a hearty chuckle. "I'm **perfect,**" she said. "Just a bit underslept. Ready for your next rotation?"

"I am," Delaney said, but Kiki's eyes had gone distant. Delaney waited while Kiki seemed to travel to unknown worlds, and finally returned.

"I got an eval recently," Kiki said, "and it said I need at least 7.6 hours. But I don't remember **when** I got that much sleep. Maybe high school? What's your number?"

Delaney had no clue. "Maybe seven?"

Kiki's eyes again traveled to far-off places. "Send autos," she said to her AI assistant. "To all forty-one." She refocused on Delaney. "How long do **you** usually take to return a message?"

Wes had set Delaney up with an elaborate system to auto-respond to all of her incoming messages, but she couldn't tell Kiki this. "Depends," she said.

"I'm trying to get quicker," Kiki said. "Because of some super-tardy exchanges, I was averaging 22 minutes, which got flagged—for good reason. I mean, that's not polite and not professional. So I asked OwnSelf to help me improve my turnaround. But Nino was sick this morning so I fell behind again, and I just had to auto-respond to my backlog, which also isn't good. I'm trying to find a balance, but it's been tough . . . Sorry," she said. "What are we doing again?"

"My next rotation," Delaney said. "You said it was TellTale?"

"Ah, good. Follow me," she said, and strode with

newfound energy across campus to a building that Delaney had assumed was an arboretum of some kind. It was a steel-paned glass structure full of plants and flowers.

"It must be exciting," Kiki said, and looked at her oval. "It must be **exhilarating,**" she corrected, and found her oval approving, "to rotate again. To venture forth into new territory." Again she checked the oval to see if points were scored. Nothing. She tried again "To venture **assiduously** forth into new and **parsimonious** territory." Two happy bells rang from her oval, and Kiki smiled.

It didn't matter, Delaney realized, where the ten-dollar words occurred, or if they were used correctly. You got points either way.

"I feel lucky," Delaney said. "But I will miss Winnie."

"Winnie . . ." Kiki said, and panicked briefly. "Winnie. Winnie in Thoughts Not Things." Her oval reacted, produced the answer, Kiki read it and smiled. "Yes, Winnie Ochoa. A truly **perfunctory** person." Another bell sounded. "**Belatedly** perfunctory, wouldn't you say?"

Another bell. "Sure," Delaney said. "Just like you said."

"So TellTale," Kiki said. "This was Bailey's last major initiative before he left the day-to-day and of course before he passed." Kiki's smiling eyes were suddenly swimming. She took a moment to gather herself. "It's really a monument to his priorities," she said. "He really was a Renaissance man. We go through here."

Kiki's fingerprint opened a heavy steel door and they entered a kind of library, if that library were designed by robots and for dinosaurs. Everywhere there were enormous Jurassic ferns and succulents, hanging recklessly near jumbo screens and gently touching an array of antique typewriters, each of them sitting atop a platform and under a heavy glass dessert dome.

"We'll meet your team leader, Alessandro, here." They were standing under what seemed to be a fourteen-foot carnivorous plant. Delaney edged away from what she assumed was its mouth.

Kiki checked her watch. "We're early, so I'll background you on the space. When the movie came out—did you see the movie?"

"I did," Delaney said.

"The actor who played Bailey . . . Darn it, what was his name? Anyway, in real life the actor collects typewriters, so that's why there are typewriters everywhere? He also wrote a book of fiction? And this got Bailey thinking he could write a fictional book, too. So Bailey, because he was so methodical, started studying made-up storytelling. He read every guide there is. And I think he even read some fiction novels? He found it difficult to concentrate for so long and finish these books, because so many of them are very long. I guess you know that from college? Is there still a lot of reading in libarts?"

"Quite a bit," Delaney said, and scrunched her nose disapprovingly. Kiki smiled. "So immediately Bailey started looking into what other people were reading, and whether everyone else is having the same trouble he'd been having finishing these books. Obviously paper books provide no useful data and should be abolished—"

"For environmental reasons alone!" Delaney added.

"I know, right?"

"And they're so **heavy** sometimes," Delaney said, gesturing as if someone had handed her an anvil.

"But the data e-books give us is so clear," Kiki continued, "and what we found was that while, overall, millions of fictional books were being **bought** every year, a much smaller percentage were being read all the way through. This was a relief to Bailey, and to people like me, because I find it almost impossible to sit through a whole movie, let alone stay still for however long it takes to read a novel. But you've read a bunch? Like all the way to the end?"

"A few, yes," Delaney said.

"Kudos!" Kiki said, and heard a happy ding from her oval. She looked up and her face eased into a tired smile. "Here's Alessandro. Alo, you should take it from here. This is Delaney." She turned to Delaney and her eyes welled again. "Sorry. All the emotion from this week. But it's been wonderful getting to know you. I'm sure I'll see you Friday at the celebration for Bailey. Until then, I wish you a **sagacious** and **immoderate** time here."

With two more bells, Kiki peeled off and Alessandro waved to her as she left the building. He turned to Delaney with the full power of his eyes, which were extraordinarily large and unblinking and seemed to be ringed in what seemed to be naturally occurring eyeliner. His long black hair sprung from his scalp in thick vines.

"Please don't call me Alo," he said to Delaney, pushing a few vines from his face. "I've filed more AnonComs than I can count, but people still call me that. Anyway, you were at Reed? I was Kenyon," he said, and closed his oversized eyes solemnly. Delaney worried there was some kind of sister-city bond between the two schools that had escaped her.

"So, like you, when I was in school, there was no chance I pictured myself here," he said. "I was supposed to be a comp lit professor. This"—here he gestured to encompass the grand room and all the people in it—"was basically everything I most despised. But obviously now I'm going to try to convince you of what I myself became convinced of. Let's go over here."

Delaney followed Alessandro to what she as-sumed was his workspace—an ergonomic stool sur-rounded by twelve screens of various sizes. It looked like a prog-rock drum set. He pushed the hair-vines from his face again, and sat down, as if ready for a solo. The screens came alive, filled with scanned pages from books, though with dozens of symbols and numbers superimposed over the text—a kind of civil war between words and data.

"Bailey's first goal was to find out why he couldn't get through certain novels, and why, by inference, others put certain books down," Alessandro said, and pulled up a second stool for Delaney. She took it. "People pick up a book," he said, "and stop in the middle. Why? With e-books we can study all of this in aggregate. We can take, for example, two thousand readers of **Jane Eyre** and see who finished it. We actually did that. Turns out 188 people did finish it. That's not good, right? People who read it all seem to like it. It's at—" He tapped one of his screens a few times and got the answer. "It's at 83 percent approval, which is high for a dead author. So we dig deeper and see that of the 2,000 or so people who started **Jane Eyre,** most quitters put it down around page 177. So then we look at what happens on page 177, and we see that people don't seem to like this character named Grace Poole. They find her scary and depressing. They want more of the romance with Mr. Rochester. Now, if the author were alive, we could tell him—"

"Her," Delaney corrected.

"Her?" Alessandro said reflexively, then went pale. Oh no, Delaney thought. She'd seen this happen. Alessandro stood up. He didn't know what to do. He allowed the vines of his hair to obscure his face completely, and seemed likely to douse himself with gas and light a match.

"It's okay," Delaney said. "You meant **Mr. Rochester.**"

"I did?" Alessandro said from behind his wall of hair.

"I **know** you did. Like, if Mr. Rochester were alive, we could tell him that his parts of the book were intriguing."

Alessandro tucked a hair-vine behind his ear, revealing a terrified left eye. "Okay," he said. "Right." He began warming to the idea, believing it his only way out of ruination. "That's exactly what I meant." He checked his oval, looking for TruVoice violations, and seemed to find none. (TruVoice did not read novels.) Finally Alessandro relaxed and sat back down.

"Where were we?" he asked. As a man just resurrected, he was still addled.

"You were saying you could fix **Jane Eyre.**"

"Well, we could," he said, "but because the author is dead, **she**"—he pressed the word so hard it erased centuries of chauvinism and ignorance—"can't learn from the data herself."

"Sucks for her," Delaney said, and saw Alessandro smile. Finally he was back, and warmed again to his subject.

"But a living author, or a publisher, can avail themselves of the numbers and act on them," he said. "And this kind of data has been invaluable to publishers and some of their authors already. Just those data points, sales versus book-starts versus completions, that's huge. Completions, of course, convert favorably to sales of the author's next book. So for publishers, figuring out where and why people are stopping is crucial. Sometimes it's obvious. Like, unlikable characters. We can help fix that. Algo Mas actually wrote a pretty simple code for turning an unlikable character into, like, your favorite person."

"Wow," Delaney said.

"The main thing is that the main character should behave the way you want them to, and do what you want them to do."

"That's just common sense," Delaney said.

"Right? It kind of makes you worry about a lot of writers—the fact that they didn't know this. But we're making inroads with colleges and MFA programs, so now they have the information. We give it to them for free, as a public service."

Delaney made a grateful, admiring whistle-sound.

"But some of the other issues are structural," Alessandro said. "For instance, people don't like epistolary novels. We found readers were skipping over most of the letters, especially if they were set off from the rest of the type with indents or smaller font size. But we found they were willing to read them if the letters were less than 450 words each, spaced every hundred pages or so, and were included in the body of the text—same size, same font, same indentation, and decidedly never italic."

"That makes sense," Delaney said.

"We found so many things!" Alessandro said. "Overall number of pages is fairly clear. No book should be over 500 pages, and if it is over 500, we found that the absolute limit to anyone's tolerance is 577."

"Even that seems undisciplined," Delaney said.

"Right. Another key was the number of ideas or themes," he said, "the number a reader would be able to tolerate in any book. I thought it would be nine or ten, but guess how many?"

"Three?" Delaney guessed.

"Exactly!" Alessandro said. "Any more than three, and people start quitting. The books that tossed out ideas left and right were always de-preferenced. Especially if those ideas get outdated. You read a book by Jules Verne and he's going to spend twenty pages describing technology that's obsolete now. That leads to high quit numbers, and a lot of in-terpaginate skims. The skimmers often technically finish their books, but we can tell by their reduced time spent on each page that they're not really **reading** each page. We find this a lot in romance novels, obviously, with readers skimming until they find the . . ."

Alessandro stopped cold. It was clear he knew he couldn't say "sex" or "sexual passages" or even "racy parts."

". . . on the vividly romantic sentences," he finally said, and instantly his face went slack. "Um," he said, hoping to forge ahead while wondering again if he'd just lost his job.

Delaney shrugged and smiled. Signaled by Delaney's blithe attitude, relief swept through Alessandro like a gust of warm wind.

"Anyway, that research led to the Fontainebleu scandal," he said. "We can't blame Bailey, because he didn't know about it, and wouldn't have approved. This was just an experiment, a collaboration with a publisher."

"Is this the thing with the AI novelist?"

"Donna Fontainebleu, right."

"When machines wrote whole books?"

"No, that got distorted," Alessandro noted. "The point was that the AI would write the parts no one read anyway—that interstitial stuff I was mentioning. The, like, **favorite** scenes, and the climactic parts and parts where there's poetical-type writing, those were still written by humans. Those parts benefit from human intervention."

"Of course," Delaney said. "Division of labor."

"Right. If we value humans, we save them from the mundane tasks. When we analyzed the reading data in the romance genre, we found that less than 4 percent of the buyers were reading all of the text. So just as an experiment, we collaborated with a few publishers on AI that would handle the stuff no one read in the first place. A fair amount of communication has been going this way anyway. Political speeches are generally repurposed using AI stitching software."

"I heard that," Delaney said.

"Listen, though. I don't see AI writing all books. None of us do. Bailey didn't think humans could be replaced or anything like that, that would be silly. But there is a role, he felt—we feel—for algorithms to play. Bailey studied some storytelling texts, screenplay guides, Campbell's **Hero with a Thousand Faces,** and started reading about the patterns, the formulas, and once he saw that word, **formula,** it all clicked. A formula is essentially an algorithm."

"Exactly," Delaney said.

"Let's start with screenwriting, which has been guided by formulas since the beginning. We did quite a bit of analysis here, and found that every successful screenplay ever written conforms rigidly to one of a few formulas, and the screenwriters we've brought in assure us that there is ready agreement in their ranks that formula, far from being a constraint, is the key to their freedom. Knowing the rules allows them to be creative within those guardrails. For example, 82 percent of the best scripts have the Catalyzing Moment on page 11. You can call storytelling a mystical, unknowable art, but there's hard science here, and to deny it would be silly. Data is just—"

"Comfort," Delaney said.

Alessandro smiled warmly. "Isn't it? Formulas are the essence of comfort. Not just for the creators, but for the viewer. **Especially** for the viewer. When viewers get **what** they expect to get, **when** they expect to get it, that's comfort."

"It's really the essence of art!" Delaney said.

"See, **you** get it. It's just another set of guidelines, within which the writer has complete freedom. Like, the alphabet has twenty-six letters. That's one set of constraints that no one seems to have a problem with. We only have so many words—another constraint. Sentences can only be so long—yet another necessary constraint."

"Constraints are the key to liberation," Delaney said.

"Exactly, exactly," Alessandro said. Delaney could tell Alessandro wanted to compliment her—to say something even as simple as "We are in sync!"—but was unsure how to say such a thing to a woman, and a woman in the workplace, and a woman in the workplace who he'd just met and with whom he'd messed up the gender of the author of **Jane Eyre.** So he smiled, for a good three or four seconds, with his mouth open. He had wonderful teeth, but Delaney couldn't say that.

"The data doesn't tell a screenwriter **what** to say," he finally said, "but it does suggest the gist of what they should say, and provides empirical evidence of **when** it should be said."

"Forgive me for saying this," Delaney said,

"but all this just seems logical. And undeniable. Otherwise you have, like, anarchy."

"On both sides!" he yelped. "On the creative side **and** the critical side. The critical side we tamed some time ago. Remember when assessments of the quality of a movie were an unruly mess? Before critical aggregation, it was totally random. For a certain movie, you had one critic saying one thing in Los Angeles, and another one in Oslo saying something else, and there was no chance of order and consensus. But when we applied percentages to each review, we could average them together, and it became far more clear. A regular human in a fast-moving society doesn't have time to read twenty-five, or even three, reviews of a movie before they go see it. But seeing it's received an aggregated score of 74.61 percent—that's clarity."

"And clarity is objectivity," Delaney said.

He looked at her and grinned. "You belong here."

"I think I do, too," she said.

Alessandro's oval dinged. "Okay, time to move," he said, and stood up. "I'm a reacher. You?" He began marching in place while also reaching high into the air, left hand then right, as if grabbing at bubbles just out of his grasp.

"I've always wanted to," Delaney said, and reached with him.

After four minutes, Alessandro's oval dinged again and they sat down. Alessandro was aglow.

"As you know," he continued, catching his breath,

"the aggregates worked so well that they quickly moved from movies into painting, dance, sculpture, poetry. I mean, you should have seen how low sonnets scored! That's why you don't see those taught so much anymore."

"Sonnet? What's a sonnet?" Delaney laughed.

Alessandro's eyes were wild with mirth and inspiration. "Then we brought numerical specificity to so-called fine art museums. In each case there was some initial pushback, but the undeniable comfort of the numbers, of simply knowing the quality of a work of art by its percentage, was soon embraced by the overwhelming majority of people. Eighty-eight percent, to be exact."

"That's the only reason we finally know who the best painter was," Delaney said. The Every had released their results a few years earlier, the product of 32.1 million respondents. The greatest artist in all of history, the survey proved, was Norman Rockwell, followed by Dale Chihuly, Frida Kahlo, Pablo Picasso and Patrick Nagel.

They shared a smile. "I liked when the Louvre started showing the aggregates," Delaney said.

"Right," Alessandro said, "I mean, the Louvre came to **us.** There were all these places doing bootleg aggregates and they wanted it done right."

"It was fascinating when **The Last Supper** was only a sixty-six percent," Delaney said.

"It had been so overrated for centuries! See, that kind of thing was revelatory. We're averaging together tens of thousands of ratings, as opposed to taking the received wisdom of a few academics. The aggregates are more democratic and egalitarian. Before the aggregates, it had all been so hierarchical and subjective."

"Subjectivity is just objectivity waiting for data," Delaney said.

"Right!" Alessandro said, and she saw him pause, again working out whether any kind of compliment would be acceptable. He decided not to risk it. "I mean, I think creatives are starting to acknowledge that we have a valuable role to play. This high wall that was built between art and data had to be torn down."

Delaney had a thought, a truly bad idea, and she had a feeling Alessandro would love it. "I wonder about beauty," she said.

"Okay," Alessandro said, his voice uncertain.

"I was just thinking that there isn't a proper measurement for beauty and artistic quality," Delaney said. "And it's something that's needed. Like Rembrandt. I know I'm supposed to believe his work is so great and important, but I don't see it. And I don't want to rely on received opinion."

Alessandro's face continued to brighten, and ten years earlier, he would have clasped Delaney's hand and said **Yes, yes! we are so similar and I enjoy talking to you!** But nothing like that could be said here, now, by him, to her. So he said nothing.

"I had this weird idea," Delaney continued.

"Obviously I couldn't do it, because I'm not an engineer or anything. But I was thinking, couldn't there be a beauty metric? When AI took over the judging of gymnastics and diving, photography competitions, all that."

"The Golden Globes," he interjected.

"Right, we suddenly had such clarity. No complaints. No questions. And for decades we've had assessments of human beauty—what's considered beautiful in each culture. Facial symmetry, size of eyes, hands, waist-to-hip ratios. That's been with us for a long time."

"Right, right."

"So how hard would it be to apply that to paintings, music, poetry, or any art form? It's just creating a set of ideals, a range of metrics that you overlay. You could take **The Last Supper** and say it has a certain symmetry score, a certain score for color harmony—"

"Originality. Boldness," Alessandro offered.

Delaney knew, then, that he would take this notion. He could make it his own. She would give it to him and watch it bloom.

"Beauty has boldness," she said, "and that can definitely be measured." She knew, now, that she needed to change the topic back to something less novel. He might feel threatened if she continued to pitch an idea he wished he'd thought of himself. Better, she knew, to have planted the seed. Ideally he'd forget it was her who planted it.

"Sorry," she said. "You were talking about movies."

He paused. Smiled. Filed away this beauty idea, now his.

"Right," he said, "before we set up our own studio, and before we bought three of the last five majors, we began working with studios. First we brought in AI to analyze what was and wasn't working in their films. We took a hundred critically successful movies, those that had scored over 86 percent in aggregate, and compared them to a hundred films that had scored under 66 percent. The results were clarifying. There were dozens of common errors in the less successful movies, and we found that certain actors, directors and producers had historically low aggregate numbers, meaning that they should, in a purely Darwinian environment, be selected out of the species."

"Personally, I don't bother with any movie that scores under a 52," Delaney said.

"Fifty-two is your number? For me it's seventy-seven. Life's too short, right? Why bother with anything under seventy-six, seventy-seven?" He sat back in his chair. "I actually had a funny experience recently. My wife convinced me to see a movie that was a 64. Normally there's no chance I would, but this one was new, so the critical sample size was small. And I'd already been zinged about it, because it did have eight other factors I'd identified in my prefs—costumes. Weddings. British accents. Horses.

I can't remember them all, but anyway, this movie had a bunch of my indicators. So I saw the film, but the aggregate didn't lie. It was definitely a 64, and I was like, 'When will I ever get those ninety-four minutes back?' "

"Nightmare," Delaney said.

"**Night**mare!" Alessandro agreed.

"I had something similar, but opposite, happen," Delaney said, making it up as she went along. "A few months ago I saw a movie without looking at the data beforehand and—"

"Yikes," he said.

"Right. So I see the movie, and afterward I walked out of the theater thinking I really enjoyed it."

"Okay . . ." Alessandro said, almost worried.

"Then I got on my phone to look at the aggregate score, and it was a 44!"

Alessandro whistled mournfully.

"So then I had to adjust my thinking," Delaney said. "I mean, how is it that I liked this movie that was a 44? Clearly I'd missed some of its flaws and inflated what I did like about it. By the next day, I'd thought it through enough and knew where I'd erred. It was definitely a 44. That's the last time I experience any kind of art before I have the numbers."

Alessandro looked at Delaney quizzically. She had the momentary fear that she'd gone too far. She was not, she had to remind herself, an actress. She had to dial it down.

"Have you been to our studios?" he asked.

"No," Delaney said. "I've wanted to do the tour."

"Oh, you won't have to do the tour," he said. "A film buff like you should get a backstage look. I wouldn't be surprised if they rotate you there for a few weeks. You know your stuff. I'll put in a word."

"That is very kind of you," Delaney said.

"Anyway, when CircleStudios started—now you know it as EveryContent or ECon—that amount of untapped data was endless. The regular studios weren't even using the vast majority of it. We hired this sort of artsy executive, and she started green-lighting projects all willy-nilly, without looking at the actual data about what actual people actually wanted. The streaming data was showing that 71 percent of what people were watching were romantic comedies, but only 22 percent of the projects she greenlit were romantic comedies. Which seemed not just unwise but kind of perverse."

"Almost willful," Delaney said.

"Willful, right," he said, and Delaney knew she'd hit another word seldom appearing in auto-fill. "So she didn't last so long. Her successors, though, have been more audience-responsive. They started aligning the content with what people wanted. And then, when we drilled down a bit, we looked closer at not just what people wanted, but when. This brings us back to Bailey. He wanted to know why people were putting down certain books at certain times. We started looking closely at that for books, for films, for episodic television, for everything. We had the data. So we've been working with most of the remaining film companies, and of course the bigger publishers, on making storytelling more efficient, audience-responsive, and successful. If you're humble before the numbers, the rewards are significant."

"Well," Delaney said, "I think that is wonderful."

XIX.

Wes working at the Every was glorious and wretched and shredded Delaney's last nerve. Delaney could make the commute with him, the two buses and a BART ride under the Bay, and that was sublime, but once on campus she had to worry about what he would say, would unwittingly reveal. He was uncontrollable, but he was so happy. After his first week, he applied to bring Hurricane with him, and though he couldn't get a dog on public transportation, he managed an ongoing rideshare that allowed Hurricane to sit on his lap. The first time Delaney saw Wes, aged thirty-six, standing at his desk in his first job-job, with Hurricane at his feet, she felt a wave of pride in her friend. But on campus, she insisted on having as little contact as possible. It was too risky, and Wes too careless. They reserved their conversations for home.

"Have you gotten one of these?" Wes asked. He was lying on his mattress on the floor, his back propped against the wall, his tablet resting on his stomach. Hurricane's sleeping head was under his elbow.

Delaney sat on the bed. On Wes's screen, the words **Idea Origination Survey** were rendered in rapturous calligraphy.

"No," Delaney said. "Nothing like it, actually."

Work had been uneventful, he said—just orientations, forms, NDAs, meetings and the med-eval. But when he arrived home that day, he'd gotten this.

"I saved it till you got home," he said.

Ready? his screen asked.

"Ready," Wes said.

We have been alerted to your brilliant new notion, "Bananaskam," and we thank you for adding so much to the Every. As part of an ongoing study to know more about where ideas come from, we ask that you participate in this brief (and entertaining!) survey. Your prompt response is appreciated.

"I love this so much already," Wes said. "I mean, this makes me happier than I've ever been. 'Where ideas come from.'"

The calligraphy disappeared, and the sepia-toned image of a frail and elderly woman appeared. She was walking in the desert, then stopped. She turned to face Wes, her eyes fiery.

"Creativity is a wondrous and mysterious thing," the woman said.

"Who's that?" he asked.

"Georgia O'Keeffe," Delaney said. "It's a repro."

O'Keeffe morphed into Jim Morrison.

"And though this mysterious process of idea-generation might remain elusive to science," Jim Morrison said, "at the Every we aim to understand a bit more about the conditions under which ideas arrive."

Jim Morrison became Akira Kurosawa.

"To that end," this resurrected version of Kurosawa said in what seemed to be a British accent, "we ask recent idea-generators to answer these sixty-five questions. Have fun and thank you!"

Now it was Georgia O'Keeffe again. The New Mexico desert stretched out behind her. "What time of day was it when the idea occurred to you?" It was dusk where she was.

"Eight-fifteen," Wes said to the screen.

O'Keeffe was now John Coltrane. "Thank you!" he said.

"Where were you when this idea emerged?" John Coltrane asked. "Please be as specific as possible. If possible, drop a pin into the map."

"At Noshville," Wes said, and dropped a pin into the Every cafeteria. "The super-cool name helped inspire me."

Coltrane changed into Kurosawa.

"Thank you," Kurosawa said. "Would you describe your state of mind at the time? For example, 'relaxed,' 'stressed,' 'under pressure,' 'under no pressure,' 'happy,' 'sad.' There are no wrong answers."

"Satiated," Wes said.

Kurosawa became Georgia O'Keeffe.

"'Satisfied.' Thank you," O'Keeffe said, and morphed into Jim Morrison.

"And I was wearing a kilt," Wes said.

"Thank you," Morrison said, and became John Coltrane. "I think I heard you say that you were wearing a kit?"

"No, I was wearing a **kilt.**"

"Okay," Coltrane said. "You were wearing a kilt. Is that correct?"

"Yes," Wes said. "A tight one."

"A tight one. Thank you," Coltrane said, and morphed into a rougher repro, this one a black-and-white man Delaney took to be Thomas Edison.

"What was your inspiration and/or motivation when creating **Bananaskam**?" Thomas Edison asked Wes Makazian.

"I wanted to end bananas," Wes said.

"Thank you," Edison said. "Was ending bananas a result of any particular creative process, life path, or think-way? For example, you could say"—the words appeared on the screen as he listed them—"grit, failure-is-success theory, siesta-revelation theory, Viking management theory, Follow-the-Light theory, quiet-mind theory, clustering, scattering, fear-based camaraderie, love-based terror, working while standing, working while ambulatory, learning while sleeping, limes, or other."

"Mostly it was limes," Wes said.

"Mostly it was limes," Edison repeated. "Thank you."

Delaney couldn't hold it together. She got up to leave.

Wes paused the survey and scrounged through a pile of mail he'd brought into his bed. "New letter from your prof," he said, and held out one of Agarwal's blue envelopes. Delaney took it to her room.

Dear Delaney,

I don't expect you to return these letters. But I do hope you're reading them, even if only to flatter an old lady.

I thought of an analogy the other day and wanted to share it with you: The Every offers the world the fruit of a poisoned tree. The early monopolies of the industrial age polluted rivers, lakes and groundwater because the government was too afraid to regulate them and the money was coming too quickly. Tens of thousands of people died.

The Every is the same. There is too much money and too little regulation. Move fast and break things indeed. They have broken three generations now. Your generation entered my classroom presenting every symptom of addiction. No one is sleeping. Half of my students are asleep during class. Each night, in bed, they're on their phones or earpods till they pass out. You know this. I wonder if you too are overwhelmed. All of my students are overwhelmed. It is not because the workload has changed, because it has not. The students now are taking a normal college courseload, which has been stressful enough for hundreds of years, but they have added a thousand messages to read, write, send, process. It is too much.

They take drugs to stay awake. They drink and get stoned to get to sleep. All of this will get far, far worse. There is simply too much. A student told me recently she'd written twelve hundred and six messages in the last twenty-four hours. She communicates daily with at least forty-nine people. That is manifestly a form of madness, of monomania. And yet this level of contact and availability is seen as a prerequisite to participating in society.

I know your employer does everything it can to counter common sense and has buried many unflattering medical studies, but the inexorable rise in suicides these last twenty years is so obviously a result of two entwined products of the digital age—the catastrophic health effects of manic (and largely meaningless) mental activity, and the lack of real purpose. No one is resting, and no one is accomplishing anything of real worth. It is, instead, the endless churning of middlebrow nonsense, of smiles, frowns, Popeyes, How U/Me fine, that keeps us from meaningful contemplation, or any hope of a new idea.

Again, please leave.

Agarwal.

* * *

Wes poked his head into her room.

"They asked about my footwear," he said. "What footwear I had on. How much I'd exercised that day and the day before."

"Did you say none and none?" Delaney asked.

"I said I sleep ten hours a day."

"You **do** sleep ten hours a day," Delaney noted.

"Wearing a shroud. Next to a wood fire."

"Vivid. Thank you."

"And I only work in rooms without doors."

Delaney pictured an army of handypersons getting to work on removing all the Every's doors.

"Walk?" Wes said.

Hurricane had gnawed his paws into raw stumps; Wes couldn't talk about it. Daily, he doused them with antiseptic, and periodically ground antibiotics into Hurricane's food, but the dog was going mad. The chief enjoyment he took from life was running on the beach, but now he could only sit like an invalid in the child's stroller Wes had bought for him. So Wes installed him in it and they made their way toward the shore. The day was breezy, the waves were good, but only one surfer had submitted to the tracking requirements. The lone figure sat up in the distance, like a black cat on the steel roof of the sea.

"You know they'll tell everyone to sleep ten hours," Delaney said.

"You think?"

"They're desperate."

"I really think they have a problem with ideas at the Every," Wes said.

"That's why they buy them. We knew this."

"Right, but then something strange happens. They buy companies, and they buy the people who came up with the ideas from those companies. Then those people come to the Every and their brains die. Is it complacency? The fatted calf?"

"It's fear."

"Yes, but it's not just fear. It's an involuntary reaction to the frozen atmosphere there. Like when testicles shrink in cold water. They retreat."

"Is it too late to add that to your creativity survey? People would benefit from your testicle theory."

"I do think Mae's in trouble," Wes said. "Think about it. She hasn't had an idea in years. They basically just update the same devices and hope people don't notice the planned obsolescence. But revenues are flat. Even when they bought the jungle, there's been no significant . . . shit, I have to say **synergy.** They've done nothing to connect their strengths with the jungle. I think she's on the bubble."

"She's not on the bubble. Who would replace her?"

"Suddenly Stenton's back," Wes said. "He's making himself at home. And the longer Mae treads water, the more vulnerable she becomes. It's like I've been saying: that's why she doesn't show her face much around campus, at any of these Dream

Fridays. She's waiting till she has something new to offer."

Delaney thought about that. It actually could be true.

"How's the AuthentiFriend team?" she asked. "Are you making it as bad as possible?"

"My power is limited so far," Wes said. "I'm just coding. They don't bring me into the conceptual meetings. That's all Holstein. I think she's beginning to think she invented it."

"Which is probably good," Delaney said. "You don't want to be noticed so much. Neither one of us should."

Wes arranged Hurricane's blanket such that he could see the surf and the dogs galloping past. On the wet sand, their reflections doubled Hurricane's envy. "The weird thing," Wes said, "is that while I was answering the survey, I had another idea. But it shouldn't leave my head. If it were enacted it would change the species. It's a bad idea. Vile." Wes threw a stick over the promenade wall. It landed on the sand without a sound, and Hurricane let out a hopeless sigh. "It's a reprehensible idea that seems, on the surface, virtuous."

"That describes almost everything the Every does."

Wes looked down the shore. "I think the company will love it, and regular people will, too. But overall it'll bring a new kind of self-hatred and personal ruination upon all humans."

"You don't have to tell me if you don't want to."

Wes looked to Hurricane, who regarded him with pleading eyes. Forced to watch all that he could no longer do, the beach was doing Hurricane no good.

"You know those carbon impact calculators we used in high school?" Wes said.

Delaney remembered them well. A person could plug in elements of their lifestyle—car, house, commute, diet—and get a rough idea of the carbon implications. Every Earth Day for twenty years, students had been inputting in their family's data and had been able to compare their carbon impact to, say, a Finnish reindeer herder. A family would think about the number briefly, question its accuracy, and then forget it completely until the next year.

"Well," Wes said, "we have the data to go well beyond rough estimates now."

"Did you just say 'we'?" Delaney asked.

"Think about it," he said. His face was grave. "For the average person, eighty-eight percent of their purchases are either going through the Every or an Every partner. The money is so easy to track. So if you buy bottled water from Iceland tomorrow, that's known."

"So?"

"Well, we can easily determine the actual carbon impact of that exact purchase," Wes said, and pointed to a pair of container ships in the distance. "That water came thousands of miles by boat. Five hundred miles on a truck. The carbon impact is

easy to calculate. You do that for every purchase—
a pair of socks made in Cambodia, a lightbulb made
in Malaysia. You could do it in real time. The moment you make the purchase, the carbon impact
of that purchase is added to your total. The total is
aggregated immediately."

"If it were private, it could be helpful,"
Delaney said.

"Right. If only you knew this number, you'd
make better decisions. Like knowing your caloric
intake. You could voluntarily change your habits. It
would lead to better buying, better sourcing."

Wes threw another stick over the wall, and
Hurricane, still in the stroller, watched its trajectory
with only academic interest.

"But it won't stay private," Wes said. "The
Every will make it public, because secrets are lies,
right? They'll call it Individual Carbon Impact. Or
Personal Carbon Impact."

"TipToe," Delaney said. "It'll have a name
like that."

"God that's good," he said. "TipToe. Jesus."

Wes crouched down next to Hurricane, who
stretched his neck from the stroller to rest his snout
on Wes's arm.

"It'll be about shame," Wes said. "Surveillance,
data and shame as behavioral modifier. That's been
where all of this has been heading all along."

"You can't tell anyone about that one," Delaney
said. "For now we stick with sillier things."

Wes stroked Hurricane's snout. Hurricane looked desperate. His eyes were restless, shining, and he was trapped in a body that no longer worked.

"Look at what they did to this guy," Wes said. "He used to be a god, a goliath. Now he sits and gnaws at himself."

Delaney didn't know what to say.

"Part of me thinks we should speed things up," Wes said.

"Speed up AuthentiFriend?"

"Everything. Flood the zone. It takes no time at all to get some moronic app out there, and we're in the perfect position. We have dumb ideas, and they have the means and motive to claim and distribute them. Ten ideas just as bad as AuthentiFriend. Ah, you like it. I see that smile."

"They will kill us," Delaney said.

"No," Wes said, "they will love us."

XX.

THEY STARTED SMALL. They created an app that told eaters, after they ate, whether or not they enjoyed what they ate. Delaney threw together some metrics that the users' ovals could detect, and applied terms like **pulse-rate optimization, endorphin count** and **pleasure center.** They called it Satisfied? and it was an immediate hit. For a week it was the most downloaded app on campus, then in California, then the world. No one thought it too silly, no one thought it evil. Instead, Wes—who got credit for it—was feted as a new force in food-related tech, given Satisfied? followed so closely on the heels of **Bananaskam.** Everyones were dazzled by his tech-aided diet dichotomy: You should not eat what you should not eat, but what you should eat should be enjoyed, and here's the app that tells you if you enjoyed it.

"That didn't work out as I expected," Wes said.

"And we shouldn't have had you take credit," Delaney said.

They invented a way to introduce ideas anonymously, and called it AnonIdea. It was a way for selfless Everyones to toss a notion into the mix, and have any other Everyone take the lead in developing it. No credit needed, no credit asked. This was seen on campus as a radically benevolent and selfless platform, and so only Delaney and Wes contributed any ideas to it.

Their next notion was simple but just offensive enough that they thought it would provoke widespread disgust. HappyNow? built on Satisfied? but was expanded to answer, in real time, whether the user was happy. They applied the same metrics used for Satisfied? but added the user's recent purchases. It only made sense that a happy person would be buying happy things—workout gear, flowers, champagne, bright clothing, sex-positive toys—and in healthy quantities. HappyNow? analyzed your purchases and provided a Happy/Healthy rating (HH), illustrated by a range of expressions on the face of a cartoon hippo. Retailers and marketers loved this, given its circularity: to be considered happy, one only needed to buy more happy things, given who but a happy person would buy so many happy things?

Building on HappyNow? Delaney came up with Did I?, which used users' ovals to determine whether orgasm was reached during any given coital session. A follow-up measured orgasm duration, intensity, and overall quality. Another update allowed the user to compare their orgasms with their friends, relatives and high-school crushes—and finally with any group in the world, the data divisible by region, demographics, income and genetic predisposition.

People loved it.

"I guess we have to get sillier?" Wes mused. They were back at the Shed, and Hurricane was chewing on his back paws. His fur everywhere was patchy and coarse; he looked like moth-eaten rug. Wes had him on hormones and antibiotics, but nothing worked. He only wanted to run. Wes dropped to the floor and rubbed Hurricane's tummy; Hurricane wheezed.

"And flood the zone," Delaney said. "There has to be a point where there's too much nonsense."

Wes looked up. "Too much nonsense," he said dryly. He held Hurricane's snout and locked eyes with the sick dog. "She thinks there's a limit to nonsense. Isn't that interesting that she thinks that?"

Delaney's next notion was obnoxious and served no purpose but to prove the limitless self-regard of the Every and its staff. **Henceforth, our campus should be called Everywhere,** Delaney proposed. **And anything not on campus is Nowhere.** This was picked up by a Gang of 40 member named Valerie Bayonne, and was codified in days. People on- and off- campus found it delightfully irreverent

and even clever, which gave great satisfaction to
Valerie, who had been irreverent and clever enough
to recognize these qualities in the idea.

Wes thought of Kerpow!, an app made to "encourage spontaneity" among the world's peoples.
"Spontaneity is the spice of life!" he wrote, "and so
important to our emotional and intellectual lives!"
Kerpow!, once downloaded, reminded the user,
every two hours, to do something unexpected. It
was a hit.

Delaney introduced Thinking of You, an app
that automatically sent a brief message—a T.O.Y.,
or toy—to each of the user's contacts, twice a day.
Thinking of you! the message might say, or could
be modified, personalized, made more frequent as
needed. Delaney hoped people would be driven
mad by the addition of hundreds, minimum, of
new messages a day, but most humans felt happy to
be thought of, even if by an algorithm, and so the
introduction of the toy, too, was a success.

Wes upped the ante with Show Your Love, which
insisted that any messages of love, support, well-
wishes or birthday greetings to family or friends be
made public and counted. It caught on immediately,
and the arms race began: it was ludicrous and
selfish and weird to send any loving messages privately, so all were made public, and had to be sent
often, to prove that love. The grandmother who
sent thirty messages to Khalil or Siobhan by lunch
loved her grandson or granddaughter abundantly,

and clearly more than the grandmother who sent only eleven. The numbers could not lie.

The natural next step was WereThey?, which called upon the wisdom of the crowd to determine whether one's parents were any good. The user supplied data, photos, emails, texts, video evidence, and the child's subsequent success with college, romance and career. Between AI assessors and the experts and laypersons who weighed in from near and far, the quality of any given parental performance, birth to present, could be deduced. Wes added a tagline—**Data for Dada, Metrics for Mama**—which Delaney considered gilding the lily, but in any case, neither Delaney nor Wes expected much pushback on the app, and none arrived. People wanted this kind of certainty and now could get it.

Delaney conjured Departy, but couldn't take credit; it was inevitable. Departy notified you of the death of anyone in your network, and then assessed who in your network knew the deceased and to whom you ought to send condolences. Departy**Plus** connected the user with florists, travel agents and estate lawyers, and Departy**Elite** handled all these things, including the messages of condolence, for you. It was adopted by millions in weeks.

Wes created PassionProject, which grew out of research proving that people were happier when they had a passion—one overarching hobby or pastime in their life. For those unsure of what their passion was, PassionProject would scour all of the user's available social media feeds, searches, purchases, posts and real-world movements and determine, "with 99.3% accuracy," Wes said, the user's favorite thing to do. People found it enormously helpful.

After seeing a child shammed one day for leaving his dog's feces on the street for a full half-minute while he retrieved a baggie, Delaney thought of Takes a Village, or Tav, which allowed the user to film and tag children for their misdeeds and deviances, and connect that evidence to the tracking-chips most children wore in their ankles. Both Delaney and Wes had high hopes that the idea of tavving would nauseate all humans, would be the last straw, but instead most people were grateful; it removed guesswork from parenting, and illuminated the few remaining blindspots between children and those rearing them.

Delaney suggested something she called FictFix, expecting, correctly as it turned out, that Alessandro would claim it. The main thrust of FictFix was to take old novels and fix them. Unsympathetic protagonists were made likeable, chiefly through aggregrating online complaints and implementing suggestions; problematic and outdated terminology was changed to reflect contemporary standards; and superfluous chapters, passages and anything preachy was removed. This could be done instantly in e-books, even those purchased long before. When FictFix rolled out, it was done gingerly, Alessandro assuming the blowback would be extreme. But there was not much, and it was confined to a few irrelevant academics, whose own back catalogs were soon fixed by their former graduate students.

"That one surprised me," Wes said.

Delaney could no longer be surprised. But she tried.

She introduced an extension to FictFix that invited the correction of all texts, from 20th-century newspapers to 16th-century treatises, to avoid offense and improve clarity. These texts were opened to group editing, wiki-style, which allowed the texts to be quickly and continuously improved. The response was universally positive.

EndDis was Wes's creation, an app where users could present a picture of anything, and ask the internet if it should exist, or if it should be eliminated in the real world and historical record. Wes's notes on it insisted the subjects be inconsequential, things like pumpkin bread and wall-to-wall carpet, but EndDis was quickly hijacked to pass judgment on people, mostly celebrities, most of whom the internet said should die and be stricken from the human chronicle.

As a palate cleanser, Wes thought of ShouldEye, a decision-making app whereby a person could ask the general public to help them make a decision. From dating to burrito-purchasing, a user could announce a conundrum, ask for a quorum, and put their trust in the wisdom of the crowd. This was the most popular idea yet, was renamed Concensus, and, when municipalities and nation-states began adopting it as their chief tool for decision-making, and when Del's parents relied on it to make any choice, and when millions began using it to decide whether or not they should leave the house, eat lunch, talk to family members or friends, or breed—given the environmental impact of baby-making, the inherent narcissism of the notion—Del and Wes decided to take a step back to regroup.

"Nothing's working," Delaney said.

"Actually, everything's working," Wes noted.

"Nothing goes too far," Delaney said. "Nothing's breaking."

"But maybe it's bending?" Wes said doubtfully.

"It could be bending," Delaney said, though she'd never been so scared.

XXI.

DELANEY'S WELCOME2ME was long past due. She'd been at the Every for almost four months, so when her proposal was approved, her relief was profound. It would be a good chance to get to know a large group of Everyones, and perhaps see soft spots, pressure points and weaknesses to exploit.

"It's perfect," Kiki said about Delaney's plan. "It's very **you.**"

Again Kiki looked very tired, but Delaney couldn't think of an acceptable way to note it, or ask her about it.

"And this **is** about you," Kiki continued. "And also you in relation to the others. So it's about both you **and** other people. But starting with **you.** And the seals—they're seals?"

"Elephant seals," Delaney clarified.

"Well, it sounds great. Kulos."

Delaney didn't have the heart to correct her. "Thank you," she said.

"It's very unusual. Again, like you."

Kiki blushed. They both seemed to recognize that her choice of words—**very unusual**—applied as it was to a fellow Everyone, would be flagged by end-of-day.

"Hello!" Kiki said, and pressed her finger to her ear. She began a very loud conversation with what Delaney took to be an elderly person. In the middle of the conversation, Kiki put herself into a plank position, with her phone beneath her, her mermaid leggings—these with a salmon-pink tint—sparkling in the sun. She carried on the conversation while her triceps strained and vibrated, and when she was done, she sat up, rolled her eyes and sighed in immense relief.

"My uncle. He's in Argentina. One of my OwnSelf goals was to have more contact with my family down there, and it's working out so well. Twenty-two calls in the last week, which is a few short of my goal. And I get some of my ab work done at the same time."

"Twenty-two calls with relatives in one week?" Delaney asked.

"It's a start," Kiki said. "I'll get better." She was planking again. "My core needs more attention," she said. "And I'm supposed to lose four pounds. Are you on OwnSelf yet?"

Delaney worried about Kiki losing any weight. She couldn't be more than a hundred pounds, her arms no thicker than a garden hose. "Who told you to lose weight?" she asked. Instantly she wondered what the AI would make of that. It was borderline.

"My body mass index is not ideal," Kiki said. "I got a notice. But it's doable. Hey, you don't speak French by chance, do you?"

Delaney did not. "No," she said in what she thought was a French accent. Kiki smiled wanly.

"It's fine," Kiki said. "I'm trying to practice, and I figured we might as well speak in French if you knew any. I'm trying to get in twenty minutes a day, but I'm thinking it'd be easier to overlap it somehow. Like I tried exercising in French but that didn't work."

Kiki's mind was pinballing, her eyes hyperalert and unsteady.

"Did I ask you before what your sleep average was?" she asked, and didn't wait for an answer. "Did you hear the new research says ten hours is ideal? The guy who did **Bananaskam** sleeps ten hours a night. In a **shroud**! A few nights ago I went to bed at eight, and I thought I slept enough, but then the sensors didn't count my hours as **high-quality** sleep. So last night all I could think about was sleeping in a high-quality way, and I ended up not sleeping much at all. So while the goal has gone up to ten hours, I'm down to 6.4."

A tinny laughtrack burst from her oval. "We should laugh. I'm low on laughter, too. Is there something funny we can talk about?"

Delaney tried to think of a joke. She could never

remember jokes. Her face must have been contorted in concentration, because Kiki let out a long, trilling laugh that devolved into hacking and coughing.

"Do you think you're taking on too much?" Delaney asked. Kiki was bent over, trying to regain control. She raised a finger to ask for a moment. A few seconds later she unfolded herself to her full height and breathed a series of measured breaths.

"Such a funny face you made!" she finally said. "Boy, I had a good laugh there." Then she checked her oval to see if the laugh had registered. Satisfied, she smiled. "What did you say again?"

"Do you think you're taking on too much?" Delaney asked again.

"Thanks for asking," Kiki said. "But OwnSelf is conscious of that. There are tons of tripwires set up to warn you of that kind of thing. Look." She held out her forearm, where an array of numbers were pulsing. None meant anything to Delaney. "It says I'm only at 71 in terms of capacity for what I can take on. So I have a ways to go. Then I'll be non-plussed." A happy bell sounded from her wrist.

Delaney found herself truly happy for Kiki, and truly worried.

"Are we good?" Kiki asked.

"We're good," Delaney said.

"Hi Nino!" Kiki said, and peeled off.

The idea of seeing the mating of the elephant seals arose from pure self-interest. Delaney did not have a car, and getting to Playa 36 (née Drake's Beach), ninety minutes north, without one, was not easy or cheap. If she could take a busload of Everyones with her, she'd satisfy the needs of Welcome2Me, while seeing what she'd heard was one of the stranger natural phenomena in the world. Every year, about a hundred elephant seals, averaging a thousand pounds each, lounged for weeks on the Point Reyes shore and weaned their young. The challenge, she'd read, wasn't seeing the elephant seals, but was, instead, not stepping over them. The viewing area was that close and the seals were wholly uninhibited as they fought and screwed and calved and returned to sea.

With Kiki's approval, Delaney began planning, and did so without malice. She wanted this to be good, and felt sure it could be. If she put on a decent Welcome2Me, she'd gain some favor intra-Every, and that could only help her gain access. She planned to bring Wes, and thought of asking Alessandro and Winnie, but was informed by Kiki that Algo Mas determined the participants on any given Welcome2Me event, and most campus events generally.

"It's the best way to ensure a good cross-section of Everypersons," she texted, "and of course most people don't want the responsibility of deciding who's included and who's not."

With the guest list out of the way, Delaney checked on the ranger presence for the coming

Saturday, and learned that at least two, maybe
three would be on the beach, explaining and guiding. Delaney wanted this to be the extent of the
planning—get to the beach where elephant seals
were gathered; that should be enough. But she knew
there would be questions.

"Write up the event description," Kiki had advised. "Make it as detailed as you can. Pre-answer as
many questions as possible. Make it searchable, of
course. I've seen these run sixty, seventy pages. The
line-dancing one came with a two-hour instruc-
tional video. But yours is . . . simpler," Kiki said.
"Have fun with it!"

Delaney wrote a three-paragraph description of
the day's plan, including six links to basic and con-
cise information about the seals, their history on
the Pacific coast, their mating cycles, Point Reyes
in general and Playa 36 specifically. "If you haven't
seen Pt. Reyes, be prepared," Delaney wrote. "It will
be spectacular." Not that anyone living in Northern
California needed to be told to bring layers, but
she mentioned this, and she mentioned sunscreen,
and comfortable shoes, and a warm hat if one's ears
were prone to chill. She sent a draft to Kiki, who,
in a distracted moment, wrote only **Food.** Delaney
took this to mean that the Everyones could not be
expected to bring their own lunches, so Delaney arranged with a deli around the corner from the Sea
Shed to create eighty sandwiches for the day, for
vegans and vegetarians, pescatarians and carnivores,

at least two options for every attendee, and a bounty of side salads and drinks—all to be brought on the bus in reusable containers. Delaney finished her summary of the Point Reyes plan, and Kiki took it from there.

A group of forty-two Everyones were selected by algorithm. It was to be a cross-campus smorgasbord, a sampling rich in variety of departments and interests. And because there would be photos and possibly group photos, a representative and perhaps augmented display of the company's diversity was essential. Once the forty-two attendees had been chosen, a message list was created, and Delaney's now-three-page description of the event—elucidating what would be available to drink and eat, and enumerating all that need be brought—was sent to the forty-two on the Tuesday before the excursion.

No info here for the lactose-free . . . said the first message, and Delaney cursed herself for this easy oversight. "Ignore that event description!" she wrote, "Better one to come!" She went through the entire three pages again, editing and adding two pages more, this time anticipating every allergy and preference. She covered gluten, eggs, nuts, nightshades, and cinnamon—recent but fast-spreading intolerances and de-preferences, respectively—and this time, in a stroke of what she considered brilliance, she mentioned the particular deli she'd engaged, Emil's on Pacheco, in case anyone wanted to pre-order and get the precise sandwich they wished.

Emil's?? Have you seen this? This message linked to a photo of Emil, the young proprietor, posing with an Israeli flag, on what appeared to be a Tel Aviv beach. This was followed by seventy-six messages from a fourth of the forty-two Point Reyes attendees, most with links to bombastic articles and messages about the rightness or wrongness of Israel vis à vis Palestine and what any given Everyone would be saying by eating sandwiches made by a man (and his staff) who were so proud of Israel and its misdeeds that he so jingoistically would pose with its flag on a luxurious beach of oppression.

"Shit," Wes said, while eating one of Emil's sandwiches, a pastrami-and-mustard for which he had a standing order. "Does that mean Emil isn't catering this thing? If so, I should tell him."

Delaney and Wes were home, scrolling through the crossfire conflating the history of the Middle East with an Ocean Beach sandwich seller, and all the while Delaney had the sickening revelation that the excursion was still four days away. The messages so far, which soon totaled 288, had all been sent in the twenty-one hours since her announcement had been issued.

Kiki let Delaney know that seven of the forty-two

original attendees dropped out in protest and had vowed, politely and menacingly, to make a note of the Every's seeming support of this Zionist sandwich-man, though it was unclear where these notes would be made and who would see them. Kiki was careful to explain, in a series of messages she wrote with, no doubt, a lawyer over her shoulder, that the Every did not take a political position on Israel-Palestine, and at the same time did not want to silence those on either side of the debate, and at the same time still, did not want to force anyone into supporting, monetarily or otherwise, any proponent of any one nation or flag or people or policy. Opting out of an activity like this was the choice that most respected all sides, and this opt-out option the Every fully supported.

This was Day Two. There were four more days before the excursion. **Is the bus using plant-based fuel?** one attendee asked. It's a standard Every bus, so I assume so, Delaney wrote. **Do I need hiking boots?** No, Delaney wrote, we'll just be standing on sand, or in the parking lot near the beach. If you choose to walk one of the trails, you can, but even then, these trails are extremely mild, and no boots will be necessary. If you have them, though, feel free to bring them! **I don't see a packing list. Usually there's a packing list for such an outdoor activity.** I provided a packing list, Delaney answered, though you might have missed it because it's embedded and short. You really only need yourselves and, like I said, layers, and maybe a hat. I'm even bringing sun-screen, so you can take that off the list! **Wait. Did we change the list? Where's the new list? And was it really a pdf? Why not an EveryDoc?** This was accompanied by a link to the dangers of pdfs, given the countless times that viruses had been attached to them. **Will I need boots?** another asked. Delaney was determined to treat every question in isolation and thus cheerfully. Only if you already have them and usually wear them to such things! she wrote. But sneakers are fine. **Now we need sneakers? What about sandals?** Sandals are fine! But it might get nippy, so bear that in mind. **How cold will it be? Forecast says 60s. Do you know something they don't?** I know only that it gets cold quick there sometimes, Delaney wrote. The fog can come in and the temp can drop to 50, even 45. Layers! she wrote, and added an emoticon. **What kind of sunscreen are you bringing, Delaney?** Delaney had not actually bought the sunscreen yet, so she looked online and found an organic brand, Sensible Dawn. This triggered an avalanche. **Wait, now we're supporting Scientology?** an Everyone wrote, and Delaney soon found that Dawn Unger, the sun-screen's founder, had been a Scientologist, though she didn't seem to be one now, and had posted no content anywhere in support of Scientology. **Delaney, seeing elephant seals shouldn't involve cult-complicity,** one helpful Everyone wrote, in the most measured of the messages. After four hours of screeds and ululations, totaling 413 messages covering the sins and virtues of every company that had or still did provide sunscreen to the world's marketplace, the group settled on an organic maker based in the Antilles. That the product had traveled a few thousand miles seemed likely to provoke a **skam** of some kind, but at the end of Day Two, had not yet done so. Many of the subsequent questions were between fellow excursioners and did not necessitate an answer from Delaney. **Anyone bringing a hat? Anyone bringing water?** We'll have plenty, Delaney answered. **I have a lemon in my bag,** noted one man. **In case we wanted to add it to the water.** Nineteen people commented on the lemon; most wanted to know where he'd gotten it. Though he'd satisfied all that he'd gotten it from his own garden, it was still spurned. **None for me, thanks! Too acidic,** noted one. **I could bring sugar, too,** the lemon-man offered. **What the fuk? Sugar?** was the answer, and this invited an avalanche of anti-sugar maxims and manifestos. Finally the lemon-carrying attendee, who was also relatively new at the Every, self-selected out of the trip and was replaced.

I heard that moleskin patches are good for blisters. This was the first message the following morning. **Delaney, do you have some of those patches in your first aid kit?** I'll bring some, Delaney wrote, but really, we won't need them. We'll just be standing on the beach looking at seals. No heavy climbing! She added a benign emoticon.

Sorry if I missed a message, wrote another, **but should we bring a hat? Wide-brim? Floppy? Cowboy? Pith?** Any kind of hat is fine, Delaney wrote. **And about the makers of those moleskin patches: company just bought by corp that does business with Chick Fil-A. Please do not support. Wake up!** An angry emoticon ensued. **Did we ever get the packing list onto EveryDocs?** Yes, it's there! **Does the bus have wifi?** It's a standard Every bus, Delaney wrote, so I would expect it to. **My bus's wifi was down on Tuesday. I was totally unprepared for a presentation.** This bus should be working fine! Delaney answered. And it's a Saturday morning, so ideally no presentations will be at risk! She added a happy-squirrel emoji.

The questions continued. Delaney felt obligated to read every message, given there might, among any one of the hundred or so daily threads, be something that required an answer of her. Soon the attendees had turned their attentions, briefly, to the mammals they were going to see. **Are these the ones we're seeing?** one Everyperson asked, and showed a picture of a leopard seal. Delaney pointed out the difference, that leopard seals were leopard seals and elephant seals, being elephant seals, were not, and in response the questioner wrote, **Phew. Those other guys seem fierce. Wouldn't want to meet them in a dark iceberg!** This joke received much praise and prompted the appearance of many laughing yellow cartoon-smiling-faces, a few of them laughing so much they were crying tears, which meant that the person who chose this emoticon was also laughing to the point of crying, too. **What did we say about boots again?** another attendee wrote. **I looked at Pt. Reyes online and found many hills, rugged terrain, a coast (!) and even some mud.** It's quite flat where we will be, Delaney answered. You could wear heels, platforms, sandals, or ride a unicycle. **Unicycle?!** came the quick reply. **I'm diabetic!** Delaney desperately stamped out this new unicycle-fire before it could spread. No unicycles! she flailed. Just a joke! I just meant that it will be very flat, very safe. **Unicycles are anything but safe!** another person wrote, with a link to a series of unicycle accidents, most of them in Poland. **What about socks?** wrote another Everyone. **I hear wool is best when near salt water, but I can't find a brand that will certify humane shearing. Anyone know?**

On the day itself, Delaney arrived at 9 a.m. and met Emil outside the gate. He'd put the eighty sandwiches in airtight bioplastic bins and stacked them on a dolly. When Delaney arrived, he was in the process of arguing with Rowena at the Every's front gate, who asserted the plastic containers were single-use and thus prohibited. After much discussion and a text exchange with Kiki, the sandwiches were allowed inside, were run through the scanners and were cleared for loading onto the buses and for eventual consumption. Along with two hundred drink-globes, the sandwiches were packed into the bus's luggage compartment, and when the cantilevered door closed, Delaney almost collapsed. That, she thought, would surely be the most complicated part of the day. With a wifi bus and trained park rangers and a hundred wondrous mammals mating and squirming like giant slugs on a pristine beach, surely all pedestrian cares would fall away before the majesty of unbridled nature.

When the attendees arrived at the bus, the vast majority of them were dressed for a final ascent of Everest. Though hiking boots had been discussed more than any other topic and repeatedly dismissed as unnecessary, all but a few of the attendees were wearing new boots, the laces and soles still stiff. Most attendees wore new floppy safari hats and scarves both decorative and functional. Most wore new waterpacks. Most wore new sunglasses with flexible neck-ties. All wore organic fleece. There were fleece jackets under fleece vests, and fleece vests over fleece jackets. There was a sameness to the pants worn by most, and Delaney had a faint recollection that on Prep Day Four someone had solved for the issue of shorts vs. pants by suggesting, for a mere $280, a pair that zipped just below the knee and became shorts. Of the forty-two Everyones getting on the bus, thirty-nine were wearing these convertible pants. They all laughed for a moment about this, but then Nestor, an earnest Everyone with sardonic eyes, made the point that once a product was well-vetted by trusted friends, it only made sense for others to follow, rather than forty-two people all going forty-two directions. "The best way was the best way," he said, and Everyone agreed.

For the bus ride, which Delaney estimated would be ninety minutes, she had prepared a mix of happy journeying music, which she activated as they pulled out of the campus gate. The first song was by Otis Redding, and the first message came via her phone. **Woman-hater,** it said, with a link to an unsigned and evidence-less post hinting that he had been unkind to an ex-girlfriend who he'd met shortly before the bay and the dock and the sitting. **Thanks for the early-morning pick-me-up!** the writer said, meaning that Delaney had ruined the day and tacitly endorsed Redding's newly alleged misogyny. Delaney skipped to the next song, Lana Del Rey's "High by the Beach," and then quickly figured it was too big a risk so skipped ahead. The third song, the Muppets' "Movin' Right Along," was unknown to most on the bus, and survived its three-minute length, during which a handful of passengers furiously tried to find a reason the song was complicit in evil committed or implied. Delaney skipped the next song, by Neil Diamond, thinking any Jewish singer dubious in light of the Israeli sandwich debacle, skipped songs six and seven (from **Thriller**), briefly considered the Ronettes' "Be My Baby" but then remembered Phil Spector, and so finally settled on a young Ghanian rapper she'd recently discovered. His first song was hunted down quickly in a hail of rhetorical buckshot—as a teen, the rapper had zinged a borderline joke about his female trigonometry teacher—so Delaney turned off the shared music, leaving everyone, for the next eighty-one minutes, to their earbuds and the safety of their individualized solitude.

When they reached the rolling green hills of Petaluma, and could see the horses and sheep lolling about, a smattering of geese in a seasonal pond, a scrum of cows poking their heads through a crooked fence, Delaney felt a kind of pride. She was not from here, but she knew country like this, and was proud of how well her home state and her adopted state had preserved open land like this, even amid frenzied development and the temptations of untold billions. They were on the homestretch, she thought—from here on out it was only beauty, and stunning natural phenomena, and when they arrived to living miracles of wayward and illogical evolution, nothing more would be required of her but staying out of the way.

Her phone dinged; a group texting session began. **For a vegan, this is the Holocaust,** the first message said, and the flood began. **Didn't know we'd be traveling through miles of animal bondage.** Delaney tried to conjure a response but the messages came without pause. **This is Trigger Valley for me.** Delaney looked back among the passengers and saw one young woman being comforted by another, their faces turned away from the window. An Everyone named Syl was sick in the bathroom. **That's two ppl sick so far,** read a text from Syl (he was texting from the toilet). **This driver needs to slow down,** said another. Another had a helpful thought: **Then again, perhaps better to speed through this animal abattoir?**

They passed Petaluma but Delaney knew there were many farms to come. Only dairy farms coming up! she wrote, and the pile-on began. **Not your milk!** I actually don't drink milk; I'm lactose unpopular, Delaney wrote, thinking that news, and her half-gag, might help. The volley continued. **These cows shouldn't have their udders yanked all day so humans can drink what's not theirs.** Again Delaney looked back to the passengers, thinking she might meet eyes with her fellow humans and find some common ground, but the eyes were downcast, fingers tapping, and so she faced forward again, counting the minutes till they parked at the beach.

Playa 36 was, like so much of coastal California, wholly unspoiled and baffling in the easy availability of almost untouched splendor. The bus parked in the sand-swept lot, next to the redwood visitors' center, and there, no more than forty feet away, were a hundred elephant seals—females, males and calves—all lying on the beach, scootching and basking and honking audaciously. The sky was azure and dotted with throwpillow clouds. There were gray-green hills behind and cliffs left and right, and before them was a beach full of enormous fleshy mammals, all of them impossibly ugly and vulnerable and loud.

Delaney stood by the bus door as the passengers stepped off and into the mulchy smell of the seals, thinking that any complaints about music, or the wrongful exploitation of cow's milk, or even the problems presented by Israeli sandwiches, would evaporate in the face of these miracles of nature so undisturbed and close at hand. Her phone dinged. **There's a lot of sand.** She looked around. Who was typing? **I forgot to apply sunblock.** This was from Syl, the man who had been sick in the bathroom twenty minutes earlier. **Me too,** said another Everyone. **I'm heading back to the bus till I get covered up.** Syl wrote again: **Hope we didn't already get cancer.**

Delaney herded the rest of group to a brownhaired ranger whose nametag read Matt Cody. Middle-aged, pink and unassuming, he was dressed in green pants and a green jacket and a green hat and wore no sunglasses over his dark, heavy-lidded eyes. He had an appealing, slump-shouldered way about him, and looked over Delaney's group with a wide, crooked smile wholly sincere and welcoming—as if he were about to enjoy meeting them all very much.

"Big group!" he said. "Welcome, welcome. I'm Matt Cody, or Ranger Matt, if you're feeling formal. You have come on a fantastic—"

"Is that them there?" an Everyone said. Her entire face was squinting.

"It is. As you'll see—" Ranger Matt began to say.

"There's no, like, barrier? Are they dangerous?" said a second Everyone, already backing away.

A third, looking at her phone, added, "This says they can cover thirty feet in ten seconds."

There was a swirl of talk about the fact that, outside of a few orange cones, there was indeed no barrier between the humans and the elephant seals, most of whom weighed in the thousands.

"Are we okay to be here?" asked a young Everyone, her eyes wide, her feet pointed to the bus.

"Folks," Ranger Matt said. "You are most welcome to be here. See, around you, there are other people present, too." He swept his hands left and right, and the Everyones looked at the other humans for what Delaney was sure was the first time.

"Why do we have to be so close?" asked another Everyone.

"There should be clearer boundaries," noted another.

"You can be anywhere you'd like to be," Ranger Matt said, now smiling broadly, "as long as you stay off the beach." Delaney was sure that he had deduced the group for what they were, and had adopted a cheerfully wry manner.

The Everyone named Syl sneered. "I mean, it seems like an invasion of their . . ."

"Their privacy?" Ranger Matt said, suppressing a

smile. "Yes, I can imagine you all are very concerned about that." And as if he knew exactly the trouble he was about to get into, he forged ahead with more mischief in mind. "Would anyone like to know what's happening here?"

A few timid hands were raised half-mast. Delaney raised hers, trying to get his attention and indicate herself as leader of the group and co-conspirator with him. He didn't take the hint.

"Good then," he said, and clapped his hands together in a manner almost dastardly. "What you see here are about forty adult male elephant seals. They're called bulls. You'll also see about twenty adult females. The little ones have been born over the past five or six weeks. The mothers have been feeding their calves all that time, but in the last week or so, the females have begun returning to the ocean. They leave their babies here, and now it's up to the calves to find their way to the water, to get in, get away, and teach themselves to swim, to eat, and to survive. Most will not survive."

"Some of these pups won't live?" Syl gasped. He had large, expressive eyes, and the posture of a gnarled tree.

"That's right," Ranger Matt said. "Sometimes three-fourths of the pups will die. Some are eaten by sharks. Some drown. Some starve. A few might die right here on this beach."

"Oh god!" a hushed voice said, and was joined in horror by a dozen others. Four ran immediately to the bus and stayed there. Six more went aboard to offer support and solidarity to the four.

"Back in '98," Ranger Matt continued, "El Niño drowned about eighty-five percent of the pups before they learned to swim . . ."

There were groans and tears. More Everyones retreated to the bus, to be out of earshot of whatever horror Ranger Matt might report next. With only fifteen or so Everyones still outside, Delaney saw a vaguely familiar face, behind large sunglasses and under a large floppy hat. "Hans-Georg?" she said. She had no idea he'd been on the bus.

"Delaney," he said, and shook her hand warmly. "This is marvelous, just marvelous," he said, in his wonderful German accent. "This I have never seen! Look at them! The way they roll, and play, and—what is the word?—bleat?"

"Bleat, yes," Delaney said. She was so happy that someone was enjoying this, was seeing it the way she saw it. Her phone dinged. It was her parents, sending her a toy. They'd begun sending dozens a day, or they had programmed their phones to send her phone dozens a day. **Thinking of you!** it said, with an explosion of teeny fireworks. She looked back to Hans-Georg, wanting very much to run into the neighboring hills with him.

"Thank you so much for bringing me, all of us here," he said. "I will never forget it." With that, he stepped away, closer to the beach, his hands clasped behind his back as if he were roaming a museum. He seemed to be communing with the sand, the sea, the seals, the wind and sun—all at once, absorbing its rough majesty with radical openness and without fear.

Elsewhere, a few hearty and curious Everyones took pictures and looked through Matt's binoculars, asking follow-up questions, but the rest of the group was not wholly sure what to do. Those still outside the bus took a few pictures of the seals, and took pictures of themselves in front of the seals, and took many Popeyes with the seals as backdrop, and took a number of group pictures of themselves in many different poses and configurations and filters. This lasted eight to ten minutes; after that they were at a loss. Two went into the visitors' center and one used the bathroom. No one else left the parking lot. Outside of the few curious questioners of Ranger Matt, no one wanted to know more about the seals they'd been driven ninety minutes to see, and one by one, the Everyones on the bright windy beach returned to the cool and dim bus, and they shared their feelings via their phones, feelings which were universally confused. The consensus was indignation, at Ranger Matt for telling them things they were unprepared to hear, and then at Delaney for exposing them to Ranger Matt, and to also sand and sun and wind, and large free creatures, for which they had also been unprepared.

After twenty-five minutes, only Hans-Georg and a few other Everyones were still near the beach. The rest of the party was stewing in their seats on the bus, so Delaney asked the driver, who was in the visitors' center buying a book for his kids, to start the engine. No one had touched their sandwiches. There hadn't been time to remove them from the bus's storage compartment.

The complaints, both signed and anonymous, began on the ride home and were universally apocalyptic. The young woman who had been shocked by the elephant seals' abandonment of their young explained that a friend of hers, a human, had also been abandoned by her mother. Had she known this excursion was going to be so horror-filled—first seeing Petaluman animals in bondage and then exposing the Everyones to this ranger person gleefully explaining the failures of mammalian mothers—she never would have come. Because it would not do to stamp the embers of her rhetoric, others blew oxygen into her fire. **Inappropriate at best,** one said, thinking herself the most reasonable. **A top-to-bottom atrocity,** said the next. There was soon a thread about how perhaps Welcome2Mes in general should be discontinued. And field trips. And forest rangers. And parking lots. Something about parking lots got the Everyones to a higher plane of anguish, and the weeping began. The crimes of the world being too many and too cruel, and parking lots being somehow entwined with the worst of these crimes, the bus erupted in wailing and consoling-without-touching. **Had enough of this kind of mess,** wrote an Everyone. **Never again means never again,** wrote another.

And all this was before the bus hit the sheep.

XXII.

DELANEY HAD SUNDAY TO HERSELF, so she stayed in bed till the walls of her room glowed white. At eleven she sat up and spent another hour staring at the window in the upper corner of her room, catching the occasional glimpse of a seagull. In the shower, Delaney remembered a dream she'd had at dawn. In it, Mae Holland was pregnant, bursting, and was sitting in a glass box, her legs spread. Then Mae pointed to the shadows between her spread legs and beckoned Delaney to enter. But in the way dreams make certain things clear to the dreamer, it was clear that Delaney was not being invited to **see** the baby, but to **become** the baby. It seemed at least plausible to Delaney that she was going nuts.

Throughout the morning Delaney heard Wes thumping through the house, making his presence known without wanting to knock. Finally he knocked and his crooked mouth smiled down at her.

"I'm done. I'm out," she said.

"Did the sheep live?" he asked.

Delaney shrugged. The night before, when she'd gotten home, she'd told Wes briefly about the trip, the complaints, the sheep whose latter half had been clipped by the bus. An Everyone had set up a camera at the veterinary office where they'd brought the sheep, heretofore unnamed and destined for chops, but now known as Athena and imbued with complex emotions and the hopes of all of those unhappy souls who had boarded the bus and regretted it. Athena was getting the best care, but after being struck by a fifteen-ton bus traveling at forty-four miles per hour, the prognosis was not good.

"I'm only sad I didn't get to know her," Wes said.

"Please," Delaney said.

"She seemed like a fascinating sheep."

"Stop."

Wes disappeared and reappeared seconds later with an envelope.

"You got another letter yesterday," he said, and dropped it on the bed. It was Agarwal again. Delaney didn't know if she had the strength. She opened it, though, hoping that hearing Agarwal's voice, even if scolding, might give her courage to continue.

Dear Delaney,

With nothing to lose, allow me to blather. I tried for years, unsuccessfully, to bring the word

technoconformity into the lexicon. Perhaps such
things are always organic, and can never be engineered. But, forgive me, I was a teenager in the
eighties. We were so comically anti-authority, anti-
corporate, anti-conformity that I remember harbor-
ing a seething anger toward even my local 7-Eleven.

Yours was the most conformist generation in
history, and the two generations after yours were
more conformist still. I do not like saying that. But
think of it. You all own the same phone. You have
willingly given all your personal data to what is the
most monopolistic, control-hungry corporation
ever to plague the world. As a generation you are so
empathetic, so intelligent, so politically active. You
boycott companies (and people) over comparatively
minor things. But this company—the company
where you now work—which more than any other
has the power to control so much of what we know
and buy and do, a company which represents the
greatest and most insidious concentration of power
and wealth in human history—you give them a
pass. I don't understand it.

Yours,
Agarwal.

Delaney felt worse than before. She got under the
covers and put a pillow over her head. Her phone
dinged; she'd forgotten to turn it off. A throbbing
warning said she was late in filling out PESSes for
everyone on the bus; they had, happily enough,

already submitted their assessments of her. She didn't look. She put her phone under her mattress and, numb and despairing, she slept, on and off, till Monday.

Alessandro said he was sad to see her leave TellTale. She'd stayed there two weeks, working primarily on the study of jokes in comedic films—how many were ideal, how many were too many (54; 77). Delaney said she was sad to see herself go.

"But I'm happy that you're only making a lateral move here," he said. "Iris Tracking is closely related to our work at TellTale, as you can imagine. Maybe if you like what Eric's team does, too, you'll stay on our side of campus. We need more like you."

After his last sentence, panic overtook his face. The words **more like you** hung in the air, as both he and Delaney examined them for offense. They sounded wrong in some way, and Delaney could understand his alarm. But after a few seconds, as they each scanned the word-triptych for toxicity, they found the cluster clean, and Alessandro—who for a moment was teetering on the edge of employment abyss, forced out of his job and made leprous for future hirers—relaxed.

They made a short journey together, from one end of Kitty Hawk to the next, and when they arrived, a very tall man with a tremendous beard—a sort of waterfall of black lichen—was waiting.

"Eric," he said, and stared long at Delaney, his

eyes amused. "Reed?" he said, and pointed to himself. "Lewis and Clark."

Delaney had no clue what this person was saying.

"Libarts schools of the Northwest!" he said, and laughed hoarsely, painfully—as if he'd been making himself laugh all his life and his lungs had finally given out.

This seemed a more logical connection than the one Alessandro had forged between Reed and Kenyon, and yet it surprised Delaney how much some Everyones identified with their colleges, and with those colleges that in vague ways resembled their own colleges.

Eric turned to Alessandro. "Just affirming: This a comprehensive NDA situation?" he asked.

"It is," Alessandro said. "I'll come back in ten. And remember the Bailey event at noon. That gives you all thirty minutes."

Though the days since Bailey's death had been thick with tributes to him, this day the whole campus would come together on the Daisy for what was billed as a celebration of his life.

"Got it," Eric said. He was the tallest person Delaney had met at the Every, and perhaps the tallest person she'd ever seen up close. She put him at seven feet. The lichen-beard somehow made him look taller. "Six ten," he said. "You didn't look it up?"

Delaney laughed nervously, and felt a surge of

gratitude that Eric was not wearing revealing leggings. Could there be a different set of rules for men of his height? She followed him into a dim room bright with blue screens.

"Sit," Eric said, indicating an ergonomic stool before a standard screen. He handed her a human version of the kind of blinders worn by horses.

"Recognize these?" he asked, and sat next to her. She was surprised to find that while seated, his head was at the same level as her own. His height must be in his legs, she thought, and then a foul smell assaulted her. It was like a window had been opened to a sour breeze. It was him. Delaney briefly smiled, thinking that of all the things the Every attempted to solve for, this—body odor—had escaped them. There was no app.

"Can you put them on?" he asked.

She put the device on her head, and indeed the headset acted like a horse's blinders, restricting her peripheral vision.

Though she couldn't see him, she sensed the rearrival of Alessandro. He placed a tablet in front of her, and she reached down to quickly scroll to the end and sign it with her finger. Eric and Alessandro burst into laughter.

"You can't do that here!" Alessandro said. "You're at the center of all the world's eye-tracking research. You have to read every word!"

And so Delaney read every word of the

non-disclosure agreement, while Eric and
Alessandro debated which of them knew Delaney
would try to sign the document without reading
every word. They decided, finally, that they both
knew what Delaney would do, and that it was very
funny, how they saw it coming, what she would do.
All the while, Delaney noted that Eric's personal
odor heightened every time he spoke or moved, and
seemed to double in potency every time he laughed
his hoarse, painful laugh. When she was finished
reading, a green light appeared in the upper-right
corner of the tablet's screen, and now she was permitted to sign. She signed, Alessandro took his
leave, and Eric cleared his throat.

"It's not just you. We do that with every new person in the department," he said. "There's no better
way to demo the tech—how it works, and how it'll
be used. Do you know the science behind it?" He
didn't wait for an answer. "Can I give you the basics?" Again he did not pause. "Look at the screen in
front of you. Just whatever your eye is attracted to."

The large monitor came alive with crudely animated shapes and pictures. She looked at an orange
triangle, a picture of a cat sitting in a tree, a series
of sperm-like squiggles swimming diagonally across
the screen.

"As you sit in front of the monitor," Eric said,
"an infrared light is being directed toward your pupils. This causes reflections in your pupil and your

cornea. The vector between the cornea and the pupil is tracked by the infrared camera, and this way we can determine what you're looking at. This also gives us the ability to track when you get fixated on something, what order you look at things—that kind of hierarchy is so crucial to study—and what things you come back to."

"So it's recording what I look at and for how long," Delaney said.

"Exactly," Eric said excitedly, and a burst of odor surged from his perimeter.

"But isn't this illegal?" she asked.

He stiffened and Delaney knew she'd made her first error of tone. She tried to course-correct. "I mean, didn't some people sue?"

"They did," Eric said, and now his odor was alive, an invisible predator stalking the air between them. "And there are laws in some cities and states that limit their use. But there are millions of systems already in place. It's been used for years within the Implicit Association Test, the Stroop Test, and of course within the gaze contingency paradigms."

"Of **course,**" Delaney said, nodding solemnly.

"It's critical in diagnosing autism and a host of other neurological disorders," Eric said. He was growing calmer.

"**So** necessary," Delaney said.

"The problem people have is with some aspects of neuromarketing. I don't think it's right to secretly implant sensation-monitors on shoppers. I objected to that in a bunch of posts that were circulated widely here at the Every."

Delaney nodded earnestly. "Yes, I think I saw those," she said, and again cursed herself. Surely he had some way to know what she'd seen?

"But using eye trackers," he continued, now back to a comfortable place of explaining methodically, "just to figure out what people are looking at and for how long—that's only logical. It started with marketing. Advertisers want to know what you look at. What you respond to. This serves the makers of ads, sure, but it serves the audience, too. A bad ad will be ignored, whoever made it will find a new line of work, and you won't see any more like it. But when something's successful, the eye will go to it, and stay there, mapping it in greater detail, and then whatever it was that attracted and kept the viewer's attention can be replicated."

"It's the perfect symbiosis," Delaney said, and finally she saw Eric smile. "It's the only meaningful way to determine what someone's actually seeing, reading and responding to."

"Well, right," he said, and Delaney felt he'd finally begun to like her again. "The utility of this tech for advertisers drove its progress in the first place. But then film and TV asked for data, and that was huge. It was kind of hilarious, because with the first test group we did, we discovered that this one very highly paid actress was actually being avoided by most eyes. She would come onscreen and the eyes—seventy-seven percent of them—would dart away like she was an infection. You can be sure that that data affected her future salary negotiations."

Delaney smiled, then thought she should be more emphatic in her approval of his joke. "Ha!" she said.

"So apply the same idea to any movie or show. Where does the eye really gravitate to? Explosions, breasts, abs—this was obvious enough. But it gets more subtle. Certain clothing tested high, certain cities, decor, facial expressions, animals, children. If you knew what I knew, you'd know how seriously it's already affected filmmaking. By any chance have you noticed a pretty dramatic increase in the number of toddlers and medium-sized dogs in contemporary film?"

"I have!" Delaney lied.

Eric nodded. "And fewer heavy people. Fewer romantic scenes between people over 65. Fewer scenes in Baltimore and the Middle East. That's the easy stuff, to be honest," Eric said. "But the thing I'm most excited about is education. I taught for a year after college. Ninth graders outside Denver."

"So cool," Delaney said.

"Anyway, I'd assign reading every week, just ten or fifteen pages, but I had no real way to determine whether any student read anything. When we gave them all e-readers, we at least knew which pages they flipped to, and for how long they spent on each page. But kids could game that, too. At the end of the year, I had a student actually show me how he flipped through Tolstoy, timing the tapping of his e-reader, while watching videos of Brazilian motorcycle accidents. He had one hand on the reader while his eyes were on his phone!"

"**Ter**rible," Delaney said.

"But imagine if that e-reader had eye tracking. You'd know if the student was reading every word. You'd have a generation that not only was assigned **Anna Karenina,** but actually **read** it."

Delaney assumed the syllables expected of her were "A-maz-ing!" so she sang them loudly to Eric, and with feeling.

"I know, right?" he said. "We just need to saturate. I mean, I guess we already have saturated. The last three years or so, all of the Every's phones and monitors have shipped with eye-tracking hardware and software installed. It's just a matter of activating it. Oh, we better go."

The celebration of Bailey's life was tastefully executed. It had been weeks since his death—enough time for the shock to wear off and a proper tribute to his life to be planned. His widow, Olivia, had asked that it take place outside, so the campus had been transformed into a kind of mournful Coachella, with tributes in person and via satellite and a rousing version of "Light and Day" by the

surviving members of the Polyphonic Spree. Three
U.S. vice presidents were present, as was every head
of state in the G8. A surf circle, typically formed on
water to honor a fallen comrade, was approximated
on the lawn, with an original poem written by Laird
Hamilton, the noted big-wave surfer (ret.), and read
by Kelly Slater, the noted freestyle surfer (ret.). It
was, as Bailey would have wanted, a party with him
as the theme, and it succeeded brilliantly. It was very
funny, too, the only two elements steering the mood
elsewhere being the brief and devastating tribute by
Gunnar, and the presence, silent but impossible to
ignore, of Stenton.

"We were always friends," he later told the Every
News Network, the company's internal propaganda
organ. "When I had an opportunity abroad, he
urged me to take it. If you know anything at all
about Eamon Bailey, it's that he believed in radical self-actualization. Holding back any person
from any experience was simply not him." Later,
Stenton toured ECon, and was filmed saying goodbye to Bailey's lair, outside of which he passed, and
briefly paused before, the iconic portrait of himself
and Bailey and Ty Gospodinov. The reaction to
his presence was uniformly polite, though in many
cases Everyones who had been at the company long
enough to know his history there were baffled and
quietly horrified.

The rest of the day was a free-for-all, with the

entire campus urged to celebrate Bailey in their own way. Delaney got a PESS reminder from Eric, finished it, and found Hans-Georg sitting on a low hill at the edge of the campus, under an apple tree. Positioned as he was, with his unruly hair and white socks pulled nearly to his knees, she thought of Isaac Newton.

"Hello, Delaney," he said, "do you have time?" He put a leatherette folder next to him and urged her to sit on it.

"Did you know him?" he asked. Delaney said she had not.

"I met him once," Hans-Georg said. "In Weimar. He came for a conference on connectivity. Something like that. I was in college and asked a question at his panel. He went on for fifteen minutes, and then found me afterward and talked to me for twenty more. He knew more about Goethe than I did, and I was doing a thesis about him. He was a generous person, a genuinely curious person."

"And loved to talk."

"I actually had to break off the conversation! I had to go to work. But what struck me was that his way was pure. His detractors, the people who question his motives, didn't realize that he really believed that tech could solve anything—that connection was all. It's the other forces that . . ."

Hans-Georg looked around him, and then into the boughs of the apple tree above him. Delaney was sure he wanted to say that it was people like

Stenton, like Mae, whose task it was and is to monetize the curiosity of not just Bailey but all the people of the world. Stenton had been behind the Right to Know laws of the 2020s and disintegrated all barriers to information, including any and all damning data about the enemies of the Every. Hans-Georg, evidently not feeling safe to talk freely, changed the subject.

"Thank you for the excursion to see the elephant seals," he said.

"You're welcome," Delaney said, wholly taken aback.

"I think there might come a time when the rest of the group can look back on the trip fondly," he said. "But group dynamics, combined with the hermetic seal enveloping so many now . . ." He drifted off, recognizing the risk in such a line of conversation.

"How have your rotations been?" he asked. Delaney said as little as she could. He said he'd just finished a week at Algo Mas. "It was overwhelming," he said, his eyes wide. "Stunning what they're doing there. The **extent.** Did you know there are sixteen subterranean floors? What you see above-ground is just a fraction of the operation."

Again Delaney knew he was withholding most of what he wanted to say. He seemed shaken.

"And it's merging with behavioral sciences," he said. "You probably knew that."

Delaney didn't know that, but it was unsurprising. The unsecret goal of Algo Mas had always been to not just track and influence human behavior but to dictate it.

"Well then," he said and hastily stood up. He looked nervous, as if suddenly realizing he'd said too much or stayed too long. "I wish you a peaceful day." He put his hand on his chest and bowed slightly. He took three steps down the hill before turning back.

"My folder!" he said. "Almost forgot. I'm so sorry."

Delaney rose to her feet and brushed a few stray blades of grass from it. When she handed it to him, he bowed again and then looked up at her conspiratorially. "Curious about what's inside?" he asked.

"Sure," Delaney said, though she hadn't thought of it until then.

Hans-Georg looked around and then flashed it open, just long enough for Delaney to see that it contained only one piece of paper, a yellowed piece of handwritten sheet music.

"Something my grandfather composed," he explained. "It's just a piece of a song. I have the only copy. I don't think it would mean anything to anyone, but to carry it around this place means everything to me." He turned and went down the hill again, weaving through the mourners on the Daisy.

When he disappeared, Delaney turned to find a wholly original face. Its eyes were large, catlike, its forehead a high unblemished dome. Its hair was black with streaks of cerulean blue. The face nodded at Delaney as if seeing her close-up confirmed all her previous assumptions. As if they were about to get to work.

"Joan," the face said. Delaney took this to be her name.

XXIII.

"I WAS ON YOUR Hell Bus," Joan said. "Joan Pham?
You didn't presearch me? Oh god. You're worse off
than I thought."

Joan was in her late twenties, thin and rubbery
and inhabiting a white bodysuit with no visible
points of entry. Before Delaney spoke, Joan peered
into Delaney's bodycam and smiled slightly when
she saw it was off. Delaney scanned Joan's own body
for recording devices and, finding none—finding no
pockets, zippers or seams—out of an abundance of
caution, she looked up into the boughs of the apple
tree, too, as Hans-Georg had.

"We're fine," Joan said. "I know the spots on
campus for candor. And anyway, I'm special. I get,
like, certain allowances. Actually, you want to walk?
Have you used the track yet?" She pointed to a
looping line of pink in the distance.

Delaney followed her, examining her. Joan Pham

walked across the campus, occasionally nodding at an Everyone, never slowing her slinky stride. She was the single-most confident and natural human Delaney had met or seen on campus.

"You're still getting used to the clothes here," Joan noted. "The sexy superheroes? Up ahead it'll be easier to talk." She raised her chin to the jogging track, a hundred yards ahead.

The track, installed a year before, encircled the campus, closely following the line of twelve-foot iron fencing—with art deco flourishes but no less imposing—which separated the grounds of the Every from the Treasure Island perimeter path. The track was wildly popular, and within six weeks had been widened to accommodate the walkers, then bikers and scooterers, and finally rules had to be established against motor-powered or motor-assisted devices, lest the speeds attained on the track reach levels considered unsafe.

As with every good thing, new issues arose. Because there were so many Everyones now near the outer gates, civilians found reasons to be walking by, or sitting, or taking pictures of the Everyones, and often talking to them, and handing them notes, and asking advice about moving from jobs outside the gates to careers within. New foliage was planted, primarily fast-growing and impenetrable bamboo, and again within months it seemed that the issues were solved, only to evolve into a new, unforeseen conundrum. Because the bamboo was dense, it became a wonderfully effective windblock, and provided needed shade.

Soon many hundreds of people who had been living in tents and shanties under nearby highways found the company's outer barrier far safer and cleaner and warmer. In a few weeks there were hundreds of humans living in tents in a ragged ring between the Bay's rough and rising sea and the Every campus, providing the starkest reminder of what happens when a society has a threadbare safety net and no plan for those who fall through it—and, more pointedly, what happens when the largest companies in the state and the nation and world somehow find ways to avoid paying taxes.

When the subject came up—in social media for there was of course no news—Mae Holland was brilliant. "These humans deserve our respect, and they deserve to live dignified lives. We're working with the state and the local government on durable long-term solutions for them all."

"So you had no idea who was on your Welcome2Me?" Joan asked.

"I had their names. I guess I could have looked up everyone, but there were so many questions before the trip, so many concerns—" Delaney felt moronic.

"There were actually some interesting people on the trip," Joan said. "You know how when you look up a flight online, and you leave the site, and the next time you go to that same flight, the cost has gone up by $500? The guy who wrote that code was on your bus. And the woman who came up with Weighty."

Delaney knew Weighty. It was an app that could determine anyone's weight using any photo or moving image.

"How are you feeling about it?" Joan asked.

"Weighty? It's wonderful," Delaney said.

"Not Weighty. Weighty's a nightmare and you know it. I'm talking about the bus ride."

"I feel . . . Fine?" Delaney said.

Joan stopped. "You're full of shit," she said.

Joan was wholly unguarded, unflinching. In the eyes of all the other people Delaney had met on campus, there was a faintly vibrating fear—of offending, of committing some small wrong, of being misunderstood and quickly ruined. The trembling of their pupils said they were never at ease. But Joan's eyes did not quiver. This struck Delaney with the force of revelation.

"It hurt a lot," Delaney said, and realized it was the first time she'd acknowledged this. She'd been bewildered, and angry, and she'd found the behavior of the expeditioners indefensible and insane, but she had not, until that moment, realized how deeply she'd been wounded by it all. In her bendy, long-striding way, Joan quickened her pace and Delaney was glad. Something about the speed of their walking, the exertion and distraction of it, the low-level chaos of moving and sweating, made hearing about her own failures seem manageable.

"I know you worked hard on that thing," Joan said. "But first of all, there were too many unknowns. Your packing list was incomplete. You know this. But more crucially, you didn't tell those people what to expect."

When Delaney protested that she'd explained it as best she could, with what was, in the end, a multi-page guide with two dozen links, Joan shook her head. "No. I don't mean sending bullet points and links. I mean explaining, step by step, with diagrams and photos and videos, what precisely will be done, and when, and what will be said, and by whom, for the duration of the event. People won't read an article without being told exactly how many minutes it will take. They certainly don't want to go on an excursion without every second being explained. They want unwavering information. Certainty, pole to pole. These are people who want to know the date of their death."

"But every day at work they aren't given—"

"At **work**," Joan stopped and looked around her. "At **work.** That's key. On campus these people know their days have been curated. Their OwnSelfs structure their every minute. On this island, they know the people they meet have been vetted and will speak correctly, that the food they get has been chosen with every sensitivity in mind. Here, they know they won't encounter a ranger who doesn't know his pronouns and tells us, without warning, about mammal moms who abandon their young. Delaney, none of that happens on Treasure Island. That kind of thing is stopped at the gate, just like plastic gift baskets and irony."

"Right. You're right."

"The Every is a closed ecosystem, and a closed ecosystem is wary of, or even hostile to, anything that might upset that equilibrium."

Delaney knew this.

"At the same time," Joan continued, "you had two other factors working against you. First, for whatever reason, your attendees were curated in a funny way. They were from all kinds of departments across campus, yes, but they all **lived on campus,** and had all expressed interest in animals and animal welfare. The algos thought this was a good pool to draw from. But the effect was that your passengers were exceptionally sensitive animal enthusiasts with that distant and reflexively terrified posture of people who live behind walls. So this was an exceedingly sensitive slice of the Every—sensitive and, if I may, a bit more prone to grievance than the average staffer here."

The path had taken them to the miniature golf course. It was packed. They paused to watch.

"See, that's the kind of thing you should have done for your Welcome2Me event," Joan said, pointing to a young woman tapping a white ball past a windmill. "Simple and already vetted. Yours was the riskiest thing since the guy who brought everyone to Modesto for bowling and buffalo wings. Another disaster. Keep walking."

Delaney had to scamper to catch up.

"So they do these Return & Restore hearings when there's an issue like this," Joan said. "It's a cross between a judicial hearing and an encounter group. There's a bit of trust-fall in there, some healing-crystal vibes, and even a bit of actual restorative justice. They've already met three times about your Welcome2Me."

Delaney felt sick. "Who met? Everyone on the bus?"

"Not **everyone,**" Joan clarified. "Two were still a bit fragile and couldn't handle it. So just about forty people. I went to the first few, and I have to say that the whole thing would have gotten a lot worse if I hadn't steered it toward some kind of balance. You know how these things escalate. Every person who gets up to speak has to be more wounded and more outraged than the one before. De-escalation is not fashionable in these contexts."

Delaney wanted to climb the fence and fling herself into the Bay.

"Sorry to be the bearer," Joan said. "But listen. It'll get better, and soon. I'll be taking you to the summary. Your schedule's been cleared. I tapped into your HelpMe. I'm impressed you resisted OwnSelf."

"Wait. The summary?"

"It's tomorrow morning. I'll meet you outside the Theater of Rhamnousia. They'll present their findings, their conclusions, what everyone learned. It's not as confrontational as it sounds. It's this guy Syl who will do it, and Syl's probably your best bet. He's afraid of his own shadow. I missed the last meeting, but I think some very interesting ideas were emerging from it all. They're also doing a presentation at Perchance to Dream next week, which I think is good for you. That means they've come around to making something positive from the experience. Oh shit. Your lip is trembling. Does it usually do that?"

"I'm okay," Delaney said. She didn't want something so small, a field trip to a beach, to affect her like this. Far greater battles lay ahead.

"I know I've put a lot on you," Joan said. She held Delaney's shoulder, squeezing it hard. "I'm sorry. Was it too much?"

Delaney was so grateful for this simple gesture. When had she been touched last? She couldn't remember.

As they walked, they were so involved that they didn't notice that they'd almost collided with a scrum of people, Stenton at the center. He was apparently being given a tour of a new organic garden on campus.

"It's really odd, having him here," Joan said. "It's got a real divorced-dad feel, am I right?" They stopped to watch from a distance. "Do you see what I'm seeing?" she asked.

Stenton, dressed in his uniform of khakis and a gray-striped button down, was looking around him like a kitten caught in a stampede. It was the clothing. Everywhere around him, young Everyones in lycra were digging, reaching, bending over, and demonstrating, and Stenton didn't know where to look. For every vegetable, there were a half-dozen bulbous body parts he was straining not to see. He seemed to have decided against watching anyone doing anything, so spent a lot of time looking up at the sky, smiling, and then, occasionally, resting his eyes on someone's forehead.

"He's drowning in dicks," Joan said. "What fun."

At the edge of the group, Delaney saw a familiar face, looking intensely at Stenton, as if studying a new species. It was Gabriel Chu, who was devouring Stenton's struggle with visible pleasure.

XXIV.

"WHICH ONE IS THIS AGAIN?" Delaney asked.

"There are two events, very different," Joan said. "Next week is Perchance to Dream, where Syl wants to make a presentation. That's public-facing. But this first one is Return & Restore. It's private, just you and the survivors of the Playa 36 Debacle."

Delaney stopped walking. She leaned against the wall.

"Sorry," Joan said. "That's what they're calling it. And **survivors** is what they're calling themselves. I know, I know. The nice thing is that they only have ninety minutes. I've seen these go for six, seven hours. Ninety minutes will go by in a blink."

And yet it did not go by in a blink.

Delaney entered the hall, a windowless third-floor space fashioned loosely on a Greek amphitheater, with rings of bench-style seats surrounding a sunken stage. The room was so dark when they entered that they had to feel their way, touching knees and heads, before they found room for two. Once they were settled, a spotlight came on, and Syl stepped into its gauzy white oval. Now Delaney could see that the room contained multitudes— a hundred people at least. Delaney's hand was found and squeezed. She looked to Joan, feeling overcome with gratitude, but Joan kept her gaze on the person standing in the light.

He was thin but for a paunch, the size of a bundt cake, which was neatly outlined by his tight lycra shirt, striped like a referee's, though in brown and yellow. The shirt was an inch too small, though, so every time he breathed, it rose to expose his belly button. He paid the exposure no mind. His heavy-lidded eyes, close-set in a round face, were carefully sweeping across the room, leaving no one unseen.

"Hello. I'm Syl. Thank you all for being here on what I hope is the last leg of this journey," he said. "We've come so far." With that, a relieved, aggrieved murmur swept through the room. "And now we have Delaney with us. We welcome you, Delaney."

The faces in the room emitted discordant permutations of the words **Thank you** and **Delaney** and **Welcome.** Delaney thought she might be expected to say something in response, but a vicious squeeze from Joan's hand kept her quiet. Syl welcomed a series of survivors who shared their feelings about the trip, though it was less about sharing and more about the making of short, apoplectic speeches. Each person who spoke was hurt by what happened

at Playa 36, and many were bewildered. One was
stunned. Two were confused. Some had been si-
lenced. Many had been made uncomfortable, and
a few were disturbed. For all, their sleep had been
affected, and their pod and departmental sleep aggregates were now down—a big problem, and
Delaney's fault. The planning had been haphazard,
it was said. No one had been properly prepared, it
was agreed. They expected more control, organization, checking-in, discussion, input, collaboration,
sensitivity, respect for the environment and for all
living creatures, and also, no one had had lunch.

Just as Joan had warned, each time a new person spoke, that person felt it necessary to be more
emotionally maimed than their predecessors, and to
reach deeper into history—theirs personally or that
common to humanity—for comparisons to what
had happened and how they felt about it. Someone's
uncle had been a hostage in Iran and they now
knew precisely how that experience had felt.
Another countered that making Iranians, Khomeini,
too, into stereotypical Middle Eastern villains, even
for the purpose of a post-p36d (the incident's ini-
tials had been lowercased to diminish its power)
anecdotal corollary, was regressive and a retraction
should be made. A retraction was made, among
many regretful and healing tears.

Finally the lights came up, and a digital wipeaway
board was illuminated. In the spirit of the exercise
wherein each member of a group would say what

kind of tree they would be if they were a tree—an exercise empirically proven, over decades, to yield intellectually provocative and emotionally cathartic results—Syl suggested that each member of the group identify, on the board, something from the day that made them uncomfortable or felt problematic, and next to it, a possible cure for that discomfort or problematic thing.

The bus was identified by many as the source of great unease, and the solutions to the bus-of-unease ranged from **Smaller buses** to **A day without buses** and finally settled upon **No more buses,** a solution seen by the majority as intoxicatingly radical and thus best. Many people spoke of the beach itself as a source of discomfort, containing as it did too much water, too much sand, too little guidance, and the presence of seal infanticide. It was agreed that forty-two people arriving aboard a giant steel machine to watch seal families mate and abandon their young was wildly aggressive and inherently exploitive. Someone called it **Darwin-porn,** and many liked that, given attaching the suffix **porn** to anything meant that thorny thing should no longer be seen, filmed, photographed, or in any way reported or discussed.

The solutions to the beach, the bus, and the uncomfortable proximity to wildlife were, again, direct and increasingly extreme. **Don't visit that beach,** was the first, and was followed by **Close the beach,** then **Don't exploit animals for our gawking**

pleasure, and finally it was agreed that **Humans should not be permitted near any animals in any context,** and that **Large groups of humans traveling together in fifteen-ton fuel-burning vehicles are so obviously environmentally offensive and metaphorically obvious that we cannot, ever, be part of the problem again.** The near-martyred sheep was not mentioned, the psychic wounds too great and too raw, but Athena was on the minds of all.

As the writing continued, spiraling upward with increasing outrage and pain, Delaney saw Gabriel. He was standing in the back, near the doorway, as if he'd come late just to audit the session. His blade-like arms were crossed before him, his torso encased in a silver fabric resembling chainmail. His head was tilted, as if trying to see underneath the event and everyone who was part of it.

When it was time for Delaney to stand and speak, Joan gave her hand a quick squeeze. "I've learned so much," Delaney said. "Your courage inspires me to do better." And, feigning emotions too strong to go on, she grimaced in Joan's direction, cowered out of the room, and then fled the building. She walked swiftly across the lawn, left the gates, and took the first shuttle off the island to return home.

Delaney slept little that night. She tried to shape her scattered thoughts into a series of aphorisms and bullet points that she could feed to Syl who, she hoped, would disseminate them to the world at Perchance to Dream. When she finally fell asleep, it was three-thirty. She woke briefly at five, terrified at the towering lunacy of her ideas, and then fell asleep again. When she woke again at seven, she was shot through with electricity. Because her notion involved the end of something enjoyed by billions, she knew it would work.

At breakfast, passing a pyramid of limes, Delaney was still pondering how to approach Syl, how to puppetize him, when she found him at her elbow.

"I'm so glad you were there last night," he said.

"And I was so happy to be there," she said.

"I wanted to find you because I know you'd want to hear about Athena."

"Yes, of course I do," Delaney said.

"She died this morning," he said. "She succumbed to her injuries."

Delaney let her head drop in sympathy. "I'm so sorry for your loss. For the world's loss. Were you with her?"

"No," Syl said, and his eyes fell. He hadn't thought of being with Athena during her last breaths, Delaney realized. But he had thought of coming to Delaney to shower more guilt upon her. This would be good, she knew. It would be perfect. He would fall for this.

"She was so lucky to have an advocate like you in her life," Delaney said.

Syl took the compliment with a beatific half-smile.

"I've been thinking of all you said yesterday," Delaney said, "and I found myself wanting more. It's like I sat in on the first lesson of a master teacher, and then he left the room."

Delaney watched, at that moment, a remarkable change come over Syl. Between this new designation as master teacher and his recent canonization as sheep advocate and shaman, his sense of himself changed fundamentally and, she was sure, permanently.

"Do you have time to eat with me?" she asked, and he and his ego could not refuse.

XXV.

"I WANT TO BUILD on Ramona Ortiz's brilliant Stop+Lük presentation the other day," Syl said.

The Perchance to Dream hall was full. Delaney sat in the fifth row, far to the left, as if hoping to go unnoticed but not wanting to seem distant or disinterested. She saved a seat for Joan, who arrived as the lights dimmed.

"Good location," Joan said. "This will be good. You feeling good?"

"The buzz is big," Delaney said, and wondered how her mind had formed those words.

"The buzz is big, hm," Joan said, and sat back in her seat. She turned to the person next to her, a young Everyperson with a helmet of black hair. "The buzz is big," Joan told him.

"Okay," Delaney said. "Now stop."

"What?" Joan said. "I'm just saying the buzz is big."

"No more."

"It's just what I heard about the buzz. And that it's big."

Delaney had engineered it. She'd sent an all-campus message touting Syl's radical brilliance. And any time there was a hint of a new idea on campus, every Everyone took note, hoping to see what new ideas sounded like, what words were used to describe them, what the new-idea-person wore and how they used their hands and feet, and by the way, were lucite podiums helpful?

Syl was wearing a simple baby-blue kilt over a powder-blue bodysuit, accented by what appeared to be shoulder pads and a utility belt. Around his neck a mustard-yellow Che Guevara scarf had been boldly, recklessly draped. It was as if the attention and responsibility had been his water and sun, bringing him to full bloom.

"Ramona spoke so eloquently about the damage we're doing to the world when we travel to excess," he said, "and I thank her for realigning our thinking about unnecessary movement through the world."

The audience nodded, for Ramona had become a legend and a member of the Gang of 40. Now Delaney saw Wes. He was sitting in the front row. She'd never seen him in the front row of anything.

Syl leveled his heavy-lidded eyes on the audience, who all but ducked. "But we have to think, too, about the damage we do every day, during much shorter, and more ostensibly innocuous, excursions."

And we're off, Delaney thought.

"As some of you know, a group of us Everyones went on something of a **field trip**"—he said the words as he might say **acid colonic**—"and on that trip, we learned a lot, and afterwards we thought a lot, and talked a lot, and finally we synthesized our findings into what we see as a revolutionary action plan that just might save the planet, the threatened species of the world, and maybe humanity, too."

Tears of joy crowded Delaney's eyes.

"First," Syl continued, "let's assume the undeniable truth of all that Ramona proposed. Elective air travel is immoral and does violence to the earth. That is impossible to deny."

The room was silent with what Delaney assumed was the shock of a principle that would never again be challenged.

"But there are two sides to human impact. There's the impact we have on the environment every time we leave our homes, and there's the impact these excursions have on our own psyches. Both present significant risk, and both are avoidable. Our group came up with a term for these phenomena, and how we feel about them."

Onscreen, the words **Impact Anxiety** appeared in bold white letters against an ominous red background.

"We've all felt it," Syl said. "Any time you take a rideshare into the city to go to a new restaurant, you're committing countless crimes against an exhausted victim—our natural world.

"Then there's the restaurant itself," Syl continued, "which becomes a magnet for endless unnecessary trips by car and other vehicles. Then the food! How many animals died for that evening at the fashionable new brasserie? How many Amazonian acres were burned to create grazing land for the beef croquettes that give you a moment of fleeting pleasure? How many pesticides have been doused upon the wheatfields that make possible your senseless breadsticks?"

He paused for effect. The effect was significant.

"Then of course we get into our complicity with that restaurant's heedless exploitation of Guatemalan banana farmers, for example. **Bananaskam,** of course, helped make us aware of this. And what of the Senegalese children sent to extract chocolate for your tiramisu? The fact is that every time we leave campus, we risk supporting exploitive, extractive, regressive and inherently violent practices. Here, we can vet what we bring onto campus, and what we use and consume. Out there, it's far more difficult, if not impossible."

Much nodding took place.

"From Stop+Lük, we've realized that we have to find alternatives to all this traveling by plane and car, and even by bus and train. By getting into that car or bus, for example, you're supporting an automotive industry that has, and continues to, extract untold resources from the earth. Metal ore, rubber, aluminum, bitomium. These vehicles aren't made from bamboo, after all. These are intensely exploitive machines that by their very existence are symbols of humanity's aggression toward its mother."

Syl closed his eyes for effect. Delaney, worried that he might be taking it too far, looked around the room briefly, and saw an audience rapt and unquestioning. Syl's eyes snapped open, as if he'd just gotten new signals from a more compassionate planet.

"Last weekend was a perfect example," he said. "One of our fellow Everyones, a wonderful person by the way," and here he looked in vain for Delaney in the audience before venturing on, "had the seemingly innocent idea to bring a group of us to Point Reyes to see the elephant seals gathered there. Our group of expeditioners thought we were innocuous travelers on a solar-powered bus and thus incapable of harm, but we learned otherwise. First, the catering for said trip had not been properly vetted, and thus made us accessories to passive but no less significant hate crimes against the long-oppressed Palestinian people, and for that we can never be wholly absolved."

He paused, closed his eyes again for a meaningful moment, then forged on. "Second, a beautiful creature died under the wheels of our vanity that day. You have heard about this, no doubt. This creature, who we have named Athena, was murdered by our desperate need to **go,** to **get somewhere,** to **be somewhere else.**" He spat the predicates like epithets. "We wanted to **put our feet in the sand.**

We wanted **to see the seals in person.** These were animals that had not, it should be mentioned, invited us to their habitat. We took a massive machine—fifteen tons of wanton privilege—and we invaded the natural domain of those seals. We did so with the violence, callousness and narcissism of a conquering army. And then, on the way home, we smashed a guiltless animal named Athena into oblivion."

Here Syl had managed to find a photograph of a sheep that looked eerily like the one they'd killed, though this sheep was alive and healthy and looked capable of intellectual rumination.

"We have come to the conclusion," he said, "that a trip like the one we took is morally wrong and impossible to justify. Had we eschewed this trip, we would have alleviated our Impact Anxiety. We would have stayed here that weekend, on campus, and by staying here, we wouldn't have risked the near-inevitable damage we have when we rush recklessly from our homes into the world."

There was a vibration in the room, a putsch-lust. It seemed that the assembled audience was ready for revolution, a revolution led by a most passive and fearful human.

"It was all wrong," Syl said. "That day, we were no better than Custer or Columbus. We should not have been there, period. And no human should have been able to **get** there, full stop."

Applause shook the room. Syl, unaccustomed to

such public approval, looked momentarily fright-
ened by the noise. Finally the clapping subsided and
Syl's shoulders relaxed.

"Now. What can we learn and enact on a
larger scale?" Syl asked. "Let's start with the
highway—the kind of road that facilitated this
uncivil destruction."

With hateful eyes, the audience looked at the
screen, which presented a real-time drone's eye view
of an eight-lane freeway.

"Humans made an immeasurable mistake when
we built the highway," Syl said, in a soft and con-
templative tone. He was looking at his shoes, as if he
himself had invented the road and now regretted it.

"We made it too easy to travel great distances
for our jobs, our errands and our touristic self-
aggrandizement," he continued. "Now the average
human in an industrialized country travels thirty-
two miles to work. Another six miles, round trip, to
get groceries. Maybe another six miles to drive the
kids to school. Our living and working and exploring has been spread out irrationally, which has led
to the overuse of the automobile and bus, which has
led to climate change, rising sea levels and potentially the collapse of civilization and the end of the
species. But!"

The audience laughed nervously. Syl smiled.

"We have the opportunity, here at the Every, to at
least set an example. How many of you commute to
work?" he asked.

About half the people in the room raised their hands.

"I won't ask how many of you drive yourselves to work in your own cars—I wouldn't want you to assume that kind of social opprobrium. But how many of you take one of the Every buses?"

The same hands that had been raised before, with a few exceptions, went up again.

"These buses are of course spacious, luxurious and convenient. Most are electric. But they should be abolished."

A few clusters of applause broke out. Syl extended his finger, asking for patience. There was more.

" 'What about trains?' you ask," he went on. Behind him a standard commuter train had been photo-filtered to look enormous and world-slashing. "Well, our trains are not without sin. They are not solar-powered, or powered by our sense of self-satisfaction. They, too, have consumed incredible energy in their manufacture, and at best they consume massive amounts of electricity, which, in this country at least, often still comes from fossil fuel—natural gas in particular—which is finite and which is extracted from under our feet at significant risk to our tectonic integrity. Trains should not exist."

Delaney watched the faces of the hundred-odd Everyones assembled. She hoped for the three waves of reaction, and they came in exactly the order she needed. The first was revulsion, rejection, given they'd heard an idea that would threaten their way of doing things, an idea that was even a bit cruel in its assessment. The second wave was the recognition that they, as Everyones devoted to eternal innovation and boundary-pushing, could not, outright or ever, reject any new notion, no matter how preposterous. The third wave was an earnest head-nodding that conveyed that they recognized the bold anomalation at hand, and that they would never deign to stand in the way of progress—and any new notion was inherently progressive. Satisfied that all three waves had passed through the eyes and minds of the assembled, Delaney turned back to Syl.

"We know the truth," he said. "We just have to affirm it and act on it. The truth is that we should be living close enough to our jobs such that no commute is necessary, period. We should either work where we live, or live where we work."

Syl let that sink in, and Delaney watched the Everyones' faces assess what it would mean to give up their houses and apartments in Noe Valley and the Oakland hills and amid the leafy shade of Atherton. Realizing they were powerless to resist this idea, which was inherently virtuous, they applauded, outdoing one another in their enthusiasm for overturning all they knew. Delaney was certain she heard someone even say, "Hear, hear!"

When the roar died down, Syl coasted to his conclusion. "I'm proposing," he said, his voice gaining strength and power, "a five-year plan, which entails building 10,000 more EveryoneIn units, all on campus"—the screen displayed a crude animation of six-story complexes going up like stop-motion plant-growth—"and that, until then, a program of carrots and sticks be instituted, whereby those who commute at the expense of the planet are dis-incentivized, and those who commute via foot or bike are rewarded. This would go for all errands, trips and jaunts. Your miles would be recorded, calculated and factored into your Personal Carbon Impact number."

Personal Carbon Impact: Delaney had given Syl that, too. She hoped Wes would not mind.

"We'd start it all here on campus," Syl continued, "in the hopes of rolling it out globally over the next few years. And our idea is that we will not only pos-itively affect the planet, but we will significantly en-hance our own wellness, too. Are you stressed about your daily impact on the environment? Stay where you are. Are you worried about frightening elephant seals and killing sheep? Stay where you are. Are you concerned about using gas, cars, roads, trains, and steel? Stay where you are."

Again applause overtook the room. Delaney couldn't have been happier for him, and for the prospect of seeing the Every try to sell this notion of never again leaving the house. If that didn't con-vince the world that the Every campus was not only power-mad but deranged, too, nothing ever would.

Many names for Syl's program were floated,
but when someone yelled out the words Stay
Still, and someone else—was it Shireen? It was!—
suggested removing the space between those words
(StayStill), and still someone else suggested spelling
it as StåyStill—to better echo the Nordic aura of
Stop+Lük—and someone else noted that if we were
using fewer resources, wouldn't we use fewer letters,
in particular consonants? Finally StayStïl was settled
upon, and there was great satisfaction all around.

XXVI.

APPLICATIONS FOR EVERYONEIN leapt a hundredfold in a day. No one wanted to be living off-campus (known now as Nowhere), unsure of their daily carbon footprint and terrified of being seen slinking onto campus (now Everywhere) from off-world each day, having defaced the planet in uncountable ways en route. The Every's senior executives, not wanting to be shamed, swiftly and quietly moved onto campus, hoping to convey the impression they'd been living there all along.

"I have to move in," Delaney said.

She and Wes were at the beach parking lot, with Hurricane in his stroller. He didn't understand why he couldn't at least be carried onto the beach. He shifted in his seat, whimpered, craned his neck to see the ocean.

"You **have** to go?" Wes asked.

"I'm already an outlier. If I'm central to this

StayStil movement, and then I don't join, it'll look hypocritical."

"Either you're getting too good at this or you've lost your mind," Wes said.

Hurricane barked three times, each weaker than the last. He had begun barking at unreasonable moments, with no prompting.

"And obviously it gets me closer," Delaney said. "To know where the levers and buttons are."

"I don't think they keep the levers and buttons in the housing pods," Wes said. "I think you'll probably find beds and sinks."

Hurricane barked again, but it came out like a wheeze.

"Where are you rotating next?" Wes asked.

"I actually don't know."

"Your eyes are spiraling," he said. "I don't think you want to be there full-time. Those people are driving you mad."

"You know what it really was?" Delaney said. "It was the ecstasy of refusal. That just hit me. That's what happened that day with **Bananaskam,** and now with all of this."

"The ecstasy of refusal," Wes repeated. "Right. That's it."

"And the embrace of the most radical refusal. That day in the cafeteria it was like an orgy of ending. No more bananas. No more papayas. The way they looked up the origins of fruit and then eliminated them from possibility. And now the end of travel, of cars, roads, planes."

"To be rid of something," Wes said. He was crouched down, trying to make Hurricane more comfortable. "There's a power there, too. This power to destroy. When we were kids, it was people. That constant erasure of people. Now it's customs and practices, traditions, history. Or like your Thoughts Not Things work. That urge to wipe something off the earth. It's like my zombie theory."

"It's not like your zombie theory," Delaney said.

Wes's zombie theory posited that in an increasingly crowded world, killing zombies was an acceptable way to express one's hatred for the proliferation of the species. The popularity of zombie films and shows and games has everything to do with the feeling that there are only a few sane people left, and that those few have the right to end the suffering of all those caught between purgatorial semi-sentience and death.

"To preside over the end of something, someone—it's a kind of lust," Wes said. "It's like purging. You start with a room full of stuff, you finish with a clean white box. You hear the new slogan for PastPerfect? **The Past Can Be Perfected.**"

"The elimination of impurities," Delaney said.

"A killing of the unknown," Wes said. "And I think it starts with Mae. She maintains her purity because she never goes anywhere or does anything.

She's never been disconnected. Outside of running the Every, she's never actually **done** anything."

"When you do things, you risk doing them incorrectly."

"Because she fears doing anything wrong, she's intellectually celibate. Never had an original idea."

Delaney sat with that for a moment, thinking of Mae's sonogram. Her mind leapt to virgin births.

"They say AuthentiFriend is ready," Wes said.

"To be released? An actual rollout?"

"They're planning to leak it in India. A lot of the coding's been done there, so the Mumbai office started creating a Hindi version. I mean, all this has been happening for a month. They just told me. Why are you smiling like that?"

"This is good," she said. "I thought it would take longer. But the quicker this happens, the better. Don't tell me you were attached to this? It was a fake app meant to embarrass the Every."

"Not attached, just disappointed in how fast it moved. This Holstein person is a force. Every week I get a huge update from her on the adjustments and improvements they're making. There's usually some language about how they want my input, but it's like they're yelling and waving from a speedboat while I'm standing onshore."

"So?"

"It's gone so far beyond what we started with."

"That's good, right?" Delaney said.

"But now it's not a joke. It's not a game or a dance app. They have real science in there now. Real sensors. Real AI. Actual scientists working on it. I actually think it works now—it can tell if someone you're talking to is lying, is forthright, is comfortable, cares about you."

"This was the entire point, wasn't it?"

"I just thought of it as a gag," Wes said. "Now it's terrifying."

"It's supposed to be terrifying!"

"But it's not supposed to **work,**" he said.

They walked home, the wind at their backs. At the Shed, Delaney checked their mailbox and found one of Agarwal's blue envelopes.

Dear Delaney,

I had to write because I just had a very enlightening lunch with a visiting academic from North Korea. She is a defector, of course, and she taught me much about the nature of information control. She lived under the world's most restrictive information-flow structure, and she's studied the system in China, too, and what she's found is quite prosaic and quite terrifying.

The prosaic part is that most people simply don't have time to care or fight. That is, in a country like North Korea, the average person is barely getting by. They work perhaps sixty hours a week, and they cook and clean and take care of their children and try to find an hour here or there for recreation.

In their spare time, which is scant, they consume highly censored television and what passes for the internet there.

If a North Korean citizen had the will, they could presumably come into contact with information and truths from the outside world. But that would take an extraordinary and sustained effort, carrying with it considerable risk. And because discovering the truth about the world outside is not the number one priority—finding enough food and other foundational concerns are far more pressing and ever-central—few bother. It takes time, and money, and gumption, to even undertake the project of accessing prohibited information. So my friend estimated that less than 3 percent of the North Korean population even attempts it.

China is freer but is not free. Again, it takes a great deal of will and effort to get beyond the information that the state wishes its citizens to have. So how does this impact your work at the Every? The Every continues to control the flow of information for most people. Most people live most of their online lives through the Every; the average user doesn't ever need to leave the platform.

Think of the power this situation gives them. Yes, we are still in a free society where anyone can write anything they wish. But how do people see these writings? If you spend most of your online life in Every platforms, you might see only that which they promote. You might be presented with a wide array of content, all of it approved by the Every, and in line with whatever ideology or business interests they have. This is not to say that a person in a democratic society could not access information that the Every is not endorsing.

But how many people will? How many people live in a state of aggressive truth-seeking? The answer is few. Remember when I tried to get your fellow students riled up about surveillance on campus? I had few takers. This makes your generation, and the ones before and after yours, a tasty morsel for autocrats and tyrants.

The world is undergoing a movement toward authoritarianism, Delaney, and this is about order. People think the world is out of control. They want someone to stop the changes. This aligns perfectly with what the Every is doing: feeding the urge to control, to reduce nuance, to categorize, and to assign numbers to anything inherently complex. To simplify. To tell us how it will be. An authoritarian promises these things, too.

I know people roll their eyes every time I mention Erich Fromm, but forgive me. Remember when he noted the young SS soldiers who felt liberated by Nazism? They wanted to be told what to do. They were free from freedom. The limitless choices of the world were suddenly made for them. Order was promised. **The streets will be clean, the lawbreakers will be gone, your days will be predetermined, and the unknown will go away.**

In related news, I have cancer. Metastatic mela-
noma, which has a certain music to it, no? It's
Stage 4, but they are optimistic, so I am optimistic. Is it hypocritical of me if I choose not to think
about it? Anyway, more news on that when I get it.
    Agarwal.

Only Agarwal would write a three-page letter and
mention her cancer as an afterthought. Delaney
ached to write her back, to fly to her, but knew she
couldn't. Instead, she put in her own application
for campus housing, and received, minutes later, a
message from Joan: **I have a bed for you.** Delaney
was aware by now that there were a thousand ways
senior or semi-senior Everyones circumvented pro-
cesses and leaped lines, and it was wholly unimpor-
tant to her how Joan had managed to slip Delaney
into the newly added bed in Joan's pod. On campus,
pods with one occupant were converted to doubles.
Doubles were converted to triples, triples became
quads. It was one way to meet the demand before
new buildings could go up.
    Syl was now something of a prophet, elevated to
the Gang of 40 and essential to climate conferences
around the world, all of which would henceforth be
held virtually. Syl and Ramona Ortiz began streaming an advice program from campus called Where
Not to Go and What Not to Do (WN2G+WN2D),
during which citizens Everywhere and Nowhere

asked questions about the environmental viability of leaving their homes.

"My daughter plays volleyball. There's a regional conference four hours away, and the only way to get there is on the interstate. Is it ethical to go?"

The answer was no. The answer was almost always no. Greenhouse gases were inevitable, and every time we take a road, they explained, we support road-building and the larger travel-industrial complex. When Syl and Ramona could not be absolutely sure of the environmental impact, they focused on Impact Anxiety, which was far more effective as a deterrent. Their refrain, which became a popular rallying cry around saving the planet by not leaving home, was, **Do you really want to risk it?**

The pod contract Delaney signed was much like her onboarding document—a manic hybrid of legalese and manifesto, self-help and willful capitalization. **The Pods are experiments in Best-Practice Habitation. Whether you're an Optimizer or a Communitarian, EveryoneIn hausing plans are the pinnacle of ease and Togetherment.** There were pictures of sunrises seen from fluffy white beds. **As with any Scientific Experiment, controls are key.** The contract had a soundtrack, which Delaney recognized as early One Direction. **Your total commitment to this Experiment is necessary for it to succeed in yielding Comfort, Mindfulness,**

and Actionable Data. There were 403 questions about Delaney's habits, allergies, eating and sleeping schedules, entertainment preferences, noise tolerance, feelings about germs, and taste in color palette and shower temperature. **Your pod is yours to modify within Certain Parameters. You are an individual of Infinite Creativity, so make it yours! Speaking of Creativity, recent evidence points to 10 Hours as ideal for idea-generation, so to that end each Sleeping Tube is equipped with white noise and pink noise, as well as UV lights and Natural Light (when possible), and Ylang Ylang diffusers.** Delaney closed her eyes. The willful capitalization saddened her, dragged her soul downward. She opened her eyes and read on. **Please see attachment for list of prohibited items and materials. Outside food, medicines and Hygienic products are unallowed without an Exemption. To request an Exemption please contact your Pod Coordinator. Attendance at Thursday Night Ultra-Exuberant Dance (THUD) is not mandatory but is encouraged. Get your bad Self down! About pets: We love Pets! However** . . .

There were more pages, 77 more pages, and because she could not sign the contract if the eye trackers found she'd skipped a word, Delaney had to read them all.

She arrived on a Tuesday with two suitcases. At the front gate, her possessions were inspected by

Rowena in her glass pyramid, and duly edited. Rowena kept Delaney's disposable razors, her shampoo and conditioner—anything containing or contained by plastic—and pointed her to the Havel where she'd live. (All the dorms were named after dissidents, freedom fighters, revolutionaries.) "The Vaclav Havel is between the John Brown and the Cesar Chavez. If you get to Michael Collins," Rowena said, "you've gone too far."

Online, Delaney had seen countless pictures and video of EveryoneIn hausing—their spelling—but in person her new pod was both smaller, much smaller, and far more full of riveting detail, at once elegant and whimsical, equal parts Zaha Hadid and Peter Pan. There were no right angles and no shape was repeated. Every cabinet door was made of bamboo and was a different, off-kilter parallelogram or trapezoid. The refrigerator was enormous and its glass door displayed its bright contents in highly organized fashion. Packaging did not exist. Snacks were available in righteous silos on the quartz countertop. Turmeric chickpeas, mushroom jerky, cauliflower crackers, ginger popcorn—everything was stored in airtight glass and tin containers. In the bathroom, toothpaste and soap were available in large pump-activated dispensers. The pod was a corner unit, with double-paned floor-to-ceiling windows, which looked out onto the Daisy, the Bay, two of three nearby bridges, and the jagged white mountain range of downtown San Francisco.

"You're here already," a voice announced. A series of squeaks followed. She turned to find a man in bright pink sneakers.

"Soren," he said, placing his palm on his chest and bowing slightly. Tall, balding, with rounded shoulders and no discernible chin, he looked and sounded like an inflatable man. He wore a snug but ill-fitting bodysuit that bunched around his ample stomach and inward-facing knees—as if he'd hastily put on a larger man's wetsuit. Over this, covering his thighs like a mini-skirt, was a kilt.

"You were supposed to move in tomorrow, right? What day is it? HereMe?" He stepped toward the kitchen, and his shoes squeaked with every step.

"Tuesday," Delaney said.

"Today is Tuesday," HereMe said.

Delaney had noticed this among many Everyones. They were never disconnected, but their relationship to the calendar was tenuous. No one seemed to know what day of the week it was, and had only the vaguest sense of where they were in any given month.

"Have you found your bed?" Soren asked. "They just built it." He crossed his arms, and Delaney noted a string of tattooed words on each forearm. IF YOU DO IT, OWN IT, one line said. This one was oriented to be read by whomever Soren was facing. The other line was, to her eye, upside-down—to be

read by Soren himself. It said the same thing: IF YOU
DO IT, OWN IT.

"That's me there," he said, and pointed to a
lower bunk, really a long plywood tube fronted by
a round wooden door. It looked like the home of a
giant gopher. "I'm a light sleeper so I need the door.
Here's yours," he said, and brought her around to
an entry point she hadn't noticed. Like his tube,
it was about eight feet long and three feet high.
But hers was situated against the floor-to-
ceiling window.

"See if you fit," he said, and Delaney inchwormed
into the box. She found it both stifling and vertigo-
inducing; she imagined it would be like sleeping
on a car dashboard, facing the windshield, four
stories up.

"It's wonderful," she said.

"Glad you like it," Soren said. "Sorry you have
a window."

"Does it get bright?" she asked.

"There should be a curtain," he said, "at the
end there?"

She found the curtain and pulled it closed. The
suffocating feeling was now complete. She was in a
coffin, against a window, four stories up.

"I love it," Delaney said, and crawled out as
quickly as she could.

"All the sleep monitors are already in there," he
said. "What do you average?"

"Seven hours?" she guessed, and he blanched at her vagueness. "But I haven't checked my up-dated average today," she said, correcting herself. "Yesterday it was 7.81."

"I'm at 7.94," he said. "So I guess we both have work to do. The company's been really devoted to making sure people are sleeping more—at least ten hours. That's the benchmark for max creativity. Did you smell the ylang ylang in there? It's a neuro-modulator, much better than lavender. It lowers your heart-rate and blood pressure."

"Right, right," Delaney said. "Ylang ylang. So important."

"I've gotten used to it," Soren said. "Ideally your brain starts associating ylang ylang with sleep, so when you smell it, your body will relax. What else? Oh. They say no screentime two hours before bed-time, but no one really obeys that one. The fridge, though, will lock at ten. Drinking and snacking be-fore sleep has been pretty well proven to inhibit true rest. For me that's been a godsend. I can't be around unlimited options. Speaking of which, can I get you anything?"

"I'm just a little thirsty," Delaney said, and looked for a glass.

"No glasses here," Soren said. "But the sink has a fountain."

Delaney discovered the fountain, took a drink and looked for a paper towel. She didn't bother to ask, and just wiped her mouth with the cuff of her shirt.

"Thank you," Delaney said.

"It's best to just eliminate the bad choices, right? That's why I can't deal with the city," he said, and Delaney smiled gamely. "I'm an addict. Booze, pills, porn. This place saved me. I know this will seem Spartan at first," he said, glancing around the room. "Maybe it is. But you can get anything you need here. You just can't get everything you **want.** Or anything you **think** you want. Are you a drinker?"

"Not so much," Delaney said.

His eyes closed in relief. "You're free to do anything you usually do along those lines," he said. "But obviously I don't drink. Joan and Francis don't drink here in the pod. I didn't tell them not to, but anyway, they don't. And you can't get pills. They probably told you that much, if it wasn't obvious."

"Right," Delaney said, and then thought, **Francis?** Not that Francis, dear god.

"My last vice was porn," Soren said, and Delaney wondered how that could possibly be kept from him, given its online ubiquity.

"I made sure my screens are fingerprint-activated," he said, and she could deduce the rest. His prints were linked to filters and blockers. Wherever he signed on, the filters kicked in and porn was blocked.

"I actually rigged it so HR knows if I've been

porning. It just helped to have some barriers," he said, and downed the rest of his water in one swallow. "I wasn't so bad off. I could control myself as long as it wasn't so easy to get. So . . . exercise? Are you a jogger?"

He swept his eyes over her and then, realizing his offense, pretended to be examining the entirety of the kitchen. "Water polo? Crew?" he asked. He'd noticed her shoulders.

"I jog some," she said. "I used to do some rock-climbing."

"Idaho, right? And then you were living in the city?" He said the words **in the city** with palpable suspicion. "Did I hear you lived in a trog place? What was **that** like?"

"It was terrible," Delaney said. "Chaos."

"I can imagine," he said. "My college dorms were based on EveryoneIn designs, so I didn't have to adapt much once I got here. How often were you shopping for food and stuff?"

"Almost daily," she said, and made an exhausted face.

Soren whistled. "I haven't been off-island in maybe two years. I don't know if I could survive." His half-smile implied he meant to be kidding, but wasn't sure if he was kidding.

"I'm sorry," Delaney said. "I forgot to ask what you do here."

Soren's head tilted involuntarily. "You haven't

presearched the people you're living with?" He seemed more amused than accusatory.

"Sorry," she said. "It's been moving so fast—"

"No, no," he said. "It's fine. It's just **in**teresting. New. It's been a while since I had to answer that question. What do I do here? Well, usually people know me initially as the smart-stop-sign guy."

"You invented the smart stop sign?" Delaney asked.

Soren laughed and lowered his head. "Guilty."

A smart stop sign had been installed on Delaney's rural dead-end street in Idaho and had driven her parents to distraction. There was no traffic on her street, absolutely no need for a stop sign, so they rolled through it, as did everyone else. But when a smart stop sign was installed, it forced her parents and neighbors to make a full and maddening stop every time they went to town or returned, six times a day, even though no other vehicle, ever, was competing for primacy of the intersection. After accumulating a thousand dollars in tickets the first month, Delaney's father had destroyed the stop sign in the dead of night, but it had been promptly replaced; the city had become enamored with the revenue it generated.

"My dad wanted to kill you," Delaney said. "**I** wanted to kill you. You probably got a million death threats."

Soren lifted his head, suddenly grave. "I don't

think you meant to say those things, Delaney." His voice was rehearsed, his eyes imploring. He glanced at his oval and Delaney understood. Her sentences would look sick once transcribed.

"Of course not," she said, her mind shopping for the right amendment to avoid a ding—a significant one, she expected, given the implication of murder. "I was kidding," she said, trying to sound as jocular as possible.

"I understand," he said, his eyes smiling approvingly. "Yes, people were upset at first. But the world has gotten used to them, and they've saved lives. Like seatbelts. I actually think they just get people used to respecting laws, even small ones. That's what Kant Kan was about from the start—making the enforcement of the law objective and universal, not subjective and occasional."

Delaney searched her mind. Kant Kan? She hoped Soren wouldn't mention the categorical imperative.

"People didn't want to think about the categorical imperative," he said. "So Kant Kan became KisKis—Keep it Simple."

Ah, Delaney thought. She'd heard about that one.

"I know KisKis," she said. "You did the automatic tickets for speeding, too? I got a few of those." Tickets were issued automatically, and fines deducted instantly from the drivers' bank accounts.

"That one saved 20,000 lives last year," he said. "I know it sounds so basic, but why make laws if we don't have an organized way to enforce them? And it frees cops to do more interesting work."

"Makes sense," Delaney said.

"You want something else to drink?" Soren opened the fridge, revealing two rows of drink-globes, piled and ordered like bright marbles.

"Anything," she said, and he tossed her a pink one.

"KisKis is such a non-confrontational idea," he went on. "When rules aren't universally observed, we have disorder and people die."

"So you're still with KisKis?" she asked.

"Not really. I moved over to Sunlight last year. It used to be called Brighten the Corners. Then it merged with Reach."

"Reach was the program where they bring the internet to unmet people?" Delaney asked. Immediately she regretted it. The program had been controversial and her question sounded judgmental.

"I wasn't part of the South Sentinel Island group," he said, his mouth drawn tight. "Those folks are gone and that program was discontinued." Delaney remembered now. They'd sent a team to a remote is-land in the Indian Ocean, where they'd been quickly killed by the locals, an unmet tribe, who evidently didn't want wifi.

"Right, right," Delaney said, and Soren regained his smile.

"Basically we find places in cities and countries that aren't seen, and we see them. We set up cameras and sat-views of the rural and out of-the-way places where otherwise bad stuff can happen."

"So, cameras in national parks, things like that," she said.

"Yup."

"Wonderful," Delaney said. **It was you,** she thought.

"We set up a nice array at Playa 36," he said. "Which is another good thing that came from out of your, you know, field trip. Now people can see the elephant seals without going there."

"What a cool idea," Delaney said, her organs burning.

"Every year we get closer to 100 percent saturation," he said, and hopped up to sit on the counter, where his fleshy thighs spread like an oil spill. "And my hope—and this was Stenton's thinking, too— is that the moment we have cams seeing every inch of the globe, two things happen: travel is unnecessary, and crime ends. The travel part is easy. Instead of going to Playa 36, just call up the cams we have there. Crime, though—that'll be paradigm-shifting. It won't be possible."

"Or any perpetrator is easily caught," Delaney noted.

"Right," he said. Soren had picked up an apple and was inspecting it for the ideal place to bite. "But I think, within a generation, crime won't be thought of anymore. There will be no point in attempting it.

That's why that moment of global cam saturation matters so much. I call that day final crime." He plunged into his apple with a prolonged crack.

Delaney didn't get the terminology at first. Finally she spelled it in her mind, in the Every way. He meant Final Crime. "Oh," she said. "Like the last crime."

"The world's last crime, yes," he said. "Then we move on down the line, eliminating the unknown, the unexpected. When everything is seen, nothing bad can happen."

"Stands to reason," Delaney said.

"One of the things we do now is move trogs into smarthomes," he said, and assessed her. "You know, I might ask you to do a testimonial at some point. We're doing a series, where former trogs explain the advantages of smart living. But only if you want to."

"Of course, anytime," she said, and hoped he'd forget. She pointed to the (ten? twelve?) glass silos on the kitchen counter. "So they fill all these?"

"Right. You'll meet those folks," he said, finishing his apple and dropping it in the compost bin. "All the basics are replenished daily. The grains, vegetables, fruits. Did you fill out your survey?"

"I did," Delaney said. "But most of it was in my med-eval."

"Of course," he said. "So if you have any variants to the diet they laid out, you make the request and they source it sustainably. If you want an orange, you know the orange you're getting has been sustainably farmed, the workers well-paid, the transport to campus has been done without fossil fuels. And if it's out of season, you're out of luck. You heard of **Bananaskam**?"

Delaney almost did a spit-take. "I have," she said.

"So brilliant. That guy Wes Makazian is astounding." He pointed to his kilt. "This is one of his things. The whimsy of it stimulates idea-flow. And he's why they got rid of doors. We had them until like a week ago. They stop creativity-streams."

Delaney smiled. She loved this so much. She'd been wrong to worry. It was a boon to have Wes on campus, to watch him move through the company, see how he was perceived, admired, deified.

"If you need something irregular," Soren said, "like cough medicine or flan, you can order it here, too, and they'll usually find it same day—a lot of products are already here on campus. But again, it's all been sourced properly. Just takes all the guesswork out."

"It's a relief not to have to think," Delaney noted.

Soren smiled wanly. "I mean, that's the tradeoff," he said. "We're supposed to be showing the rest of the world how it can be done. Last year our pod ended a twelve-month cycle with exactly one bag of actual landfill waste."

Soren's watch emitted a faint whistle.

"Shit," he said. "I better go." The color left

his face. "I shouldn't have said that first word. You're staying?"

Delaney remained, happy to be alone. The pod had an open floor plan, with the bed-tubes discreetly tucked into corners at the edges of the room. In the middle, the kitchen bled into the sitting room, which was dominated by a large paisley-shaped couch large enough for seven or eight adults to splay themselves. It faced a large screen, around which were a grid of shelves, where eleven or twelve books had been collected and arranged by the color of their spines. Otherwise, the pod was devoid of objects or clutter. Delaney got a few minutes of churning in, sending smiles to a Thai nurse who sang "Over the Rainbow" to a dying patient, and a sham to a Peruvian parent who had allowed his daughter to walk in the rain unjacketed. In the bathroom, she used the mirror to take a Popeye and sent smiles to the Popeyes of three dozen others. Her father was using Concensus and needed help deciding on a brand of butter. She added her vote to the majority—vegan, organic, unsalted—and put her phone down.

The bathroom was large and airy, dominated by a sunken expanse of poured concrete stained a Mediterranean blue, candles lining the rim. She didn't know when she'd be alone again, so she slid the frosted glass door closed. Her phone dinged. She'd gotten a Personal Encounter Satisfaction

Survey from Soren. She pressed **remind me later** and undressed.

The shower head, directly above the sunken tub, emitted a most perfect rain, heated just so. The sun was bright through the skylight overhead, and Delaney lathered a faintly fragrant handful of soap until she was immersed in an intoxicating mist of steam and jasmine. No shower she'd ever taken was so soothing, but after two minutes, a polite ding sounded from somewhere beyond the walls, and the flow of water slowed until, a few seconds later, it ended. She hadn't touched a knob. The steam evaporated and she was left standing in the sunken shower, looking for a towel, when a shape appeared in the frosted glass.

"That you, Delaney?"

"Joan? I'm in here. Does the shower turn off automatically or . . . ?"

"Two minutes, yup," she said. "Are you still sudsy?"

"I'm fine. I just didn't know. I'm getting out now," Delaney said, hoping Joan would realize the awkwardness of their proximity, and exit the bathroom. She sensed no such movement, though, so she looked in the tub area for a towel, or a perfect arrangement of sumptuous towels, and found none.

"Are the towels here or . . . ?" Delaney asked.

"I'm getting the impression someone didn't read their EveryoneIn contract carefully . . ."

"It was a hundred and ten pages long," Delaney said. "I might have drifted." She began to shiver. "So towels?"

"Step out," Joan said. "I'll explain."

Delaney stepped out, covering herself with her beaded arms, feeling slightly warmer as she stood closer to the skylight. Joan had politely turned away.

"We do something here," Joan said, "called meditative air-dry. Look up."

Delaney looked up to the skylight as its glass slid open, allowing air to flow in.

"I don't know the physics," Joan said, "but these are positioned in such a way to capture the wind off the Bay and lead it inside. It's why you don't need towels. Breathe. Breathe slower. You're almost dry."

Delaney did her best to regain control of her body.

"Obviously," Joan continued, "I don't have to mention the billions of gallons of water that go into making and washing towels. Think of the insanity. You get into the shower, where you get clean. You step out and you have a bit of water on you. You use a towel, fine. Then you wash the towel? You just cleaned yourself, so how is it that a towel gets so dirty drying clean water off you?"

"I'm still cold," Delaney said.

"It's good to be cold!" Joan said. "That's the other thing. Think about cold-water swims, ice baths, the polar-bear club. The health benefits are undeniable.

Here you're drying under the sun, helped by a gentle breeze. If you surrender to it mindfully, it's really lovely. Just close your eyes."

Delaney closed her eyes. She was almost dry now. Her shivering had slowed. Her skin tingled. But she was still naked before Joan Pham, which seemed too odd, too soon.

"We call it madding," Joan said.

Dear Baby Jesus, Delaney thought.

"How good does it feel to do without?" Joan asked, "to eliminate something from your life?"

"Podmate arrived!" a man's voice said.

"We're in here," Joan said, stepping into the space where a door had recently been. "Francis," she said to Delaney. "He's the other roommate. Stay out there," she said to him.

Delaney's skin went cold again. It couldn't be the same Francis. But when she was dressed again she found him in the kitchen. It was that Francis. She would be living with him. At the moment, he was glancing, with extreme caution, at Joan's ass as she bent over, her bodysuit shiny with exertion. When he sensed Delaney's presence, he turned to her, unabashed.

"You! We meet again," he said. "Now I can get you to finish that survey I keep sending." His tone attempted good cheer but was laced with grievance.

Delaney had already committed. She'd signed all the contracts and NDAs. She couldn't leave.

"What survey?" Joan asked. She walked past him, en route to a low kitchen cabinet full of dried fruit. Her body language indicated comfort with him, trust, even respect.

"Initial meeting questions, basic," he said. "Never got an answer."

Joan walked toward Delaney, rolling her eyes.

"Was it lack of time?" he asked. "If so, there are myriad tools to help with that. Tools that were made to prevent anyone feeling slighted."

"Maybe I'll start using them," Delaney said. She looked around the pod for something she could claim she was allergic to. She had to leave. She could not live with this man.

"Maybe, maybe," he said. "You're a puzzle, you know that?"

"Okay, Francis," Joan said.

He smiled meanly at Delaney, then softly at Joan. "It's just that much of my work at PrefCom is about the elimination of maybes."

"Of course it is," Joan said, and patted him gently on the cheek.

When Soren returned, just before ten, Francis called a pod meeting, at which the topic of pod aggregates and quotas would be covered.

"Given we have a new podmate," he said, nodding to Delaney, "and given there are some new numbers the Havel as a whole is shooting for, we should go over expectations. I'll make it brief, given the best practices say six to eight minutes is ideal for meetings like this."

Joan was smirking at him. He stared at her, through her, and continued.

"So quotas. Delaney, this was in your onboarding but just to refresh: the Every goals begin here, in the pods. The podmates' data is collected and aggregrated. If we hit our numbers, that's good for the whole floor, which is averaged together. Then the floors are averaged into the building as a whole. If we do well, the floor does well, the Havel does well, the Every does well."

Now Joan was fake-yawning. Francis pursed his mouth but otherwise did not react.

"First, laughing. The updated research says 34 to 36 minutes is ideal. That means each person should be shooting for that, individually. It's not cumulative. We've been slagging here, with . . ."—he flicked at his tablet—"Soren at 12 minutes, Joan at 14 and me at 21.5. So let's enjoy ourselves a little bit more, okay?" He looked at the group with a frozen smile and sour eyes.

"Next, consumption and waste. We're doing fine here but could be better. We've consumed 82 percent of the food delivered, with 16 percent rollover and 2 percent waste. That's high for the floor and in the upper 7 percentile for the dorm. So kudos. But we can always improve." A ding came from his oval. "Okay. We're almost out of time. You can look at the majority of the quotas on your own but I did want to mention the most important one, which of course is sleep."

Joan yawned again, this time for real.

"As you know," Francis continued, "the company's taking sleep seriously, as they should. The Everywhere goal, as per Wes Makazian, is at least 10 hours per person. And recent studies say that group dynamics are a big factor. Some pods have very low aggs, and they're attributing that to, for example, one or two podmates staying up late, or being noisy in the morning, that kind of thing. So the hope is that the pods self-police a bit, work together to make it a conducive environment for measurable rest and creative minds. Are we in agreement?"

He looked at Soren, who shrugged, and then Joan, whose eyes were filled with mirth but hinted at something else, too.

"We have some of Wes's helping tools coming—shrouds and a firepit—but until then, we'll make do. Keep your ovals on so the system knows when you've hit REM. You can't get into the tube and scroll for two hours. Everyone good with that?" His oval dinged again. "Okay, that's nine o'clock. We should get to bed. Ideally you're asleep in twelve, thirteen minutes. If we all hit that, we're good. If not, penalties will ensue." He looked meaningfully at each of his roommates, saving a bit of extra eye-menace for Delaney. Finally he bowed and slunk to his own bed-tube. "I wish you all a restful and rejuvenating sleep," he said, and ducked inside.

Delaney crawled into hers.

"Are you ready to sleep?" a voice asked. It sounded like Judi Dench.

"Yes," Delaney said.

"Excellent," the voice said. It **was** Judi Dench. It was a repro, but a good one. "You have forty-four unanswered messages. Would you like to take care of those now through dictation? Many people find it easier to rest when they know there are no loose threads or unfinished work." Her tone was warm but with an acid fringe.

"No thank you," Delaney said. She was wide awake now, fascinated by this voice and what it might say next.

"I'll dim the lights now," Judi said. "Can I play a soothing selection from your musical preferences?"

"Yes please," Delaney said. A Chopin sonata began. Delaney hadn't heard it in years, but the algorithm had easily found it on her playlist.

"The music will fade over the next eight minutes," Judi said. "A slight increase in ylang ylang is being added to the air."

Delaney lay flat in her bed, waiting for Judi's next utterance.

"Your preferences indicate you're a side-sleeper,"

Judi said. "Would you prefer to turn to one side now?"

Delaney smiled. "Thank you so much," she said, and turned to her side. She closed her eyes but found they were rattling. She opened them, turned over to the other side.

"Should we increase the ylang ylang level?" Judi asked.

"No thank you," Delaney said. "Silence for a few minutes, please."

"I think I heard you say, 'Silence for a few minutes.' Is that correct?" Judi asked.

"That's correct. Please be quiet."

Judi was quiet. Delaney thought of Wes. Outside a few days here and there, she hadn't slept away from him in almost two years. She didn't need his I love yous, no, but wasn't there an animal comfort in knowing he was breathing on the other side of their paperthin wall? The Chopin was halfway finished, and she knew Judi would appear again when it ended. But she couldn't slow her mind down. She saw Athena, the dead sheep. She saw Syl and his smarmy grievance. She saw herself as Athena, being struck by an Every bus, hurtling down the embankment. Stop, she hissed to herself. Stop.

"Excuse me?" Judi said.

"Please be silent," Delaney said, and was sure she heard from Judi the faintest, frustrated, huff.

"Would you prefer another voice?" Judi asked.

Delaney said nothing. She was at once exhausted

and fascinated at who might come next. Somehow she expected Jared Leto. Before she could answer, a new voice emerged.

"Hello Del."

It was Delaney's mother. Delaney gripped the bedsheet.

"Are you comfortable, sweetie?"

Good Christ, Delaney thought. She tried to discern whether these were her mother's actual recorded phrases, or an assemblage taken from their smart speaker.

"Is there anything I can do to make you feel more comfortable?" the voice asked. Now it was clear that these phrases were pasted together, word by word. This last one sounded awkward, with odd pauses—the product of a computer pasting together stolen sounds.

"Please bring back Judi," Delaney said. She surprised herself, preferring the obviously fake reproduction of a distant celebrity to an algo-pastiche of her own mother.

"Here I am," Judi said. She seemed quite satisfied, her tone implying a gently annoyed **Told you so.**

"Good night," Delaney said.

"Good night," Judi said, and the Chopin returned.

Delaney thought of peaks. For years she'd done this when she couldn't sleep. It was a task just mundane enough to occupy the mind, to crowd out unwanted thoughts. She started with Idaho's, in descending order, tallest first. Borah Peak, she thought, and pictured its snowy cap. Leatherman Peak. Her mind slowed, shrinking from a frantic, thousand-tentacled monster into a simple doe, in a field, chewing fresh wildflowers, thinking of mountains.

Mount Church.

Diamond Peak.

Mount Breitenbach.

Lost River Peak.

The eight minutes of Chopin ran out and Delaney braced herself.

"Sleep should usually come within twelve minutes," Judi said. "It's recommended now that you get up, walk around, or perhaps I could read you some content. Would you like to continue reading **Middlemarch**? I believe you left off on page 177."

"No thanks," Delaney said, and turned over again to face the window. Through a crack in the drapes she could see, below, what appeared to be a vole. There was a small island of ivy on the lawn below, and the vole would scamper a few feet onto the lawn, and then return to the ivy. She watched the vole come and go, terrified to be out of its ivy for more than a second or more. She watched the ivy island closely, but the vole stopped appearing, so she closed her eyes, and conjured a picture of the vole's home hollow, rich with vole-smell, so warm and—

"My sensors say you're not asleep," Judi said, now louder than before. "It's recommended that you get up, perhaps walk around for a few minutes. This helps you to avoid overthinking your sleep. When a person spends too long in bed trying to sleep, it can make it difficult to actually sleep."

Delaney had a revelation. Could it be that Judi Dench was sending people to their deaths? Was this sleep tube and this tremulous voice part of an experiment to see what would drive a human to self-annihilation? Could she survive this, or would she wake up in Valhalla?

"I'm fine," Delaney said. "You can turn yourself off."

"I think I heard you say turn myself off. Is that correct?"

"That's correct. Please turn yourself off and remain off."

"Understood," Judi said, and went quiet.

Donaldson Peak, Delaney thought. She'd summited that one.

Hyndman Peak. Hadn't seen it from the highway.

USGS Peak. Didn't know what that was.

No Regret Peak.

Ha. A real place, a beautiful place. She'd been there once. She sat atop it near sunset, and watched a shaft of godlight sweep the valley, slowly, so slowly, touching every creature and thing, one by one, caressing rocks and wildflowers and mice and moose with a melancholy golden touch. Delaney had been alone at the time, not a soul for miles, and was sure she was the only human who had witnessed the sight. It happened, a moment so beautiful it burst the heart, and only she had any record of it.

XXVII.

DELANEY WOKE to a series of texts from Wes.
Did you hear? Did you know?
Where will he go?
Let's meet to talk.
I'm dying.
Delaney had heard rumblings and now it was
done. In the wake of her Welcome2Me and the
Death of Athena—the incident was now a proper
noun—a vocal group of Everyones had begun questioning the rightness of pets on campus and the
idea of pets in general. **Problematic** was the first
word agreed upon. This led to **unacceptable** and
barbaric and finally **prohibited.** A digital poster
was circulated showing a cat behind bars, the words
LIBERATION! below, rendered Soviet-style, and from
there, the momentum was impossible to reverse.
For a second, the emotional-support animal cau-
cus put up a fight, but support animals were seen
as another example of animal subjugation and they

were quickly shamed into silence. The word **pet**
would soon be banned and the animals' former
owners ostracized.

In her tube, Delaney tapped on her phone and
found the notice.

"Everyones will be given a Workweek to remove
their animal captives from campus. Thank you for
your Cooperation!"

I'm so sorry, she texted back. **Talk later.
Solutions will ensue.**

But she had no idea what the solution might be.
There was no chance at an exception; the righteousness of the anti-pet movement was at an apex and in
the heat of revolution, purity was all and no exceptions could be made. With nowhere to go, the vast
majority of these animals would be brought to shelters, where most would eventually be euthanized.
Hurricane was lucky to have an alternate home;
he could stay with the moms, though they did not
much like dogs.

"I notice you're up," Judi said. "You have slept
6.3 hours. Would you consider returning to bed for
more rest?"

"No thanks," Delaney said.

Wes had never been separated from Hurricane.
Unstated in his text was that she was ultimately
the source of this pet ban. Her trip to the elephant
seals had triggered a wholesale separation between
humans and animal-kind. This, she realized, was
the idea underpinning many of its recent rules:

separation between Everywhere and Nowhere, separation between travelers and nations, between states, cities, groups, species—all of it lessened the chance at harm, the perception of harm, the possibility of momentary discomfort.

They banned meat, too, Wes wrote. Seconds later, he wrote again. **All pet videos have been removed, too.**

Delaney checked, and saw that this was true. She couldn't find any videos of pets doing adorable things anywhere on the Every's platforms. No pets in human clothing, no pets forming unlikely friendships with unexpected species, no pets saving their owners from catastrophes. The videos were gone, the word "owner" was banned, the word "pet" allowed only when referring to romantic contexts—and even then, not advised. Delaney checked the video of the murder of the Widower's wife; it was still there. She checked the video of Bailey's death: still there. All the murders and suicides were left up, but the pet-videos were gone and would stay gone.

Hurricane will be fine, she texted, not believing it.

"Let's go!" Joan said. She was in the doorway while Delaney was still tying her shoes. Joan, too, now knew about Delaney's slow shoe-tying, and she was determined to introduce her to new footwear.

This was one of many goals Joan had for Delaney

at Are You Sure. She had arranged Delaney's next rotation to be there—they'd recently removed the question mark, to imply the service offered both question and answer—and Joan was sure Delaney would remain there indefinitely. Delaney, for her part, was looking forward to an atmosphere of relative calm and liberation. Joan had somehow inured herself to the vast majority of constraints that bound Everyone else, and Delaney assumed her department would be a haven of comparative freedom.

"It's the fastest-growing division on campus, outside of PrefCom," Joan said, leading her out of the Havel and into the sunlight. "And you'd hate those people. I didn't just say hate," she said, pointing to her ear. She mouthed the words "call" and thereafter, as Joan led her across the Daisy and through the bamboo forest, Delaney trailed her in silence.

Delaney had heard of Joan's work before she'd come to the Every. She'd started a site, considered frivolous by some and visionary by others, called Supple, which curated a high-end fashion and wellness lifestyle so economically out of reach for most of humanity that it would be dismissable were it not so earth-friendly and weirdly prophetic. Supple favored well-made, well-sourced products that, Joan and her co-founders asserted, "cost what they should cost." They knew it would take some time to convince a global consumer base accustomed to paying $18 for a shirt that, for a shirt to be environmentally sustainable, its sourcing ethical and its workers fairly paid, it should cost at least $80. But they also knew these consumers would pay extra for environmental assurance, as it came to be known, and did not want to make every last decision.

Supple, with a staff of eight, had vetted and celebrated products, mostly clothing and décor, and sold them through its site, taking a percentage. By the time Every acquired the company, Supple had revenues of $67 million a year. Weeks after buying Supple, Mae Holland also bought Fewer Better Things, another tastemaking site dedicated to ending disposable fashion. The two teams were combined at the Every and were recast as Are You Sure?—AYS—soon known as the company's conscience of consumption.

Delaney had been getting AYS alerts for the last eighteen months or so; everyone she knew got them. She'd choose a pair of shoes on the Every commerce portal, and the trademark AYS sunburst would appear. **Are you sure?** The consumer would be invited to look at AYS's better-sourced choices, and though these alternatives were always more expensive, they were also better designed, sturdier and far more environmentally responsible. If a consumer made the AYS choice, rewards followed. If a consumer agreed to an AYS membership, discounts would ensue. There were consumers who had come to trust AYS implicitly, and let Joan and her team do all the vetting for them; if that buyer stayed 90 percent within AYS's purchasing suggestions, the discounts they received, cumulatively, erased the overall difference between the AYS goods and those unapproved.

"Ready?" Joan said.

Delaney pretended she was nervous. "I think so," she said.

They arrived at what looked like a cross between a treefort and a Fabergé egg on stilts. The main floor was fourteen feet above land. Below, under the dome, on the grass, there was a pile of discarded products—handbags, mittens, pants, a toaster, a chair. The objects looked like they'd been dropped from one of the dome's triangular windows.

"You'll like everyone," Joan said. "They might say something about this"—she swept her hand over Delaney's clothing—"but that's only because they can't help it."

Delaney had taken great care choosing her outfit—recycled cotton jeans she'd bought through Supple, vintage shirt and ballet flats. Joan had seen her before they left the pod and had said nothing. Now Delaney wanted to go home and change.

"Up here," Joan said. A spiral staircase led up to a second-story open-plan workspace, a hive of feverish movement.

"Told you!" someone said. A willowy woman in a faux-fur pantsuit wafted by, bathed in clerestory light and smelling of lilies. She smiled at Delaney, pointed to her earbud and rolled her eyes.

"That's Helen," Joan said. "Supply chain."

Delaney looked up to see the words **Limitless**

Choice is Killing the World laser-cut from plywood, hanging from the ceiling. Opposite that was another maxim, this one in neon: **Your Whims = Their Suffering.** In silver letters stenciled onto a skylight were the words REMEMBER THE FIVE Cs!

"This is an official rotation," Joan noted loudly to the room, "so she needs the full introduction to all of you and all we do."

"Delaney? Berit." The speaker was over six feet tall, blond and holding an enormous staff. "It's a kind of walking stick, they say. You like it?" She held out the staff doubtfully.

"It's wonderful," Delaney said.

"You don't mean that," Berit said, and dropped it out the window.

"This is Ro," Joan said, and Delaney turned to find a woman in an ivory catsuit, her black braids dyed blue—phosphorescent streams racing down her shoulders.

"Those are like yours, Joan, but synthetic," she said, pointing to Delaney's pants. "Last fall, right? Hi Delaney. Welcome. Actually, can you smell this?"

Ro produced a small vial and sprayed a tiny mist onto Delaney's wrist. Delaney smelled it, recognizing the same smell she'd caught trailing Helen. More lilies.

"It's lovely," Delaney said.

"Lovely," Ro said, nodding, amused. "What about this?" she sprayed another cloud into the air. "From Cairo."

It smelled faintly of cardamom. "I like it," Delaney said.

This was not enough for Ro. She tossed it out the window, and with it, the dreams of whatever Egyptian entrepreneurs had created it.

There were twelve members of the AYS team, as far as Delaney could tell, and even if they hadn't been at Supple, they called themselves Supples. Everyone's name was offered in a dizzying lightning round; Delaney struggled to remember four. Preeti was about thirty, short and curvy, with an undulating mass of rippling black hair. Saba was pink and freckled, her eyes green and bright, her lips thin and her teeth tiny.

To the last person, all women or non-binary, the AYS staff was the most effortlessly glamorous and magnetic group of people Delaney had ever been among. They were strenuously individualistic, their style personal and seemingly indifferent to trend. There was linen, bright cottons and the occasional feathered embroidery, a good deal of hemp, and a surprising amount of corduroy. There was no leather, no pleather, nothing synthetic.

"Come," Saba said, and took Delaney's wrist. In the center of the room there was a tall round table, messy with dozens of products, from pants to hats to juicers and a leaning tower of snow-white pillows. Ro handed her a pair of sunglasses. "You like?"

They were flimsy to hold and stylistically bland; Delaney assumed it was a trick question.

"Not so much," Delaney said.

"Dammit," Saba said. "They're made of corn. But they're ugly, right? I know they're ugly. But I want to like them. Sunglasses made from corn, could be good, right?"

"We have to clear this table, people," Helen said.

"This is just the stuff that arrived today," Joan noted. "And after it's been vetted by the advance team."

"There are others?" Delaney asked.

"Oh, this isn't the whole group!" Joan said. "Lord no. How many screeners are there now?"

"Eleven hundred," Preeti said.

"This is just the leadership," Joan said. "I thought you knew that. When things get to us, they've already gone through at least six rounds of vetting globally. Wait, we should get Delaney's take on the espadrilles. Helen, show her."

Helen overturned a canvas bag and a half-dozen pairs of espadrilles tumbled out onto the tiled floor. Delaney saw that most of the tiles bore slogans. SPONTANEITY KILLS KOALAS said one.

"We have to pick one of these espadrilles today," Helen said. "I wanted the ones from Barcelona. They still make them by hand there, but they can only do a hundred a day. We need scale. Del? Are you Del or Laney or what?"

"Del is fine."

"So?" Joan asked.

Delaney had no opinion. She'd never
worn espadrilles.

"The clothing industry is responsible for ten, fif-
teen percent of global greenhouse gases," Joan said.
"That's more than air travel and shipping combined.
And that's mostly during manufacturing."

"I'm going with this one," Helen said, and walked
away with one of the espadrille samples. That decision, Delaney realized, would forever change
the lives of everyone at whatever company manufactured them—and would likely doom half of
its competitors.

"Worse is the overproduction," Joan added.

"Millions of garments are made that are never
sold," Ro said. "And the high-fashion brands won't
discount their unsold stuff, much less give it away."

"Gucci doesn't want a homeless person wearing
one of their jackets," Berit said. "Or shitting into one
of their bags."

Delaney was struck by the coarseness of the
language, a kind of candor she hadn't heard at the
Every. But as Joan promised, the Supples seemed
to exist on a different plane, not subject to the
same constraints as anyone else. She hadn't seen
any cameras.

"The real problem is overproduction," Joan said.

"The real problem is the traditional retail model,"
Preeti said. "Every part of it is an environmental af-
front. First, you build these monstrosities, malls.

Then you ship goods to them from all over the world at untold ecological cost. Then you display the goods for a month, hoping they'll sell. Half of the stuff doesn't, and you either ship it back or burn it. It's an absolute travesty."

"Zhay were zhooing zha best zhay could," Ro said. She was testing a teeth-whitening mouthpiece. She took it out. "They were doing the best they could. Before the certainty we have now."

"Now, something's only shipped when it's ordered," Joan said. "One shirt, one buyer, no mystery, no waste. That's why retail must end. People act like brick-and-mortar stores are inherently good, when they're the root of the problem. Just about everything about them creates and perpetuates waste. We throw away 100 billion tons of stuff each year in this country alone. Carbon dioxides are at a three-million-year high."

"The next step is controlling production," Ro said.

"Even with a direct-to-consumer model, manufacturers are still making more than they can know they can sell," Preeti noted.

"Traditionally, they would get orders from stores," the woman Delaney took to be Gemma said. "A store in Bozeman would say, 'Give me twelve of those shirts.' A thousand stores would do the same thing, and the maker would know approximately how many to make."

"They could still return them, though," Joan said.

"Right," probably-Gemma said.

"So the challenge is to pinpoint demand with greater accuracy, so there's less waste," Preeti said.

Delaney waited for someone to say that the Every was in a prime position to do this. Helen reappeared.

"Obviously," she said, "the Every is in a prime position to do that."

For the next ninety minutes Delaney was passed around the room, told to watch over a shoulder, asked to come see this, sent over there to visit with Berit and then back to watch the presentation just finished by Preeti or Ro. At eleven, half the staff broke for a snack at a high table. They stood, sharing from a buffet that Delaney had seen brought in and set up by a trio of men in yellow jumpsuits. Again there were no plates. Delaney ate a scone and fennel salad while Berit examined her shirt.

"Synthetic," Berit declared. "Why?"

Delaney was ready. "It's vintage," she said, and thought that would be the end of it. Somehow she'd assumed that re-using old things was preferable to just about anything else—certainly better than the making of new things. **Extant is exlent,** she'd been taught in high school.

Berit looked to Joan for permission. Joan shrugged.

"Your shirt is shedding," Berit said. "Not because it's old, but because it's inevitable. Micro-fibers are coming off it all the time. As you walk, when you move your arms. Definitely when you wash it. And every one of those microfibers ends up in the water supply. That's why people passively consume so much plastic."

Delaney had no words.

"Basically," Berit said, pulling at a stray yellow hair, "at some point, we're drinking your shirt."

"Thank you," Delaney said, and was instantly embarrassed. How did she not know this? And then the simplicity of AYS became fully clear. To avoid social embarrassment, to avoid complicity in the decline of the world, all she had to do was choose their chosen products. **Tell me what to buy. Tell me how to do no harm.**

"I liked regular shopping as much as anyone," said another woman. Mansa? She seemed very young, a heart-faced high schooler in four-inch cork heels. "You'd go to a mall and touch a hundred blouses and you'd have no idea where any of them came from, the materials-sourcing, how the workers were treated."

"Once we were able to give a product our imprimatur, sales of that product skyrocketed." **Was** that Gemma?

"Stratospheric," said Berit, eating a peach.

"That's why we can't be seen here," Ro said. "The stock market was watching our meetings, and things would rollercoaster all day. The SEC actually got involved. So now we're unseen."

"At least in this space."

"Anyway, an endorsement is obviously good for the manufacturer," Ro said, taking a peach for herself. "It rewards good corporate behavior. At this point they're trying to outdo themselves to please us."

"Then other companies in the marketplace emulate those methods," said possibly-Gemma. "Once they felt ready, they would invite one of our reps out for an inspection. If we were able to endorse that new entrant, we saw that as a net positive for the world."

"Another conversion," Helen said. "Fifth C."

Delaney had somehow missed the first four Cs. One had to be Curation. What else? Caution? Consumption?

"But it only works," Joan noted, "if we have a large enough consumer base. That way, if they migrate to or from a product or manufacturer, it has real impact. That's where the subscriptions came in. It's a commitment to buy from these companies we've vetted. Essentially, AYS is a pair of hands saying 'Whoa. Whoa. Hold up. Do you really want to buy that cheap plastic toy for Siena, your beloved baby daughter? It's full of toxins and unsustainable polymers, and will be in a landfill by the end of the month.'"

"You have to give up a bit of choice for the sake of the planet," said Berit. "You probably saw that sentiment above. Though phrased in slightly stronger language."

"Oh God, have you seen this?" Preeti said. The Supples gathered around and started talking about something called Friendy. Preeti's cousin in Mumbai said it was everywhere. In a week it had amassed 41 million users there.

"Put it on the screen," Joan said. "I don't want to huddle around your little phone."

Delaney looked up to the central office screen. An app came to life, revealing a face in a frame. "That's my cousin Urmila," Preeti said. Delaney did not breathe. It was AuthentiFriend. Everything was the same, but far more developed, and now it was called Friendy.

"Terrible name," Joan said. "I hate it already."

"No," Preeti said. "It's like a lie detector test. It tells you if someone's honest, candid. You know dogs can sense cancer? This senses any untruth. Anything hidden, withheld. Is the word guile?"

"It can sense guile? That is fucking **dark,**" Joan said.

"What's the big number in the corner?" Helen asked. In the upper right of the screen, above Urmila's face, a number—88—was pulsing.

"That's overall quality of friendship," Preeti said. "You know the stats about friendship. You live longer and healthier if you have quality friend-ships. That's why the slogan." She pointed to the screen's upper left corner, where the words "Who are your **real** friends?" were written in a sharp and accusatory font.

"It's about quality, not quantity," Preeti said. "We're always worried about the **number** of friends we have, when we should be assessing the **quality** of those friendships."

She really thought she was explaining it in a helpful way.

"This is sulfurous," Joan said, and Delaney loved her for it.

"It's just for fun," Preeti said.

"That is some diabolical fun," Joan said.

Her opinion was in the minority. The other Supples were trying to decide on someone they could call—a test subject. Berit had a college friend she thought would be appropriate. Minutes later, a dark-haired woman named Anita appeared on the Supples' main screen. She was in Uppsala, Sweden.

"Hi Anita!" Berit said. She had positioned herself across the room, in a quiet corner. To Anita, Berit would seem to be alone, talking to her on a tablet. But all of the Supples were watching Anita on the large screen.

"How are you?" Berit asked.

Anita's answer, "Good!" was deemed untruthful.

"Are you sure?" Berit asked.

"Yes. Why?" Anita asked.

Friendy's red lights were pulsing—lack of candor, guardedness. The Supples, silent and huddled out of view, were having a ball.

"I've always meant to ask you," Berit said, "when we were in college, you went to the Stockholm

archipelago one summer with a bunch of
people. Remember?"

"Of course," Anita said. She seemed distracted.
There was a gardener in the backyard, and a cat that
periodically tapped across her keyboard. "Why?"

"My boyfriend at the time went with you," Berit
said. "Remember Per?"

Delaney's brain was on fire. A moment ago Berit
had seemed confident and kind, and now, with this
weaselly tool, she'd become a weasel.

"I do," Anita said uncertainly.

"You always seemed to have a thing for Per, am I
right?" Berit asked.

"I wouldn't say it was a **thing,**" Anita said. "Berit,
why are you bringing this up now? It was eight years
ago. I haven't seen Per since that summer. Isn't he
in Toronto?"

"I just always had a feeling something happened
between you two on that trip. And remember I
couldn't go. My brother was dying."

"Yes, I know. I've always been sorry you couldn't
be with us," Anita said, her voice quavering and
eyes growing wet. Friendy's sensors were going wild.
"Nothing happened between us."

A green light pulsed. This was truthful. The
Supples were impressed. Berit pressed on.

"Just tell me," she said. "You were attracted to
him, yes?"

"Oh Berit," Anita said. "When are you coming

home next? Maybe we can talk then. I don't
like this."

Overall Anita's truthfulness score was in the
low 20s.

"Never mind," Berit said. "I got the answers
I needed."

And she ended the connection. She returned to
the group of Supples, accepting their condolences
and smiling grimly at their many cursings of Anita
and all like Anita.

"This is a good friend of yours?" Preeti asked Berit.

"Since we were six," Berit said.

"Berit!" Joan snapped. "Have you regressed to
thirteen years old? You can't take this seriously. It's a
fucking app that some nerds here developed."

Berit laughed. "I know. I know it's silly. I'll call
her again some other time and get a read on things."

Ro comforted her. "Give her a few more chances.
Average them together." Her eyes were soft and
magnanimous, almost saintly. "She deserves
that—an aggregate score."

As Friendy caught fire in the next days, Delaney
waited for the outrage. It did not come. Friendy
burned through South Asia in a week and then
went east and north. In Japan and South Korea, it
was the most downloaded app in a decade. Delaney
planned to check in with Wes, to see what he knew
of an American rollout, but before she could, it was

everywhere. There had been no announcement, no fanfare. It was simply on everyone's phone and then the topic of half of all conversations. Friends used it on friends, and when all friends became wise to its ubiquity, they used it on relatives. A billion lies, small and large, were told and were caught, and a remorseless wave of sorrow and suspicion swept over humanity. It was far worse than Delaney had imagined.

And yet no one blamed the Every. The company had done a brilliant job of concealing their role in its rollout, wanting to first see how it played out before taking credit. A smattering of family-welfare associations issued admonitions and a handful of psychologists and pundits explained the problems with friends and family subjecting each other to data-driven analyses of sincerity, but in short order, the app was instantly as acceptable and common a tool of measurement as the thermometer or yard-stick. Because, humanity said in one unified voice, a person has a right to know if they're being lied to, and who in their midst was a true friend.

XXVIII.

DELANEY COULDN'T UNDERSTAND it. She passed weeks boggled and benumbed. She sleepwalked through her time at AYS, hearing the vaulting praise attached to Holstein, who had managed to seize credit for Friendy, though she did, once or twice, mention Wes's valuable contributions. On a sunny Saturday, Delaney got a text from Wes: "Come see the moms. We're meeting at El Toro."

She took the BART to the Mission District, and when she arrived at 16th Street, she found Wes standing at the top of the escalator. This interception, and his large floppy sunhat, made clear that the meeting of the moms, had been a ruse. He smiled, greeted her blandly, and gave her a sunhat, too. Hers was covered in tiny anchors. The Mission's camera density was middle-range, but Delaney understood Wes's facial-rec protections. She followed him silently and soon realized he was taking her to TrogTown.

TrogTown was only sixteen square blocks, but it was a radical throwback to what cities had once been, or perhaps never were. Delaney had no point of reference, really. She'd arrived in California only a few years earlier, but this, to her, was some semblance of a mythical urban past. At the outer fence, blocking a narrow alley, they met an elderly trog volunteer in a white vest. Without a word, Delaney and Wes dismantled their phones and handed them over. The volunteer bagged and locked them in one of a grid of small lockers.

"Welcome," the volunteer said, finally smiling. "I'm Jackie. Do you two need any directions or help?" She offered a crudely printed brochure with a map included on one side.

"Post office?" Wes asked, and Jackie provided guidance to 16th and Bryant, the city's only post office located in a trog zone. They made their way through the alley until it opened up to a sensory riot. The stench hit them in seconds—a melange of hot garbage, urine, feces, spices, barbecue, human sweat, cigarettes. The streets were crowded with a chaotic mix of hippie holdouts, anarchists, apostates and eccentrics—and thousands who simply couldn't afford to live anywhere else. Half the buildings in TrogTown had been converted to SROs, and makeshift homes had been carved out of vestibules, garages and rooftop pigeon coops. Disorganized density abounded. A stray dog rushed past them, then turned briefly, as if to assess the likelihood they might feed him. Delaney stepped over a woman's sidewalk display of old paperback books, batik handicrafts and glitter art.

"Trade for the hat?" the woman said, and Delaney declined.

"Satay! Satay!" a hairless man yelled, holding chicken skewers out in an unwittingly threatening manner. The tiny wooden spears were the first sharp objects Delaney had seen in months.

"Sorry for the cloak and dagger. Here," Wes said, handing her one of Agarwal's distinctive envelopes. Delaney folded it and put it in her pocket. "You have to get a post office box," Wes said. "We'll forward your mail there. It feels unwise to get your mail at the Shed."

They watched a man of about thirty speed by on a bicycle, without a helmet, riding no-handed. With his black hair flowing behind him, he looked like the freest human on Earth.

"Sorry about Friendy," Wes said. "I thought that would have been a turning point. Not just a cliff, but an abyss."

Delaney could barely hear him. An street orchestra was playing "Rhapsody in Blue." It was good, very good, and no one was recording it. No phones. Delaney had a reflexive moment of panic, knowing that something was happening that would not be captured, would be heard only by the few dozen people within earshot—and lost forever.

"Del!" yelled Wes. He was halfway up the block. She caught up.

"Maybe we can market it to kids," Delaney said. "That's the only way to get it regulated. Tweak it so kids use it on their parents."

"You don't understand," Wes said. "Half the Friendy users **are** kids. Mostly girls. The parents just shrug as the girls go at each other with a new level of ferocity. It's so terrible, Delaney. And the divorces! You can't get an accurate number, but it's got to be thousands. In **weeks.** In a year it'll be the main hiring tool for most companies. There are already apps that promise to improve your Friendy scores. Therapists who say they can make you more trustworthy. A plastic surgeon in Dallas is claiming he can make your face Friendy-proof. Something he calls facial dulling."

Delaney and Wes walked around a ladder. From the top rung, a man in a puffy jacket was examining the eave of an old warehouse. Something caught his attention, and he pulled out a telescoping tool and jabbed it upward. A tiny SeeChange cam fell free and crashed on the sidewalk. He climbed down the ladder, crushed it underfoot and picked up the pieces. He held out a shard to Delaney.

"Souvenir?" he asked.

She declined, and they walked on. They passed a row of apartments carved from warehouses, thumping basslines coming through bootleg windows.

From somewhere above, a rooftop squat maybe, they could hear a screaming argument between middle-aged lovers. A man walked by on stilts, smoking a blunt and cackling. A pair of junkies emerged suddenly from an alley, scared by the barking of a desperate labrador. In the distance, someone was setting off firecrackers. But amid all the clatter of TrogTown, one sound was not heard, not yet by Delaney and Wes at least—the sound of children. The law prohibited them from living in trog homes. It was assumed by all that they were here, that hundreds lived in TrogTown, but today they were invisible.

"How about," Delaney said, "Friendy can read your friends' texts and find all the times they mention you. That would be so—"

"Already done," Wes said. "You have to understand, they have the best people on the planet working on it. And the AI is fine-tuning itself every hour. It grabs every available piece of information. Body language in videos, photos. It sees things you can't even personally control. You can't train yourself like you could with an old-time lie detector test. It's measuring minute muscle-indicators on your face you have no way of suppressing. And there's a new tool that measures not just truth, but **degree** of truth. You say something, it assigns a numerical value to its candor."

"What does Holstein say?"

"She's so happy. I mean, it's the first significant and profitable idea the company's had in years."

"What about Stop+Lük? StayStïl?" Delaney asked.

"There's no **money** in those," Wes said. "But Friendy, god. You have no idea how many ways they're monetizing this. The Gang of 40's doing everything but removing Holstein's brain to study it. Did I tell you that they've brought me into some meetings?"

"At the Gang of 40?" Delaney was astonished, aghast.

"Not like I'm a member yet. Still, though. It's interesting."

"Interesting?" It was like Wes being invited to UN Security Council and acting like he'd been brought to a neighbor's fantasy football meeting.

"Have to say, they are some high-minded weirdos," he said. "Profit and purity are mentioned in the same breath. It must come from Mae. This idea that anything concealed hurts humanity and the bottom line at the same time. The two are just inextricably linked. So Friendy is like their ultimate tool—it straightens out the last few hidden thoughts, motives, private opinions. The software sees it all. If you say you like something but you don't, it calls you on it. Instantly. And what can any opposition say? That we should have more lying? Deception? Duplicity? How do you defend our right to lie?"

Delaney was sick. "I thought it would be some silly thing. Like one of those apps teenagers use to put funny noses on each other."

"This is another purging," Wes said. "That's the thinking among the leadership—that these moments are necessary cleansings. That the improvement of the species, its perfectibility, is only possible by shaking off all our frailties and deviances. And anyone who can't adapt is part of the culling. The brash or incautious are eliminated, and the species moves on, only tamer. Step back."

Wes pulled Delaney into an alley, where they crouched behind a dumpster. A self-driving police cruiser, designed for surveillance, hummed by. Even the most truculent trogs couldn't stop police from sending vehicles through their neighborhoods and photographing faces, capturing voices. The sweeper passed slowly and stopped, blocking the alley. Delaney put her hand over Wes's mouth. A rooftop sensor spun for a few moments, and finally the sweeper continued down the road.

"You don't want to know about the government contracts," Wes said. "Think of the uses by police, the army. Interrogations. I mean, even simple negotiations between diplomats. Think of those without any ulterior motives, or possibility of deception."

In a window above the dumpster, a handwritten sign read END THE EVERY, SAVE THE MANY. Delaney squinted beyond the glass, and was sure she saw the silhouette of a tiny girl, no more than five. But another figure appeared and hustled her away.

"Speaking of which. Did I tell you my Stenton theory? It was confirmed, but no one's talking about it. He went to Huawei to ruin it. He went in, insisting that they make their phones lighter, cheaper. No one bought them, their stock cratered, and Every phones dominate the market. Then, conveniently, he leaves Huawei and comes back to the Every. It's so diabolical I almost respect him. Let's go."

She and Wes stood and rejoined the flow of people. They dodged a magnificent woman on a magnificent horse, who was momentarily spooked by the sound of a pair of men on a nearby rooftop shooting drones for sport. A pair of middle-aged women serpentined by on roller skates, heading toward a kind of forbidden marketplace—every urban trog zone had one—where tables offered those things banned or unsellable anywhere else: cigars, suede shoes, peanuts, Barbies, bison jerky, busts of Lincoln and Churchill, sheepskin condoms, books by Garrison Keillor. At the makeshift entrance to the market, a rail-thin man in a red satin vest was selling balloons. Delaney almost bought one in the shape of a panda; she hadn't seen an actual rubber balloon since she was twelve.

They stopped at a stall filled with copies of the world's remaining newspapers. One from Austria, three from Germany. A magazine put out by the Cuban diaspora. And of course a whole section dedicated to Liberia, the last trog nation. Their print media was thriving, and in English. A headline read **New WTO Director General Exploring Ambitious Anti-Trust Agenda.**

A fortysomething woman wearing a vintage vendor's smock, with wide front pockets for change, assessed them. "You can't bring these back to the Every," she said, and waved them away as if she were sweeping dust from a mantlepiece. "Look and leave."

Delaney and Wes hustled off, past an effigy of Mae Holland hanging from a powerline. Down the block, in the middle of the road, a Cold War–era missile, nonfunctional but still unsettling, was pointed in the direction of Treasure Island. Someone had painted **Thinking of You** along its length.

"I need to sit down," Delaney said, and collapsed on the curb. "How'd that lady know we were from the Every?"

Wes shrugged. "I haven't been to TrogTown in a while. People are angrier now." An elderly man walked by carrying a boombox on his shoulder, Public Enemy radiating through the man's remaining brain-tissue.

"You see that your beauty-assessor is out there?" Wes asked.

"I did," Delaney said.

Delaney's suggestion, tossed off to Alessandro, had yielded an app called Hermosa. The original marketing encouraged users to submit paintings, photos, flower arrangements, and the ever-learning algorithm would assess the submission and provide a rating, 0 to 1000, based on composition, symmetry, color harmony—hundreds of inputs.

"You hear about the art students?" he asked.

She had. A growing number of undergraduate and graduate art students were lobbying for the app to be given equal or greater power than the subjective assessments and grades traditionally given by their professors. **Fairness and Objectivity in Beauty,** these students insisted in a fast-moving meme, quickly nicknamed FOB. Humans are error-prone knots of biases, they insisted, and should not be involved in determining what was beautiful or good.

"That British talent show is moving to an algorithm," Wes noted.

"No one wants to be judged by a human. Too painful," Delaney said. Baseball umpires had been replaced years ago, given computers were better at calling balls and strikes. Then diving judges, gymnastic judges, figure skating. No one resisted. The subjective was being hunted to oblivion.

"Let's head out," Wes said, and they began weaving through the crowd, toward the exit.

"How's Pia?" Delaney asked. They passed a table offering fake fur coats, ziplock baggies, wet-wipes and eggs.

Wes's face smoldered. "So you know."

"Know what?"

"Why did you ask about her right after I brought up Hermosa?"

"No reason. Jesus. I just asked."

Wes squinted at Delaney. He'd never done that before, a sort of truth-assessing. Satisfied, he went on.

"You know they're testing a version of Hermosa for human beauty. You heard of FaceIt?"

Delaney had not.

"You will. It uses the same tech, same principles, same scale. And Pia's rating wasn't what she expected. Don't smirk. I know you never liked her, but she's devastated."

"I'm sorry. I didn't smirk." She reached out to him, took his hand in hers. He examined the cluster of fingers as one would a tangle of snakes. She let go.

"I didn't create the app," she said. "I mentioned it to one guy."

"I know. Alessandro. I know Alo pretty well now. One day he said it's not supposed to be used to judge the physical beauty of living people, but the next week he introduced FaceIt." Wes looked up at the white sky. "Pia got a 628." His voice broke on the 8. He really believed this number. Delaney wished she had another friend, another Wes, the previous Wes. She and this proto-Wes would have a good laugh about all this.

"Wes, c'mon. You and Pia can't take it seriously. It was a joke."

"Of course she takes it seriously!" he said. "The science is actually good. Alessandro incorporated every beauty standard, every micro-measurement of symmetry and proportion. And Pia bought the deluxe package, where every deviation from the ideal is explained. It's tough, Delaney. Most of it is stuff she can't change. Did you know her eyes are laterally uneven? And too close together? That her breasts are considered conical and the tissue not dense enough?"

"Wes. Listen to yourself. How can you buy into this?"

"Del, how can you not? It's like not believing in science. I'm an engineer. This is science."

"But it's **not** science!" Delaney said. "Everything isn't science! Fucking hell, Wes. Beauty's the most subjective thing we have."

Wes stopped at a stall selling cassette players and turntables. **Nothing fucking connected or connectible** read a sign above. An 8-track player was asking $2,000, a Discman twice that. Next to it, a box of Krispy Kreme donuts sat in a Lucite box. **Likely still edible,** read a sticker. It was going for $180.

"Anyway," he said, "once the number's in your head, there's no erasing it. I did yours, too, from a photo."

"Don't tell me."

"722."

"Fuck, Wes, what is happening to you?" Delaney

knew this number would never leave her. "Why would you tell me that?"

"You said it was meaningless, so why do you care?"

Delaney's mind cycled. She was happy hers was higher than Pia's, then ashamed that she cared—that she believed for a moment that a machine could judge her beauty or anyone else's. Then happy again hers was higher than Pia's.

"Anyway, she's getting surgery," Wes said. "Her nose is too wide, so that's the easy part. The surgeon says he can get her into the 700s."

They stopped at the last booth, called ONLY STRAWS. True to its word, it only sold straws, most of them plastic, some of them decades old. There were models for the budget-minded and the extravagant.

Delaney took Wes's elbow. "Wes, you two have lost your minds. Did you tell her she's beautiful?"

"I do! I have! Every day. You know this. But these are words, and they're just mine. FaceIt is consensus. It's definitive. She won't be happy till she's in the 800s. At least. It's a long road."

Delaney knew that if Pia was going through this, millions, tens of millions, of others were, too. She had to stop it, stop everything. Or just quit, flee, leave this city, leave all cities, hide in the mountains, never connect again. She looked into Wes's eyes and saw, for the first time, that they were trembling.

"How are the moms?" she asked.

"Fine. Gwen's retiring. Forced into it, actually," Wes said. "There were only a few trogs left in
her field anyway. She and Ursula might move to
Liberia." As the last trog nation, Liberia provided
steep tax benefits for skilled tech refugees willing
to emigrate.

"And Hurricane?"

"He's holding on. He just stares out the window,"
Wes said. "He has a place, just inside the front door,
where he sits in the sun and looks outside. I don't
know if he's content or waiting to die or what."

"Sorry you couldn't keep him on campus."

"I don't blame you," Wes said, meaning he no
longer blamed her. "It's been a relief not to have to
watch you tie your shoes. For Hurricane, too. It's
been a real weight off him."

They planned to connect again in a month, same
place. Wes crossed the street before they reached the
post office. He didn't want to take any chances—
a government building was a government building,
and the likelihood of tracking was high. They
waved a quick goodbye. Delaney lowered her
sunhat and went inside.

Instantly she spotted the cams; there were no
federal buildings without them. But these were
pointed in useless directions—at the acoustic tile
ceilings, into a dim corner. Someone had taken
pains to make them ineffective without discon-
necting them. Delaney waited in line behind an

elderly woman holding a box she'd packed and addressed. There was one young and bearded clerk behind the counter, safe behind what appeared to be bulletproof glass.

The threats against the USPS had been growing for years, fueled by Mae Holland herself, who declared open war on paper mail in the name of safety and decency. "This is the last safe haven for terrorists and white supremacists," she declared. Since the beginning, the Every had done the very minimum to thwart the efforts of the far right, and yet Mae found in this segment a useful bogeyman. Digital media could be scanned and hate discovered, she noted. But paper mail was inherently opaque, and thus the perfect vessel for its dissemination. There was no evidence of terrorism being conduced via the USPS, but enough people took the bait to make the agency the target of a wide range of cranks and counterterrorists.

When Mae proposed the abolition of the post office, it received widespread support. The agency was perpetually broke, used by an ever-shrinking clientele. When historians pointed out the Founding Fathers' repeated references to a federal post as key to a healthy democracy, she pulled back and focused on something more palatable and achievable—the reading of the mail en route. The Every proposed the rolling out of new paper and envelopes—not unlike the European air mail formats—that could be machine-read during normal processing. The

Every even offered to pay for all necessary software, machinery and cloud storage of the contents.

"No humans will be reading your mail," Mae assured the public. "But if the machine-readers are triggered by certain keywords, then that mail will go through a second-level, human, scrutiny."

The program was piloted in Kansas, with the hearty support of Governor Pompeo, who saw the processing as a useful bulwark against domestic terrorism. The rollout's results were mixed. Of some 320 million pieces of mail processed in Kansas in the first eight months, fully 12 million were flagged for human scrutiny. There was not nearly enough staff to do this, of course. One of Pompeo's advisors was outed for pricing offshore processing; there was a Malaysian contractor who had claimed his employees could read and assess 500,000 pieces of mail a week. But having U.S. mail sent to Malaysia for examination seemed burdensome and possibly, said some, unethical.

"This is a happy day for domestic extremists," Pompeo said when the program was abandoned. "And a sad day for the safety of our republic." The defeat wounded him, and was reportedly an ever-present thorn in the side of Mae Holland.

Delaney rented her post office box without incident and was given a small silver key. On her way out, she tried the lock. The tiny door of her box opened with a happy squeak, and inside her little compartment she found a pink slip of paper. It was

bulk mail, metered; someone had paid to have copies slipped into every box.

"You are COMPLICIT," it read in bold letters.
"You are GUILTY. What are you HIDING? What
FILTH and TERROR are you SENDING through
THIS INFERNAL SERVICE? The . . . **P**ostmaster
Educates **D**emented **O**ppressors . . ."

The missive went on for a while, full of biblical
recrimination and conspiracy gibberish, but was unsigned. She folded the flyer and stuffed it into her
back pocket.

As she was locking the box, a clerk on the other
side slipped in another pre-paid circular. In a sober
font and without all-caps, it began, "Dear Friend
of the USPS, if I am elected, I will fight to maintain this crucial pillar of democracy. We all have the
rights to privacy in our communications, digital
or analog. . . ."

She flipped it over. **Tom Goleta for President.**

XXIX.

Tom Goleta was popular among the Supples. His online appearances were increasing in frequency and ferocity as the day of his visit to the Every campus drew closer. The Supples watched his speeches together and afterward debated the efficacy of each new broadside.

"Monopoly," he said during one, staring into the camera, his flawless forehead pinched in consternation. He'd mastered the thirty-second speech, clearly and sometimes even lyrically written, delivered in shirtsleeves, his forearms flexing strategically. "It's as un-American as communism, as treason, as mass incarceration. Every one of these things are affronts to liberty. Monopolies drive out the small businessperson. They kill the Mom and Pop store with cruel efficiency and no remorse."

Delaney pictured her parents' grocery store. They let her run free there. She remembered the milk-spill smell of the storeroom, the impossible colors of the bell peppers and mandarin oranges. She remembered climbing the bags of coffee in the basement, she remembered her parents putting her in charge of giving Smarties to any child who wanted one. The store was disorganized, often messy; the signage was loopy and the prices only occasionally profit-making. Everything about the store was inefficient, but the customers all loved it anyway—until FolkFoods did everything her parents had done better, quicker, and cheaper.

"If we agree that the United States is a country built on free enterprise," Goleta continued, "then we have to agree that monopolies are the enemy of free enterprise."

The camera pulled back, revealing that Goleta was indeed standing on a Main Street, once adorable, now a graveyard of boarded-up stores. "The Every killed this Main Street, just as it killed a thousand more. And why? Because we allowed a monopoly to grow like an invasive weed and kill every other living thing."

Now the camera pulled closer again.

"A monopoly is an autocracy in business clothes. And the Every is a monopoly. I'm Tom Goleta, and I'm running for small business. For free enterprise. For freedom. For president."

"I don't understand," Joan said. "I thought he was a Democrat. Since when do Democrats denounce Communists?"

"I think it's brilliant," Ro said.

Delaney agreed. Somehow Goleta had reclaimed the words **free enterprise,** which had been more or less trademarked by conservatives since the 1960s.

"Who cares about monopolies when we're facing the death of the planet?" Berit said. "This is an argument from a different century. It's untethered capitalism that'll end our species. Isn't that obvious?"

"But all this is so unnecessary," Joan said.

"What is?" Gemma said.

"Campaigns in general," Joan said. "Hundreds of billions of dollars are wasted, when the outcome is almost entirely pre-determined by party affiliation. Mandatory voting was a half-measure."

"She wants AYS to get into politics," Berit explained to Delaney. She was now wearing sunglasses with star-shaped lenses. Finding them unacceptable, she dropped them out the window. "You register your party, you vote that way always. If you stray, you get an Are You Sure?"

"Or a visit from PrefCom," Ro said.

"Why not?" Berit said. "Political affiliation is already part of your preference profile. Why not have it like an auto-pay?"

"Auto-vote," Delaney said.

"Right. It would make democracy far saner," Berit said.

"You automatically vote your party line, up and down," Joan said. "Whoever has more voters registered, wins. You know where you stand at all times."

"What about undecideds? Independents?" Ro asked.

"Euthanize them," Joan laughed. "Seriously, this country loses far too much productivity to these chaotic elections, all this bullshit. Two years for every presidential campaign. It drives us all mad."

"When's Goleta coming again?" Berit asked.

"Friday," Joan said. "I got us good seats."

It was hard to know, though, who had thought of the idea first. Goleta announced that he would be visiting the Every campus, and he and his campaign presented it as if he had made the request in the form of a demand, with the Every cowed by his power to acquiesce. A counter-narrative emerged in the days leading up to the visit, which posited that the Every had made the first overture, and was seeking to make friends with Goleta, to sway or seduce or bribe him (in the perfectly legal form of a donation), as they had thousands of elected and non-elected leaders for years, and with universally positive outcomes.

In any case Delaney was baffled. Goleta was formidable, and very quick on his feet, and the last thing he would do in his maverick-styled campaign would be to come to the Every campus without a plan and a message. Anything but a "Tear-down-this-wall" sort of speech would be anathema to his campaign, which put much weight on his crusade against monopolies, algocracies, and everything associated with the Every. But the Every had never hosted such a speech, and they were brilliant at eliminating risk, especially on campus. Inviting an assassin into their home was uncharacteristic and seemed unwise.

"I'm trying to parse this," Berit said.

Goleta traveled in a solar-powered bus, and from the AYS tower, they were able to see it pause briefly at the gate before being guided in. The itinerary known to Everyone was to include first a brief tour, live-streamed but otherwise intimate and without media, and then, at noon, a speech on the Every lawn, where all staff were invited, and selected local officials would be present. In the morning, a few hundred white chairs had been set onto the kelly-green lawn, a podium facing them all. From a distance it all seemed as innocuous as a small-town wedding.

"It's a campaign. What's the question?" Ro said. She was testing a kind of tea made from kelp. After a sip, she made a face and set her cup aside.

"I can't understand what's in it for the Every," Berit said. "We've never hosted a candidate. There's no upside. We give money to everyone, play every side. So why this now? Why pick this one person?"

"Has Mae said anything about it?" Helen asked.

"Nothing beyond this-is-happening-stay-tuned,"

Joan said. "Anyway, the speech isn't for 90 minutes. Let's try to accomplish something before that."

For half that time, they did. Then the dings began.

"Oh Jesus," Helen said.

Delaney looked at the time. It was just after 11:30 a.m. and she'd gotten dozens of notices via audio and screen. She rushed to the window to see Goleta's truck leaving.

"I don't understand," Ro said.

Over the next hour, via hundreds of video clips and eyewitness accounts, they pieced it together. Goleta had arrived at 10:44, twenty-four minutes late—somewhat significant, given the punctuality that reigned on campus. Greeted by ten of the lesser-known members of the Gang of 40, Goleta and his entourage were led through the new edible garden by three of its caretakers, two men and a woman, and stopped briefly at a dragonfruit plant, touching its leaves and saying encouraging and innocuous things. Altogether, between the camera crews, Everyones and Goleta's own staff, there were about sixteen people gathered. But Goleta seemed increasingly distracted.

"He'd never seen all the dicks," Helen said.

Things began to get complicated. Witness messages were gentle at first. "Check out Goleta checking out Farmers Yuri and Dion." "Goleta sees some other organics he'd like to pluck." These comments were not seen by many and were unknown to the candidate's staff. The tour continued, around the rainwater pool and then through the expanded Cathedral of Wellness, and there, amid its glass and ferns and ceilings re-creating Miwok village life in mosaic, all of Goleta's political dreams died.

Footage of his eight minutes in the gym, surrounded by forty-seven men and women (mostly men; the internet counted) dressed in standard Every shape-hugging clothing, was tragic.

"Poor man," Berit said. "His eyes like waterbugs." She popped a pink-lemonade globe into her mouth and crushed.

Goleta could not keep his eyes off the curves, the muscled edges, the gleaming bulges and buttocks. Eye-tracking software later calculated 112 unique visits of Goleta's irises to body parts of thirty-two unique members of the Every staff. There were fifty-four visits to male genitalia, forty-one unique visits to twenty-two Every breasts, and—interestingly enough—only seventeen unique visits to the faces of those owners of those body parts. Delaney felt for him. He'd never seen anything remotely like the feast of barely veiled flesh in the Cathedral of Wellness. Clearly he didn't go to contemporary gyms. And hadn't been in a French disco or on a Spanish beach. He was a sheltered and monogamous Midwestern man, and this was, compared to Iowa, a fever-dream bacchanalia. He stuttered. He soaked himself in sweat. He coughed, he looked at the ceiling and its calming mosaic depicting pre-genocide Native American life, but then returned, helplessly, to the feast of body parts.

"I can't watch anymore," Ro said, and kept watching.

"What time is it?" Goleta asked.

It was clear he thought he could escape from the gym to his speech and salvage the day, but no such luck. He was told it was 11:15. He'd only been on campus twenty minutes, and the speech wasn't scheduled till noon.

"Maybe we should see something else," he managed to say, and he stumbled from the gym. But the gym led to the volleyball court, in which ten men, wearing far less than those in the gym, were engaged in a sweaty game, and he had no choice but to watch, for his hosts had stopped, ostensibly to talk about the recycled plastic that stood in for sand. He nodded, squinted at the tiny shards of what had been bottles and cups and plates, but his eyes could not stop wandering.

"Poor thing," Berit said. "In way over his head."

"It's not good to leer," Preeti said, "but this makes me never want to go outside. You glance someone's way and it's recorded?"

"I have to say," Joan said, "this feels like a setup. This has the feel of a Gabriel Chu production."

"You think?" Ro said, and laughed.

Halfway through the visit it was obvious that even Goleta, a former campaign manager himself, knew he was cooked. He knew his eyes were wandering, were darting and landing and groping, but he couldn't stop them. He knew how all this would live, forever, online, and what this meant.

Everyones continued to engage with Goleta, innocently greeting him, palm to sternum and even the occasional handshake, while his eyes continued to land on their bulbous regions. Meanwhile, one by one certain Everyones left his orbit and posted messages, video, photos, many using eye tracking on their cams, quickly confirming that Goleta, candidate for president, had just ogled their phalluses, their buttocks and breasts and abs and lats. In twenty minutes, edited versions of the footage began to appear, and compiled this way, with his oglings counted and punctuated with cash-register dings, the effect was catastrophic.

It was 11:38 a.m. when Goleta's handlers whispered to him—this was easily caught on SeeChange microphones—"We're out. Regroup on bus." And then he was gone.

He didn't give his speech that day, and never mentioned the Every again. He hadn't even gotten to meet Mae. In days, his poll numbers plummeted, donations dried up. The clips of his eyes lost in a sea of bulbous and brightly displayed body parts were seen hundreds of millions of times, and in three weeks he was out of the race completely.

* * *

The global debate about the ethics of eye tracking, which began that afternoon, was vigorous, but
anyone hoping to hold back the advent of ETR was
proven a fool. The unexamined glee with which
it was embraced followed a familiar pattern. First
hobbyists explored its limits, producing results both
innocuous (which parent does your baby prefer?)
and terrifying (which parent does your teenager prefer?). Heedless capitalists leaped in, apps and related
products proliferating; first and most popular were
those that built on the Goleta incident, enabling
anyone with a self-cam to determine where the eyes
of any other humans around them were landing.
The software and hardware necessary had been built
into Every phones for years; it was only a matter of
activating it.

In a rare formal statement issued through her
feed, Mae Holland provided guidance. "Like every
other progression from darkness to light," she said,
"ETR allows the truth to emerge." She was in her
glass office box, dressed in a white bodysuit sprin-
kled with faint purple sunbursts, staring unblink-
ingly at the camera. "What had been hidden is now
known. What was in doubt will now be certain.
And the more we know each other, and the more
our behavior is seen and recorded and illuminated,
the better we become. Overnight, there can be no
doubt, countless lives have become better. Those
who leer have been tamed. Those who ogle have
been shamed. We've caught child predators, we've

caught potential thieves and prevented assaults and soon we'll thwart terrorists, too. The eyes are the windows to the soul, and they tell no lies."

She signed off, never having taken her eyes from the camera. It did not appear she would have trouble with eye tracking herself, but elsewhere in the world, some—or billions—would. Over the next few weeks, it became clear that because half of humanity's iris scans had already been stored, their owners could be singled out within seconds. If a man ogled a woman at a New Jersey dog park, those eyes could instantly be paired with the offender's name, and his family, employers, and the public would be duly notified of the transgression. A new wave of suicides ensued, the embarrassment and discredit being too much for certain caught and called-out persons, mostly men. In the first week, one hundred and seven humans in Tokyo took their lives, thirty-one by throwing themselves in front of trains, the scene of their eyeshame. Tens of thousands followed elsewhere on Earth, and a few hundred, nicknamed Oedipals, chose a middle path—they gouged out their eyes.

Whatever the name for the offenders, **eyeshame** was the term that stuck to the crime. The Every resisted it, tried to push **ocular offense,** but eyeshame was more direct and descriptive. It was not strictly speaking a crime, of course; no laws prevented anyone from looking where they shouldn't. But shame ensued, and shame was deserved, and shame was the internet's currency and lever for change. As ETR spread without resistance among the vast majority of the species, there were occasionally calls to ban it, and trog areas did so preemptively and predictably, but otherwise, like most innovation in the twenty-first century, the spread was caterwauling, without organization or caution, and thus unstoppable.

XXX.

IT WAS ANOTHER REASON TO STAY INSIDE. A few billion people, who did not trust their own wayward eyes, huddled in their homes. People were accustomed to being inside anyway; the pandemics had given the human race much practice in isolation and fear. In the wake of the Goleta Pivot, sunglasses were quickly invented that thwarted eye tracking and saved people from eyeshame, but soon ETR was improved to see through all lenses. More people, called **isos,** chose to work from home, refusing to be seen, lest their eyes wander. Alessandro had become an iso, as had Dan Faraday. Isos used cartoon avatars for their teleconferencing, and many refused to speak with real-time audio, for fear of a misplaced word being recorded and tipping their Shame Aggregate. Meanwhile, enterprising developers created software that could discern eyeshame in old footage, and a half-million reputations turned to ash.

Staying home was safer. Since the 1970s, houses had grown with every passing year, and ballooned during the pandemic years. In most developed nations, smart tech was required for all new construction, for a host of reasons that no one attempted to debate. Energy and water consumption was minimized and optimized, burglaries were near-impossible. More and more homes in neighborhoods had linked themselves, sharing surveillance footage, the locations of pets and pests, and more than anything, the threats of suspicious characters in their midst. Environmentalists couldn't justify living in a trog home unless they were carbon-zero and off the grid, so they had become, every year, more the bastions of freaks and anarchists, the selfish and the insane.

On campus, Delaney had more or less mastered her own irises. When meeting people in person, she began by focusing on the tops of heads; this worked wonderfully for days, until she was notified, via AnonCom, that her lack of eye-to-eye contact was being noticed. She developed a way of moving across Treasure Island quickly, stealthily, with eyes down, on her phone, or oddly elevated, focused on some far-distant destination. It was exhausting, her brain in an ever-present state of high alert. She was sure she'd developed the vibrating-pupil syndrome she'd seen in Everyone else, but she couldn't know for sure; trembling eyes weren't discernible by the eyes that trembled.

The only place she could relax, to some extent, was in the Havel. The official workday always ended at 5, and she arrived home at 5:18. This gave her about forty minutes, usually, before Joan would arrive after working out. The solitude was key. After a day of AYS chatter—the Supples talked without end and there were no walls—she needed the time to form her own thoughts again, to bring eight hours of conversation and noise into some coherence and shape.

"Start shower," Delaney said, and went to her section of the communal closet for her robe. The HereMe assistant knew her voice, and her shower-heat and water-pressure preferences. She was entitled to six minutes of water a day, which she chose to split in two brief but restorative sessions.

"End shower and I'll mad," she said, and then stood, naked, under the skylight, her skin awake everywhere to the touch of the breeze from the Bay.

"Open curtain by my bed," Delaney said, and crawled into her tube, feeling warm and comfortable in her robe.

Delaney was getting accustomed to the conveniences of pod living, studying her own reaction with scientific detachment. She found, to her surprise, that there was little about the Shed she missed. She didn't miss the drafts, the gaps in the 100-year-old floorboards, the squeaks, the ants, the occasional mouse. She didn't miss the cold at night, the strange smell of the house, like a man's

stale sweat after a day of direct sun, or the scaly salt-
water stench of the neighborhood as a whole. She
didn't actually miss shopping for food. She missed
Hurricane, and the moms, and the smell of the
ocean, but the pod was more civilized, and something in her physiology responded to it. The warm,
soundless floors. The perfection of the cabinets, the
reliability of the ice machine, the instant and un-
failing hot water, the ylang ylang. Everything was
in its place, nothing was ever broken, and her time
was never spent on anything that should have been
working but wasn't. She grew to accept that she deserved this ease, these conveniences, and she padded
barefoot through the pod with a sense of belonging
that occasionally startled herself.

In her tube, she wrapped her comforter around
herself and peered out the window for her vole. The
whole back-and-forth was never more than two or
three seconds, and it was never clear to Delaney
what the vole was seeking or getting. But each time
it darted out it was a minor event, and its forays
kept her entertained while she waited for her evening nap to pull her under.

"Delaney?" It was Francis.

Sometimes she didn't get to sleep. Joan and
Soren's schedules were steady, and if anything, they
were occasionally late (and were never early). Francis
slithered into the pod at irregular hours, and with
an uncanny ability to arrive wherever and whenever
he was least wanted.

"Yes," Delaney said.

There was little point in him asking or her answering. The podbrain knew she was there, and Francis's phone, among six other indicators, would also tell him who was in the pod. But it was impossible to know why Francis did the things he did.

"You in your tube?" he asked.

This, too, was a fact without an alternative. The rest of the pod was empty; he'd heard her voice emanating from her bed. Sometimes she felt for him. He had been born annoying, and seemed to know it. He was so eternally needy, and eel-like, and shifty-eyed, that his every compensation or adjustment only seemed more needy, less convincing, and more pitiable. The pod did everything they required and a hundred things they wouldn't have thought of themselves, but somehow, each day, he found reason to send them a notice nudging them toward better domesticity. **Um guys,** said that morning's message, **bathroom floor extra-wet this morning. Someone could have slipped.** And with a link to research about the alarming number of broken bones caused by bathroom-slippings.

It wasn't that he almost slipped. Or that he was tidy—he was not. It was, for him, a way of loving, or seeking love. No one talked to him willingly, and so his way of crossing the void were these reminders, questions, notices, these grave slippage findings.

"Trying to take a nap," Delaney said.

"I picked up our shrouds on the way home

today," he said. "Do you want yours now? The research says they improve sleep and REM and idea-generation."

"Not just now," Delaney said. "But thanks."

"Do you know when Joan's getting back?" he asked.

"No," Delaney said, though she knew it would be about six, as it always was. "Trying to nap," she repeated. "Sleep quota, you know." She rolled over to face the window.

The vole below was out in the open again, and this time stayed longer than she'd seen him before. Treasure Island had a fair amount of birds of prey, and occasionally the shadow of a red-tailed hawk would sweep over the green and Delaney's breath would still until her vole was safe.

"Hoping we can have a pod meeting later," Francis said. "There's a new plan for projects undertaken together. You hear about that?"

"Maybe," Delaney said. It was probably embedded in one of the thousands of messages she hadn't read that day.

"Good. You'll be around?" Francis said.

"I will," Delaney said.

"Have a good nap," he said, and then rattled the fridge for the next three minutes.

Delaney closed her eyes but saw Francis. She needed, she knew, to remain friendly with him. She expected PrefCom to be key to her murder of the Every, and wanted to rotate in with Francis soon. She tried to relax. She inhaled the ylang ylang. She tried to think of Idaho peaks but thought, instead, of the conversation she'd had with Francis about PrefCom. It had been a week ago, and when she'd asked him about the department, and quizzed him about his work, he was so startled and flattered he prattled on for ninety minutes.

"PrefCom," he had explained, "is a crucial companion to Joan and your work at AYS." He briefly reminded Delaney that what he was about to say was covered by the blanket Every NDA and was being recorded, too. "At AYS you ask the consumer to reconsider. The Five Cs, right?" Delaney made a mental note to figure out what those were. She kept forgetting to ask.

"You ask them to choose well," Francis continued, "to be conscious consumers. When they become AYS members they agree to purchase within AYS parameters in exchange for steep discounts and exclusive offerings. Did I get that generally right?"

He was exactly right and knew it.

"Well, PrefCom is the stick to that carrot," he continued. "If a consumer indicates, through their purchasing history, a taste for vegan food, and various Every partners have invested years in gearing offers to this preference, departures from this are painful for the workings of those partners' business models. If the vegan suddenly starts ordering meat, then the customer profile that's been carefully created over years or even decades is damaged. So PrefCom is a way to make consumers aware of the advantages of staying within their established preferences."

He wouldn't go into much more detail about the ways PrefCom could right an errant consumer, but Delaney could make certain assumptions. The credit scores of the 1980s and '90s eventually evolved into a more holistic Consumer Rating, in which that person's predictability was factored in. Loyalty programs were subsumed and aggregated until the advantages of regular spending patterns were so great that there was obvious financial disincentive to deviate. Anyone could request their credit rating and get it from one of the three major assessing companies. But the exact numbers attached to Consumer Ratings were, in the Every era, opaque. The Every preferred to keep the numbers a mystery to each consumer, in the belief—Delaney assumed—that having them scared into compliant behavior was better than having them knowledgeable about the precise effects of their actions. Delaney gave up on her nap.

It was after six now and she crawled out of her tube, knowing Joan would arrive momentarily. Joan was usually first home, fresh from the gym, smelling sweet and feral. Soren was usually back by six-thirty, and would want to know if anyone had thought about dinner. He was a gifted cook who said, every night, that he did not feel like cooking and was sick of everything they'd been eating for

weeks and months. As he complained, he would
begin tossing ingredients onto the counter with
thumps and clicks. He would turn on the stove, and
add a wok with a low tick—he was a loud chef, as
if making sure his roommates knew the labor being
expended—and he would drop a lasso of soy sauce
in the wok. And when it was clear he was beginning, and there would be good food that night,
Joan would play some song she knew he liked,
something mindless but upbeat, and she would leap
onto the counter facing him, kicking her heels into
the cabinets.

Delaney sat on the couch and checked the time.
6:07. She woke her phone. By now she knew the
general parameters. There were about 120 all-Every
messages a day that had to be at least eye-scanned.
This took her about eight minutes. The 15,000 or
so humans on the Treasure Island campus produced,
daily, about 14,750 memos, notes, reminders and
invitations, which Delaney's AI auto-sorter cut
down by 88 percent. The sorter would auto-decline
all the invitations that conflicted with her own calendar settings and commitments. Her auto-sum
skimmed longer messages and boiled them down to
their essence, usually less than twenty words. These
would go to her Actual Essence (AE), which would
filter the messages through her own custom filters
for relevance. Her settings, for example, filtered
out anything related to sports, childcare, pet care,
yoga, and kayaking. These messages would not be

deleted, though—they would appear, to the sender, as if she had opened and read them. Wes had given her an app which remembered friends' birthdays and sent them original, personalized messages the night before the birthday, so as to be first. For zings and pops, again Wes had set her up with an auto-smile algorithm, which would scan Everyone social media accounts and smile at things she was known to like—marmots, mudskippers, three-legged dogs, Idaho, trees, mountains and anything like that she figured people would figure she'd like. At the end of any given day it would seem, to any aggregating algorithm, that she'd read about 8,250 messages and sent about 750 smiles.

The door opened suddenly. Delaney jumped. It was Soren. He was wearing a headband, indicating he'd attempted exercise. "Joan here?" This, too, was a ruse. He knew where she was at all times.

Soren and Joan had lived together for just over a year and it was clear that she loved him as a room-mate and that he loved her romantically and un-requitedly. Joan knew he loved her but pretended she did not, and he knew he could not act on his feelings unless given some overwhelming signal. He did not get such a signal from Joan, who said often, aloud, that she would never date anyone at the company, given the complications—even though the Every had recently begun encouraging such arrangements, seeing Every unions and marriages as somehow strengthening the fabric of life on campus.

Soren opened the fridge. "What are we thinking tonight? Can you eat with us?"

Delaney was supposed to be adhering to her med-eval diet but was allowed three cheat meals a week.

"I can eat here," she said.

"You think Joan's home for dinner?" Soren asked. Though he tried to toss the sentence over his shoulder, it was freighted with limitless longing. **How can I live with this person I love?** he was asking. **Wouldn't it be so easy for her to love me back? Why not do the easy thing?**

Joan expressed no need to date, and only occasionally referred vaguely to a longtime college boyfriend. She told embarrassing stories about herself, her frequent flatulence and persistent body odor, none of which Delaney knew to be true, and all of which made Joan more appealing.

Just then she burst through the door. "Who wants to smell a stanky lady?" she asked, and rushed over to Soren, who was cutting bell peppers, and pressed herself against his back. She was cruel to him this way—so familiar and physical. She raised her bare underarm and thrust his head into it. "You like? ¿Te gustas?"

Soren turned away, continued his cutting, but his body language encouraged her to stay. She jumped up on the counter next to him, interlocking her legs and letting them knock against the cabinet.

"You're a sexy man, Soren," she said. She reached for his bicep and squeezed. "These muscles, when you chop—they make me crazy. Delaney, don't you think Soren should wear tighter clothes?"

Delaney refused to aid the torture. She looked to Francis, who was facing the wall, murmuring.

"Francis, did you want to talk to everyone?" she asked.

He raised his index finger, his back turned.

"Is this about the service projects?" Joan asked. "Didn't you get the memos?"

"I did," Delaney said. She'd scanned one of the messages, which announced If You See It, Solve It—a month of commitment to social justice. "Ten Ways to Engage" were listed. **Send a smile to a cause you like; send a frown to an agent of injustice . . .** Everypersons were encouraged to find, analyze, address and fix a societal shortcoming, and in short order.

"A month?" Soren said. "Too easy."

Delaney was surprised, actually, that service would be introduced now, after Bailey's death. Service had been Bailey's purview—even if pursued sporadically. He had attached himself to certain causes, and would, for two months or so, highlight the work, the injustice, and then, just as quickly, lose interest.

"Francis?" Delaney called out.

Finally he turned around, finding Joan's eyes first.

His look was annoyed and intimate, as if the two of them were aligned somehow—parents exasperated by their two children.

"Okay," he said. "I was actually clarifying the objectives with the Gang of 40. So I'm sorry if I kept anyone"—he meant Delaney, but didn't look her way—"waiting. You probably know the general parameters of the service suggestion. The new wrinkle is that pods are being encouraged to take on projects together, to work quickly, nimbly, and to deepen our interpersonal bonds. I took it upon myself to volunteer us to take on what I think is one of the thornier but most pressing issues affecting not only society, but our immediate surroundings—the houseless persons' encampments on the perimeter of the island."

"Oh hell," Joan said.

Delaney's heart leapt. If there was any place the relentless hubris of the Every would be revealed, it was this.

XXXI.

The next evening, after dinner, Delaney led
Francis, Joan, and Soren to the island's outer ring,
where a few hundred tents and shanties sat rippling in the winds that howled through the Golden
Gate corridor.

"This seems ill-advised," Soren said. "Don't you
think we need permission?"

"We're anamolizing," Delaney said.

"We're filming?" Soren asked.

"We should," Delaney said, and Soren turned on
his cam.

They approached the front gate, a periwinkle
sunset to the west hinting at a warm and windless
dusk. But immediately after passing through the
fence, they felt the Bay's assaulting gales. Delaney
turned east, and they walked along the perimeter
path, with the hillside homes of Berkeley and
El Cerrito glowing gold in the distance.

"I don't remember us coming up with a plan,"

Francis shouted over the wind. "Was there a plan but I didn't hear it?"

"No plan needed yet," Delaney shouted back. "We're just listening today."

They approached the first few dwellings. One was a squat sky-blue camping tent, facing a far bigger one, tall enough for a person to stand up inside. A woman's figure within took notice of them.

"Hello?" she said. A long yellow cigarette extended from her hand. Delaney hadn't seen a cigarette in weeks.

"Hi," Delaney said. "Excuse us. Do you have a minute?"

Francis placed his hand on Delaney's arm, as if horrified by the question. She shook herself free. The woman stepped out of the tent. By her build and posture, Delaney guessed her to be about forty, though her face, sunburned and largely toothless, appeared far older.

While Delaney took her in, the woman did the same with her four visitors. "What are you all wearing?" the woman asked. "Ramón, come out. Wake up." She banged her flashlight on the smaller tent, and cigarette ashes fell onto her hand. She brushed them off with her free hand and took a long drag.

A shadow in the smaller tent sat up.

"Who's out there?" he asked.

"Some people from the Every," she said to him. She turned back to Delaney and the group. "I'm assuming? From the clothing."

"We're from there, yes," Delaney said. "I'm Delaney."

The woman raised her eyebrows in faux-deference, and extended her hand, as if Delaney might kiss it. "Charmed, I'm sure!" she said, and laughed hoarsely. Then she used this same hand to bang on the tent again. "Ramón, get out here!" she roared.

Now a second figure emerged from behind the larger tent. He was an imposing man, well over six feet and built like a longshoreman. He had a graying beard and wore wire-rimmed glasses.

"I called for Ramón, not you," the woman said. Delaney realized the woman hadn't given her name yet, and wondered if it would be rude to ask.

"I'm not invited?" this new man said. "I'm sorry for my friend's lack of manners. I'm Victor. She's Glynnis. Ramón's inside and too hung over to move with any . . ." He looked into Ramón's tent, as if the right word might be inside. "Alacrity," Victor said, and he extended his hand.

Delaney took it, and Victor shook hers earnestly. Joan and Francis made no movement to physically engage with Victor or Glynnis. Soren, farthest away, now stepped forward and shook Victor's hand, and for Soren, Glynnis performed a brief curtsey.

"Is this about the body last week?" Victor asked. "We told the other team what we saw. And it was down the shore a bit, so we weren't even the main people that found it."

"No, no," Francis said. Finally Delaney understood. There had been another suicide, another
body in the Bay. Of course the tent-dwellers on the
perimeter would see the corpses washing ashore.

"Don't you guys usually throw yourselves
off that one building?" the man inside the
tent—Ramón—asked. "Algo Mas?"

"I'm sorry," Victor said. "His manners."

"Usually can tell when it's an Everyperson,"
Glynnis said. "From the clothing." She pointed her
cigarette at Francis's bodysuit.

"You know what Algo Mas means?" Ramón
asked. "I always wondered if any of you people
knew. **Something more.** It means **something more.**
Did anyone know that?"

"Again," Victor said. "I'm sorry." To the tent he
said, "Either come out or shut up, Ramón."

"They can't tell us to leave," Ramón said. It
seemed clear he didn't plan on joining them outside.
"Public shoreline."

"We're not," Delaney said.

"Not our purpose at all, sir," Soren said.

"How about telling your people to stop drowning
themselves?" Ramón said. "It's pretty fucked up."

"For the last time, I'm sorry about my friend,"
Victor said, and banged on Ramón's tent. "And
what brings you to the ring of shame?"

"We're actually here to see how we might help,"
Francis said.

"Do you have money?" Ramón asked from within his tent.

"Shush," Glynnis said to him.

"Normally I would offer you a tour," Victor said, "but there's been trouble in certain quarters, a few squabbles over turf and resources, so I'd propose we stay here to chat. Does that sound agreeable?"

Delaney glanced at her group, who seemed greatly relieved to not have to venture further. "That's fine," she said.

"I would offer you all a chair, but we only have the one," Victor said, and indicated a large over-stuffed recliner. The recliner had cup holders built into each arm, and each was filled with a billiard ball—the 9 and the 3, as far as Delaney could tell.

"We're really just here for fact-finding," Delaney said. "Just to listen, really. To see if there's a way we could be of use."

Joan cleared her throat and Delaney turned to her. Joan shrugged, unsure or unable to articulate her complaint.

"Well, that's very kind of you," Victor said.

"Are they wearing wetsuits?" Ramón asked from behind the walls of his tent.

"Shh," Victor said in his direction, and turned back to Francis. "I'm sorry. He knows better. He was quite a surfer in his day."

"Give us money!" Ramón sang out. "You have money, and we need money."

"They're not giving us money, shithead," Glynnis said.

"Or homes!" Ramón yelled.

"Again, I'm sorry," Victor said. "Ramón is right in that we're unhoused, and would appreciate being provided housing of some kind, but I'm assuming that's not in the cards?"

"We're looking to help with a durable solution," Francis said.

"Homes would be durable!" Ramón said. He was ignored by all.

"Where do you get food?" Soren asked.

Delaney looked to Soren, thinking his question crude. But in his eyes there was a compassionate outrage that made the question plain and logical.

"Can I take this one?" Victor asked Glynnis. She threw up her hands. He pivoted to Soren. "The official food banks require us to come to them, at which point we're provided meals. But how do we get off this island and to one of the food banks? It's a conundrum."

"So why—" Francis began.

"Why do we live out here, apart from such services? Good question. The answer is that despite the winds, this is quieter, cleaner, and far less plagued by crime. Here we can live without the other troubles associated with urban life. The catch of course is food."

"Money buys food," Ramón sung from his tent. His voice was a very pretty alto. "Give us money!"

"So we rely on three sources of food," Victor continued. "The first you might call scrounging. Once every two or three days, a few of us make their way into the city via the subway, stopping at a dozen known spots where restaurants and grocery stores are willing to give to us what they otherwise might throw away. These scroungers bring their takings back and we distribute it."

Soren paced back and forth along the waterfront. The injustice of the unhoused seemed to have just hit him this day.

"The second way," Victor said, "is through the guerilla food banks you may have heard about. The ones in TrogTown. They're not sanctioned by the city, but every so often, they come by with a truck or van and unload whatever food they've been able to assemble."

"Their food sucks," Glynnis said. She watched Soren's pacing. "Is he okay?"

"And the last way?" Francis asked.

"Cardboard signs," Ramón said.

"The third way," Victor said, clearing his throat, "is from simple panhandling-and-purchasing. For example, Glynnis here might beg for cash from the commuters and tourists near the Ferry Building, and she might take home fifteen to thirty bucks on a good day. With that we buy whatever else we need. Kerosene, for example, for the grill."

"And drugs," Glynnis added.

"Right," Victor said. "As you probably can

surmise, many of the residents of this ring of shame are addicts."

"So if we gave you money, it'd just go to drugs," Joan said.

"And booze!" Ramón yelled.

Victor smiled grimly at Joan. "Well, yes. We eat food here, and we try to stay alive, and many among us also use drugs and booze. So cash would inevitably go to those two things. Food to stay alive, and the servicing of our vices. That and the occasional blanket or tarp."

There was a long pause. Seven humans stood and sat in proximity to one another, and no one knew what to say, for the sadness and intractability of the situation overtook them all. Then a light appeared in Victor's eyes.

"Now, I realize that there are liability issues that preclude the Every from providing meals to us," he said. "And I know that simple cash handouts would likely be seen as treating the symptoms, and not solving the problem." As he spoke, his eyes rested briefly and warmly on each of the Everyones' faces.

Francis nodded vigorously. "Well said," he said.

"Thank you, Francis," Victor said. "And if I know the Every, you all are problem solvers. After all, if you weren't problem solvers, how could you have built such an imposing empire in such a short time?"

Francis leaned closer to Victor, with what appeared to be unexpected affinity. Victor removed his wireframed glasses, cleaned them on his shirt, and reinstalled them on his wide face.

"You know what?" he said. "I'm just thinking aloud here, but there are so many governmental and nonprofit services out there in the digital realm, and often we don't know about these services, and can't access them, because we don't have the technology."

"Web-based services," Francis said.

"Precisely," Victor said. "As you know, most of these services are best accessed digitally—updated information about offerings for people in our situation, food-access programs, drug-rehabilitation projects. And as you know, the job market really requires internet access. Without it, we're further disenfranchised."

"I know this sounds like an inane question," Delaney said, "but none of you out here have phones or . . ." She had a sense of where Victor was heading and wanted to make sure he got there.

"Laptops and phones, no," Victor said earnestly. "But imagine if we did!" He turned his palms upward and looked to the sky. He was good, Delaney thought. "Being able to scroll through new employment listings, even possible housing opportunities . . . Well, that would be transformative."

"Francis," Delaney said, "I would think someone with your seniority and pull might be able to pilot a program to provide meaningful help here."

Delaney watched Francis think. He was nodding,

working out the logistics, the numbers, picturing himself accepting humanitarian awards from the Every, the city, the White House. She caught Victor's eye, and was sure he knew her gambit.

"Victor," Francis said, and seemed to relish the radical generosity enshrined in his knowing and repeating the unhoused human's name, "do you think that this technology—laptops, for instance—would help you all get back on your feet, and even maybe leave this island, this ring of shame, in your words?"

"Francis," Victor said, taking his glasses off again, and looking deeply into Francis's black ferret eyes. "There's nothing that could change our lives quicker than having the technology to access web-based services and communicate via text and email to providers of help and agency."

Now Francis was standing on his tip-toes. He seemed inclined to hug Victor, thanking him in advance for the Nobel he'd just won, but decided against such extensive contact. "Victor, we'll keep talking," he said. "I'll come back with news. Good news, I bet."

"I'll be here," Victor said, and bowed deeply.

It did not take long. Delaney had never seen—no one had ever seen—Francis work so hard and with such passion. For a week he used every spare moment messaging Gang of 40 members, city supervisors, sending innumerable unanswered messages to Mae.

"He's so cute, all this activity," Joan said. "He hasn't had an idea in a decade."

It did seem likely Mae would take notice. As Francis's project became known—and known as Ring of Opportunity, Francis's idea—there was a general buzz on campus about turning the embarrassment of the encampment into a triumph.

"Think of it," Francis said. "It's so on-point. Think local. Act . . . Wait. How does it go again?"

"You have it," Delaney assured him. She was tempted to mention that the Every had never paid taxes locally, or in the state, or federally, or anywhere, nor had its founders, and that the paying of taxes might go a long way toward feeding and housing and empowering the unhoused among them, but she would be wasting her breath.

"Godspeed to you," she said instead.

Francis thanked her and did a bit of shadowboxing. This was new, and it continued. Whenever he was excited, he jabbed and jogged in place. But first Francis needed approval to give away some vast number of free phones and laptops. Delaney was unaware of the Every ever giving away anything, so she was startled when Francis burst into the pod two nights later, breathless and aglow.

"They approved the phones!" Francis announced, and smacked the wall, producing a triumphant

sound. He paced the pod, smiling to himself, looking for other things to smack triumphantly. He pretended to kick Soren in the crotch. "I'm so hyper!"
he said.

Two days later he got word on the laptops. The
laptops were a no, but the Every was introducing
a new tablet in a month; the Gang of 40 suggested
giving the ring-dwellers the first batch.

"You're doing it, friend-o," Joan said, and
punched him playfully in the arm. Francis boxed
back at her feebly, and then, inexplicably, pretended
to kick her in the crotch.

Delaney was impressed, too. Giving Victor,
Glynnis, Ramón, and everyone else living on the
perimeter hardware was of course silly, but it was
simple-silly, maybe even harmless.

"Ovals, too," Francis said the next day.

"Ovals?" Soren asked. "Why would they
want those?"

Delaney was watching Soren's conscience come
alive, even if just a bit. These sorts of questions—
e.g., **Why?**—were new for him—for anyone
on campus.

"The Gang insists," Francis said. "The recipients
will have to wear them for the machines to work.
And I have to say, it makes sense. They'll get real-
time health data, and you have to assume there are
some serious health issues among them."

Now Francis was bouncing in front of the mirror,

jumping rope without a rope. "We're going to do a photo-op next week. This'll finally show the Europeans how we deal with the unhoused. Will you all come?"

"You did the work, sweetums," Joan said.

"We'll watch from afar," Delaney said.

"Okay," Francis said. He jabbed at himself in the mirror, delivered a slow-motion uppercut. "I've got to think about what to wear. Do you think we give clothes to Victor and Glynnis? Or just have them be . . ."

"Broke? Destitute?" Soren asked.

"Don't," Joan said. "This is good. You know it is."

"Is that when they get the hardware?" Soren asked. "At the photo-op?" He slumped into the couch.

"Nope," Francis said, "we're actually bringing the hardware to them tomorrow. No cameras."

Soren looked up, his brow knotted in grudging respect.

"That was Victor's idea," Francis continued, "which is brilliant, if you think about it. They get the tablets, phones, and ovals, and then they have a week to get used to the tech, to access services, get some experience. Then, when the cameras come, they'll already have some familiarity, some anec-dotes, and they can describe how it's all been work-ing for them. Wouldn't it be great if someone had already gotten a job?"

"How many are you giving them?" Joan asked. "And I hate to ask a dumb question, but how will they power all this stuff?"

"Victor said there are 1,137 people living on the ring," Francis said, "so we got approval for one set for each resident. And we'll have a solar charging station set up at the end of the week."

"Wait. There's over a thousand people out there?" Soren asked. "I would have said three hundred."

Delaney had a strong sense that Victor had made the number up, and had been savvy enough to choose a highly specific number; any hard number was instantly fact, even that number defied what could be surmised with the naked eye.

"That's part of the issue," Francis said. "And the opportunity. Once we distribute the machines, and get the ovals on the wrists, then each resident can register. We'll confirm their numbers exactly, match them up with official state and federal records, and get a much better sense of everyone's background and needs. It'll be like a census, but far more precise."

"I hope," Delaney offered, "that you'll be tracking their usage once they get up and running?"

"Of course," Francis said. "They'll activate the phones and laptops with their fingerprints, and the prints will go out to the police database, to see about overlap with known offenders and outstanding warrants. The phones, too, will help with tracking—see how often these folks are near, like, spots where crimes are committed."

"Finally," Joan said. "That at least sounds practical."

Soren was pacing again. "Why do the police get access to all that again?"

"Beyond the fact that it will make us all safer?" Francis said. "It was also the only way we could get the city to pay."

"Pay for what? The hardware?" Soren asked. "The **city** paid for the phones and tablets and ovals? That we **make**?"

Francis tapped his ear. Soren threw up his hands.

"The police have a right to some quid pro quo," Francis said. "And the city has a budget for services for the unhoused."

"They **should** pay," Joan said. "**We** didn't make them homeless."

"Houseless. Unhoused," Francis corrected. "And anyway, the city didn't pay retail. Just wholesale plus."

It was to be done at night. Victor didn't want Everyones gawking at the distribution, so he'd asked for the delivery to be made after sunset—a plan Francis and the Gang of 40 found agreeable and dignified.

When the time came, Francis skipped out of the pod, shaking his shoulders like a boxer weaving through the crowd on his way to a title fight.

He jogged across the Daisy and to the outer
gate. Delaney found a vantage point at the Yelapa
Cafeteria, from which she could see Victor
and Glynnis's tent. At just after nine p.m., a few
dozen Everyones pushed large dollies through the
gate and to the outer ring, where Francis met them.
Each dolly was stacked high with phones and tablets
and ovals, all in unmarked brown boxes. The train
of dollies stopped at Victor's tent, and Francis and
Victor greeted each other like allies and friends.
Delaney turned away; she had an inkling what
would happen next.

In the morning, Delaney found Francis on the
couch, tapping his tablet, his face pinched.

"Everything okay?" she asked.

"It's fine," he said.

"I saw you bring the boxes out there," she said. "I
was really touched. How was the distribution?"

"Well, Victor and Glynnis did that part," Francis
said. "Victor said it would be better that way, and
I agreed. I didn't want it to be a big show. So we
made plans to do some trainings in a few days,
and left. I assume they handed out everything in a
low-key style."

He continued to tap and sigh. "It's just
strange," he said, "how few of the machines have
been activated."

Joan stepped out of the bathroom. "How many?"
she asked.

"Sixteen," Francis said. "Does that seem off?"

"Out of eleven hundred? I would say so," Joan said. She opened the fridge and grabbed a mango globe.

"You think I should go see if they need help?" he asked.

"Maybe they're too drunk and high," Joan laughed.

Francis tapped again. "The crazy thing is that even Victor's isn't activated. Why would that be, do you think?"

That evening, when there was still no word from Victor, Francis asked Delaney to go with him to the outer ring.

When they arrived at Victor and Glynnis's tents, everything seemed in order. Nothing was moved or altered. The recliner was in its place, the 3 ball and 9 ball snug in their armrest homes.

Francis stood between the tents.

"Victor?" he called out. "Glynnis?"

He was oddly respectful of Victor and Glynnis's privacy, and it took him five minutes to get up the nerve to peek into the larger of the two tents. It was empty. They looked in Ramón's and found it empty, too.

"They could just be out and about," Delaney said.

She said this while knowing that something was amiss—and confirmed what she had seen coming.

Francis had never met any of the other ring-
dwellers, so it took him some time to build up the
nerve to continue down the perimeter to the next
cluster of tents. A weatherbeaten woman, wearing
on her bare torso only a fleece vest emerged from a
half-plywood, half-tent home and squinted into the
setting sun.

"Oh, Victor and his crew left last night," she said.
"They said they'd gotten some delivery work from
you guys? I'm thinking they said they were going
downstate? Or maybe to Canada."

Francis made the sound of an animal caught in
a trap.

"Delivering what?" he asked. "Do you know? Did
you see them leave?" He was near tears.

"All those little brown boxes you guys brought
out. Middle of the night, a truck pulled up, and
they loaded them in no time. Very efficient. What
was in those boxes, anyway?"

XXXII.

BECAUSE THERE WAS NO LOCAL NEWS, and the event had not been filmed, word that a small coterie of unhoused people had made off with a half million dollars' worth of new Every hardware did not spread widely. Still, enough people Everywhere and Nowhere knew, and Delaney held out vague hope that the comic level of incompetence and gullibility displayed would be an embarrassment to the Every.

But days passed, a week, ten days, and the only chatter was that the remaining ring-dwellers were up in arms that they didn't get any hardware they could sell, too. Though their protests were muted—only the occasional demand or disgruntlement yelled through the fence—it unsettled the Everyones who liked to walk or jog near the perimeter; they decided to exercise outside of projectile range of the encampment.

Francis was livid, Soren was devastated, and Joan showed no particular feeling one way or another.

Francis worked with the local police department, then the sheriff, the state troopers, and finally the FBI—all to no avail. They had nothing to go on, really, outside of the first names of three unhoused people, and those first names, it turned out, had likely been false. Photos of the truck had been taken as it crossed eastbound on the Bay Bridge, but the driver had been wearing a mask—the face of Popeye, as it turned out—and the license plates had been stolen. There was brief hope that whoever bought the hardware would somehow err in stripping them of their tracking devices and serial numbers, but no such luck—not so far.

Francis's anger and investigative zeal gave way to despondence. In the pod, after work, he did his customary watching and murmuring, but with an air of catatonia that was new and unsettling.

"He's cooked," Joan said one day at AYS. "They won't get rid of him, but he's at the end of the road. Not that he was climbing the Every ladder at a brisk pace, but now he's knocked down to private with no hope of ever being more."

Not even the coming of the new pod firepits cheered Francis. Wes had doubled down on his assertion that sleeping near an active fire was key to creative fertility. **Where were cavepeople sleeping when they invented the wheel?** he asked rhetorically. And so all the pods were being retrofitted with firepits, and the unspoken hope was that propane-driven flames would be just as creatively fruitful to

Everypersons as woodfires had been to Paleopersons. The research, though, was not yet there.

At home, Delaney felt for Francis, and hoped for his sake he might leave. He stared into the fire, and Delaney tried to cheer him by reminding him of the pod's sleep aggregate, which had gone up by 7 percent since the firepit had been installed.

Francis nodded, said nothing, and continued to stare at the flames.

The stolen-goods episode shook the dynamics of the pod in other ways, too. Delaney was sure that Soren yearned to have someone to talk to about Joan, and finally, as she was walking back to the pod from work, he caught her in the hallway just before their door.

"Hi Delaney," he said, and, with a few mimed gestures, he moved her into a position in the hallway he determined right. "Just a quirk of the building, but happens to be a blind spot. We're not seen or heard here. As long as we're quiet and don't move."

"Everything okay?" Delaney asked.

"I have to be quick," he said. "I don't know how much time we'll have. Now that you've been around us a few months, do I seem pathetic with Joan?"

"Oh," Delaney said. "I don't—"

"Sorry," he said. "This isn't fair to spring on you. I know I look like an idiot. I can't help it. The way I look at her, the way she toys with me. I'm ashamed."

"You shouldn't be. It's pure. You love her, right?"

"It's hardly love. I wait under the table for crumbs. I didn't mind when it was just us and Francis, because he seems oblivious. But now I see myself in your eyes, and I'm horrified."

"No, no," Delaney said. "It's fine."

It's fine. That wasn't right and didn't help.

"Have you ever told her?" Delaney asked.

"Told her what?"

"That you like her this way," Delaney said.

"She knows. She knows a thousand times over. You **know** she knows. That's why she plays with me," he said, rubbing his forehead with his palms. "She owns me but doesn't want me."

"Then maybe you should leave," Delaney said.

"What?" he said.

"You're too familiar to her now. You're too available, too easy. Get away. Move out. Make yourself scarce."

Soren's eyes were pained. "What are you saying?"

The sound of footsteps reaching their floor echoed from near the stairway. Soren listened closely, and when it was clear the feet were Joan's, he quickly ducked into the pod and avoided Delaney the rest of the night.

With her pillow over her head, Delaney heard only a muffled version of the sound, later described as a metallic pop followed by a whoosh like an old window thrust open. She heard voices outside her tube, then the rapid tapping of bare feet on concrete floors.

"Del, get up," Joan said.

Delaney shimmied out of her tube and followed Joan into the hall.

Red EXIT signs on either end of the hallway illuminated the figures running to and fro in a blood-colored light.

"What is it?" Delaney asked.

"Explosion, fire, something," Joan said. "We're supposed to go to the basement." Delaney checked the time. It was 3:13.

A figure swept behind them. "Outside. Go to the Daisy."

They came to the stairwell and took the stairs three at a time.

A man was standing on the landing and contradicted the last directive. "Basement, people, basement! Keep moving. Nice and easy. Get there and wait for an announcement."

Delaney had never been to the basement. She didn't know there **was** a basement. They took the rest of the stairs quickly, as more sleepers awoke and joined the river of people fleeing downward. At each landing, a handful of people stood, unmoving, staring at their phones, incredulous that there wasn't more clarity.

As Delaney and Joan reached the last landing, an announcement came over the speakers. "We've had an incident at the northeast corner of campus.

Please go to the basement of your building and await further instruction."

"The homeless," Joan said. "It happened out by them."

The basement was a warren of pods and small common rooms. Delaney and Joan found a kitchen in the corner of the building and sat on the floor. A woman entered wearing a ghostly white nightgown. "Bomb," she said, and then wandered out to the hallway.

"A **bomb**? Why a bomb?" Joan asked.

The kitchen grew crowded as the residents of every floor spilled into the basement and filled every corner. They continued to check their phones.

"I can't believe there's nothing," a man near Delaney said. "No information. It's been nine minutes. This is insane."

"Was it the firepits?" someone asked. A vigorous discussion ensued about whether the firepits in the pods had something to do with the explosion at the perimeter. And with each passing minute of communication blackout, the dread grew more florid.

"Maybe they cut the power. The towers."

"Who? They blew up the satellites, too?" the man said.

Finally the lights came on. Those who were reading their phones got a series of notices. **Stay where you are. Do not leave campus. You are safe. The threat has been neutralized.**

A few minutes later, another message.

Please do not go to the perimeter. This area is unsafe. No one will be allowed to exit campus for the time being. Please stay where you are.

Fifteen minutes later, a final message.

There has been an explosion at the northeast end of campus. Please return to your pods and stay inside your dorms. You are safe there. Police and fire are here and they assure us the threat is over. Try to sleep and we will update you as needed.

Back in the pod, Francis adopted the role of unflappable elder. "I know this is probably very scary for all of you," he said, though he seemed strangely unaffected himself. "From everything I'm hearing, this was a very isolated and minor kind of event."

"But they said northeast side," Delaney said. "Wouldn't that be the houseless perimeter?"

Francis nodded gravely. "Let's hope no one was hurt."

Delaney studied him. He seemed to know something. Or he was simply gratified that some karmic justice had been visited upon the unhoused humans who had wronged him.

In the end, Francis's assessment was not far off. It had been a van carrying a small amount of C-4. It had been driven through an area of the outer fence that was undergoing adjustment and was vulnerable. It was assumed by police and the FBI that the driver intended to drive the van all the way to one of the central Every buildings—most speculated that Mae was the target—but was thwarted when the van's front axle was split in half by a cement cornerstone that had been there, unnoticed by anyone, since Treasure Island's Navy days. The van's driver had abandoned the vehicle and detonated it remotely, perhaps figuring that an explosion at the edge of the campus was better than none at all. Though the conflagration was only twenty yards from the closest tents, no one was hurt at the perimeter, and that was deemed miraculous.

Reaction was swift and decisive. The encampments were gone in hours and did not return. All Everyones rejoiced their departure, though silently, and what had been a flat perimeter was now studded with sharp stones—ostensibly a sea-barrier—that made any future tent-habitation impossible. The San Francisco Police Department, which had been a sporadic and unwelcome presence on the island anyway, arrived to do a cursory investigation, but was overshadowed by the Every's security detail—four dozen armed guards, chiefly ex-Mossad, imported from a DC-based private security company. Wearing tactical gear, they roamed the outer gates and were stationed on the streets around campus. Airspace around the Every was restricted, and a team of former Kurdish intelligence officers arrived to install a drone-jamming tool they'd perfected in northern Syria. A marine detail circled the island 24-7 by

boat and there were rumors of a mini-submarine pa-
trolling San Francisco Bay. The majority of Treasure
Island businesses were suddenly shuttered, never
reopened, and the chatter of helicopters overhead
became constant.

There was widespread consternation about
the inability of investigators, public and private,
to find the perpetrator, given the vast powers at
their disposal. The vehicle driven through the gate
was thirty-two years old, and had no digital tools
aboard. Cam shots of the van passing various inter-
sections were unhelpful; the driver was wearing a
mask of Tim Berners-Lee. The Widower—the griev-
ing husband who protested daily at the entrance to
Treasure Island—was brought in for questioning
and released. There was much on-campus speculation about the involvement of a cabal of disgruntled
banana-growers, but there was absolutely no chatter anywhere online about the planning of such an
attack, and responsibility for it was not claimed by
any individual or group.

Life on campus grew more anxious. The
perpetrators—somehow consensus emerged that
it had been a group—were still at large, and might
have the capacity to make another run at their target. The Everyones living on Treasure Island were
terrified but agreed, to the last person, that things
were far worse, far more chaotic off-campus.

In the weeks before and after the bombing, there

was a series of ineffective but unsettling attacks on the Every buses that took staffers from the campus to their homes in San Francisco and Walnut Creek and Atherton. Rocks were thrown from rooftops, shattering a few windows and adding a smattering of side-panel divots. The damage was minimal but the psychological impact was significant. Applications for EveryoneIn hausing surged and the available units were quickly filled (and the rapid construction of more dorms was planned). Between the chaos of Nowhere, the sporadic animosity expressed toward Everyones there, and Impact Anxiety, Everyones were now unwilling to leave campus, ever—and conveniently, they never had to.

XXXIII.

THE BLIMP WAS BOTH unexpected and inevitable. In all her research, Delaney had not come across the existence of surveillance zeppelins, but two weeks after the bombing, its shadow circled the campus, never stopping. Bailey had bought a Turkish blimp company years earlier but hadn't done much with it; his interests had migrated to Io. Now, with the blimp flying silently overhead, two hundred feet up, the majority of Everyones couldn't figure out how they'd ever lived without its soothing shadow. It saw everything, and everything it saw was available to everyone. At any given time, anyone sitting on the Daisy lawn could watch themselves as the blimp watched them, and this delighted all. The lens was so powerful it could read the text on your phone; it could count the hairs on your head. And most important, it could detect any unauthorized thing coming from any direction—land, air or sea.

Stenton took full ownership of its existence

and messaging. A contest to name it was held, with Blimpie McBlimpface a close second to the Eye of Bailey—Wes's idea, a winking tribute to their departed founder. Stenton released a video celebrating it.

"Can any of us remember life before the Eye of Bailey was watching over us?" he asked. "Do we want to? Now we know a new kind of security. A sense of relief. The unexpected is no longer possible."

Delaney watched the announcement with the Supples.

"Stenton is fully back, I take it?" Berit said.

"I feel like my stepdad got out of jail and moved back in with my mom," Ro said.

"And then bought a blimp," Joan said.

"Anyone notice the blimp is smiling?" Preeti asked.

The blimp had been humanized with large anime eyes and a toothy smile. The effect was like being watched over by a beluga whale crossed with a slow-moving B-52.

"Just watch," Joan said. "Stenton will be running this place in six months. This is the Reichstag moment."

The usual shifting and clicking of goods at AYS stopped and the room went quiet. All eyes were on Joan.

"What?" she said. "You know I'm right. Mae

hasn't had an idea since she took power. Stenton's making a move."

The assembled Supples glanced at each other, and then back at Joan, silently telling her, **Enough.** After the bombing, even at AYS there was an increase in caution, in attention to every word said. Joan returned their admonishing stares, her own eyes saying **Fine. You know I'm right.** Activity resumed, and a few of the Supples took an early lunch, as if to flee the damage.

Joan turned to Delaney. "You sure you want to rotate again? What's the point? You'll end up back here anyway."

But it was time. She'd been at AYS for three weeks—far longer than she'd intended. She needed to seed ideas elsewhere.

"People, Del's leaving," Joan announced, and the remaining Supples gathered around. "She's going to HereMe."

"It's just a rotation," Delaney clarified.

"HereMe?" Preeti said, and wrinkled her nose. "Why HereMe?"

After the bombing, Delaney had heard rumblings that Stenton was taking an interest in HereMe, and she felt she had to be there to exacerbate whatever horrors he had in mind.

"Just curious," Delaney said.

"She'll be back," Joan said, and then said it to Delaney. "You'll come back. Everyone comes back."

* * *

"Delaney!" Kiki squealed. They had planned to meet at the Daisy, and Delaney had duly arrived at the Daisy, but as always, Kiki was thrilled that the Delaney-dot on Kiki's screen had become a real-Delaney in front of Kiki. "Ready for another rotation?" she asked and smiled, then raised a finger. "Hi Nino honey! And Ms. Jolene, good to see you." Kiki turned her head away.

For the next two minutes Kiki engaged in an intense, hushed conversation with the two faces, her son's and her son's teacher's, on her arm-screen. Delaney couldn't help hearing, and wanted to hear, in case she needed to save Kiki from this latest drama.

"I didn't mean to touch her," Nino said. "I was by the Legos and Mia came over. She and I do this thing where we tap our Legos together. Like it's a fist-bump. But today I missed and my Lego touched Mia's arm."

"Nino, I'm sure that—" Kiki began.

"I'm afraid this triggers a mandatory review," Ms. Jolene said, her voice utterly without warmth. "It's automatic. You know the school's policy on interpersonal contact. I couldn't stop it if I tried. Luckily we have quality video so there won't be debate about exactly what happened. Check your feed about next steps."

"But Ms. Jolene—"

"I'll see you at pickup," Ms. Jolene said, and the screen went dark.

"You heard any of that?" Kiki said to Delaney.

"I did," Delaney said. "I'm sure it'll be fine."

Kiki was already back on her screen. The next steps had already appeared; Delaney glanced at what appeared to be a contract of some sort that Kiki had to sign.

"This isn't the first issue," Kiki said. "Look." She showed Delaney her screen, which was filled with incidents involving Nino. Delaney saw a handful of entries—**knee-to-knee contact 3-11** and **singing along to inappropriate song 5-23**—and looked up to find Kiki breathing through a straw.

"It helps with my stress," she said. "You have an EveryStraw?"

Delaney said she did not.

"We're late," Kiki said. "You're going to HereMe, right? Where is that?"

Delaney could see the building, no more than a hundred yards away; its façade bore the word HereMe in four-foot letters. Kiki was looking at her screen.

"Oh no," she said. "It's telling us to get on the highway. That couldn't be right. Just let me . . ." She tapped away for a few moments as Delaney tried, gently—for she felt anything could send Kiki over the edge—to tell her that the building was in front of them. Finally, as Kiki waited for her screen to re-fresh, Delaney managed to lead Kiki's eyes to rest on the HereMe sign.

"Okay," Kiki said, "but I want to be sure." And again she waited for her screen to confirm what was before her.

"I can make it from here," Delaney said, and Kiki gave her an exhausted, grateful, half-mad look, and then tapped her earpiece, through which a new call had arrived.

The HereMe building was a spiky mess of glass and timber, meant to evoke a seashell, purportedly a conch. Delaney arrived early, just as the shadow of the blimp spidered slowly across the building. Inside, Delaney was greeted by an enormous sign laser-cut into brushed steel.

HERE YOU ARE HEARD, it read.

More than any other aspect of the Every, smart speakers fascinated Delaney, and had since she was a child. Delaney's parents had fiercely resisted having one in the home, until they began work-ing at FolkFoods, bought one for the home—at a discount—and they soon found it indispensable. In college, Agarwal had spent weeks on the topic, view-ing smart speakers as proof, the most convincing proof, that humans will resist no level of intrusion if it saves the trouble of walking across the room.

Smart speakers had an awkward introduction to the world. They arrived in the 2010s to phenomenal sales, with hundreds of millions of households adopting them within the first few years. Before the Every entered the picture, the makers of the devices—at the beginning there were three main players in the field, including the jungle—assured the buyers that the AI assistants were never activated unless their designated name or code word was spoken. This reassured the users that their private everyday conversations were not being heard, that only brief requests were audible, and even then, never stored. But a few months later, it was revealed that the smart speakers were in fact listening all the time, or **could** listen all the time. In fact, they could be activated by their manufacturers any time at all. For this, the manufacturers apologized; perhaps there had been some confusion, they said. Were we unclear?

The users, though momentarily upset at this foundational and central deception, were assuaged when they were told that under no circumstances were their conversations **recorded.** It would be, both users and manufacturers agreed, an egregious breach of trust to have a machine that a customer brought into their house—a machine, everyone noted, that was purchased primarily to play music and inform them of the current traffic—actually **recording the conversations conducted in these private households.** That would be unethical. And so it was assumed that no recording was being done by these home assistants, until one day the manufacturers admitted that they had in fact been recording just about every conversation every user had ever had, from the very beginning.

Again the makers were contrite. When you were asking before about whether we were recording conversations, they said, we didn't quite understand what you meant. We thought you meant recording and **listening** to these conversations, and that of course we would never do. We would **never.** We record the conversations of hundreds of millions of users, yes, but no humans ever **listen** to any of these conversations. Conversations in the home, between family members, are private, are sacrosanct! they said. We simply record these conversations to improve our software, they said, to optimize our services, to better serve you, the customers, better.

And for a while the users, though feeling wary and burned by the series of revelations, looked askance at their smart speakers, wondering if the tradeoff was actually worth it. On the one hand, their private family conversations were being recorded and stored offsite for unknown future use by a trillion-dollar private company with a limitless litany of privacy violations. On the other hand, they could find out the weather without having to look out the window.

Fine, the users said sternly, fists on hips, you can continue to record everything we say, but—but!—if we ever find out that you manufacturers were having **actual humans** listen to our conversations, that will be one step over the line.

We would never! the manufacturers said, hurt by the inference, which, they felt, was offensive even to think about, given how open and transparent they had been from the start. Didn't we reveal, they asked, after we were caught, that our smart speakers were turning themselves off and on at their own behest? And didn't we admit, after we were caught, that we were listening to and recording anything we wanted at any time, anything that was said in the private homes of hundreds of millions of users? And didn't we reveal, after we were caught, that we were recording all the private conversations every user had in the privacy of their own homes?

After all this openness and contrition, they said, it stings to think that customers would wonder aloud if other shoes might drop. No more shoes, said the manufacturers, would be dropping. We stand before you barefoot and humbled.

When it was revealed that the manufacturers had in fact hired 10,000 humans, whose only purpose was to listen to, transcribe and analyze the private conversations that had been recorded by these smart speakers, the manufacturers were amazed at the outrage, as muted as it was. **Yes,** they said, we have all along been recording and listening to your conversations, they said to their customers, but none of these 10,000 workers **know your names,** so what possible difference would it make that we have all of your private conversations recorded, and that we could with one or two keystrokes de-anonymize your conversations at any time? And, given the fact that every database ever created has been hacked, these recordings could be accessed by anyone at any time who had will enough to get them? What, the manufacturers asked, are you getting so worked up about?

In fact, no one got worked up at all. Lawmakers were mute, regulators invisible, and sales skyrocketed.

And so when the Every swallowed the jungle and created a next-level smart speaker, privacy was not promised or expected. But a new name was needed. For a decade, since the assistants had been activated by saying names like Alexa or Siri or Bobo, there had been unnecessary problems and even lawsuits from people who had been given those names at birth. The activating phrase, the Every decided, would be "Hear me." It was a phrase that no one said in daily life, and yet it was clear and to the point. The user simply said "Hear me," and could begin. The words were then combined to make the device's name, HearMe, and shortly thereafter, the slight change in spelling, to HereMe, was just one of those unfortunate Every-isms that diminished the dignity of the species and shamed whomever had to type it.

* * *

The blimp's shadow overtook Delaney again, followed by a woman of about thirty standing above her. The words **eye shimmer** pulsed in Delaney's mind in neon letters. Karina's was cerulean, luminescent. When she blinked, it was like the flutter of a morpho butterfly. Delaney tried not to squint.

"Delaney," she said, and looked at the screen strapped to her arm.

"Yes," Delaney said.

"Karina," Karina said, her hand to heart. "I'll be your guide today," Karina said. She wore a loose boho blouse over black leggings—the most demure outfit Delaney had seen in weeks. Karina was oddly unsteady in her heels, though, so when she walked, her earrings, enormous gold hoops, shimmied frantically from her high-piled hair.

"I'll show you to your play area later," Karina said, as she led Delaney into the building. "But we have a sort of an unexpected opportunity if you're interested. I know this will seem sudden, but we do have a very interesting topic today being discussed in an all-staff. Your NDA covers this, so you're welcome to come in and listen. Otherwise you can lounge for an hour or so until we're done."

Delaney tried not to seem too anxious. She managed to convey that she'd very much like to sit in if no one objected.

The room was dominated by a conference table in the shape of an amoeba. There were twenty-two Everyones tucked into the various inward and outward curves of the amoeba, with seven isos on screens, their avatars mostly copyright-free cartoon characters from the early twentieth century. Of all the departments Delaney had visited thus far, the humans in the room seemed the most characteristic of what she'd expected at the Every. The faces she saw were focused, sober, the clothing and haircuts more or less conservative; she assumed a good number of them had come from the jungle via the merger. A door behind her opened and closed and a familiar voice spoke.

"Greetings," he said gruffly. It was Stenton. He swept past Delaney and took his place at the head of the amoeba. A woman in a yellow, impossibly snug business suit followed him and took a seat at his side. The presence of a business suit was so incongruous it seemed to alter the chemistry of the room. Finally a third person, a beefy man of about fifty, took Stenton's other side. He was mustachioed and wore a snug golf shirt. Stenton introduced the woman as an attorney specializing in audio-surveillance law; the man was the former police chief of Miami, credited with quelling the city's riots during the second pandemic.

"My hope in the next hour is to figure out what we have and what we might be able to find," he said. There had been no preamble.

Delaney had heard little about Stenton's return to the Every, but here he was, quite comfortably leading a departmental meeting. From behind Karina and the large bowl of fresh limes on the table, Delaney was able to take surreptitious glances to gauge the effect his presence was having on the assembled. Almost uniformly their eyes were avoiding his. It was remarkable. She couldn't find more than a few of the many faces focused on him, and when he swept his gaze around the room it seemed clear why. His eyes were dark and held no spark. They were dull, reflectionless, the eyes of a shark.

"As you know," he said, "the authorities are not making demonstrable progress in finding who drove a van laden with explosives onto our campus. Our own investigations have been fruitless. The car, as you know, had no tracking devices aboard and the last ownership papers were thirty years old. There were no fingerprints, and though the car was photographed by highway and bridge cams a few times, the driver was wearing a mask. So we have no leads. But I'm joined today by a specialist in audio-surveillance law, and my hope is to find out what HereMe might do to help bring this terrorist, or these terrorists, to justice. How many American homes currently contain HereMe assistants?"

The woman in the snug suit answered, her fingers in a victory-V. "Two hundred and sixty million."

"Right now, how long is audio being stored from each speaker?" Stenton asked her.

"The law says all recordings have to be deleted after thirty days," the expert said. Delaney looked down on her tablet for the person's name. It seemed to be Metzger. She was fine-featured, red-haired, sharp-eyed. It was unclear if she was a full-time Everyone or a consultant. Stenton seemed to have a mandate to bring in anyone he wished.

"How far back do we actually **have** audio?" Stenton asked her.

"It depends," Metzger said. "Some we've kept for some time, for research purposes . . ."

"Ballpark," he said.

"Eighteen months."

"Good," he said. "There will be no deleting of any of these past or future recordings until further notice. Understood?" He didn't wait for a response—had never in his life waited for a response.

"Now," he said. "Morris, can you explain a bit about what we're looking for?"

He turned to the former police chief. Morris placed his heavy arms on the table; it looked like a butcher setting down two hairy lamb shanks.

"Back in the day, we'd spend weeks, **months** even, getting intel," he said. His accent seemed outer-borough New York, but there was an unhurried calm atop it—the monied veneer of a well-paid consultant. "A name, a stray address, date, contact. We'd shake down CIs."

"Confidential informants," Stenton clarified.

"Right," he said. "Just to get a name that might lead to a name that might lead to a name who might know **someone** who might have heard

someone who'd heard a perp brag about a score. Now you have all that audio at your fingertips. Any plan these bad guys make in the home or hideouts. And it's searchable. Back in the day, getting a home or bug installed—just getting the warrant alone was this holy hassle, not to mention how you were always running up against liberal judges who wouldn't grant you . . ."

Stenton made the slightest gesture of impatience, just a movement of his clasped hands a few inches outward, and the police chief wrapped up.

"HereMe," he said, "is the best tool law enforcement has both to prevent crime and investigate crime. All we need is access."

"And now we have access," Stenton said, and by that he meant that the Every would not be waiting for a judge's warrant. "Morris and I are working with our security team, as well as our Mossad and NSA friends to come up with a series of words that we'll search for—anything related to the planning of a bombing. If we hear these words, we de-anonymize the user and we can work with law enforcement to issue search warrants and such. Meanwhile, we'll be collating any of this audio with location and movement data we have on the users' phones and ovals. We'll first start with the five Bay Area counties and—" He stopped. A hand had been raised. "Yes."

The raised hand belonged to a fresh-faced man of about thirty. He had the look of an assistant district attorney—an earnest civil servant in a white button-down shirt.

"Sir," he said, "those are two of the specific tasks we can't perform with the recordings. We can't specifically search for words, and we can't de-anonymize any users. I mean, that's the core of the Wyden Law and the Quinterelli Guidelines."

Stenton looked at him, his blank black eyes resting only briefly on the man's pink, unlined forehead. Stenton said nothing directly to him, paused almost imperceptibly, and then continued. Plans were made to search all audio from the five counties closest to the campus and report back in thirty-six hours. If that yielded insufficient results, the radius would widen. The van had an old Utah sticker on what was left of the windshield, and though Morris thought that was probably misdirection, Stenton wanted the recordings made by all of Utah's HereMes scanned, too.

"Nevada, too," Stenton said. "There's no reason not to."

The work began the next day. Delaney signed another NDA and Karina introduced her to Every software called Everyword. She was given noise-cancelling headphones and an oversized tablet. On the screen, a simple transcript, with two speakers, Speaker 1 and Speaker 2, were identified.

"There's never been simpler software," Karina

said. "The audio will play, and your screen will follow the transcription. See the highlighted words?"

Delaney saw that the first word of Speaker 1, **Wait,** was highlighted in yellow.

"As the audio plays," Karina explained, "the highlighter will go word to word, and your task is to make sure the transcript is getting it right. Your team is working on the more difficult accents, so the software sometimes has trouble with the English. I think this one is Eastern European?" Karina checked the metadata in the document. "Yes, so those accents are tough for the AI sometimes. Why aren't they speaking Bulgarian or Russian, you might ask? That's the second wrinkle. These are generally mixed groups. Maybe a father and son. The father's from Sofia but the son was born here. So they speak English at home. Maybe it's two friends, one a Russian speaker, the other speaks Croatian. So they meet in the middle with English. The result is that you have heavily accented English, and that sometimes needs human oversight to make sure we're not missing anything."

"Okay," Delaney said. "And if there's something incorrect?"

"You type in the correction. The AI will learn from that. And your correction will be part of the record, too, in case it needs to be triple-checked later."

Delaney felt ready. She looked back to Karina,

who was holding her phone's lens up to her. "Can you acknowledge that you're analyzing these transcripts and audiofiles with no preconceptions?"

"Yes," Delaney said.

"Can you acknowledge that it is against Every policy to make any assumptions or inferences based on the accents of any of the speakers in these audio files?"

"Yes."

"Can you acknowledge that you are only looking for discrepancies between the audio and the transcript?"

"Yes."

"And can you acknowledge that you are not an investigator, member of law enforcement, or of the Every security system?"

"Yes. I am none of those things," Delaney said.

"Finally, can you acknowledge that you will not venture any further than the task assigned, that you will not make inferences or assumptions about the persons speaking, nor will you make any attempt to personally de-anonymize these persons?"

"Yes. I will do none of those things," Delaney said.

Karina lowered her lens and smiled. "Legal. The thing to remember is that you're fixing the words. So if you do hear a word that's incriminating, AI will flag that, too. If you hear 'bomb,' you'll type that in, and the security team will take it from there. Got it?"

* * *

The work was plainly immoral and Delaney was
sick every minute she did it. The first conversation she analyzed was between a father and a son.
She was no expert on accents, but she guessed the
older man's first language was Russian. The son had
a British accent, with some odd European touches
thrown in. The fantasy in Delaney's mind was that
the father was a wealthy Moscow industrialist who
had sent his son to a Swiss boarding school, then
Cambridge, and now one or the both of them had
settled in Palo Alto. Somewhere along the line
the son's Russian became worse than the father's
English, so they spoke in the latter tongue.

> Speaker 1: HereMe, can you check the traffic
> into San Francisco now?
> HereMe: Traffic is heavy on 101 but 280 is
> moving. The average speed of traffic is 34 miles
> per hour.
> Speaker 2: See? 280 is always the better op-
> tion. 101 is a nightmare. And so ugly. 280 is
> actually beautiful.

Delaney took Speaker 1 to be the younger of the
two. Speaker 2 sounded like a man in his 60s.

> Speaker 1: HereMe, shut off.
> Speaker 2: Is it off?

Speaker 1: You heard me. I just shut it off.
Speaker 2: So I spoke to Vlad yesterday.
Speaker 1: Has he admitted he's sleeping with Amina?
Speaker 2: Please. He's not sleeping with Amina. Amina's in London.
Speaker 1: Vlad was in London for a month!
Speaker 2: He would never. Vlad's a unit.

Delaney paused the audio and reversed. She listened to the sentence again. The last word hadn't been **unit.** It was **eunuch.** She keyed in the change and was rewarded with a tiny ping.

Speaker 1: HereMe, activate. Is Vlad sleeping with Amina?
Speaker 2: [Laughter]
HereMe: This question is a good one. Let me think and get back to you.
Speaker 1: [Laughter]
Speaker 2: [Laughter]
Speaker 1: HereMe, shut off.
Speaker 2: You catch Chelsea yesterday?

Delaney lay in her bed that night with a terrible idea. It was world-wrecking and immediately she knew she would have to let it loose. The day had repulsed her, had fascinated her, had enthralled her. She'd heard thirty-six conversations, all of them desperately private. In almost every instance the speakers had said "HereMe, activate" and "HereMe, shut off," with no effect whatsoever; the recording was activated automatically whenever any voice was heard. The owners' control over their HereMe devices was akin to a child in the backseat of a car, playing with a toy steering wheel.

Delaney needed a vessel for this new idea. She'd spent two days at HereMe and had met one person, Karina. Karina could be the lead on it. She had that kind of presence. But perhaps she was missing that hint of fury necessary. The soul of a crusader. This notion needed passion and stubbornness, for if it met any resistance, it would be at the outset, and that initial resistance would have to be shamed by righteousness, by outrage. After that, after even the first wave of implementation, it would be unstoppable.

Delaney asked to remain at HereMe for the next week, too. She needed to gather material, and she needed to find her crusader.

Speaker 1: Because you're an ass, that's why.
Speaker 2: [inaudible]
Speaker 1: HereMe, activate. What's a plane ticket from Oakland to Maui cost? Tomorrow.
HereMe: A coach seat on American Airlines on tomorrow's 12:15 flight from Oakland to Maui is $1,290.
Speaker 2: Get the fuck off of that.

Speaker 1: I'll spend the money. I need a break. It'll be worth the cash.

Speaker: 2: To get away from me.

Speaker 1: Right. You're never not here. You do nothing.

Speaker 2: Know what? You're welcome to leave any time. Not just to Maui. You can move out, you can die, you can drink bleach. I do not care. Is this thing on? HereMe, deactivate. Cindy, do not touch that. That was Rena's.

Speaker 1: I'll touch anything.

Speaker 2: You will not touch my shit. Don't be a child.

Speaker 1: I'm the child? You know what I need? A man who doesn't need perpetual vali- dation from every ex-girlfriend.

Speaker 2: And for you it's always drama. These endless one-act plays. Soliloquies. You're always at the edge of the stage in the spotlight, singing your pain to the audience in the dark. Hey! Put that down before I have to take it from you.

Delaney's screen dinged. "Time to stretch and walk around! Three minutes is the window."

Dazed, Delaney made her way to the hallway, where she found Karina.

"Anything interesting?" Karina asked. She blinked and the blue morpho flickered.

"The recordings?" Delaney said. "Yes. Very interesting."

"Anything relevant to the investigation?" Another flash of blue.

"No," Delaney said, and then had a thought. She hadn't planned for it to begin at that moment, but she'd been thinking it through, practicing her overtures, anticipating reactions, counter-arguments, and she felt she was ready. Karina was in front of her, and while she wasn't sure this was her crusader, another opportunity was not guaranteed.

"I've heard a lot of strife," Delaney said.

Karina nodded, her eyes wide, as if to say, **This comes as a surprise?**

"Do we report it?" Delaney said.

"No," Karina said. Morpho-blink. "Remember, none of this is admissable. We're not supposed to be listening at all. So no, and no. But you know the two cases where actual murder-plans had been caught on HereMe? That's different."

"But regular domestic abuse gets a pass?"

Karina lowered her chin. "You being serious?"

"I don't know," Delaney said. "I mean, are we for transparency or not?"

"Outside of a terror investigation like this, which is not strictly authorized, by the way, the home is always going to be a legal no-go zone," Karina said.

"But think of the implications," Delaney said. "We're basically saying that things that aren't socially acceptable in public are acceptable at home. We're condoning bad behavior as long as it's in someone's house. I mean, haven't you heard arguments when you listen to your audio?"

"Sure."

"I have, too. A lot. And I'd call much of it abuse. Emotional abuse, and that's the gateway to physical abuse. I'm actually surprised I haven't heard any violence yet. But it's just a matter of time."

Karina closed her eyes again, and shimmery blue filled the room. "We have caught crimes on audio, in many countries, and those have been reported," she said. "We have an agreement with law enforcement in some other countries. The Philippines. Poland. I forget where else. Turkey, I think."

"But see, that's random, and it's after the fact," Delaney said. "What I'm talking about is something different. I'm talking about full access, and **known** access. The same kind of monitoring there is in public. I don't think anyone argues anymore that the precipitous drop in crime is a direct result of the prevalence of SeeChange cams."

"But what do you mean? Someone from the Every is listening in the whole time? To every home in the world. The cost would be—"

"No. No one has to listen, not in real time," Delaney said. "It's AI monitoring first of all. And the key thing is that everyone assumes they **are** being heard. That would provide the same behavioral inhibitor as cameras in stores and streets.

People assume they're being watched in public, so they behave better. Now we take it into the home. And we already have 260 million HereMes already in place."

Delaney watched Karina think, then pushed it further.

"We have smoke detectors, right? Those are legally required. Because they save lives. Any surveillance that saves lives is inevitable."

Karina's face froze. She saw the light. "Okay . . ." she said.

"This is no different," Delaney said. "Instead of sensing smoke or carbon monoxide, it's sensing strife. Signs of trouble. Prelude to abuse or violence."

Now Karina was nodding vigorously. "I get it. Raised voices, sharp tones, certain inflammatory words," she said.

Delaney knew immediately that Karina would sell it. She was already taking leaps. "Okay, okay," Karina said, her eyes wide, seeing the world changed, changed by her. "And what would trigger a 911 call?"

"I was actually thinking," Delaney said, "that once certain inflammatory words were spoken, or tones of voice or volume were reached, then a series of protocols would kick in. First, AI would flag it, and local authorities would be notified that something was potentially happening. Just a yellow dot on a screen. If there's a police car in the area, they know to stay close. Then our AI tracks it to see if it escalates."

"Cops could patch in if they wanted to," Karina added. "They see the yellow dot, patch in and listen in real time."

"Right," Delaney said.

"It'd be a First Amendment fight for a minute, but it'd lose on the fire-in-the-theater grounds. Imminent violence. And cops would have probable cause to at least knock on the door. It would probably cut spousal abuse down to a fraction of the current rates."

"Not just spousal abuse, but **child** abuse," Delaney said. And she realized it was true. What did it mean for humans if this was true? In a moment she knew, unequivocally, that this is where the species was heading. Resistance to home surveillance would be a tacit endorsement of domestic violence. Anyone without home surveillance would be presumed guilty of horrible crimes.

"Hold on," Karina said. She was already on her way to the conference room. "We have to bring everyone in. Do you mind?"

The Every had encouraged its teams to Follow the Light—a management strategy that dictated that when there was an idea being birthed, it should be followed and fed, and immediately, lest the flame dim.

* * *

When the twenty-one team leaders had assembled, nine of them isos, Karina summarized the conversation thus far, and Delaney was invited to continue where they'd left off. Delaney kept her foot on the gas.

"The debate about smart speakers has been puzzling to me from the start," she said, "because I see these as possibly the best weapon we have against child abuse." She'd decided to focus on this angle. There could be no resistance.

The reaction of the team was swift and startled. One woman looked down, her eyes welling. Karina turned to this reddening countenance. "Rhea, did you want to say something?" Rhea had a round, friendly face framed by Bettie Page bangs. She sipped obsessively on her waterpack tube.

"No. I'll add on maybe later," Rhea said. "Finish your thought . . . ." She glanced at Delaney, but couldn't remember her name.

"Delaney," Karina said helpfully.

"Right. Delaney. You keep going."

Delaney continued. "Okay," she said. "Imagine smart speakers are just as common as smoke detectors. As far as I know, smoke detectors and sprinklers are required in all new construction."

"They are," one of the isos said, his voice disembodied and digitally altered.

"So why wouldn't a smart speaker be required, too?" Delaney asked. "And for the same reason—to protect the inhabitants of the home from harm. The two things are virtually identical, when you think of it. The smoke detector senses smoke or carbon monoxide, and sounds an alarm. The people inside hear the alarm, and the fire department is notified."

Now Rhea had her face in her hands. Karina nodded to Delaney, closing her butterfly eyes, urging her on.

"Just like any situation where you feel you're being observed," Delaney said, "your behavior improves. That's been demonstrated here in myriad ways, from SeeChange on. But I would argue that the most dangerous place in the world is the home. The majority of violent crimes are perpetuated by someone you know."

Now Rhea was weeping openly, and she was quickly surrounded by Everyones attempting to comfort her without, of course, touching her. Meanwhile, Karina was patting the air above Rhea's shoulder, and a half-dozen other Everyones were near her, making sympathetic faces and sounds. Finally Rhea wiped her face and straightened her posture and her face took on a determined cast.

"I'm sorry, everyone," she said. "I was abused at home. Some of you know this. It went on for years. It was such a shitty cliché. The one where the molester-stepdad is protected by the mother with low self-esteem."

Now half the people in the room were crying, too. Delaney wanted to hunt down Rhea's predator and deliver frontier justice.

"This would have caught him," Rhea continued. "I know we're talking audio through HereMe, but that's the start. These should be required for any home where there are kids."

Delaney saw the future. Cameras would be required in any place where there were children: schools, churches, libraries, homes. There was no possibility of it being any other way. Anyone refusing or resisting would be **de facto** allowing, planning, or engaging in abuse. And Rhea would be the ideal person to create and justify this new reality.

"Goddamn it!" Rhea said. "Right now some kid like me is being abused, and we're complicit because we have the tech but it's not being implemented already. It should be everywhere. Today. **Yesterday.** People are dying because we're not listening."

XXXIV.

THE NEXT FEW DAYS WERE FRANTIC, full of mission and fury. Karina and Rhea had set up a meeting with the Gang of 40 and the Every's top legal minds, including a dozen former prosecutors and four former ACLU attorneys. For the day, the HereMe team created a presentation that they believed irrefutable. Karina insisted she go alone, and she did so, with the HereMe team tearfully bidding her good luck.

She returned two hours later, her eyes apoplectic. She looked around the room and composed herself.

"We have more work to do," she said steadily. "At this moment it seems that the constitutional obstacles are significant—the Fourth Amendment being chief among them."

Rhea's face went purple, then pale, and finally fell apart. The team gathered around her, patting the air near her as more tears were shed.

"This is government-sanctioned abuse," Delaney said.

"Exactly," Karina said. Now her hand was stroking the airspace above Rhea's head.

Delaney was mildly shocked at the outcome. It was highly unusual for the Every to give in to legal boundaries. They had long been inclined to try new notions in the real world and let them play out—well before inviting any regulation. The playbook would have had them try the program locally, with acquiescent households and the local police. After six months, the concept proven, it would quickly spread, as had doorbell cams and their lockstep alliance with law enforcement, reaching saturation far before any legal challenge could be contemplated.

"Take the rest of the day to . . ." Karina couldn't finish.

The next step, to Delaney, was painfully obvious. But she was already far more visible and central to this particular idea than she wanted to be. She was dangerously close to getting credit for it, so she waited a day for the HereMe team to propose what she thought was inevitable.

The team was despondent. Rhea had taken a personal day at home. Karina solicited ideas and got none—none but the coining of the term **dungeon** for homes without HereMes; the social media team programmed bots to popularize the slur. Otherwise, the team lobbied Every attorneys, but with no additional arguments or evidence. After three days, Delaney had no choice. She asked for a private meeting.

Karina met her on the perimeter track. Her eyes were vibrating. "We don't have much time," she said. "I hope this has something to do with how we make this work."

"We need proof," Delaney said. "You're giving them the vague promise of abuse prevented. But what if you gave them actual proof?"

"Catch someone abusing someone?" Karina asked.

"The AI is searching for words related to the bombing, and that's fine. That should continue. But what are the odds the bomber has a HereMe in their home? They used a thirty-year-old truck. They left no digital trail. They know what they're doing."

Karina glared at the Bay. The view was far clearer now, without the tents and shanties. "Okay, so?"

"This dovetails with the bombing, but it's bigger than it. We're talking about requiring all families to have a HereMe in the home, activated at all times. We need to prove the concept. We need to program the AI to listen for the indicators we were talking about—raised voices, broken plates, slammed doors, certain keywords."

"Okay. Then?"

"We have hundreds of police departments that

have been working with the Every for years. Whose work has been made far easier with our data, doorbell cams, neighborhood cams, license-plate readers, search histories, downloads—"

"Right, right."

"Well, we begin a program whereby AI dings when they hear trouble, that address is sent instantly to the local cops, they come and prevent an incident before it happens. The cops have bodycams on, so they get footage. In a few hours we can edit together a 90-second sample. Potential child abuse in the home caught by HereMe AI, relayed to the cops, cops arrive in time, wife and children relieved, crime prevented."

"The lawyers will hate it," Karina said.

"Maybe on this one we go around the lawyers. We prove the concept to the public, and it becomes something the public wants. The lawyers and the law follow the people's will. Security cameras in ninety percent of the places they are already are blatantly unconstitutional, but the public wants them. And no one challenges them. Who could prove they're harmed by the presence of surveillance cameras? Criminals? A class-action suit brought by burglars?"

"Right, right," Karina said.

"The main thing is that we're preventing abuse. It's that simple," Delaney said.

"The cops will make mistakes," Karina said.

"We're not talking about them busting down

doors. But arriving, doing a wellness check, maybe removing the kids from the home for a few days. The evidence will be obvious. The abusers will be exposed, neutralized."

"They can turn off the HereMes."

"But they can't. That'll be the law, eventually," said Delaney. "Just as it's the law to have smoke detectors. It's the law that cams are in every classroom and church. The one place kids aren't protected is the home—and that's where most abuse happens. This is screamingly simple."

"Good. I'll give you two days," Karina said.

"Me? No, I'm not—"

"You just proposed this. What's the problem?"

"I'm not the right person. Rhea should—"

"You think it's more appropriate for Rhea to be re-traumatized by searching through audio of imminent domestic-abuse cases?"

The next day Delaney was sitting next to a programmer named Liam. He was a pale, sharp-featured man of about twenty-six, educated at MIT and completely surprised to be brought into such a project. Karina essentially locked them in a room and gave them two days to produce results. Liam had a habit of looking directly into Delaney's eyes, locking them into a vibrating ocular clench, which helped her keep her eyes away from the vents cut into Liam's bodysuit—two inner-thigh windows for testicular cleavage.

"I'm sorry," Delaney said. "I know this is probably a lot."

"We'll end abuse somewhere?" he asked. "That's the goal, right?"

Look up, Delaney told herself, but the flashes of strained flesh kept summoning her eyes downward.

"In theory, yes," Delaney said.

"Where do we start?" he asked.

Grateful for a task, Delaney looked up the top ten counties in the United States for child abuse. After listing them for Liam, he found they had a relatively low saturation rate for HereMes in these homes—only 58 percent. Still, that was 1.6 million homes.

"That's our search area?" he asked.

"Yes, that's our search area," Delaney said. She stared at the spreadsheets on his screen until the numbers took flight and blurred before her. Finally he looked to her. "And we're searching for what words?"

Because the project had to be secret and the results quick, they had no time to find linguists, domestic violence experts, any authorities of any kind. It was up to Delaney.

"Just type them, send them to me, and we'll make a list," Liam said. "Send as you go."

"And the searches happen instantly?" she asked.

"It's current, yes," he said. "Not always, but after the bombing we started real-time searches. We get dings the moment the criteria are met. Eighty,

ninety percent match. Like, if the phrase we're looking for is 'I'm going to kill you,' then anything close
will get us a ding. 'Gonna kill you,' 'I'll kill you,'
'I plan to kill you,' 'Someone should kill you,' 'Get
back here or I'll kill you.' Anything like that."

He said the phrases with no affect. And then he
waited for Delaney.

"Start with those," she said. Beyond a handful
of films she'd seen on the subject, Delaney had no
point of reference.

Liam typed them in and again turned to Delaney.
She was blank.

"How about, 'You little fucker'?" he asked.

"Sure," she said, and he typed it. His oval pinged,
and he sighed elaborately.

"Ready?" he said, and from under his desk he retrieved an enormous rubber band, each side ending
in a molded hand-grip. He connected it to a hook
on the wall, and began furiously pulling at it, as if
desperately swimming away from the wall. Thirty
seconds later he took a break. "You want?"

Delaney took hold of the grips, attempted her
own tragic swim, and relinquished them to Liam.
They traded for a few more minutes and Liam sat
down again.

"How about 'You little **mother**fucker?'"

Delaney, out of breath, made an approving
sound, and for the next hour, Liam's fingers flew
and Delaney occasionally added or amended.

I'm gonna beat you.
You whore.
You worthless whore.
You worthless little whore.
Get your ass over here.
Get your worthless ass over here.
You deserve a beating.
I'm going to beat your ass.
I'm gonna beat your worthless ass.
In an hour they had 188 phrases and Liam
thought it enough. He stood before her, stretched,
and now Delaney could not avert her eyes. When he
turned around, his rear vents revealed themselves.
They were vertical, bisecting each buttock, and he
seemed intent that she have a look.

Sleep was a challenge. Delaney lay in her tube,
knowing she would wake up and have to eavesdrop
on the private conversations of unsuspecting fami-
lies. She cycled through the peaks of Idaho.
Borah Peak.
Leatherman Peak.
Mount Church.
Diamond Peak.
None of her work at the Every up to then
had been so direct; all else had been abstract
by comparison.
Mount Breitenbach.
Lost River Peak.

Donaldson Peak.

Sleep pulled her under, if only for a few hours. She woke, turned over, pictured the deaths of children in twenty variations.

Hyndman Peak.

USGS Peak.

No Regret Peak.

And finally she slept through to morning.

When she arrived at their workspace, Liam was sitting and for this she was grateful. She quickly crossed the room to him so he wouldn't get up. She rushed through greetings, staring at his blank screen. In her peripheral vision she saw nothing but black vinyl.

The process of the AI readying itself to search for these keywords and phrases took longer than expected, he said, and he'd been working late, finding and squashing bugs, and building in filters designed to sort out television and radio noise, and to focus on adult voices.

"Thank you," she said, looking at his hair.

"With the bombing," he said, "we got tens of thousands of matches in the first few days. It's too much to wade through. In that case, of course, it was a rarer breed we were looking for. There are more abusers in the world than there are people who drive bomb-laden vans onto our campus, I'm betting."

For no reason at all, her eyes fell to his lap, where she found he was wearing not a similar bodysuit, but the same bodysuit, with the same upper-thigh vents.

"I also put in kids' screams," he said. "Like, the AI will search for screams. High-pitched screams, wails, that kind of thing."

"Thanks," Delaney said, and left the room.

In the bathroom, the cartoon skunk met her, grinning.

"Hi Delaney!"

She ran to the stall and defenestrated her breakfast in a peach-colored flood.

"Is someone sick?" the skunk asked, its face a sympathetic pout.

"I'm fine," Delaney said.

"Remember, the clinic is available 24-7. Should I tell them you're coming? Your EveryMed plan recommends you visit after an event like this."

"Just nerves," Delaney said. "Just excited about all the progress we're making," she amended.

She left the stall and began to wash her hands, thinking the skunk would focus on that, and begin the birthday song. She did sing the song—in the background. In the foreground, a second, louder, voice emerged. It wasn't the skunk's. It seemed to be coming from the cartoon tree next to the cartoon skunk. "There are many things that vomiting can indicate. Food poisoning, bacterial infections, even pregnancy. We do recommend you seeing a clinician. I'll arrange with your OwnSelf system to find a good time today."

Delaney declined, went back and forth with the skunk and the tree for a while, and finally escaped. When she got back to Liam, he was on the floor, apparently in the middle of a strenuous set of burpees. He finished, settled back in his chair, and informed Delaney that he'd already found thirty-eight matches. They were broken into batches tied to each phrase they'd programmed in.

"The most common is 'I'll kill you,'" Liam said. "But I almost think we should go for one of the more specific ones. Remember when I added 'Get over here you little bitch?'"

Delaney didn't remember that. But Liam had been typing furiously, as if channeling the phrases from memory.

"There's a few hits with that phrase," he said. "I checked out one that's in progress. You want to hear? I'll back it up a few minutes."

His finger was on his touchscreen. Delaney's skin was on fire. **Damn,** Delaney thought. **Damn, damn, damn.** She nodded. He touched the screen and the audio came alive, all over the room. The voices were in stereo surround-sound, a simultaneous transcription on the wallscreen. Delaney read the words, if only to dull the effect of the audio, which was so loud it seemed to be coming from the recesses of her own skull.

Male voice: You don't have a fucking clue, do you?

[Pause 2.1 seconds]

Male voice: Your bitch of a daughter thinks she can fuck with me.

Female voice: Don, put that down. It's not funny.

Girl voice: Let him talk. Every time he opens his mouth the house gets stupider.

Male voice: Get over here, you little bitch!

"Turn it off," Delaney said.

"The scream comes in a second," he said. "Sounds like he hits her, or throws something that hits her."

"Turn it off!"

Liam killed the sound.

Between burpee sessions, the project continued. After much discussion with Karina and Rhea, Rhea agreed to lead HereMe, SaveMe. Karina's concerns about re-traumatization, it turned out, were unfounded. Rhea wanted to be the face of the project and threw herself into the work like a warrior.

Focusing on the same household, Rhea led the team to the planned 90-second demonstration. She fed the audio and address to the local police, who got a warrant and arrested the stepfather on suspicion of abuse. The police bodycams provided dramatic footage of the drive to the house, the knock

on the door, the stepfather's shock at their appearance, his brief resistance to arrest, his head being
guided into the squad car and, most importantly,
the utter disbelief, the barely hidden glee, of the
young woman, about fifteen, standing in the doorway, watching her oppressor sent away.

And yet the Every lawyers still wouldn't authorize
its release. Using it as evidence would be tricky for
the district attorney, that much was known. But re-
leasing in-home audio to the public was counter to
the HereMe's consent agreement, and had no precedent, they said, in the Every's history.

But what about social media? Rhea asked.
Postings and photos and video have been admissable
for years, she insisted.

Those are posted, the attorneys said. They are
voluntarily self-published, they said. Or those
people are caught, in public, in the committal of a
crime. At home, in the privacy thereof, it's different,
they said. It's different when the evidence is accu-
mulated without consent.

Of course the HereMe minds went to the obvious
solution—alerting HereMe's terms of consent—and
yet the attorneys again were obstructive. In buying
a product manufactured by a private company, you
cannot consent to the breach of your rights—not in
terms of the judicial branch at least. Our terms of
consent don't alter the law, they said.

And that was the end of Rhea's patience. She did

what she felt she had to do, and what had been the
way of things for three decades now, and would
be the way of things forever more. She leaked the
video, with all identifying characteristics intact but
the Every's participation opaque. The video was
a sensation, viewed a hundred million times in a
week. She authorized more; they made one each
day, and pushed them out through a variety of
cloaked accounts.

Each video began with an exterior shot of the
home—this was easy to find, given the Every had
photographed every American home, from satellites and the street, multiple times. The audio
caught by HereMe then began, with the transcribed
words scrolling over the home in white type. When
a given speaker began talking, his or her face appeared and could be identified in seconds. When
offending words were spoken, when the conversation escalated and tensions rose, the POV switched
to the police dispatcher, who, alerted by the AI,
began listening. Squad cars were sent, and the
POV switched to their car- and bodycams, and the
view from the local surveillance blimps (most self-
respecting cities had blimps). The slam of car doors,
the rush to the front porch. Now the video had
both perspectives—the audio in the home and the
video outside. They were merged into a tense and
cinematic cross-cutting confrontation, ending with
the arrival of Social Services, the saving of the child

or children, the arrests of fathers or uncles—in one case a grandmother—and finally a coda enumerating charges and court hearings pending.

The clips were hugely popular; the most dramatic of the first batch was the most-watched video for eight days, amassing 420 million views. The father in that particular instance was caught screaming threats and obscenities at his eight-year-old twins, was arrested and kept in jail for seven days before being released on $500,000 bond. The district attorney, though, had no evidence to go on beyond the vague threats and loud voices in the HereMe audio. It was not against the law—not yet—to yell inside the home. The twins had not yet been abused, it was determined.

Still, a new kind of justice was done. What the letter of the law could not or would not do, the public would. The father was fired from his job on the following Monday. On Tuesday, the mother—who public opinion determined was complicit—was fired from hers. The nation seemed satisfied, and while the legality of HereMe, SaveMe was being worked out, the program proceeded at an urgent pace.

Partner police departments were identified—eighty-eight of them in cities large and small, with some sorting for those with higher-than-average instance of domestic violence and child abuse. The departments were given link-ups to HereMes in their towns, and the program triggered hundreds of police visits. In some cases, the AI was hearing voices from television, music, video games and even audiobooks, and this provided much helpful information for HereMe's programmers.

It was not perfect, no, but the AI was still learning, and of the six hundred and nine visits that first month, fully eleven of them yielded actionable results. In three cases, siblings were fighting and those were settled after the children had spent a month or so in foster care. In two cases, parents and children were rehearsing plays, and these situations were explained after single nights in jail and effective lawyering. The key takeaway, though, was that in six instances, real trouble was likely prevented. "I'm gonna kill you!" was heard in three cases; "You're getting a beating" was recorded in two. The crack of a belt was correctly ascertained in one.

From the public, Delaney expected a deluge of resistance. There was something off-limits, she was sure, about the home—something far beyond the reading of emails, or the surveillance on the street, or the presence of cameras in taxis and subways and libraries and stairwells and schools and restaurants and bakeries and offices and government buildings and groceries and corner stores and boutiques and candy shops and movie theaters and the DMV and art galleries and museums and hospitals and retirement homes and boat-supply retailers and off-track betting centers and chiropractic practices and hotels and motels and vape shops and public bathrooms.

The home, though, was different. She expected a hundred million people a day to do what she'd done at her old place with Wes—she expected a mass tossing-out of the HereMes in one global show of disgust.

But this did not happen. Instead, people saw the wisdom in it. They saw the gains in safety and security. They wanted to show their virtue by demonstrating it, all day and night, to the AI listeners.

People grew quieter at home. They were more careful with their words. They did not yell at their spouses or children. They did not threaten. Sex became quieter, laughter more cautious. Those who shrieked when they laughed or sneezed or came found a way to suppress their noisemaking. The happy screams of children confused the AI for a long while, and brought authorities to a few million homes before the machines learned. By then, children knew to be quieter—or, better yet, just quiet.

And only the most lunatic and criminal attempted abuse. The world grew safer for all humans in weeks, and would grow exponentially safer in the years to come. Just as the insertion of microchips into children had eliminated all but a few child abductions, the universal adoption of HereMes would guarantee the safety of children wherever they were required. Which was everywhere.

It would begin with private companies. They would require their employees with children to install and keep HereMes awake in the home. Churches would follow suit, then private schools. Homeowners' associations would have no choice but to require them, too, then co-op boards and landlords. Then hotels, motels and vacation rentals. Outside the obvious issues of child safety, it was a liability matter, too. Towns and states, and finally nations, would find ways to make them mandatory, and after some desultory legal opposition, they would become ubiquitous and beloved in most every corner of the globe, giving humanity a new sense of control and safety, and all this would be vastly improved—and the human race far closer to perfection—when HereMe added video, and this became law, too.

XXXV.

IT WAS SUNDAY NIGHT and Francis was gloating. In the kitchen he boxed, his feet dancing around the firepit, his little fists jabbing. Delaney's next rotation was at PrefCom, and Francis couldn't wait; he'd already begun a kind of preliminary onboarding in the Havel. After the catastrophe of the unhoused humans, he'd been subdued, even cowed, but now he seemed on the verge of a comeback.

"I know you've signed an NDA," he said, "but it's still a big deal you're going to see what you'll see. And you have me to thank for that." Realizing that might not sound Everypropriate, he amended. "I mean, we should **both** be grateful for the opportunity."

Delaney had watched HereMe proliferate like a plague. Rhea and Karina were apostles of a world message of peace-through-surveillance. No one objected. And anyone who was tempted to object was quickly cowed into silence: fighting for unseen and unheard homes was fighting for spouse abusers, child molesters, terror-planners. Every week brought some story of a plot thwarted, an adolescent saved from harm. And more than being shy about being on camera in their homes, the vast majority of people welcomed it, and were tickled when AI monitors identified funny or adorable things they or their children or pets did in the home, and then broadcast, automatically—it was so convenient—these funny and adorable moments to the world without their knowledge or permission.

Delaney said nothing, numbed to the unintended consequences of every goddamned thing she and Wes had proposed. The travel industry was flattened by Stop+Lük, and its now-unemployed millions were apoplectic. A cruise ship even sailed by Treasure Island, its skeletal staff mooning and middle-fingering the Every campus in pitiful defiance. The ship was otherwise empty. No one was going anywhere.

And no one was eating bananas. Or pineapples, or any fruit or good that had heretofore traveled more than a few hundred miles. Angry entreaties from the Papaya Industry Association—a real thing—had no effect. Millions more became unemployed with every new thing the Every canceled, but there was always work in the Every warehouses, where humans were invited to work beside robot package-pickers and while monitored by AI, and be paid a fair minimum wage for it. It was an orderly system.

Delaney wanted to scream and rage and plan more urgently, but Wes was nowhere to be found. Or rather, he was easily found, because he'd moved onto campus. But he'd become busier every day, what with having been elevated to the Gang of 40, a development Delaney saw as a key way they might probe the company for soft spots. But she couldn't reach him. Her most innocuous texts—**I thank you**—had gone unanswered. She expected a simple **I love you,** for no one could object to that, or wonder about it, but she got nothing. One day he hinted in the most cryptic of texts—**Big things afoot. So interesting. Catch up later**—that he was unavailable for the sharing of new ideas of silly-subterfuge. And so she waited, and continued the rotations, which led her to this one, at PrefCom.

"AYS is great, of course," Francis said, and did a very sad kung-fu kick in the direction of the fridge, "but PrefCom has teeth. PrefCom has power. You step outside your prefs, you feel it. But I've already said too much. The rest is need-to-know."

Delaney knew that the department had grown more furtive in recent months—that there were new plans afoot. It was no secret that they'd added a few hundred staff, and were absorbing much of the Every's advertising and financial operations.

"The growth is astronomical," Francis said.

"You'll see. Some of it at least." He pretended to chop the counter with a weak fist. "I'm not the one who you'll be working with, though. It'll probably be Ladarious or Allyson, but I don't know. I'll walk you in, though. That'll be cool. Take your roomie to work day!" he said, and threw a punch.

But Monday morning, after madding and dressing, with Francis at the door—at the opening where the door used to be—Delaney received an audio message from Gabriel Chu. "Hello Delaney, this is Gabriel Chu. I'm hoping you can meet me at the Aviary at 8:40 this morning. I've checked with your OwnSelf and cleared all obstacles. You can visit PrefCom another time. See you soon."

Delaney searched her mind for the Aviary. Oh god, she thought. It was the top floor of Algo Mas, the observatory from which a dozen or so Everyones had leapt to their deaths. It had been closed as long as she'd been at the Every.

Delaney checked the clock. It was 8:28. She told Francis her visit to PrefCom would be delayed, and she thundered down the steps to the Daisy. She needed Joan, and texted her, hoping she would be at the AYS office. **Working out. See you soon!** was Joan's auto-reply. Gabriel's message had been cryptic, almost aggressive. He left no room for debate or alteration of the plan. Delaney stood in the shadows before the Daisy, pondering her options. Pretend she hadn't gotten the message? Impossible—he'd have already received confirmation that his message had been heard. A surge of protest welled within her. What authority did he have to summon her like this? Did she have to go? What if she just didn't respond, didn't come running?

Across the Daisy, she saw someone who looked like Wes—he had Wes's bowlegged cattle-rustling swagger—walking across the grass. But this person was dressed like a male figure skater. He was wearing a form-fitting lycra wrapper with pastel swooshes of color, a sort of marzipan camouflage. She stared, then checked her phone, tapped for Wes's location and realized it was him. He was surrounded by Everypersons, like Socrates leading a peripatetic lesson, and he seemed very happy, positively aglow.

It was 8:40:54 when she arrived at Algo Mas. She'd decided she had to at least show up. She didn't have to go to the roof. She'd see Gabriel and assess from there. And what was she worried about? That he was secretly throwing people off the observatory? She wasn't sleeping enough. Her mind was disintegrating.

"There you are!" It was Kiki. She'd appeared out of thin air—and had no reason to be there. Delaney didn't need her help finding the building, and this wasn't a rotation.

"I saw that you were coming here," Kiki said in explanation, and tapped the screen on her arm. "Do you have a meeting inside? Maybe in the Aviary? I don't have an appointment, but I've always wanted to see it. Maybe I go in with you?"

Now Delaney saw that Kiki was wearing heels. And that her leggings were torn at the knees. And she had a sunhat in her hands, and in the sunhat were a collection of wildflowers and stones.

"Kiki, are you okay?" Delaney asked.

"So good!" Kiki said, altogether too loudly. "Shall we go?" She opened the door to Algo Mas and Delaney stepped in. Kiki rushed to the elevator bank and tapped every button she could. She planned to go up. "The Aviary!" she said. "The views are very dramatic up there. Where are you going? I can hit whatever floor you're going to, and I'll keep going up. It's not a problem."

"I think you should rest," Delaney said.

"Rest? Yes! Later!" Kiki sang, and pushed the buttons again. "Do you have a meeting here? With Gabriel? Hey, I've been meaning to ask how you're adjusting to life at the Every. It seems like you're doing **assiduously.**" Her oval let out an affirming bell. "How are you sleeping?"

"Kiki," Delaney said, and reached for her hand.

"Hey!" Kiki wailed and hid her hand from view. "Hands off, she's mine. She's mine to do what I wish. **Crepuscular!**" Her oval's bell rang and Kiki smiled. **"Magnanimity!"** she yelled, and another bell rang.

"Hello," a man's voice said. Delaney turned to find Gabriel Chu standing next to the elevator. He was wearing a dark-blue bodysuit, and with feet planted widely, he assessed the scene, his blade-like arms crossed before him. "Kiki, should you be here?" he asked.

"I was bringing her," Kiki said defensively, averting her eyes.

"The Aviary's closed," Gabriel said calmly. "You know that, Kiki, and you know why."

"I know," Kiki said. "I was just bringing her." She looked at Delaney for a long moment, and Delaney realized she couldn't recall her name. Finally Kiki looked at her screen. "Delaney," she said.

"That was very kind of you," Gabriel said. "What are you carrying with you?" He approached her so he could get a better view.

"Nothing," Kiki said. "Just some rocks I picked. And flowers."

"Okay," he said. "Again, the Aviary is closed."

"Nino's fine," Kiki said.

"I'm sure he is," Gabriel said.

"He's surrounded by love," Kiki said.

With his sculpted arm, Gabriel showed Kiki the door. "I trust you can show yourself out? I'm sure your day is full."

Kiki's eyes were wild, her mouth moving, shaping possible responses. But finally she said nothing, and spun out of the lobby and into the sunlight.

"Delaney," Gabriel said, completely unperturbed. "Thank you for coming." He looked at the lighted buttons on the elevator bank. "It doesn't work. We've discontinued the elevator in the interest of encouraging exercise. Will you come with me?"

Delaney followed Gabriel up the winding stairway, thinking of lighthouses and Kiki, and whatever Kiki planned to do once she got to the Aviary. Eight stories up, and Gabriel said little all the way. At one point he asked if Delaney was managing okay, and then corrected himself. "You're the mountain climber," he said. "This is nothing for someone with your background, I assume?"

When they reached the top floor, Delaney expected to find an open-air observatory, but instead it was closed everywhere—the Aviary had become a dark room lit only by makeshift track lighting. In the center of the room, two cushioned chairs sat side by side, separated by a portable screen. The screen was translucent but rippled, allowing a kind of funhouse privacy.

"Thank you for making this walk. This is one of the quietest places on campus, so I've sort of commandeered it. Can I ask for your cam?"

Delaney took it off and handed it to him.

"Please sit. Either chair," he said.

In the few steps she took to get to the nearest chair, she glanced around. She saw no cameras. Delaney's heart hammered. Her mind cycled through possible outcomes. She found herself wanting the safety of being watched.

He sat down on the second chair, and once he did, she could see only a blurry version of him. "Thank you for meeting me," he said. "I'm going to turn your cam off. But we will be seen through Friendy. Have you used it?"

"I have," she said, trying not to seem guarded.

"With your permission, we'll begin, and as you know, Friendy will be assessing your truthfulness. Do you consent?"

Delaney knew she couldn't refuse. But she'd never been subjected to Friendy in its present form—far more powerful and accurate than she and Wes had ever envisioned.

"That's fine," she said.

"Okay, then we'll begin now. Don't be nervous," Gabriel said. "You're not in any trouble. Just the opposite, really."

She glanced his way again, and saw that he had a small tablet on his lap. She hadn't seen it as he entered the room. She looked forward again, but from her peripheral vision she was sure her own face filled the screen. There was no camera visible in the blank wall opposite her, and yet her face was being captured and transmitted to Gabriel's screen.

"Relax if you can," he said brightly. "I know this is unexpected and without precedent, at least in your own experience here at the Every. Are you comfortable? The chair, the setting, that is?"

"I'm okay," she said.

"The chairs being side by side like this is an innovation of mine. I've found that eye-to-eye contact sometimes alters results. Some people get anxious and that sets off stress hormones. Sitting side by side, without the tension of eye contact, puts people at ease, at least relatively speaking. And again, you have no reason to be nervous. This should be enjoyable for us both."

Delaney laughed nervously, as if to underline to Gabriel the joke of him suggesting that a surprise interrogation in a blank pink room, between herself and this head-melter, could be enjoyable. Beyond that, Delaney was not ready. She looked down at the floor, at the faintest saber-shaped scratch in the timber. She thought of the work of her onetime boyfriend Derek. Though going undercover with Idaho Fish and Game was far afield from this white-box interrogation, the key to lying remained the same. The crucial thing was to simply say things that were true. Turn the question in your head, rephrase it—even reconstitute it—until your response could be truthful.

"Hold on," Gabriel said, and tapped his screen a few times.

She expected him to begin with easy questions and wend his way up to whatever purpose he had in mind, so she girded herself, taking some comfort in the fact that she would have some time to practice on banal queries before he went deeper.

"Why are you here?" he asked suddenly.

Delaney felt slapped. He knew. He knew all her plans. Her body instantly soaked itself in flop sweat, but she knew to keep her mood light. She forced herself to smile, then to laugh. She tried to pour a kind of carefree mirth over her voice, her face. She felt half-crazy as she laughed, dropped her head and laughed more.

"I consider myself a funny guy," he said, "but not that funny. And not when I haven't made a joke." He chuckled a bit, to indicate he was amused, not cross.

"Sorry," Delaney said, and laughed more. She really did sound insane, she realized, but it was better than seeming scared or caught. "I expected you to start with questions about pets and favorite foods. Your first question just struck me as funny in its directness."

"Oh, okay," he said, and he sounded genuinely curious, and maybe even a bit off his game.

"Can you repeat the question?" Delaney asked, and laughed again, this time for real. She was funny, she thought. Asking him to repeat a four-word question—that was funny. That was a good one.

"Why are you here?" he repeated.

There was no affect in his voice. She realized two things: first, that his questions were carefully crafted, such that he would not alter their wording. And second, when he asked them, he kept his own tone neutral. This must be part of his method.

Delaney decided to maintain a blithe tone. She smiled and turned to the blurry version of him available through the blind. "Why am I here in this room?"

"On campus," he said evenly. "At this company. Why are you here?"

Her mind iced over. He had to know. For a moment she felt like giving up. Lying was exhausting. Whenever she watched cop shows she identified strongly with the perpetrators who didn't run, didn't argue, who quickly raised their hands in surrender. She stalled.

"Why am I at the Every?" she asked.

"Yes, why?"

Should she give up? Tell Gabriel the truth—that she had entered the Every with the plan to destroy it? She pictured herself being escorted from campus, and found the image vastly appealing. She would go back to Idaho, rest for months, live for years alone in the woods. Then again, if she were to be expelled from the company, why not fight her way out? Why give up—why give in to a man like Gabriel Chu, who wrote **online surveys**? She slowed her breathing and a smile spread over her face. Embrace the absurd, she thought.

"I wanted to be at the center of the world," she said.

He looked down at his screen, but otherwise gave nothing away. "Where is your favorite place?"

Now relief spread through Delaney's every

filament. Maybe this was just a randomized test, an inscrutable mind-maze?

"Ghost Canyon," she said. She was relatively sure he was getting a level now, comparing her initial answers, which no doubt rattled the sensors, with a few benign answers.

"Your hometown," he said.

"Yes."

"Have you enjoyed your time here on this campus?"

She smiled again, looked up at the ceiling, pretending to think of all the things she loved while racing through all she loathed. Focus on what you love, she thought. She thought of Wes, of Joan, of the feel of the Bay air as she stood naked under the skylight.

"I have," she said.

His head dipped briefly.

"Do you have a roommate named Soren Lundqvist?"

"I do."

"Did you tell him that you wanted to kill him?"

Delaney's throat cinched shut. "It was a joke," she said hoarsely. "My father used to hate the smart stop sign and—"

"I understand," Gabriel said. "But do you now wish harm upon Soren Lundqvist?"

"No."

"Do you intend to kill him?"

"No."

"Is Wes your friend?" he asked.

"Yes," she said.

"Did you invent AuthentiFriend?"

This is a nightmare, she thought. **Speed through it.** "Yes," she said.

"Did Wes also invent AuthentiFriend?"

"Yes. He did the coding for my concept."

"Did you invent StayStïl?" he asked.

"No," Delaney said quickly. This, she felt, was true enough.

"You were close to its creation," Gabriel said.

"I know Syl," Delaney said.

"After that, I had to move onto campus," Gabriel said. "My kids had been happy at their school in Pacifica. Friends, teachers they liked, playgrounds they knew, the beach. Now we all live here."

Delaney didn't know what to say, so said nothing. Gabriel continued. "Were you part of **Bananaskam**?"

"I was with Wes when he thought of it," she said.

"And AnonIdea?"

"Yes."

"You seem to often find yourself in the room where things are invented. How do you account for this?"

She could frame this in her mind, Delaney felt, in a way that would register as truthful. "I hadn't thought of it," she said. This was accurate, in some way—she hadn't thought of herself in a room when these ideas had been formulated.

"You were at HereMe when they proposed a massive expansion of their listening programs," he said.

"Yes."

"What do you feel about their ideas?"

"Which ideas?" she asked, and Gabriel sighed a disappointed sigh.

"The notion that HereMe should be a tool to prevent domestic violence and child abuse—that accessing all in-home audio and working with police should be a right of the Every and the state."

Again Delaney thought of a truthful sentence. "It will save lives."

"Why are you here?" he asked again.

"You asked me that a minute ago," she said. This, she knew, was a tired tactic. A guilty person would provide a rote answer. An innocent mind would do the natural thing—note the repetition.

"Would you lie for a higher purpose?" he asked.

"Excuse me?" She'd heard him clearly but needed time to form a response.

"If you felt it necessary to achieve a noble objective, would you lie?"

"Yes," Delaney said. There seemed to be no risk in saying so.

"Your name, Delaney, means **dark challenger** in Irish. Do you know why your parents would have named you that?"

"I didn't know it meant that," Delaney said.

She really had no idea. "They told me it was a family name."

"Are you a dark challenger?" he asked.

"No," she said, sure this would read as a lie.

"Do you know the work of Meena Agarwal?" he asked.

Delaney looked down, to prevent whatever cam was in front of her from seeing the shock in her eyes. He's playing all the hits, she thought.

"Yes," she said. "I took two classes with her in college."

"Tell me about Professor Agarwal," he said evenly.

She focused on Agarwal's health. "She was brilliant. **Is** brilliant. She's sick. Do you know her?" Delaney decided to return to an upbeat, even playful conversational style.

"Did you agree with her theories?" he asked.

"Which theories?" Delaney asked. Again, she felt this was the most natural style. "She's written a hundred papers."

Delaney could feel Gabriel smiling.

"Would she have approved of you working here?" he asked.

Easy one. "No," Delaney said firmly.

"Have you spoken to her since you were hired?"

"No," Delaney said quickly. This satisfied her greatly. She'd been smart to make no contact. Mistakes precipitate lying; planning and discipline eliminate the necessity.

"Is this company a monopoly?" Gabriel asked.

"No," she said.

"Why not?"

"There is no barrier to entry for potential competitors. I wrote a paper on this. You might be aware of it?"

His head was bowed, looking at his screen. "Do you agree with Agarwal's theory that we're undergoing a species-level evolution?"

"I'm not sure," Delaney said. True enough, Delaney thought.

"Agarwal says people do not want to be free. Do you agree?"

"She says **most** people don't want to be free."

There was an oddly long pause. She saw Gabriel's hand touch his screen and perhaps even type a word.

"And do you agree?" he asked finally.

"I don't know what percentage of people fit that description, but there is some percentage of humans who prefer to be told what to do."

"Is it over fifty percent?" he asked.

"I don't know," she said, and was certain this lie would be sensed. Delaney had in her mind a number, as accurate as she could conjure and catchy, too: 82-82. Eighty-two percent of people want eighty-two percent of their lives dictated for them.

"Do the people working at the Every fall into this category, of people who do not want to be free?" he asked.

"I'm not sure," Delaney said. She scolded herself. That answer was not wise. The correct answer was "No." She had just tipped her hand, and was certain this answer alone would cause the termination of her employment. Any loyal Everyone could not possibly think her coworkers were indifferent to freedom. Should she amend the answer? The pregnant pause after her answer meant he was giving her the time to do so, as if he knew she might.

"I think," she said, "there are people everywhere who fall into that category, and always have—long before the advent of the Every. So it stands to reason that there are people here, too, who don't recognize the difference between being free and not free, or don't care much about the difference."

Gabriel stared ahead for three seconds, five seconds—an epoch.

"How is freedom best exercised?" he asked. He hadn't looked down at his screen. This seemed to be an improvised question.

"Willfully," she said. "Irregularly. Through the refutation of custom. The breaking of patterns. The rational flouting of irrational rules. Keeping secrets. Being unseen. Solitude. Social indifference. Fighting ill-wrought power. Irreverence for authority. Moving without limit or schedule through the day and the world. Choosing when to participate and when to withdraw."

When she finished, she knew she'd said too

much. Gabriel took another long pause, and she saw him scrolling on his screen. While he paused, she cursed her blathering. Then again, many at the Every, and she expected him to be among them, respected freedom of thought and expression as long as it didn't threaten their business plan.

"Why were you upset at the park ranger at the beach?" he asked.

"Excuse me?" she said. She had no idea what he was talking about.

"Shortly after you were hired, you tried to go to Ocean Beach, and were confronted by a city sentry. He was checking your phone and oval. Why did that upset you?"

"I wasn't upset," Delaney lied, and knew the lie was obvious. "I was surprised. It had never happened before at that beach."

"Did that upset you when you were a forest ranger—the requirement that hikers have phones with them?"

"No. It keeps everyone safe," she said. Now her lies were childish.

"You wrote a complaint," he said.

"I did no such thing." She had, but she'd written her complaint on paper, in a field office in New Mexico, a thousand years ago. Delaney could not believe that note had somehow been saved, digitized and was discoverable by Gabriel Chu. But of course it had.

"I don't remember doing that," she added.

"Why did you choose to live in a trog house?" he asked.

"It was cheaper," she said. This would read as partial truth.

"Research has found that, in terms of overall expenses and convenience, they're more expensive," he said.

"In terms of rent, it was cheaper." She laughed. Should she go back to the laughter strategy? Why had she abandoned that?

"Why do you have a post office box?" he asked.

"I get letters from trog friends, older relatives," she said, then realized the most authentic response would have been shock and outrage that he knew such a thing. "This is a paperless campus, as you know." Again she tried a little laugh.

"Do you like living on campus?" he asked.

"Yes," she said, and it felt true enough.

"What was in Hans-Georg's folder?"

"I don't remember," she said. The lie was reflexive and she couldn't take it back.

Gabriel suppressed a smirk. "Did you see anything unusual in your medical evaluation?"

And there it was, at last. All she could do was tell the truth, and quickly.

"Yes," she said. "I saw what appeared to be Mae Holland's sonogram."

"Did you tell anyone about this?"

"No," she said. His eyes were on his screen. His goddamned face, she thought. This was his experiment all along. He'd just confirmed it, and his face revealed nothing—no satisfaction, surprise, not even mild interest.

"Do people want to be free?" he asked. He read this from his screen. Either the questionnaire was ordered elliptically or it was intentionally repetitive.

"Many people appreciate boundaries," she said.

"Do **you** appreciate boundaries?" he asked, as if genuinely curious.

"In many cases, yes," she said.

Again she pictured herself fleeing through the gates and never coming back.

"I'm going to suggest you wait a few weeks before visiting PrefCom. Is that okay with you?"

"That's fine," she said.

He knows, she thought. He must know. She felt cold mercury racing through her veins.

"Why are you here?" he asked. "Sorry to ask again."

He absolutely knows. She gripped the chair, ready to get up. His eyes turned to her, surprised. Something in his look, some faint mirth that mitigated her terror, put her back in her seat.

"You invited me here," she said.

"Why are you working here at the Every?"

"Didn't you ask me this before?" she said.

"Forgive me. Can you answer again?"

"When you asked me the first time, I said I wanted to be at the center of the world. And that's true. I also want to make an impact. Here and in the world generally."

She felt good about that last sentence. It was true enough, and bland enough. Her peripheral vision caught his head nodding, as if she'd confirmed all he suspected.

XXXVI.

It was liberating to give up caring. Delaney left the Aviary shaken, expecting at any moment to be escorted from campus or thrown into the Bay. Did they do that? She believed they could. Now, anything was possible. She'd just been experimented on. Interrogated, toyed with. She thought helplessly of lawsuits. Hadn't Gabriel done something illegal there? She searched her mind for applicable laws broken and found none. Was it emotional abuse? Were mind-games protected by the NDAs she'd signed?

When she left the building, her fury lost strength, but she was torn between wanting more than ever to destroy the Every and wanting to flee. She was just a person, she thought. She deserved a life, deserved to be happy. Why couldn't she simply leave all this? Leave her species to their inevitable devolution? Each minute on Treasure Island would only make her more paranoid, her mind more bent and frayed. She could simply go. There was that freedom still. She could walk away and nothing could compel her to return.

She crossed the Daisy in a state of nihilistic euphoria. One moment she was leaving, ready to pack her few belongings and walk to the subway and ride to the airport, where she'd get on the first plane to Boise or even Seattle—she'd find a way home. The next moment, driven by righteous vengeance, she wanted to go back to the pod, to plan, to scheme faster, better. She'd been fucking around and now she needed to work quicker, more intentionally. She'd give herself a month. A month and she'd bring the place down, or leave.

The sun was out, a breeze was coming from the north, tousling the hair of a group of Everyones squatting and murmuring in the grass. Some were being comforted. She saw an Everyone—was it Fuad?—crying on a berm, shoulders shaking as he looked at his phone. Delaney checked her own screens and realized it was the quarterly deëmployment moment. The bottom 10 percent of every department was being let go, via text, determined by an algorithm. Those let go had no one to complain to, for no one was responsible. The Eye of Bailey passed overhead just then, and in its shadow Delaney could see more clearly: It was Fuad. He was being comforted by Syl, who seemed to be having a rough time, too.

"They're both out," Joan said. She'd appeared at Delaney's side. "It's just numbers."

"But Syl? After all his acclaim?" Delaney said.

"The algos don't see it," Joan said. "He spent too much time giving talks and not enough time on measurables. He's interesting and prominent and all that, but he lost track of what can be tracked."

Far away, she spotted someone waving to her. She waved back, squinting to discern who it was. Winnie. Winnie? She seemed cheerful. Maybe she wasn't among the culled?

"Is the list public?" Delaney asked.

"Is the list public? How long have you been here?" Joan said. She sent Delaney the list, and Delaney searched for Winnie. There was no Winifred Ochoa among the deëmployed. She looked up to find Winnie waving again. Delaney waved again, too, relieved.

"I'd never want to fire someone," Joan said, looking up at the passing blimp. Its screen directed the deëmployed to a counseling app called Going Nowhere, or GoNo. "Berit is gone, by the way," Joan said. "She and I were both happy that it didn't have to be personal. There's twelve of us, so someone had to go. The numbers are the numbers. This way she and I can still be friends."

"Right," Delaney said. "Such an elegant system."

Joan's eyes searched Delaney's. "It **is** an elegant system. **You** try firing someone."

"That's what I said. Elegant system."

Syl and Fuad had left their perch on the berm, and a breeze from the Bay blew through the grass where they'd been, erasing whatever imprint they'd made.

A text from Wes came through.

"Can you meet me at my moms' tomorrow?" he asked.

Delaney had seen animals die. Wolves and foxes and coyotes caught in traps. She'd hit two deer in her time in Wyoming, and both times she'd had to help them find the next world. In Oregon she once came upon a black bear dying from an arrow shot through his back. Teenagers with a crossbow, she figured. They were ten miles from a road, and they both knew he wouldn't survive. So she sat with him until his breathing stilled.

She knew Hurricane's death was coming, and didn't want to be there when it happened. But Wes was asking for her, and as grim as the trip would be, she welcomed a reason to leave campus.

The moms had moved to The Pinnacles, a smartpartment complex just across the water from the Every, in the Mission Bay neighborhood of San Francisco. After Gwen's fall (in the kitchen, wet tile, broken hip, then sepsis), Social Services had determined that their trog home was grossly unsafe for two women in their early seventies, and had arranged for them to move to a mixed-age, mixed-income development where they would have ready access to on-site medical care.

Delaney arrived in the early evening. The

construction was so new the manufacturer's stickers were still on the floor-to-ceiling streetfront windows. When she approached the entrance, she heard the buzz of the door unlocking; the moms had told their HereMe that she'd be coming, so the doors could open automatically upon her approach. She didn't know what floor they lived on, or what apartment, and she didn't need to. The elevator opened and took her to the seventh floor, and an illuminated sconce pulsed by their door, guiding her to them.

"Del," Ursula said, and hugged her. She looked haggard but smiled warmly. "Come see Gwen. She'll cry."

The apartment was spacious and full of light and in many ways resembled Delaney's pod. The appliances were the same, the fixtures, the ceiling lights, the painted concrete floors. Sitting in what seemed to be a cross between a hospital bed and overstuffed recliner, Gwen held out her hand and Delaney took it. She looked ten years older, utterly helpless, but her eyes were enraged.

"I'm so ashamed to look this way," she said.

Now Delaney's eyes welled. Wes emerged from a back room, sniffling—though Delaney sensed this was for Hurricane.

"This place isn't so bad," Ursula said. "First of all, it doesn't smell of fish. Only now do I realize how much our old place reeked. I swear **we** must have reeked, too. What kind of life was that, two old ladies walking around smelling like fish? Where's the dignity in that?"

"We didn't smell of fish," Gwen said.

"Anyway," Ursula continued, "it took some time to get used to this place, but I don't miss the headaches. The old house—between the bad wiring, the drafts, the spotty water, the constant repairs. I don't know, I feel like I have about three extra hours a day."

"Which we fill doing nothing," Gwen said.

"We do plenty," Ursula said.

"I can't smell the ocean. The windows don't open."

"You want fresh air? The sky's full of smoke," Ursula said.

There were wildfires burning a hundred miles north, and the smoke had just reached the city.

"They don't let us leave," Gwen said.

"The residents here have agreed to collective carbon neutrality," Ursula explained, and raised her fist to show her oval. "So the building tracks overall carbon footprint. It just means we don't make decisions on excursions unilaterally."

"Excursions! They don't let me walk around the block!" Gwen wailed, her voice cracking.

"You have a fractured hip, hon. You can't walk right around the block anyway," Ursula said. "And every trip is a carbon moment." She turned to Delaney and whispered, "We're learning."

"We're **dying**," Gwen hissed. "They have me as a suicide risk."

"Just based on searches, habits, neural patterns, Mom," Wes said. "It's just a tool to help you and your doctors."

"If you wanted to help me," Gwen said, "you'd let me leave. I'm a prisoner here." She turned to Delaney. "You were always so sane. Do you say shit like **carbon moment**?"

"Hush, you," Ursula said, and swatted Gwen's knee. "We haven't figured out how to fill the time," she said to Delaney. "But OwnSelf is helping. Are you on it?"

Delaney's throat went dry. "Yes," she managed to say.

"Gwen's skeptical, and I was too, at first, but I've actually found it to be a godsend," Ursula said. "Gwen's got medication she has to take at certain times, and between that and just feeling productive here, it helps me sort out the days. I'm learning classical Portuguese online. Did Wes tell you?"

"He hadn't," Delaney said.

"There's this Everyone named Roderick. He has a club for all things Portuguese. Have you met him?"

"Heard of him," Delaney said.

Gwen was staring toward the window. Not through the window, but **at** the window. At the glass.

"And then there's the shopping. No shopping anymore. Have you seen one of these?" Ursula pointed to the smartfridge. "Of course you have.

Anything that doesn't come to the door we can get at the store on the first floor. So food's taken care of."

"I miss my garden," Gwen said.

"There's one on the roof, but—" Ursula said.

Wes went to the door. "Actually, I'll take Delaney up there to see it." He turned to her. "We'll be back in a few minutes," he said, and she followed him to the elevator.

On the roof, it was windy and overcast and the acrid smell of the wildfire was far more pronounced. Wes led Delaney to an enormous cooling fan which spun with a loud thrumming fury. Delaney understood—this was the one place in the building they wouldn't be heard.

"Gwen seems sad," Delaney said.

"She's getting better," Wes said. "I actually think this place is good for them. Or will be good for them. They're adjusting."

"I hope not too much," Delaney said.

Wes's face darkened. "They're in their seventies, Delaney. They can't take care of a run-down shack forever. We're lucky the accident wasn't worse. People die like that."

"Okay," Delaney said. "You're right. She's safer here."

"She is. Don't be a smartass," he said. "And they're saving money. Their expenses are half what they were. Remember, they're on a fixed income.

You know what their power bill was last week? Seven dollars. Water was four bucks. Nothing's wasted here."

"It sounds wonderful," Delaney said.

"Fuck, Delaney," Wes said, and spun away. "I'm pretty tired of your self-righteous individualist bullshit. There are issues larger than getting to run the water as much as you want. I've evolved a lot since all this began. I've learned a lot. They gave us a breakdown between the carbon footprint in the old house and this one, and I have to say the old house was just irresponsible. **Indefensible.** That kind of living is cloaked in the language of personal freedom, but in the end it's just selfish. It's anarchic, really. It's anti-community. It's anti-social. It's anti-human."

Delaney couldn't speak.

"Don't give me that look," Wes said. "I might as well tell you now. I can't be part of your plan anymore."

"Obviously," she said. "You were so quick to surrender."

"I'm not surrendering. I'm planning to take bad ideas and make them better. And I'm going to improve the good ideas."

"Are you kidding?"

"People listen to me. They respect me there. I can improve things. I already have."

"Like with Friendy."

"We've made it far more humane."

"Wes. My god. It's a horror."

"They wanted to add a feature for kids," he said. "So parents could tell if their kids were lying to them. It was being specifically reconfigured to the irises and facial musculature of kids, all the rhythms of their speech. I put a stop to that."

"That justifies your existence there?" Delaney was sure he'd lost his mind.

"Neither of us is operating from a place of purity and honor," he said. "Your approach is predicated on deceit. Your very existence there is a lie."

"But I have a **plan,**" she said.

"Do you? It hasn't worked so far. Every terrible idea you've fed them—that **we've** fed them—has been embraced inside the Every and out in the world. How are you calling that success?"

"It's building to something. The outrage will grow."

"There is no outrage, and it's most assuredly not growing. You're making the company stronger."

"It's bending. It'll break."

"It's not bending and won't break," Wes said.

Delaney worried that this was likely true. "But don't you see that you moderating things there is working against what I'm trying to do?" she asked. "That kid-trust thing—if it had been released at its most offensive, it would have started a conflagration."

"Really? You think so? People have been tracking their kids for twenty-five years. They put **chips** in their fucking **bones,** Delaney! You think an app that determines whether kids are lying is some bridge too far? For anyone?"

"Then why did you curb it?"

"Because **I** saw it as an evil. **I** did."

"All the more reason to blow the place up," Delaney said. "You think you're going to catch every evil thing before it happens? You're one of twelve thousand people in that place. And don't you think they'll catch onto your game soon enough? They'll identify you as a pollyanna and you'll be neutralized. They'll call you a Product Philosopher or put you on the ethics team, and you'll never be heard from again."

"Which is still better than your plan."

"Then help come up with another plan."

"I don't want to," he said.

"You don't **want** to?" Delaney asked.

"I don't believe you'll succeed," he said. "All along, we thought we could steer it off a cliff. That there would be some new app that would be too far, too corrosive and inhumane. But you and I both know it won't happen. There is no cliff."

"I don't believe it," Delaney said.

"You have to believe it. And we have to stop adding to the madness. Our ideas are too good. Too horrible. People love them. So we have to stop."

"No," she said, though much of her really did want to stop.

"You won't succeed," Wes said. "And actually, I

don't think you **should** succeed. Just standing here talking to you, something clarified in my mind. And it's that your plan is worse than theirs. Yours is weirdly self-serving and ineffectual."

"Are we done?"

"Delaney, no, we're not. I've been wanting to tell you that stuff like Friendy—it's minor. It's small potatoes compared to the climate impact the Every has. There's only one entity on earth that really has the power and reach to turn around catastrophic climate change. You smell the fires? You notice the sky is orange? Have you been watching the sea levels? Any meaningful impact will have to be enacted on a global scale, and there are no countries, no organizations that have remotely the power that the Every does. If they disappear, the power vacuum will only invite a new kind of chaos. There'll be no attention paid to an ethical supply chain. I don't know how you could have spent so much time at AYS and not realize the good they're doing. Stop+Lük has already reduced carbon by 22 percent. The people of Kathmandu can see the Himalayas again. Respiratory problems are down 74 percent. The impact the Every can make in weeks is more important than whatever little privacy offenses they commit."

"Like the end of freedom and free will."

"I'm not excusing that. But I'd call it the end of the society of the self, and the birth of a more communitarian one."

"The tidal rise in suicides?"

"Then we get into population growth."

"Don't say the suicides are good for the planet."

"I'm not. I'm not," Wes said, and looked at his sandals. "I'm not. I'm just saying that the planet is at war for its survival. And during wars, we need war powers. You have to remember that the Every was bombed and we still don't know who did it."

"So?"

"So I'm beginning to like the idea of a world without bombings. Without crime. Without violent death or the possibility of it. And to get there, we need a streamlined decision-making process. Coordination. We can't have a multilateral mess."

"So you'd give unlimited power to the Every."

"There would be checks, of course. But Del, you have to acknowledge that they get stuff done. They bring order."

Wes looked from the rooftop toward the wildfire smoke coming from the north. "The Every has a plan to fight fires with drones, but they can't get it through the FAA. Drones could bring water to places where people can't get to. It's ridiculous to watch the planet suffer because of bureaucracy and sloth. Just seeing how my moms' lives are simpler, easier now—it makes me think there's a symmetry here. We eliminate so much of the chaos of life, so much of the struggle, so much of the unnecessary running around, driving, shopping, choosing, throwing away, overspending, overconsuming—this

goes hand in hand with a more sustainable way
of life."

"And those who can't be part of this new system
die off."

"If they choose to, sure."

Delaney had nothing to say. He was right, and he
was wrong, and she could not convince him. They
would always be friends but were no longer allies.

"That's new from you, Wes—that kind
of callousness."

Wes scoffed spitefully. That, too, was new.

"What?" Delaney said.

"Nothing," he said.

"What, Wes?"

"See, just that," he said. "You're not so nice
yourself. You're not so pure. And you're not
so trustworthy."

In the yawning silence, as Delaney took in the
violence of his words, she knew he'd used Friendy
on her. Every bone within her turned to water.

"Jesus, Wes," she said.

He looked into her eyes, then at the floor.

"What did I score?" she asked.

"Doesn't matter," he said. "It just helped me see
some things."

Delaney was ruptured, ruined and she didn't care
about anything. And then there was Hurricane.
She'd come to say goodbye, and it was as good
a diversion as anything, so she walked past her

friend and to the elevator and went down to see the old dog.

When they entered the room, Hurricane tilted his head just enough to focus on her. He was lying on a faux-fur mat in the corner, under a tinted window. His ribs protruded, rising as he breathed. Delaney crouched before him and reached out to stroke his head; his fur was brittle as he leaned into her touch.

"He won't go outside," Wes said. "I tried to put him in the stroller but he growled."

"He's so tired," Delaney said. **And I am tired, too.**

"The moms wanted to put him down," Wes said, and stroked his graying snout. Delaney took Hurricane's paw and rubbed the leather pads of his tiny toes.

"Will you stay an hour?" Wes asked.

Delaney lay down in front of Hurricane, looking into his tired eyes. Wes arranged himself against the wall and put Hurricane's head on his lap. Hurricane's eyes closed immediately, as if in profound relief. Wes closed his eyes, too, and stroked Hurricane's fur, and they heard Hurricane's breathing grow slower until it reached an almost beautiful steadiness, like the push and pull of a gentle tide. And finally the tide went out and did not return.

XXXVII.

DELANEY SLEPT OVER, on the floor, waking up in
the cold silver morning with a blanket draped across
her. Wes and Hurricane were gone. The moms, too.
It was a Sunday, and Delaney thought to stop at the
post office box on her way back to Treasure Island.
She went to the basement of the Pinnacle, hid her
phone in a crack in the foundation, and borrowed
one of the moms' bikes. It gave her at least a chance
of making the trip unknown. She kept her head
down, trying to stay uncammed, until, at Geary
and Masonic, she ran a red light and got shammed.
The cam's flash immortalized her crime, and, for
good measure, a teenaged boy filmed her from
the sidewalk.

When she got to TrogTown, she was patted down
by a different woman this time, a twentysome-
thing in a peasant dress. Again assaulted by the
smells—patchouli among them this time—Delaney
parked the bike and saw a flash of rust-colored fur.

A fox darted in front of her and disappeared into an alley.

At the post office, she found only one letter. It was from Agarwal. She knew it was unwise to read it there, on the counter, but she opened it anyway.

Dear Delaney,

I should have talked to my colleagues in the Religion department years ago. Now I understand surveillance.

God is not old. He/she/they were invented, all across the world, not more than ten thousand years ago. When human societies were small, they were close-knit and moral boundaries were clear. In a tribe of twelve, if you stole your fellow caveperson's favorite club or wheel prototype, it was known and could be rectified. You were always seen, and all was known.

But as societies grew, the wayward could do things unobserved, and crimes could be committed. So it became necessary to invent a being who saw everything. Watch out, God's creators said, you are being watched by a morally righteous eye in the sky—even when no one else is around. (The concept of Santa works in a similar way.)

Now, the decline of God and the imminent collapse of so many faiths seems tied directly to the rise of surveillance, and the collective enforcement of social norms through instant global shaming. God promised punishment after death. Now it's meted out in minutes. Karma was vague; digital shaming is specific. And I would argue people prefer the reliable nature of morality-through-surveillance over the ephemeral promises of the gods/Gods of the past.

Prayers to God were rarely answered, while shouts into cyberspace always receive a response, even if misspelled and hateful. Everything God offered—answers, clarity, miracles, baby names—the internet does better. Do you know how many times **What is the meaning of life?** was searched on your platforms last year? Twenty-one billion times. Every one of those queries got a reply. The one question that could not be answered, until now, is **Am I good?**

I think we're on the verge of the Every, or those who want to be subsumed by the Every, of determining this—or claiming to. This will be the last step. The number will tell us. Homo sapiens will become homo numerus. Millions more will suicide, yes—those who bristle at the numerification of our species—but for so many billions more, the new certainty will allow them to sleep.

I'm keeping up with my treatments, and things for the time being seem stable. Which is a bit of good news that might lead to more good news. If my tumor shows no growth for the next month, I might qualify for an experimental treatment. The irony is not lost on me: I have to be healthier to be given medicine.

Agarwal.

Delaney stared at the letter, numb. She folded it back into its envelope, looked up and jumped out of her skin.

A man was studying her from the other side of the glass. She backed away. He didn't move. She edged toward the front counter. He didn't move. His face was hidden deep under a hoodie, his eyes behind bug-eyed sunglasses. She was about to yell for help when the man threw his hood back. It was Gabriel Chu.

She was pressed against the wall. He waved in-nocently. She mimed a heart attack. He mimed an apology, then pointed to his left. He wanted her to follow. She steadied herself. Her heart had relocated to somewhere near her right shoulder. She nodded. He walked on. She left the post office and walked up Bryant, followed by a pair of stray dogs, both beagles, seeming like siblings. Gabriel stayed a block ahead, glancing her way as he crossed the street. They passed an alleyway full of tents. A pair of city workers were in the process of trying to clear them out, while the sound of someone practicing the trombone came mournfully from beyond.

She passed under a sign on the corner. YOU ARE ENTERING A PATH WITHOUT SURVEILLANCE CAMERAS. CITIZENS CHOOSING THIS PATH ASSUME ASSOCIATED

RISKS. SFPD. Somehow all the subterfuge she'd engaged in the last month seemed pedestrian next to this, following Gabriel Chu through TrogTown. She followed Gabriel down two sloping blocks overgrown with ivy and wisteria until he ducked into the Senello Animal Shelter. Most shelters were now in trog zones; scrutiny online was too unhinged.

Delaney followed him in. There was no physical danger inside, she assumed, and she could leave any moment. The moment she opened the door, she was blown back by dual assaults of noise and stench. It was loud as a monkey house and smelled far worse. The ceiling was eighteen feet high and cages were stacked to the roof. Dogs, cats, guinea pigs, birds. A banner across the rafters said **These animals cannot be released into the wild. We try to find them homes. Support the Senello Animal Shelter and Proposition 67.** The anti-pet movement had grown exponentially. Prop 67 would codify the right of humans to keep pets, but was expected to fail.

Delaney heard a deafening bray. She turned to find a pair of goats in a large corner cage. When she turned back again, Gabriel was at her side. "Have you been here before?" he asked.

She said she had, and he glided away, leading her to a silver cage in the middle of the floor that held what appeared to be a chinchilla. The enclosure reached Gabriel's chin, striping his torso. Delaney stood on the other side of it, making the chinchilla an unwitting eavesdropper.

"I'm sorry we're in here," he said. "I know you guys just lost Hurricane and this is probably triggering."

"Thank you," Delaney said, "and it's okay."

The woman at the counter, fully twenty feet away, noticed them. "You can bring that chinchilla home today," she called out. "If you live in Nevada, of course. Not here."

"Thanks!" Delaney shouted back to her.

Gabriel hadn't taken his eyes off Delaney. "I know what you're doing and it's okay," he said. "I approve."

Delaney tensed.

"Don't worry. We're safe here," he said.

Those words meant nothing. He could be wearing a hundred devices. Delaney tried to think of a response that would survive playback scrutiny. "What is it I'm doing again?"

"I know you're at the Every to destroy it," he said. "Or at least to gather information. It's obvious. You're a bad spy. Why do you think I interrogated you?"

Delaney stared at the animal in the cage. Its expression said both **End my life now** and **I have everything I need.**

"I've watched you from the moment you got onto campus," Gabriel said. "I read Agarwal in college. Then a student of Agarwal's comes to the Every after six years in the forest? It was all too intriguing. Then I watched your presentation with Wes. I know it fooled Carlo and Shireen, but please—it was terrible. You were terrible. And when I questioned you, Friendy ripped you apart. Your ratings were abysmal. But it was fun watching you lie, thinking you were fooling your own software."

Delaney couldn't stay. This was too much. This was not the way to reveal herself, amid braying goats and chittering rabbits and to a man in burgundy pants. She felt ambushed and wanted to run.

"We have pot-bellied pigs," the shelter woman said. She was now standing behind Gabriel. She was wearing a soiled lab coat and a knit beanie. "They're out back. We can't keep them here."

"We're just looking around for now," Delaney said.

The woman didn't move. "Something smaller? We have a kangaroo rat. It's really just a hamster with big feet. Adorable."

"Thank you," Delaney said. "That sounds tempting."

"These animals will die," the woman said. "Hundreds every week. When the Every canceled pets, they all ended up here. You have no idea. How about a cat? We have seventy out back."

"Please," Delaney said, "please give us a minute."

She retreated to the shrieking back room.

"Delaney, you need our help," Gabriel said. "There are a lot of us. Did you think that out of twelve thousand people on that campus you were the only saboteur?"

Delaney stared hard at the mound of fur in the cage.

"Is Joan involved? I know Wes is," he asked.

She couldn't say anything—that would confirm his presumptions—but she needed to absolve Wes and Joan. How, though, without admitting her own culpability?

"My best guess is that you're trying to plant terrible ideas at the company in hopes they cause some chain-reaction and bring the company down. Am I right?" He was craning his head to catch Delaney's eyes, while Delaney was determined not to meet his. "Delaney, say something."

By staying this long, by not denying anything he'd said, she'd already opened herself to catastrophic scrutiny. If he was indeed trying to trap her, he'd already won. Delaney didn't trust Gabriel, or the existence of any Every underground. But as soon as she thought of those words, **Every underground,** she had the sense that Gabriel had a name for his movement. And she knew that if the group did have some name, that name would be idiotic.

"We'd like you to join the EveryThrow," he said.

Delaney laughed involuntarily. Of course they'd named it.

"Listen, I like your plan," he said, "but you should go further. We can help. You've met Holstein. I hope you're pleased with how far she's taken Friendy."

Gabriel smiled. "Yes. Holstein is one of you. One

of **us.** She's trying to drive the program off a cliff. Same idea as you. And then of course there's Hans-Georg. He's been key."

Delaney's neck tingled. Hans-Georg could be trusted. He was a man without guile. "I thought he left," she said.

"No, no," Gabriel said. "Well, yes and no. He's been bouncing around the world, making some arrangements and connecting with hundreds of others. It's not just this campus, Delaney. There are insurgents all over. He sends his greetings, by the way."

Gabriel tapped his index finger against the chinchilla's cage.

"Tell him hello," Delaney said, and knew she shouldn't say more. She needed to flee, to think.

The shelter woman emerged from the back, holding a white rabbit in each hand. Their eyes were pink. "These are great pets," she said, and made her way toward Delaney and Gabriel. "Ignore the eyes."

"Thank you," Delaney said to her and to Gabriel, and weaved toward the exit.

"I'm assuming no snakes?" the woman yelled.

"Even if we don't work together, we'll be watching," Gabriel said over the cages, two fingers raised to signify victory, as Delaney fled the building.

XXXVIII.

DELANEY MADE PLANS TO GO HOME. Home to Idaho. She'd take a leave of absence. Or she could quit. The idea that there was an insurgency at the Every seemed impossible. But if there was one, she was intoxicated by the idea that she was not alone. That people like Gabriel and Holstein, far better placed than herself, were already working to destroy the company. But she did not trust Gabriel Chu. He'd inhabited her nightmares for weeks; no one who wanted to position himself as her ally would have performed an interrogation as ruthlessly as he had. It showed a sadistic side that couldn't be reconciled with an idealist. And by following her, Gabriel had compounded her paranoia when he was trying to gain her trust.

This was the Every way.

So she needed Idaho. She needed to sit by the river and think. She put in a request for time off, and in the meantime she requested a low-pressure rotation, citing the emotional drain of HereMe. She was placed in New World Order, where the team of six was tasked with ranking all that could be ranked, which was everything. That week was M-themed, so she ranked the world's best mammals, mothers, monarchs, magicians, mail carriers, Malawians, Malaysians, mannerisms, maps, masseuses, and Marxists. They ranked mathematicians, MBA programs, medicines, measurements (No. 1 = millimeter), Mercurys (Freddie first, then the element), midwives, meteorologists, middleweights, mimes (Marceau 1, Melania 2), Misters (Rogers 1, Mister 2), mountains, mutineers, and muffins.

The work occupied her mind while she awaited approval for her vacation. Meanwhile, Gabriel wanted an answer. Was she in or out? **Let me know,** he wrote. He was good, Delaney knew. The message was vague enough to refer to anything. He sent a slew of texts in a similar vein. **Answer please,** he wrote. **Join us,** another said. If examined, all the messages could refer to anything—he'd even invited Delaney to a brunch for anyone interested in the nutritional value of bark, considered a new superfood. When the invite had come through, she was confused, but now she saw it as a red herring for anyone investigating. She didn't want to answer any of the missives, but finally, in a noncommittal attempt to bide time, she wrote back "I'll try!"

Decide by tonight, came his answer. **Things are moving.**

* * *

Delaney returned to the Havel late that night. On her phone, she got a message from Soren before she stepped through the door.

Quiet, he texted.

She entered silently. Inside, she found him sitting on the floor, his back against the couch. He pressed his forefinger to his lips and pointed to her phone.

Interesting happenings tonight, he typed.

She stood in the middle of the room. Now she smelled something sour around him. A tall coffee cup half-full of what she assumed was vodka sat next to him on the floor.

You're drinking, she wrote. **Shouldn't you not be drinking?**

Been drinking for months, he wrote. **You wondering where Joan is?**

Okay, where is she? she wrote.

Where is Francis? he wrote.

Please tell me what's happening, Delaney wrote.

Want to check Joan's bed?

Delaney's heart hollowed. **No, I don't.**

I got home earlier than they expected, he wrote. **Then they were too embarrassed to get out. But I heard enough.**

And now?

They're still in there. I think they fell asleep.

Let's get out of here, Delaney wrote.

No thanks, he wrote.

Too drunk anyway, he wrote.

I really have nothing, he wrote.

Delaney sat down next to him and reached for his hand. They sat in silence while Joan and Francis remained entangled in their tube. The scene was grotesque.

"Come," she said to him, and pulled him up and into the hallway. He had changed, and was wearing a loose T-shirt and basketball shorts. The effect was dramatic; he looked comfortable for the first time since she'd known him. Far more attractive, too—when every extra pound wasn't straining against the limits of lycra. He nodded gently to her, moving her to the unseen spot where they'd spoken before.

When they were finally hidden, he exhaled and looked like he might cry. "What are we doing here?" he asked.

Through the window, over the roofs and over the mountains to the north, Delaney saw Venus. It twinkled like a drop of honey.

"Venus," she said, nodding to the light.

"Could be," he said, and all at once broke down. He buried his blubbering face in his hands and his large round shoulders shook.

"Go ahead," she said. "You're invisible." With the suicides soaring, Delaney knew the sensors would pick up on a big soft man crying uncontrollably.

"I'm sorry about Joan," she said. "And—"

"It's fine," he said, cutting her off before he might

hear the name Francis. He straightened himself and wiped his face. "I asked for a transfer. I'll move tomorrow, into one of the newer buildings."

"You're leaving the pod?" Delaney asked. She couldn't contemplate being alone with Joan and Francis. Their unholy coupling seemed far worse without Soren.

"You'll miss me?" he asked, and smiled. "I've had a hard time reading you." He turned to her. "I've been wanting to tell you I'm not a zealot. I'm not hellbent on seeing every unmet tribe or putting cams everywhere. Reach was the job they gave me."

"I didn't mean to judge," she said.

"You should judge. It was needed. It was the first even mild opposition I've heard since I've been here." He looked outside. "Huh. Look. Venus isn't Venus. It's getting closer. It must be a helicopter."

The honey-colored light was twinkling but was growing larger, flying low over the Bay.

"It's been good to have you here," he said. "You woke me up. I've been here four years and something's different now. A different chemistry in the air maybe. Or it's just Stenton being back. The smell of sulfur."

Delaney was shocked by his candor. It was seductive. And she felt a responsibility to show him uncomplicated affection. Joan's was a ruse, was teasing and cruel, so Delaney thought she might simply hold him tightly, human to human. She moved to him, filling the gap between his body and the glass. She put her arms around his waist and pressed herself against his soft shape, smelling his gentle scent—a mix of sweat and floral deodorant and a bit of lemon.

"Oh," he said, and took her in.

He was soft everywhere. It was like holding a waterbed. His arms rested high on her shoulders but slowly dropped to her waist. She had no plans beyond this. She hadn't held anyone in months. She closed her eyes, inhaling him, feeling so tired, so content. But then he began tilting. "I need to sit," he said, and laughed.

Finally he slipped away, soundlessly, and smiled, and returned to the pod, and to his spot on the floor.

"Just working on passing out," he whispered to her, and blew her a kiss. No one, ever, had blown her a kiss. She returned the gesture and climbed into her tube, feeling that Soren deserved to be loved, and loved correctly, and though she couldn't imagine that person would be her, she thought, in a short and irrational life, it might as well be. Maybe she would be the one to love that man correctly.

She was drifting off when a heat pressed against her eyelids—a brightness, as if she were staring into a sun coming quickly toward her. Then all was heat and noise. She watched herself fly away from the light. For a moment she saw the night so clearly, for there was no wall, no windows. The walls were shards, dust. Everything was gone. She contemplated the wholeness of the sky, now unimpeded by the window, saw the shimmer of the water, felt sure she could hear the water, and finally her back struck a wall.

Her mouth was open but her lungs went limp. Bomb, she thought. The coming light had been a bomb. Another bomb. A plane carrying a bomb. A drone, a larger drone, packed with explosives. She heard a scream but it was not hers. She tried to breathe. She thought she was gasping but there was no sound, no movement, no air. She was sitting up, she was sure, but then she could no longer keep her head upright. Her face met the floor with a sickening slap. When she opened her eyes again, she saw her arm but couldn't move it. She reached for it but she had no hands. They were connected but nothing worked. She slept for a year, a hundred years, or didn't sleep at all. When she opened her eyes again, the air was cool. There was no more wall. She could see, she could name what she saw—stars, water, blood, twisted metal. But she couldn't breathe or move.

She heard screams. Her hearing had returned. Joan was talking, moaning. Low animal howls. "Get me up," Joan moaned. "Get me up." Then the floor was vibrating. Delaney sensed people around her but now her eyes seemed to be stuck to the floor. More screams were both loud and miles away. She was shifted onto a gurney. She tried to scream as they moved her but she made no sound. Nothing she thought became words.

She was awake enough to think she had lost her limbs, that her spinal cord had been severed, that she'd lost her ability to speak. Now she was moving through the room, heading for the window. To where the window had been. Now there was nothing, just sky. Not through the open wall! she wanted to scream. She could feel the night air. It was so cold. But no. She was not being sent into the night air. They turned and rushed down the hallway and again she saw the body, part of a body, a body shredded, faceless. The hair was yellow and red. She passed out again.

Then she was awake and flying. Together they seemed to be flying, she and the paramedic. They were moving through space at unimaginable speed, she knew, but then again she and the paramedic were not moving at all. She was weightless but also her head was one with the ambulance. Her head, she was certain, had been fused with the metallic floor. She was looking up from the floor. She tried to blink, but she couldn't speak or move any part of her. The head of the man above her swung around like a balloon on a string. He smiled down at her. "Hold on," he said. "A few more miles."

The siren was too loud. It shouldn't be so loud, she thought. She tried to speak, to ask the balloon man to turn the siren's volume down. She closed her eyes to quiet the sound.

A crash woke her. They were inside now. The lights above flew above her, bright as doves. Her head crashed through three doors. Four. Stop the crashing, she said. She couldn't speak. Stop the lights, she begged, though she had no voice.

"We knew Soren was dead," the paramedic said. He'd come to visit her. Where was she? She had no idea. He'd introduced himself as a paramedic. His name was Roger, he said, he was an EMT. But he looked like a child. He had acne. She thought of a summer camp counselor. Buoyant and excited to make plans.

Where am I? she asked, but her mouth still wasn't working.

"We were the second team," Roger said. "The first team got the other two. As I said, my partner, he thought you were gone."

Had he already said this? When? Had she met him before?

"The first team said no more survivors," he continued. "He even took your pulse and found nothing. But I had a mirror. You know that mirror test, under the nose? My mom taught me that when I was a kid. She was an EMT for a while, back in Pakistan. She said, 'Roger, if there's one thing I need to impart, is that the pulse is sometimes hard to find, so have a back-up plan . . .'"

He talked a great deal but Delaney didn't mind. Delaney liked him and wanted him to stay. "I'm probably rambling on," he said, and laughed. "I just wanted to check on you. My day off, as I said. We go off three days, but I have nowhere else to be. The nurses know me. They think I'm strange for visiting people I bring in, but where else am I going to go? I don't have kids."

He stayed another hour.

"You were covered in blood," he said. "Just covered in blood. A bomb hits a building, half the place is blown to hell, and when we got up there, we see a bloody lump. You were just a wax head in a pile of bloody linens." He smacked his lips, as if tasting his analogy.

"That's why we didn't even go near at first. We thought your head had been severed. So we didn't get close. So much blood, but not **your** blood, as it turns out. We actually went to the blond guy first. His body was in better shape, but when we turned his head, we knew he was gone. His face was gone. I mean, **gone,**" he said, then realized his enthusiasm was inappropriate. He apologized.

"Then, as I said, my partner went back to you and didn't find a pulse. That's when he realized you hadn't been decapit— You know. Then, like I said, I came and did the mirror test and you were breathing."

When had he said all these things he said he'd said before? Delaney thought she might be living in a kind of time loop. Did she have amnesia? How would she know? Roger was still talking.

"So I yelled, Over here, over here! It was crazy. The craziest thing I've ever seen, and I've been doing this for almost three years. Mostly we pick up drunks and junkies."

Delaney passed out and slept for days. She woke up and saw her parents. Their faces were close to her. And were they singing? They seemed to be singing. She woke up again and they were gone. Then someone was drilling in her head. Someone was pulling string from the backside of her eyes. Now rope, pulling and pulling ever-lasting lengths of rope. Now she was being moved. Why was she being moved? My fucking god that hurts. Why move me? Why would it be a good idea to move me?

XXXIX.

IT WAS A DRONE, a military-grade model developed
at the Every. It had ripped the walls off the Havel,
blasted a twenty-foot-high hole in the side of the
building. Soren was gone. Four others had died,
too—no one Delaney knew. No one could figure out why the toll hadn't been higher. Eighty
could have been killed, security said, had it not
been for the tubes. The tubes! Wrapped together
in theirs, Joan and Francis had suffered only con-
cussions, scrapes, mild burns, mild embarassment,
nothing more.

Delaney had four broken ribs. She'd been burned.
Her feet had been scalded. Her palms were simmer-
ing, seemed to be burning still. She was in a hospital, she realized, then forgot. She heard the voice
of Wes, speaking to her from the bottom of a well.
Joan's face appeared and she seemed to be talking,
but Delaney couldn't hear her. One morning she
realized she had no hair. She asked a nurse where

her hair had gone. The nurse seemed to have no idea. She looked at Delaney's chart. "Ease the swelling in your brain, I'm thinking," she said. "They probably opened your skull. You broke four ribs, too. And it'll be painful to walk for some time."

Delaney spent weeks in intensive care. In the hospital, between glorious morphine flights, wild thoughts overtook Delaney's mind. The assumption was that this was the work of anti-Every trogs, that this was their 9/11 moment, and of course the logic tracked. They had motive. So many had motive. Millions unemployed when the Every began to kill travel, planes, buses, cars, trains, roads. Those ruined by Friendy, eyeshame, OwnSelf. But when Delaney closed her eyes she saw Mae. Mae had done this. Mae and Gabriel. They'd found out about Delaney's plans and arranged to be rid of her. But could they really know what Delaney was at the Every to do? It seemed both possible and highly implausible. Delaney was one of twelve thousand Everyones on campus. Over a hundred thousand worldwide. It was mathematically impossible that Mae had any idea who she was. But Gabriel knew. He knew quite a bit.

Or it was Stenton. With perfect clarity she saw it. He'd engineered the bombings—all of them. Only he had motive and capability. Joan's Reichstag comment made more sense now—the consolidation of power in the wake of violence. Mae couldn't do such a thing, but Stenton would. Stenton was made for such a moment. But just as quickly, she dismissed all these theories. These people were too visible, too transparent to plan terrorist attacks on their own company. No, no. Even Stenton couldn't. But someday the truth would come out, she thought. A journalist, a news agency, would piece it together, would conduct interviews, examine documents, make actual phone calls, check facts, start over, and in six months or two years finally figure out who was behind the bombing—who had killed Soren and the others, and had almost killed Delaney. Then she realized she was going mad. There were no journalists and there was no news. How had she forgotten? She wanted less morphine—or more.

She slept most of her days and dreamed of Wes. Or Wes visited. Wes seemed to be next to her for long stretches, or perhaps he was hurt, too? No, no. He was visiting, but nothing he said made sense. His words were concrete poetry, and in a different language. She had nightmares. Nightmares of Jenny Butler on a rocket, the rocket with no radio, no guidance, just speeding into space at the cruelest speed. She dreamt of Gabriel Chu sitting next to her in priest's garb, listening to her jabber away before suddenly seizing her thighs, his eyes suddenly before her, searching through her own eyes as if peering through cracks in a fence. But most of her nightmares involved babies. Usually Mae's baby. Always silent babies, alive but with terrible plans. One night she dreamt of a thousand babies emerging from

Mae, all of them quiet and scheming. But the last
baby was not a baby at all, but a lamb.

One dawn she woke up in a new place. It wasn't the
hospital. The view was all water, the Bay, the same
northern water view she'd seen when the walls had
been blown off the building. Her head was suddenly
clear, the clearest it had been in weeks. Her oval told
her she'd slept eighteen hours of the last twenty-
four. She felt a brief flush of pride and wished she
could tell Francis. She looked around her and realized she was back on Treasure Island, but the vantage point was different. The view looked down
upon the water from a hundred feet, the boats like
waterbugs. Then she knew: she was in the Overlook.
　Now she was wide awake.
　There were no clocks in the room. She swung
her feet from the bed and felt a screaming from her
ribs. She touched her side and found her torso still
tightly wrapped. Her feet were bandaged lightly. She
dropped them gingerly to the floor. It was her arches
where the burns were worst.
　She padded around the room, noting the lights
on her bracelet awakening. Her movements were
being monitored. She expected someone to arrive
any moment. But who? She knew so little about this
place. Would it be doctors? Counselors? Security?
The people around her seemed to be sleeping peace-
fully. There were no bandages, no injuries. They

were just Everyones, and this seemed like any other
pod, and as she approached the window she saw
the slashing reflection of the moon on the water.
A sharp ache radiated from the back of her skull.
She squinted, turned her head, and finally dropped
to her knees. The pain had seized every nerve. She
managed to crawl back to her bed, and when she lay
her head down again, the pain receded. Too soon to
walk, fool, she thought, and passed out.

She awoke to Winnie. She hadn't seen Winnie in
months, and now Winnie was sitting by her side,
knitting what appeared to be a sock. In the window beyond, Delaney saw a series of clouds, dots
and lines, a kind of Morse code. When Winnie
saw Delaney's open eyes, her face lit up. "Look at
you!" she said. She rested her first two fingers on
Delaney's temple. "You look so much better than
yesterday. Yesterday I really worried about your face,
like it'd be bloated forever. I told my husband . . ."
    Delaney closed her eyes and slept. When she
woke, she saw her parents, whose faces were pressed
together, as if peeking in on her from a small window. They said the word prognosis far too many
times for normal conversation, and each time they
were very happy about this, her prognosis. So
happy, they said, and soon were gone. When she
woke again it was hours later, or a day. The light was
different, the clouds were gone.

"You again!" Winnie said. She was still knitting. Now it really was a sock. How can Winnie spend a day here? Delaney thought. It must be Saturday.

"This place is so crowded!" Winnie said. "No beds left, no chairs. A lot of people needing help. You have one of the last private rooms. Oh! Did you hear? You probably didn't hear. I don't know if I should tell you, but maybe you want some distraction? I know I like to be distracted when I'm in pain. Are you in pain?"

Delaney closed her eyes to say **Yes. And your talking hurts me, too. It's too fast, too loud. Please stop. And who will wear that misshapen sock?**

"They don't know who did it," Winnie said. "The bombing. It's driving everyone nuts. But Stenton's on it. He's the one, I think. He says leave it to him. Everyone's turning to him to figure it out, to get the security here in order. Strong leader, right? They brought in the Widower for questioning. You know that guy, the one with the sign by the bridge?"

Delaney closed her eyes in assent.

"Well, the police brought him in. Or we did. Someone did. I mean, he had motive, right? Then they let him go and guess what? They find his body washed up on the shore of Treasure Island. A suicide. Someone saw his body while they were jogging on the perimeter. He must have jumped from the Bay Bridge. Which means, I'm thinking, he had something to do with the bombing?"

Delaney didn't have the energy to bother dissecting or debunking.

"Oh and!" Winnie said, her voice rising, "Maybe you don't know this. You probably don't know this. We haven't told the customers yet, so don't tell anyone off-campus, okay? Actually, don't say anything to anyone for now. Wait, can you even talk?"

Mute, Delaney looked at her with exasperated eyes.

"Oh," Winnie said. "Sorry. Well, there was a hack of Thoughts Not Things. We're assuming it's Russians, but it could be someone posing as Russians to make us think it's Russians. They do stuff like that. Or it could be the same person who did the bombing. If it wasn't the Widower."

Delaney reached for the morphine button but realized she had not been given a morphine button.

"You looking for painkillers?" Winnie asked. "That's not something you control here. They don't let any people do that. Definitely not the doctors. Too many mistakes! I like this color on you," she said, and took the corner of Delaney's robe between her thumb and forefinger.

Delaney saw a figure shuffling past her room. He looked familiar, a middle-aged man with a faint smile on his face. He was holding a leather folder to his chest as if to keep it warm. Winnie turned to follow Delaney's eyes.

"Oh, I saw him before," she said. "He walks

around with the folder, like as if someone might take it from him."

The man turned and Delaney knew it was Hans-Georg. He looked right at her with his pale eyes, but he showed no sign of recognition. He smiled blandly and shuffled on.

"And there's nothing in the folder," Winnie said. "Isn't that sad? What was I talking about? Oh, the hack. You didn't hear?"

Delaney shook her head. The pain stabbed her in both temples.

"Everything's gone," Winnie said. "They deleted all of Thoughts Not Things. All the scans. All of them. Every last one. If people downloaded them, they're fine, but who downloads anymore? It was all in the cloud, and the cloud got hacked, knocked from the sky. Now we're trying to figure out why they targeted Thoughts Not Things. Why not some other department? And does this have anything to do with the bombings?"

Delaney closed her eyes again. She couldn't stand more news, more words. She thought of all she'd scanned and burned. The wedding dresses, the photos, the baby shoes, toys and letters. A grandfather clock! When she opened her eyes again, it was night, and the moon through the window was a sinister void shrouded by fog. The Supples visited. There seemed to be thirty of them, forty. They were touching her face, her arms. Someone—Gemma?—was trying to cinch the waist of her hospital gown. There

were many opinions about the gown. Was it synthetic? We can do better, they concluded. Delaney
closed her eyes and thought of snowy mountains.

Mount Breitenbach.

Lost River Peak.

Donaldson Peak.

Hyndman Peak.

USGS Peak.

No Regret Peak.

When she awoke, it was dawn. The Supples were
long gone, replaced by Carlo and Shireen.

"We wanted to visit," Shireen said.

"We had to visit," Carlo said. "Being
your friends."

"Definitely your friends," Shireen said. "We were
so worried."

"Not because the care here would give us any
worry," Carlo said, and gave Shireen an imploring
look. "But just because what you went through. The
care here is unparalleled."

"Right," Shireen said, and giggled nervously. "Of
course it is. It's so good. I would never have implied
otherwise. I needed help here, too, once and—"

Carlo squinted sidelong at her.

"We're just so glad you're awake," Shireen said.

"Of course she's awake," Carlo said. "Because
she's getting the best care available."

Delaney closed her eyes, hoping they would disappear. When she opened them, it was nighttime
again, and she saw the same sinister moon. Her

head throbbed, and she looked for a doctor. Where were the doctors? She had watery memories of doctors and nurses visiting between Winnie and Carlo and Shireen, but couldn't remember what they'd said or done, and as she tried to recall anything about them, anything they'd said—where were the doctors?—sleep took her again.

XL.

WHEN SHE WOKE, Delaney found Kiki sitting on her bed, wearing a chartreuse robe. This was a new room, a pink room, a bright recovery room with a powder-blue couch and a row of cacti on the windowsill.

"I heard you were here," Kiki said, and tapped Delaney's knee with her tiny forefinger. "I'm here, too. Getting better, just like you." She blinked cheerfully. "Don't you love this color?" she ran her hands over the lapels of her robe. Delaney looked down and saw that she, too, was wearing a chartreuse robe. She tried to sit up.

"Let me help," Kiki said, and pushed a button on the bed until Delaney was nearly at ninety degrees. For a moment, Delaney's head throbbed like a dying star.

"I've been sleeping," Kiki said. "Finally, yesterday I slept six hours. **Restful** sleep. You probably didn't hear that the sleep metrics have been improved. Turns out that the previous measurements were off by 33 percent. So we all were sleeping less than we thought we were. And very little of it was Truly Restful Sleep—TRS. But now it's been measured better. See?" She raised her fourth finger, which bore a thin white ring. "Let me see yours."

Kiki reached for Delaney's finger, which bore the same ring.

"Eight hours! Wow!" Kiki said. "Maybe I need to survive a bombing, too." A ding came from her oval. "Just a joke," she said to it and to Delaney. "Anyway, I do feel rested," she said.

Delaney tried to find evidence of Kiki's restfulness, but she still looked wan. Her face was puffy, her eyes red and trembling. Delaney looked beyond her, and in the pink hallway saw others in chartreuse robes, shuffling through.

"At first I was so bored here, and I missed Nino," she said. "But I know they're caring for him. I see him every day on FaceMe and he seems really happy." Kiki looked out the window at the shimmering silver water. Her mouth dropped open and her eyes lost focus. Then she returned.

"I'm just glad I'm here and not someone they fished out of the Bay. I guess they were worried about me. The AI flagged my word choices and movements and . . ." She drifted off again. "But I wouldn't even know how to even go about that. I mean, how does it work?"

"How does what work?" Delaney asked.

"Drowning. Like, how do you do it? What are the steps?"

Delaney desperately wanted to change the subject but Kiki was one step ahead of her. She turned to Delaney with a bright smile just short of insane.

"And I saw Gabriel Chu! He was so helpful. He explained everything. It turns out some of my goals were out of reach," she said. "Which is funny, because one of my main OwnSelf goals was to set goals that **were** out of reach. Growth mindset, right?"

She stared at Delaney's forehead for a disconcerting amount of time. She was lost again, and then returned.

"I failed, for sure," Kiki said. "It took me a few days here to admit that. But failure's good—we know that. It's even better than grit. Gabriel said that. You've met Gabriel Chu?"

Delaney nodded.

"It turns out my OwnSelf settings were too loose," she said. "I had all my goals in place, but gave myself too much leeway in meeting them. You know how I was always late in getting you places? You were probably like, 'Why are we always late?' That's on me. I'd stop and FaceMe with Nino when I should have been just getting from one place to another. I was pursuing the right goals, Gabriel said, but just needed more structure."

Delaney swallowed, coating her throat, determined to speak.

"Less freedom," she managed.

"Exactly!" Kiki said. "If I want to meet my goals, I need to just be told how to achieve them—with far greater specificity and chronology. I've started that here in the Overlook, and I've gotten a lot better. The stress is gone, because all those decisions are gone. It used to be that I'd set a goal for 18,000 steps a day, but how I would go about getting there would be up to me. And even though OwnSelf was reminding me dozens of times a day about the goals, and where I was in meeting them, it became doubly stressful, with me trying to decide when and where and how to achieve them. So I'm on OwnSelf: Total—OST. Are you on OST?"

"No, but—" Delaney began.

"Oh you should!" Kiki said. "It's the last step that gives all the other steps meaning. I finally can relax! Even now, see how relaxed I am?" Kiki appeared utterly wasted, hollow.

"You look wonderful," Delaney said.

"Yesterday, when I found out you were up here, I set aside forty minutes to talk to you. OST figured right now would be the best time to find you awake and free, and coordinated with your auto-meds so you'd be awake. And here we are!"

"Miracle," Delaney said. She wanted to spirit Kiki out of here with Nino, bring them to an island

and nurse Kiki back to health. But how? What were the steps?

"When did the doctors say you could leave?" Delaney asked, her mouth still gluey.

"Doctors? They're in the mix, sure, but the numbers will determine when." She tapped her oval. "I'm serious about my recovery, Del—I'm not going to leave it up to some random doctor. And the nurses are worse!"

Delaney found no words.

"And you shouldn't, either," Kiki continued. "Get the data. You have to, actually. They don't let people leave here unless the algos are right. That makes it error-proof."

"Right," Delaney said, and suddenly wondered if that were true, or just something Kiki misunderstood. Would an algorithm really determine when Delaney could leave?

"Listen, though," Kiki said. "I didn't come to just talk about me. Can I?" She shimmied her buttocks into Delaney's bed. "I wanted us to watch the Stenton presentation together. Did anyone tell you about it?"

"Sorry, no," Delaney said. "I think I've been asleep the better part of a month."

"Well, I knew you'd want to see this," Kiki said. "It's all prompted by what happened to you and the people who died." She got a ding on her oval. She read it and looked back to Delaney. "And I'm so sorry about Soren."

Kiki was using Departy, Delaney realized. "Thank you," she said.

"Can I?" Kiki said, and shimmied further. Delaney allowed her to place a tablet on her lap, and Kiki pulled up the frozen image of Stenton.

"This happened earlier this morning," Kiki noted, and pressed Stenton's frozen face to give it life.

"Greetings," Stenton said. "For those of you who were here before I left, I say hello again. Thank you for welcoming me back with such graciousness. For those Everyones who have come on staff since I was last here, and I'm thinking there are about two thousand of you, I say hello."

"He's back full-time now," Kiki said. "It's been so good."

"When I returned to the Every," Stenton continued, "my wish was to prove my value to this company. To this movement. And now Mae has given me an opportunity to do that. As you likely know, in China one of the projects in which I was involved was security-oriented, and I became very familiar with the ways we can continue to make ourselves, our families, and our world safer. And of course our workplaces. It's unacceptable for anyone to come to work and feel at risk of an attack like that which happened last month here. We lost five of our own in that attack, and many more are still hospitalized, on a long journey of recovery."

Kiki squeezed Delaney's shoulder, and Delaney

noted her long fingernails. Had they always been so long? She looked into Kiki's dark, trembling eyes. Everything about Kiki seemed strained now—her face gaunt, the veins in her forehead manically searching.

"And I know each of you has been blindsided by these two assaults. You've wondered, How can this happen? How can something so unforeseen elude us? Sneak up on us like it did?"

Stenton's eyes were enraged, as if the bombings were less about violence and more about deception.

"One of my strengths, I'm told, is that I'm practical," Stenton said. "When confronted by a problem as we now find ourselves, I can see it clearly and arrive at a solution efficiently. I think I've done that in this case. We were able to merge some existing tech, like SoulSearch of course, and fast-track some new projects with lightning speed. So I want to give a—" he paused for a second, as if double-checking he could pull off the word—"**shout-out** to the team, two hundred and eighty-seven of us who have been working day and night on this, which we are calling KnowThem."

On the screen, a satellite map of the Bay Area appeared, the Every campus heralded with a pulsing yellow dot.

"As you know, the drone that delivered the bomb was an AH-32, a model designed here. Notably, it has one of the shorter transmittal ranges of any of our drones. So we know that the perpetrator of this

violent act was within a five-mile radius of our campus. That's right. The person who committed this
crime was not operating from halfway across
the world. They were in our midst. For all we
know, they might still be in our midst—living
among us, because the operator of this drone has
yet to be apprehended."

Stenton's face shrunk to a small square in the
lower corner of the screen, while the majority of
the screen showed the streets of Oakland. Delaney
had no clear sense of what time it was, but this
seemed to be the morning commuter hour, with
thousands of people emerging from the subway
into downtown.

"This is a live feed of downtown Oakland," he
said, "but this could be anywhere. Anywhere people
come and go, we all have to simply trust that the
people we're moving past don't mean us harm. Must
we live in this precarious state, knowing nothing
about the people around us? Having to trust their
intentions? It's obscene. It's irrational. It's not right."

The screen now showed an overhead view of a
suburban neighborhood, a blimp's shadow fitting
nicely into a high-school football field.

"As you know, for decades now, we have been
given the right to know if sexual predators are living among us. Whether these criminals were caught
with child porn or were convicted of assault, we
have the right to know where they live."

In the neighborhood of fifty-odd suburban

homes, seven red Xes were placed on three free-standing homes and four were concentrated in what appeared to be an apartment complex near a freeway.

"This registry was our right and has been, for millions of families, a safeguard and comfort. As parents and indeed as citizens, we have not just a right, but a duty, to know this. When you commit a crime on the public, that crime itself should be public and forever knowable."

Now the screen went back to the commuters in downtown Oakland. As they walked up and down San Pablo Avenue, over every head, a question mark appeared.

"And yet we're deprived of the right to know what other criminals live and walk among us. The Sexual Offender Registry came into effect in the 1990s, and still, in all those years since, we have no registry of addresses for those convicted of murder, assault, burglary, or any other felony or misde-meanor. Years ago, with SeeYou, we tried, but the tech wasn't there. Now it is—it's available to anyone with a phone. Wouldn't you like to know, when you're walking down the street, if there's someone close to you who's been convicted of theft? Wouldn't that be useful information?"

Again Kiki squeezed Delaney's shoulder.

"As we speak, in the Bay Area, there are more than 1 million people who have been convicted of some crime, and yet there is no comprehensive database that lists them in an easily accessible way—in a way that we can act on quickly."

An animation onscreen showed the silhouette of a woman being approached on all sides by threatening cartoon men.

"The tragic thing here, the exasperating thing here, is that we already possess all of this information. The Every has it at this moment. In fact, here it is."

A satellite map of the Bay Area, in its lushness and the crystal white of its cities, now began to bleed from a million red pinpricks.

"Most of you are already ahead of me," Stenton said. "Anyone with a phone and a TruYou account—and that represents 93 percent of the population of California, by the way—can be easily known. We can discern their location at any time. And with one quick filter, we can single out those convicted of violent crimes."

The sea of pinpricks now shrank, but still soaked the map in red.

"Now, those convicted of car theft."

A different set of red and pink dots overtook the map.

"Now rape," he said.

Thousands of dots sprung from the map. Stenton quickly ran through other categories of crime, from embezzlement to petty vandalism.

"You'll see that there are not just red dots but pink, too," he said. "The pink are those who were arrested for a certain crime but not convicted. We have a right to know where those people are, too."

Delaney glanced at Kiki. She was looking out the window, where a three-quarter moon was visible in the daytime sky.

"You know where I'm heading here," Stenton said. "Let's find those accused of acts of terrorism." A handful of red dots appeared—far fewer than the previous crimes. "And those arrested on charges of possessing explosives . . ." A different handful of red dots appeared, one of them just a few miles west of campus.

"It's my assertion that all of us, as citizens, have a right to this information. Do you have a right to know if a man in your building has been arrested for breaking and entering? For assault? For rape? I believe you do. And I think it should be as easy as a tap on your device. Let me demonstrate." He lifted his fist in the air and talked to the phone strapped to his arm. "KnowThem, how many convicted felons are currently within a five-mile radius of the Every?"

"One thousand, eight hundred and eleven," his phone said.

"Wait. There's more," Stenton said, and smiled. "I want to show what it looks like in more visceral, personal terms. Right now we have one of our own, Minerva Hollis, on a BART train. She got on at Lake Merritt and she's heading toward campus."

Minerva's face overtook the room. "Hi!" she said, each of her teeth an inch tall and gleaming.

"Now this is where the information becomes far more useful," Stenton said. "Minnie, will you do a sweep?"

Minnie's cam took a quick panoramic video of the other passengers in her BART car. There were nine men, six women, and four children. None seemed to notice her, for all but one of them was looking at their own phones.

"Now when we apply KnowThem to Minnie's fellow passengers, we see with whom she's sharing such close and contained quarters."

The shapes of three of the men were shrouded in a red filter. One more man, and one of the women, went pink. "Okay," Stenton said, "Minnie's got an interesting crew with her now. Three convicted felons and two more with arrests, no convictions. She can leave it at that, and get off at the next stop, or she can dig deeper, and find out what each person's offense was. I believe Minnie has a right to know this. Do you?"

Stenton addressed Minnie. "So you got onto this train, and you saw nineteen strangers. Now you know a bit more about what risks there are around you. Do you feel safer?"

"Well—" Minnie said.

Stenton's easy smile, which had been conveying his happiness at what was his finest public moment, tightened.

"I have to admit I'm a bit freaked out," Minnie said.

Stenton glanced backstage and cleared his throat.

"Yes. Yes. It is concerning. The level of crime around us. The chaos. The proximity of those who might do us harm. All the more reason we have a right to be informed."

"He's so strong," Kiki said. "Don't you think he's strong?"

Delaney nodded to appease Kiki, and was suddenly certain that Stenton planned to edge Mae out. He had a vision and she had none—that would be the perception. He had a plan, and after the bombings she had only platitudes. Smiles would keep no one safe.

"For the past week, we've been experimenting privately with this tech, tracking the few miles around campus," he continued. "When we note a felon in the radius, AI helps us sort them and alerts us to those who have been accused or arrested for more violent crimes, or those pertinent to the safety of the campus. Our security teams then take a closer look, sometimes politely asking these men and women a few questions, and letting them know we know who they are. We've found," and here he issued a studied chuckle, "that this is usually enough to keep them off our island. Now, the question is, would this tech have prevented the attack that took the lives of five innocent souls? We can't be altogether certain. But my personal belief is that it would."

Now Stenton's eyes took aim. "I have lost patience with the chaos of the world. And chaos is possible because we allow it to fester in the shadows. Well, I vow to eliminate those shadows. One of the Everypersons who lost his life in the bombing was Soren Lundqvist. He was a member of our Reach and Sunlight teams, dedicated to brightening unseen parts of our world. He died in this pursuit—the pursuit of illumination. Of safety through transparency. And it's my vow, and I hope it's one you will join me in fulfilling, to eliminate every last shadow on this planet. To that end, I want to introduce someone many of you already know. His name is Wes Makazian."

Delaney gagged as the camera angle opened to include Wes, wearing an immaculate bodysuit, black and stitched to emphasize his wiry muscles; he looked like a sleek assassin.

"Thank you, Tom," he said. "As we mourn the many we lost in this horrific act, I want us to remember that there are many survivors, too—many who will be scarred by this experience. Among them is a close friend of mine, Delaney Wells."

Kiki let out a thrilled eek. Delaney's heart stopped.

"And to honor her pain," Wes continued, "we on the Friendy team have been working day and night to expand the software to prevent anything like this from happening again."

Delaney watched the screen closely, wondering if this was some kind of hostage video, or a Stasi-style forced confession. But Wes seemed utterly calm and wholly sincere. He was gone, gone, gone—intoxicated by the power he'd been given. Delaney was nauseous.

"Friendy's not just for truth-finding between friends," Stenton added.

"No, Tom, it isn't," Wes said. "There's no reason we can't use the same tools, the same diagnostics, to find clues. To see patterns. To identify those inclined toward malfeasance."

"Great crimes start with small lies," Stenton noted. "And Friendy, better than any tool humans have yet made, can identify those small lies before they become dangerous acts."

Wes and Stenton then demonstrated how AI would scan all conversations—anonymized, of course, they were quick to note—and when they found instances of a certain level of dishonesty or guile, that person would be flagged for closer scrutiny. A disproportionately dishonest or cagey person would be referred to the proper authorities, who could keep an eye on them as needed.

"Friendy will continue to assess the quality of your relationships. Don't worry about that, L-O-L," Stenton said, and forced a mirthless chuckle. "But in addition, it will be one of our primary instruments in keeping you safe. Thank you,

Wes, for your vision and your sacrifice." Stenton turned briefly to Wes and then back to the camera, which zoomed in, removing Wes from the frame.

"And thank you, Delaney Wells, for your role in all of this. We wish you a speedy recovery, and we can't wait to get you back on the Every team."

Delaney remembered to breathe, and wanted to vomit, but she was too tired, too wrecked. She heard a sniffle, and found that Kiki was crying. A ding sounded from her wrist.

"That's my signal to go," Kiki said to Delaney, and straightened herself. "You should be proud. Proud of what's come from Soren's death and your own suffering. None of it was in vain. Kudos, Delaney. Kudos."

XLI.

DELANEY COULD HAVE SUED. Even the threat of a lawsuit for the Every's failure to protect her would mean she'd walk away with an eight-figure settlement. But she'd signed every release the Every had given her. She did not hold them responsible, she said. And she did not want ten million dollars from the Every. She wanted them to cease to exist. The alacrity with which she signed the forms kicked off a steady drumbeat of admiration and gratitude from an ascending colonnade of Every executives.

With bandages still covering her feet and hands and ribs, she was feted at a private dinner in one of the senior pods, with twelve Gang of 40 members in attendance. They thanked her in tones of great sincerity and promised they would find the culprit, would do so within the week. They asked about Idaho and her work as a ranger, and they all wanted to know her hopes for her permanent placement at the Every. What did she want to do when she was

done rotating? they wanted to know. She was offered roles in advertising and marketing and design.
There was room on the ethics team, they told her,
or—or!—she could be a Product Philosopher.

She wanted to continue to roam, she said. She
loved every minute she'd spent in every department,
she said, and this was largely true. It was a dream to
be able to get to know each lever and button, and
see the minds at work in all quarters, she said.

They were so grateful, so relieved. They said absolutely. They knew she wanted to spend some time
at home in Idaho, and they gave her a travel bonus,
offered to get her home in a carbon-free manner.
She even got a message from Stenton: **Integrity. You
have it. S.**

And at the end of the night—as if the dinner
were a final audition before she was cast—they
said that in the morning, Mae Holland would very
much like to meet her.

"Damn it," Joan said. "I shouldn't have listened
to Francis."

Francis had counseled Joan to stall for a
few days, perhaps a week, to see how things
shook out. He was hoping for some kind of
settlement-with-continued-employment, and had
convinced Joan to do so, too. She and Francis had
not signed anything yet, and though they had been
assured they could take their time, Joan had sensed
from the Gang of 40 that her delay had already been

taken as a sign of mercenary betrayal. Delaney was shocked that Joan, who had always appeared to have the place wired, had read the situation so wrongly; the Every valued loyalty, and had since the beginning rewarded loyalty and discretion with mountains of stock options and cash. They were miserly with settlements and vicious with shakedowns.

"Where are you meeting?" Joan asked.

"I think in her box," Delaney said, though she had not actually been notified of the location.

"Just you?" Joan asked.

"I think so. But I actually don't know."

"I'm not asking you to bring me," Joan said.

Delaney hadn't thought to bring Joan along. "I can ask," she said, knowing the idea was ludicrous. "When they give me details, I'll ask."

"No. Don't," Joan said. "I know I fucked up. I don't want you to be sullied by my avarice. Just watch them demote me to Product Philosopher or something like that."

"They won't," Delaney said, but realized that was exactly where people like Joan were relegated. "I'll ask if you can come."

"Sure, but she'll say no. Anyway, listen. You should be ready. You'll be on camera. Can we get your hair cut? I like your wounded pixie look, but it could be improved."

Delaney hadn't factored in cameras, but of course it was true. Joan called in a favor from one of the Every stylists.

"This might be seen by millions," Joan said. "If she sends out an alert that she's meeting one of the bomb victims, **tens** of millions. In case that informs what you wear." Joan's eyes swept across Delaney's clothing without further comment.

The meeting was in the same nondescript building where Delaney had first met Carlo and Shireen—a blank and purgatorial room, neither here nor there, invisible to the outside world.

Delaney was now free of bandages and able to walk largely without pain. The morning of the meeting, she ran her palms over the little hair she had, feeling sure her every thought and plan was now unhidden. The stylist had done what she could, but the result was more alarming than chic; her skull was still swollen and bulbous. Her phone dinged. She'd been told that the audience would be at 9 a.m., and the location would be provided that morning. Now, at 8:48, she was given the building's address, and told to come alone, and that Mae would be alone, too.

It didn't seem possible. When Delaney arrived, there was no one near. No cameras, no attendants, no assistants. When she knocked on the door, Mae answered, looking precisely like herself, only far smaller than Delaney had imagined. She was tiny.

"Come inside, come inside," Mae said, as if ushering Delaney from bad weather and into a warm cabin. When Delaney entered and the door was closed, Mae squared up on her, reached up for Delaney's shoulders and brought her in. Her embrace was tight and instantly Delaney found herself sobbing. Shit, she thought. She blinked madly.

"Is that too tight?" Mae asked, pulling back. "Your ribs?"

"It's fine," Delaney managed, and the sobbing continued. What was happening? She loathed herself. Mae was manipulating this whole situation, she told herself, and yet here she was, holding Delaney tightly, without caution. Surely if Mae were some calculating monster she would be more careful about physical contact in front of millions. She would have given some advance warning about an imminent embrace. But she had not, and the embrace continued for a full minute—it was, she realized, one of the longer clutches of her adult life, and it was not until the end that Delaney's breathing slowed and her eyes dried. Mae pulled back again and held Delaney by the shoulders. She found Delaney's eyes and locked hers to them.

"I'm so sorry," she said.

Delaney blinked furiously. She was furious at herself. Her fragility. What was happening? Who was this person? For a moment she was on Mae's side, Stenton's side, Wes's side. The bombing was a towering crime and the Every and all humanity should do anything they could to prevent it, or any crime, from happening again.

"Just cry," Mae said, and Delaney found herself

in a chair. How did she get into a chair? She was sitting on a comfortable stuffed chair and was doubled over, choking, with Mae standing behind her, stroking her heaving shoulders.

"Go, go," Mae said. "Cry and cry and cry."

Goddamnit, Mae was a human. Her hands were making circles on Delaney's back, and finally Delaney's breathing slowed, and her tears slowed, and she raised her head and looked around and it was still just her and Mae, and whatever millions had been watching the pathetic breakdown.

"You aren't on camera," Mae said.

Delaney scanned Mae's body for her cam. There was nothing. She cried again, heaving. Again Mae rubbed her shoulders. It was pathetic, Delaney thought. What kind of spy was she? She was nothing. Spineless.

Delaney knew Mae had only turned the camera off a few times in all the time she'd been running the company. She'd done so now, and that was the right thing to do. Mae was real.

Lord, Delaney thought. This will be so hard. How to ruin all this without hurting her new friend, this being of pure light? She looked into Mae's eyes. They were wet but her cheeks were dry. She was a being of righteous love and was also a highly evolved angel of control. And now she had a tissue. Not just a tissue. A bundle of tissue.

"They're so flimsy. One is never enough," Mae laughed.

Delaney blew her nose and soaked the first bundle. Mae had another ready. Delaney soaked this one, too. Mae took the first two handfuls, wet with Delaney's mucus, without hesitation, walked to the compost bin, tossed them in, returned and gave Delaney a third fistful of tissue. Delaney dried her nose and eyes and cheeks, and her right wrist, which was laced with stray strands of tears and snot.

"I can't imagine," Mae said. "So scary."

"So fucking scary," Delaney said.

"I bet it gets scarier the further away from it you get. The more you realize truly what happened."

"It does. It does get scarier," Delaney said, realizing that this was true. "Every night it gets more real."

"You could have **died,**" Mae said, and again Delaney couldn't see. Again she was underwater and her nose let free a flood of mucus.

"I'm sorry," Mae said. This came in a whisper to Delaney's ear, because Mae had once more taken her into her arms and was saying, hotly in her ear, "I'm sorry" and "Shhh, shhh," the sounds wonderfully hushed and loud.

"Thank you so much," Delaney said.

"Shhh. Shhhh," Mae whispered in her ear, so hot and so loud.

When Delaney's breathing slowed again, Mae stepped back. "The Every has made some enemies, I'm afraid," she said. "So many people and entities who don't appreciate the evolution we're undergoing as a species. I'm thinking this was some kind of violent last gasp of the old ways and the people who benefit from keeping things as they are. As they **were.** But listen. I want this to be just the beginning with you and me. Okay?"

Delaney didn't believe this part, was sure Mae was simply saying what a kind person would say.

"I'm going to Idaho, too," Mae said, "You know the Allen & Co. retreat they do in Sun Valley?"

"I do," Delaney said. Every year, a hundred of the wealthiest and most powerful tech and media CEOs and venture capitalists—and the occasional Winfrey or Soros—took over the town. Hotels were closed, restaurants rented out, the galleries stayed open late. In general, though, it drove the locals mad.

"I'll be going," Mae said, "but I have free time. I built in an extra day, actually, so you and I can spend time together. Can you plan a hike for us?"

"Yes. I'd like that."

"Somewhere only you know."

Delaney laughed. "I know so many places!" She was so happy. The idea of showing Mae, her new guardian and close friend, the back country filled her with pleasure. "There's a waterfall—"

"Don't tell me!" Mae said. "I want it to be a surprise. We'll hike, and we'll talk, just us girls, and we'll make plans. Just make sure it's off the grid. Somewhere where it's only you and me."

"Okay," Delaney said.

"I have such plans for you," Mae said.

XLII.

It took Delaney a few days to return to sanity. Or at least to her previous state of mental disarray and paranoia. She had regained her healthy cynicism regarding Mae and her motives, and had regained her rage at the Every for co-opting her friend Wes and turning their gag software into a tool of global interpersonal suspicion. But she wondered if the real problem was Stenton. Was it Stenton who turned every innocent-enough idea into a weapon of control and suppression? Was it possible to separate Stenton from all of this, and to save Wes, and to bend Mae into a less dangerous purveyor of internet diversions?

These things were on Delaney's mind as she waited for Kiki and her next rotation. But instead of Kiki, a very tall woman with ink-black hair approached. She was wearing a white taffeta tutu over a blue bodysuit; it looked like the splash she might make entering the ocean feet-first.

"I'm Siggi. The new Kiki," the woman said, and walked right past, intending Delaney to follow. "So, the Reading Room! I think this was a good choice. Given all you've been through, a low-stress rotation seems best." Delaney followed Siggi to the south end of campus, the Bay Bridge above. "Especially given you seem to really enjoy reading." She said the word **enjoy** with the hint of bewilderment some-one might apply to a hobby of canning or catalog-ing grubs. They came upon a shaded doorway and stepped in. Silver stairs led them two flights down.

"It's underground, for obvious reasons," Siggi said, but Delaney couldn't imagine why a reading room would need to be subterranean. Siggi knocked on a steel door, and it opened upon the drabbest room Delaney had seen on campus. She had ex-pected something like Bailey's famed library—an antiquarian's room rich with mahogany and brass and ladders for the higher shelves—but the room was instead a sloppy modernist mess. It looked like a junior high classroom on the first day of summer. There was the tinny sound of mournful chamber music coming from one corner, where a middle-aged woman stretched on a plush pink divan with a stack of yellow papers on her lap. She did not look up.

Delaney counted eight people in the room; only one appeared younger than forty. She stood at Siggi's side for an uncomfortably long time before a man, who had been sitting no more than ten feet from them at a round walnut table, raised his head to them and smiled. In no hurry at all, he rose and walked to them with a quieting finger at his lips, and beckoned them to follow him into a courtyard. It was a small outdoor space, two stories underground but full of light and potted plants. With a heavy glass door between them and his colleagues, he spoke.

"This is sort of our conversation area," he said, his voice like a woodwind, his accent East African. He bowed ever so slightly.

"Delaney," she said, and mirrored his bow.

"Yes, I made the leap. I'm Gregory, the ostensible head of the Reading Room," he said, and handed Delaney a business card, printed on cardstock with rounded edges, that read:

GREGORY AKUFO-ADDO
[OSTENSIBLE HEAD]
The Reading Room

He wore loosely knit jersey under a V-neck sweater. His leather shoes seemed to have been through great trouble, cross-hatched with a thousand wounds.

"I can get you a pair," he said, noticing Delaney's noticing. His eyes were quick and penetrating, and she realized that while he was finishing this sentence about one thing he'd noticed, he had noted a dozen more things about Delaney, stored them away—all while consciously keeping his eyes smiling kindly.

"I'll leave you to it," Siggi said, with a terrified smile that spoke of her profound discomfort with Gregory, his watchful eyes, his unkempt environs and his odd coterie. Before she left, though, Siggi presented Delaney with another non-disclosure agreement, on her tablet, and watched her sign it.

Gregory looked through the glass at the puddles of papers inside. "I'm done apologizing for the mess," he said, and seemed to be waiting for Delaney to comment on it one way or the other.

"It doesn't bother me," she said.

"I want to say that I'm sorry that you were injured in the bombing," Gregory said. "It's the one thing I know about you. And I'm deeply sorry. For your own suffering and the loss of your friend Soren. It must have been harrowing."

"Thank you," Delaney said. His sincerity was total.

"You have physically recovered?" he asked. His eyes scanned her for visible injuries. She smiled, yes. "That is a blessing. And you haven't been here before?" he asked.

"No," she said.

"Very fine," he said. "Out of curiosity, what have you deduced thus far about this place?"

Delaney had the sinking feeling that this introduction, and possibly all of her time at the

Reading Room, would be conducted via the
Socratic method.

"I'm assuming you read the things no one else has
time to read," she said.

A tight smile pinched his face. "Close," he said.
"The rest of the Every does, and must, exist near the
surface. We are deep-sea divers. We are missioned
with reading about a hundred long-form texts a
week, from books to scripts to contracts to manifestos. The incoming texts we examine for libel, sabotage, legal exposure, and existential threats to the
Every. For the outgoing texts we act as content curators, copy editors, tonal judges and proofers. Does
any of that need further elucidation?"

"Nope, got it," Delaney said.

"This department has no cameras, no internet,
no signals going in or out," he continued. "We read
sensitive documents on paper. As you know, as texts
are digitized, they can be altered. You may have
heard of a diabolical recent thing called FictFix,
which so-called improves classic texts to meet contemporary standards and reading tastes?"

Delaney's stomach cinched. "I think so," she said.

"Here we deal with original, definitive texts and
we go slow. Bailey set the department up after noticing that with every passing year, errors in outgoing messaging were increasing, pivotal words and
clauses in incoming contracts were being missed,
and in general he could not depend on the rest of

the Every staff to catch these things. So here we read carefully and slowly, and we miss nothing. Does that interest you?"

"It does, very much," Delaney said.

"I assume, because you are here, you are, or were, a reader?" he asked. It occurred to Delaney that Gregory really had not researched her, and was asking her questions in order that he might know more about herself. It was jarring.

"No, I don't presearch people before I meet them," Gregory said. Again he'd read her mind. "I ask them questions and learn about them from their answers. I realize how radical that is."

Delaney wanted to ask him why he was working at the Every, but again he knew her thoughts.

"What am I doing here then," he said, removing the interrogative aspect of the sentence and stating it like the most obvious next topic.

"I was Bailey's college roommate," he said. He paused long enough that Delaney was forced into speaking.

"I'm so sorry for the loss," she fumbled. "For **your** loss."

"Thank you," he said. "We were close. We met as freshmen, and I used to write his history and English papers. When the Circle grew, he realized the need for close readers to pore over every word in every meaningful company communication, and he called me. You've been to eye-tracking perhaps?"

Delaney said she had.

"They confirmed what Bailey had suspected, which was that people were reading less than half the words they saw. Even in text messages, there was a new tendency to get the gist, and of course in contracts and sensitive documents, the gist does not suffice."

"No," she said.

"Remember when Mueller issued his report? It was 448 pages. About two million people downloaded it. For those who downloaded it to be read on e-readers, of course we were able to deduce how many people read every page. Would you like to guess the number?"

"Twelve?" Delaney said.

"Very impressive," he said. "But the actual number was eleven. And five of those readers were in one family in Bend, Oregon. Remember the second report, the one that summed up the first was much shorter, but only seventy-three people read this abridged version."

"I read it," Delaney said, and instantly regretted saying so. She still didn't want to be noticed, here or anywhere.

"It was quite delicious," Gregory said. "Wall-to-wall crimes of all varieties, and yet it was not read. The documentary was watched, of course . . ." He drifted off for dramatic effect. "But back to Bailey. He gave me free rein and gave me this room and a budget to hire a team of readers. My rules were that this room remain free of all incoming or outgoing signals, that I run it exactly as I wish, and that I never have to speak to Tom Stenton. In turn, Bailey's request was that this department turn any document around within a reasonable amount of time, usually within forty-eight hours, and that we eliminate all outgoing errors. Are you a grammarian?"

"I believe I am," Delaney said.

"What is a gerund?" he asked.

"A verb in noun form. The i-n-g form," she said.

"Close enough," he said. "You may or may not have noticed an overall degradation of the language, and a proliferation of errors of spelling and grammar in even the most official documents?"

He didn't wait for an answer, just led her back inside, opening the door with the hush of heavy glass. "Of course you have. I don't want to believe otherwise. Now, I thought the best way to give you a sense of the range would be for me to simply tell you what everyone is reading today. Fair enough?"

He led her to a wingback chair of yellow wool, in which a large man sat. He was wearing a pageboy hat.

"Marcus is reading a 256-page contract between the Every and a supplier of cobalt. This has been read by a number of company attorneys and outside consultants, but the attorneys miss a lot. Given the proliferation of auto-fill and AI in the legal profession, lawyers no longer know how to write. Some

ninety percent of contract boilerplate is now generated by algos and AI, with only minor human
intervention or augmentation. This can lead to
ghastly problems."

Marcus nodded and they moved on to a fortysomething woman in a puffy black coat, a wool
blanket over her legs.

"Brenda, who is always cold, is reading a pre-
publication galley of a book, to be released in three
months, by a popular technology columnist. It con-
tains a chapter about the Every and all its terrifying
power." He said the last two words without any affect. "It will be Brenda's task to see if this book pre-
sents any real threat, though of course no book of
its kind ever has, given these books are rarely read.
You've met Alessandro, I assume?"

"I have," Delaney said.

"Thank you Brenda," Gregory said, and they
crossed the room and found a wary-eyed woman
who had been hidden behind a bookshelf. She had
shaved half her head and was wearing a City Lights
T-shirt.

"Minka is reading the work of Italo Calvino. Mae
Holland is meeting the Italian prime minister in
Sun Valley, and her team asked for a lesser-known
Calvino quotation—something that would indicate she'd done more than a cursory internet search
of his name and his famous quotations. Minka has
read six of Calvino's books in the last three days and

has so far compiled a list of twenty-two options. When she's done, Minka will winnow the list down to seven. Mae's team asked for seven."

They thanked Minka, and Gregory led Delaney to a wall of glass, behind which sat two preternaturally calm people in their fifties.

"You'll see two people in our sound-proof pod. That is Larissa and Fyodor. Larissa has been with us for many years, and she's brought Fyodor, a noted expert on Russian literature, on as a consultant. They're examining four versions of Dostoevsky's **The Idiot.** One is the original Russian publication. The second is the latest human-generated translation into English. The third was translated by AI and its characters and plot improved through FictFix. This morning they were sixty-seven pages in, and had indicated that thus far, our AI-FictFix version had improved upon the human-generated translation, a fact I found fascinating and which will likely eliminate much of the profession of editor, archivist and translator. Do you have questions?"

"No," Delaney said, but there was the obvious one.

"What will you be reading?" Gregory asked. "That is the obvious question. Given you are a visitor—not to say interloper—I urge you to seek out what pleases you. Does that sound agreeable?"

No one but Gregory spoke to Delaney that day or the next, and she was invited to roam the room and the stacks. There were two levels below the Reading Room containing papers, books, newspapers, academic treatises.

If only to be alone, she wandered the lowest levels, feeling like she was in some nineteenth-century archive assembled by hoarders. The organizational system was difficult to grasp. There were sections of boxes and bins, each with an author's name or topic on the outward-facing side. There were file cabinets based on subject—anti-trust, privacy, libel, pornography, fascism, warrantless data collection. And then on tables and without label, there were unbound manuscripts, crudely printed manifestoes and self-printed screeds. No one in any of the rooms took the slightest interest in Delaney, so she meandered, picking papers up, examining them, putting them down.

And then she found the box called OwnSelf Studies. It was an unremarkable box, looking precisely like all the rest, and without any whiff of self-importance. Inside, though, were documents labeled SENSITIVE AND PROPRIETARY and NDA REQ'D—**see Jacob.** But because Gregory had insisted that anything in the Reading Room was open to her, she took the box to an empty corner of the room illuminated by a shaft of natural light. RANDOMIZED STUDY, read the cover sheet of the first packet, and in smaller type: EFFECTS OF LONG-TERM OWNSELF USAGE AMONG SUBJECTS AGES 34–47.

Her heart thrummed. She flipped to the middle.

"Subject 277 was found today at the bottom of the stairwell, unable to discern how to get to the second floor. Her OwnSelf had not been updated. Subject was conscious of the humor in the situation, but was still unable to conjure a way to get to the second floor without OwnSelf guidance. She laughed about her failure, and was quite apologetic. When offered the chance to cease the OwnSelf experiment, she could not make that decision, either."

Delaney looked up, certain she was reading something forbidden. But no one was paying her any mind. She flipped to another page.

"Subject 112 presenting with acute mania and insomnia. OwnSelf had set modest sleep-hour goals but Subject 112 has been unable to meet these, despite multiple interventions. Subject's stress levels then increased, and insomnia was exacerbated. This cycle continued until she was admitted to Overlook by her direct reports."

This could only be Kiki, Delaney assumed. And if it wasn't Kiki, it was someone like Kiki, and there were dozens like this, not just at the Every but all over the world, people who had ceded so much control over their lives that they'd lost the mind-map that could take them from the first floor to the second.

The next day, Delaney found a loose sheaf of papers written by Mercer Madeiros, whose name rang a bell but whom she couldn't place. He'd written something called **On the Rights of People in the Digital Age.** She began reading it when she felt a presence nearby. It was Gregory.

"If that's of interest, we just got this," he said, and handed her a gray box containing a brick of freshly printed white pages. The cover sheet said **Bending and Breaking** by Meena Agarwal, PhD.

"You heard of her?" Gregory asked.

"I have," Delaney said, and hoped to say nothing more.

Gregory paused for a second longer than was comfortable. "Well, she's quite compelling," he said finally. "You should read this. It's new. I think we might have one of the only copies. Maybe the **only** copy."

Beyond the letters Agarwal had sent, Delaney hadn't read anything new of hers for years. She'd been careful not to look Agarwal up online, and even ordering Agarwal's papers had represented un-tenable risk. So to find herself being encouraged to read Agarwal inside the confines of the Every sent Delaney into an out-of-body experience. Afraid she'd be caught any moment, Delaney jumped to the middle.

"Each year, we spend more time examining each other, judging each other, mentally murdering each other. And we wonder why the pills continue to get stronger. We are numb and want to be number."

Delaney looked up. No one had moved. No one seemed at all interested in what she was reading, and yet she felt sure she was being watched. She skipped ahead.

"We are a species in contraction. The age of exploration has given way to the age of introspection.

"Of fear. Of caution.

"We seek nothing,

"We invent nothing,

"We forgive nothing.

"A species that sits still, in a circle, staring at each other, cannot survive. We sit in constant judgment of each other, and thus we are a species in decline. Nothing great can be created in such a climate. An authentic human life cannot be lived this way. We become more tame and fearful every year, every day, and every hour brings another thing we cannot do or cannot say, and in all cases, the penalty for violators is that they are thrown away—a kind of digital capital punishment. Every new generation purports to be more empathetic, and yet every new generation is less forgiving. And of course, with every coming year, technology ensures that no errors go unrecorded."

Delaney looked up. Sunlight was shooting through the subterranean door and casting a watery reflection on the ceiling. Though she trusted Gregory's assurances, she searched the ceiling for cameras. But she was still alone, unwatched, unseen. She flipped ahead in Agarwal's manuscript.

"The question now is whether we have become a different species. Never before has humankind evolved so quickly and so uniformly. Globalism has enabled the Every to touch nearly every human on the planet at the same time. Never has it been possible to introduce a movement, or goal, or product, and have it reach every person the same day. And in my research we've never been a more pliable species. The ready adoption of virtually any new application has almost no historical precedent.

"This leaves a very small group of non-adopters who struggle to participate in society in analog ways. But with every passing year, the ability of these resisters to function in society becomes more challenging, if not impossible. Children need the latest hardware and constant connection in order to get an education. Seniors depend on algorithms to receive pills. Cash and paper will soon be outlawed, and every transaction and communication will be digital and thus public and tracked and open to interpretation, speculation and judgment. Though they try, trogs in the end are no more politically powerful or culturally influential than the Amish."

Delaney did not believe her unsurveilled reading could last. Again she looked around the room, expecting to find a camera she hadn't noticed before. The ceiling's acoustic tiles were full of tiny holes. Surely they could rig a camera in one of those? She flipped to the end.

"I want to have hope, though," Agarwal wrote. "Monopolies have been broken in the past, tyrannies have fallen. Usually these entities go too far, and always there is someone who sees this and has the power to not just ring the bell but actually stop a flood of lemmings from following each other over the cliff and into the sea. I have spent decades now trying to think of just how this message could be conveyed—how I could convince the species to turn back. But I have failed. I've stood at cliff's edge for generations now, and watched thousands leap. Whether they heard me or not I don't know, but in any case they sailed over the edge."

This was new, this despair in Agarwal's prose. Always there had been outrage, and fury at the prevailing apathy of her students and humankind, but Delaney never knew her to be resigned, despondent. Was it the cancer? With a sudden dread she worried Agarwal would end her life. Not for a moment did she rule it out. Agarwal was the type to do it; she'd get hold of one of those Swiss euthanasia kits. Delaney's heart awakened. She had to see her. How?

Then she knew. She was already going to Idaho. She'd make a detour. A ten-hour detour, but not impossible. She could do it undetected. She could surprise her. She could simply arrive unannounced. They'd embrace. They'd touch each other's mutilated hair. Delaney would apologize for her silence and they'd plot the end to the Every. It was time.

Delaney looked up. The clock said six. Gregory was at the door, shaking himself into a heavy coat. He glanced toward Delaney, winked almost imperceptibly, and left.

XLIII.

DELANEY FLEW TO BOISE AND took a bus home
to Ghost Canyon. She walked the two miles from
town, and when she approached the door to her
home, she heard an unfamiliar sound: her parents
were fighting. They were at the back of the house,
and for no reason she could justify, she crept around
the side of the house so she could eavesdrop. She
leaned against the wall near the living room, next to
an open window.

"It's just insulting," her father yelled.
"Disrespectful."

"There isn't any insulting happening. Or disre-
spectful," her mother said. "There's nothing at all.
There was only golf. He asked me to play, I played.
You don't play."

"I **could** play," her father boomed.

"You've never played. You want to start now?"

"Yes. I really do."

"You lie," her mother said.

"No," her father said. "No. This is about **you** lying. You're not going to turn it around. Just admit what I already know."

"I'm not admitting something because some app told you I lied. I'm shocked you'd take the machine's word over mine."

"I'm not," he said. "It just confirmed what I suspected."

"What? That I'm having some fling with Walt?"

"I didn't say you were! I only said there was something more to this golf business. It's disrespectful to me. You purposely made sure I wasn't there."

Delaney sunk lower against the wall. She needed to tell them what she'd done—that Friendy was a gag, that it meant nothing, could do nothing—but that was not quite true anymore. It worked, or at least was able to sense certain discrepancies, certain elisions, tension in the mouth, a telling posture. Something mildly, distantly inappropriate had happened with her mother and Walt, she was sure of it. The situation had invited suspicion and Friendy had confirmed it. Her father was right. But was her mother right, too? Was she entitled to this, golf with flirtatious undertones at age sixty-one? So the harm was what? The crime was what? The crime was a private moment—something apart, something for herself after thirty-seven years of marriage. But there was no more nuance, no more give, no more gray. Only absolutes.

Delaney entered the house through the back door and her parents went pale. They'd never fought in front of her before. She put her finger before her lips and they quieted. She unplugged their HereMe and tucked it, and their phones, into a closet, under a stack of linens. When she turned from the closet, ready to tell them everything, the police had already arrived. It had all happened as Karina and Rhea—as Delaney herself—had designed.

After an hour of explanations, of Delaney defending her parents, of the three of them trying to tell the police that what the AI had heard, and what the police themselves had access to, was not the whole truth of their marriage, the police left, having issued a court summons and insisting on the re-activation of their HereMe. Delaney's parents would thereafter be subject to what the police called **heightened observation.** As the police were wrapping things up, Delaney went to bed. Her hope was to feign sleep, so she could escape quickly later in the night. But they came to her door and did not leave till she sat up.

"We're so embarrassed," her mother said.

"Mortified," her father said. "This isn't how we wanted to greet you. Especially after not seeing you for so long."

"But you saw me a few weeks ago," Delaney noted.

Her parents looked at each other. "Oh hon," her

mother said, "we didn't come in person. Did you think we were there? In the hospital?"

"That was a video visit," her father explained. "You thought it was us there with you? That is so sweet. The tech has gotten so good."

Delaney had stopped breathing. Her memory of them at her bedside was so vivid. They'd read to her, sang to her.

"We wanted to come," her mother said. "But you know how the store tracks our carbon impact. The company is pretty serious about StayStil goals. So when your vitals were stable . . ."

"We could access them any time," her father interjected. "You were never in any mortal danger. We followed closely."

"You understand," her mother said. "You have a higher-level sort of job than we do. At the FolkFoods level, the Personal Carbon Impact limits are pretty strict. And we took that trip to Mexico last year, so . . ."

Delaney told them she understood. Completely. It was fine, fine, she said. She was fine, all was fine, and finally they left her alone. She stared at the ceiling, her teeth grinding, her mind imploding, and when she was sure they were asleep, she slipped out, borrowed her father's car, a 1998 Subaru, left her phone and a note for her parents, and drove, as untrackably as she knew how, into Oregon. For the next nine hours she thought a thousand thoughts of destruction and revenge. She drove in a state just short of hypnosis, seeing only the occasional truck or Every delivery van, and it was not until she crossed the Oregon border that the fear of what she would encounter blew through her like an icy wind.

At best, Professor Agarwal would be emaciated and bald, at home with caretakers, maybe graduate students. At worst, she would be dying or dead. What was the utility, Delaney wondered, of seeing someone days before death? Agarwal had no belief in an afterlife, so for whom was a visit like this? If Delaney sat with her on one day and she died the next, in what ways did that matter? A kind of shallow self-satisfaction, to be able to say she visited—did the right thing, just in time? She stopped the car two blocks away from Agarwal's house. It was five in the afternoon. She'd driven all night, all day, and was still wide awake. She still had a vague fear of being discovered. How and by whom she had no idea. And how leaving the car two blocks away would create some bewildering fog for whoever might be watching her . . . It was absurd.

There were wet branches all over the neighborhood, black slashes on lawns and the road; there had been a storm, she surmised, no more than a day ago. A tree near the sidewalk had dropped a great branch onto the ground. It lay there, as though it had fallen straight down, too tired to be flung. Delaney walked through curled leaves toward Agarwal's house, and had to remember to breathe and breathe evenly. She was already overcome. She'd planned this arrival a hundred times, knowing that the best thing would be to rush to Agarwal and embrace her. Any hesitation would allow Agarwal to see the agony in Delaney's eyes, and everything after would be a struggle to regain some equilibrium.

At the steps, she saw that the main door was open; only Agarwal's broken-down screen door separated them. Delaney took the first step and a light went on inside, but only by chance. Then she was at the door, smelling the undefinable musty smell that Agarwal complained about and apologized for. No matter how much she aired out the house it lingered; it had been there, she said, when she moved in.

Delaney looked through the windows, thinking she might find Agarwal lying on the couch by the front window. Or in a hospital bed. She had the frantic thought that the home seemed much too open for Agarwal in her condition—that Agarwal was dead and a new family had moved in, had replaced her.

But the house, for all its light, was quiet. Delaney knocked on the warped screen door frame. No response. She turned to the street, knowing the visit was wrong. She should have called. Who surprises a dying woman like this? Normal people call, they write, they give warning. When she turned to the house again, thinking she'd leave a note, Agarwal was at the door.

"That's not **Delaney**?"

Agarwal looked the same. Her face at least looked precisely the same, utterly alive and radiant. The door flew open and Agarwal was in her arms. Now Delaney could feel the illness. She was so **small.** She had lost weight—twenty pounds or more—but her skin was aglow.

"I've been writing to you for so long!" Agarwal said. "Come inside. Tea or wine or something? Sit in the living room and I'll come right out. Or stay close to me."

Agarwal's hair was far shorter than Delaney remembered but stylish, silky. She wore a sleeveless blouse, showing off her toned arms, which looked, somehow, more fit and ageless. And a skirt! It flared a bit, and seemed to be made of black pleather. And then her boots, the same boots that Delaney knew well, with the carved cacti and sagebrush. From twenty feet she would look like a teenager.

Delaney lingered by her side as Agarwal filled the kettle. Delaney remembered this kettle, dented and most assuredly unsanitary.

"This thing still," Delaney said.

"Shush, it works. You got my letters then?" Agarwal asked.

"I did. I'm sorry. I couldn't write back."

"That's fine. I didn't expect a one-for-one ratio," she said.

"I want to explain. There's so much I have to tell you. Two main things, really. But first I have to know what happened. The last you wrote . . ."

"It was dire, yes. I'm sorry to have burdened you with that."

"No, no. I was so glad. Humbled. I mean, you were open about it and I felt lucky you thought me worthy . . ."

"Stop. Don't get saccharine. I was worried about you, and I wrote, and I was confused, too. And then I was sick, and in some cases it all got wrapped into the same letters."

"But then, what? Some miracle cure or . . . ?"

"No. Nothing like that. But I am in remission. They put me on a very aggressive regimen. Steroids and Pembroli-something. It doesn't work for everyone but it worked for me, and Delaney, don't. Don't cry like that. It's not . . ."

Agarwal's small hands were on Delaney's back, circling. "Thank you," she said. "It moves me that you were this worried."

"I didn't know what to do," Delaney said. "I couldn't do anything."

"Well, you're not a doctor, Del."

"I know. I just—"

"These doctors I had were unbelievable. They're nuts, in a way. They're renegades. I gave them carte blanche and they did some radical things. And you? I almost came to see you when I heard you'd been hurt in the bombing."

"I'm fine. Just a concussion, really."

Agarwal noticed the burns on Delaney's hands. She took Delaney by the elbow. "No residual effects? Dizziness?"

"No. And you're not that kind of doctor."

Agarwal slipped her hand to hold Delaney's. "When I heard about the bombing I just thought of you immediately. And I had the worst thoughts. Just horrible images." She gave Delaney's hand one more squeeze and let it go. The kettle whistled and Agarwal filled two cups, both chipped. She handed the less-chipped to Delaney.

"And the second bit of news?" Delaney asked.

"Oh gosh. Well, it's related, actually. And so strange, really, given everything I've been writing to you about. I don't think I told you, but some unsettling things have happened here on campus. The main thing is that from now on, tenure will be determined by AI. So—"

"You're kidding."

"I'm not. It's been in the works for some time. Here and everywhere. The younger professors prefer it that way. You may have heard that a war on subjectivity is on?" She chuckled grimly. "Well, we have not been able to remain neutral. After so many complaints of bias and caprice, so many lawsuits, the powers that be have determined that their best defense is to cede the process to algorithms."

"But for you—"

"I'm fine. I've been tenured for thirty-two years.

But I lost a friend to this new philosophy. I don't think you knew her. Lili Ulrich? She got here after you. Anyway, she's been an associate professor for years and should have gotten tenure last year, and this new system just sent her over the wall. The tenure process became too contentious, so they left it to algos. No one wants the responsibility. The blame. The algos didn't see her value to the school, and that was that. Del, this is where it's going. All of it. She took her life a month ago."

"Jesus. I'm so sorry."

"Six students this semester, too. And an adjunct. I'm assuming it's the same sort of thing that's affecting people all over the world. And at your company, too. Having ceded all control to algos, it's the last decision a person can make."

Delaney's eyes must have betrayed her concern, because Agarwal smiled and said, "You were worried about me? Taking my life? No. That wouldn't be my path. I enjoy the fight too much. But I'm in the minority there. We've lost most of the art faculty, too—not suicides, but just a mass exodus, after the students refused to be graded by humans. This place is collapsing. It's all collapsing, really."

"They should have listened to you," Delaney said.

"Maybe, maybe not," Agarwal said, and sighed. "I don't know. It came from both sides. I didn't quite see the complicity coming. The motivations of the companies, yes, to consolidate and measure and profit from the data, I saw that. But the everyday human side, no. Our overwhelming preference to cede all decisions to machines, to re-place nuance with numbers . . . It surpassed all my nightmares. Every day, we make another machine that removes more human agency. We don't trust ourselves or each other to make a single choice, a diagnosis, to assign a grade. The only decision we'll be left with is whether to live or die. This is the changing of the species from a free animal to a kept pet. Like so many others, Lili chose not to be part of where the species is going. The last resisters will either be co-opted or will fall away. So I'm leaving, too."

"Leaving what?" Delaney asked. "The world?"

"The college," Agarwal said. "I've told them. But it's actually for something better. You really don't know? I thought maybe they would have told you."

"Who?" Delaney said. In a brief moment of blindness, she had no idea.

"The Every. You're still there, I hope! They gave me a grant and offered me a job. You truly didn't know? I'm allowing myself to be co-opted. To be digested by the monster. I can't believe you didn't know."

The floor seemed to tilt. The ceiling sagged. Delaney needed to sit but the kitchen had no chair. She leaned against the sink.

"You okay?"

Of course they'd found Agarwal. Of course they'd subsumed her.

"When did this happen?" Delaney managed to say.

"I guess the first call was three weeks ago. Do you know someone named Gregory Akufo-Addo?" Agarwal asked. She was riffling through a drawer of tea boxes. "He calls himself the 'Ostensible' something. I have his business card somewhere. Here it is. Do you know of the Reading Room?"

"I think so," Delaney said hoarsely. Agarwal didn't hear.

"Well, if you haven't visited that part of campus, you should. They seem very scholarly, and the man in charge is quite formidable and sincere. Apparently they've been studying my work, and they want me to take my criticisms and help them make the company better. Isn't that just remarkable? I see how you're looking at me. **Of course** I'm skeptical. **Of course** it's safer to have me inside than out. But my ego allows me to think I can make a difference. You sure you're okay?"

"Can I lie down?" Delaney asked, and didn't wait for a yes. She stumbled to the couch, where she was overwhelmed by the smell of Rasputin, Agarwal's cat, now five years dead.

Agarwal followed her to the living room. "Are you all right?" With a click she placed Delaney's tea onto the glass coffee table and sat beside it on the table, facing Delaney.

"And if not for you, I wouldn't have considered it," she said. "The fact that you went to work there got me weighing that old dichotomy about change: are we more effective agitating from outside, or creating structural change from within?"

Delaney couldn't think of a rational thing to say. She was unmoored. "So you're coming to California?" she finally asked.

"Well, I don't know about that. I'm not likely to be bunking with you anytime soon. I'm still recovering, and this is my home. But they've been so accommodating. They want to see everything I write, when I write it, and they want to set up monthly calls where we discuss my ideas. They really seem committed to reform."

Delaney didn't mention that she'd seen Agarwal's paper at the Reading Room. There was no point. She looked out the window, at a black bough stripped of its leaves. She didn't think she'd ever be able to look into Agarwal's eyes again.

"I know it sounds incongruous," Agarwal said, "but things here are untenable, and . . . What's wrong?"

"Is that a smart speaker?"

A next-generation HereMe stood on Agarwal's windowsill.

"I know, it's madness for me to have one. But they sent it for free. Someone even came out to set it up. And if I'm going to work there, I might as well get used to the devices."

Delaney had no choice but to pretend. "Yes," she said. "They're so generous."

"I mainly use it to play music," Agarwal said. "They taught me how to do that, too. Now I get it. To be able to simply tell it to play 'The Long and Winding Road' and it begins . . . I mean, that is life-changing."

The song began, and they both smiled. Delaney knew that Agarwal hadn't said "HereMe"—that the device had been listening all along.

Delaney was numb, hollowed out. There was nothing she could say to Agarwal that would have any effect on the course of events, not now at least, so she could only think of leaving. She turned the conversation away from the Every—to Agarwal's son, a pediatrician living in Portland, and finally to Delaney's own family.

"Well, my parents always said twenty minutes is the limit for an unannounced visit," Delaney said. She thought Agarwal might push back on her departure, but she didn't. She looked tired.

"So you'll come to Treasure Island sometime?" Delaney asked brightly. "Even if just to visit?" And soon she backed away, to the door, held Agarwal tight, then was gone.

XLIV.

DELANEY DROVE THROUGH THE NIGHT, adrenaline animating every moment. She encountered few fellow travelers along the way; only twice did a trucker's headlights scream from around a bend and light her world on fire. Darkness and quiet followed each time, and with each mile she grew more determined and more serene. She had nothing left, and nothing left to lose.

"You're back!" her mother said, when she arrived just after dawn. "How was Agarwal?" Delaney gave her mother a thumbs up and went to her bed. She needed to sleep, even for an hour. She napped in the feral warmth of her old room and when she woke, her father was in the kitchen. He was playing poker on his phone.

"You leaving again, Del?" he asked.

"Just a bike ride," she said. She clicked her helmet strap and stepped onto the porch. Her mother was sitting on the swing, her head lowered to her tablet, which emitted screams from zombies being beheaded by the planet's last sentient heroes.

"You're leaving your phone?" she asked.

"I am," she said.

"Okay," her mother said. "Be safe out there!"

Delaney had insisted on meeting Mae on a trog trail off a trog road, fifteen miles north of Ghost Canyon. The bike ride was sublime, utterly silent but for her own dusty rattling, and she found her mind wandering, then empty, then at one with the sun. She hadn't been like this in months, maybe years—body and brain in one place, thinking of nothing but the turns in the path and the pressing of foot to pedal. **I could live out here,** she thought. Why had she put herself in the middle of the fight for the soul of the species? It was useless. Wes was lost, Agarwal was lost, her parents were lost. **I am alone and will be alone,** she thought. **No one else wants what I want.**

She made it to the trailhead thirty minutes early, and had time to rest, splaying herself on a vast flat stone to warm in the late morning sun. She decided to play out the day, to pitch Mae one last idea, the idea that would end all ideas—that would finally drive the company over the cliff. On the one hand, thinking it would make any difference at all was absurd. Somehow she had a perverse gift for conjuring ideas that sounded terrible to her but tickled the rest of humanity. This last one, though—if there were any bite left in any nations, any regulatory bodies, any monitors of global trade—it should trigger an avalanche of revulsion. She held out the remote hope that this final proposal would finally trigger the collective outrage she'd expected so many times. This would go so far that any free being would be rattled into rebellion.

She expected Mae to love it, and if the people of the world wanted it too, so be it. Delaney could live out her days in a place like this. The Every, with the wholesale complicity of humanity, wanted a different world, a watched world without risk or surprise or nuance or solitude. Why not just let them have it, and she could have this? She could build a cabin, be alone, drift away, and leave the ruined world to those who had created and embraced it.

When Mae pulled up, alone, in a burst of gravel and dust, in a car she'd driven herself, Delaney was surprised. Twice now Mae had shown herself to be a person of integrity. She kept promises. She was precisely the person she seemed to be. Delaney felt a brief flash of shame, given that of the two of them, only she had ulterior motive. Mae stepped out and looked around her, at the carpeted hills surrounding them and the jagged peaks beyond.

"It's beautiful out here," she said.

She was tying her boots on, and Delaney couldn't help noticing how big they were. They seemed intended for a man—a large man.

"They're weighted," Mae said, double-knotting her laces and standing up. "I'm trying to boost the cardio impact. And you? Your feet are healed enough for a climb like this? It was your soles, right?"

"They're okay," Delaney said.

"You're so strong," Mae said, and seemed to mean it.

"Well," Delaney said, "this is my favorite place in the world. I guess it helps me forget any residual pain."

"But this is totally off-grid!" Mae said, and stamped a few times in the white dust, settling into her boots. "Without your directions, I never would have found it. It doesn't even have a name!"

Delaney wanted to say **That's why I love it, you monster,** but she only smiled. She prepared herself for a few hours of pretend, where she would feign friendship, candor, allyship.

"You know what I'm going to say next," Mae said.

"Why not share it, right?" Delaney said.

"Sharing **is** caring," Mae said, and turned her torso left and right in a kind of stretch. "I know it's facile but isn't it true? The Dalai Lama said, 'Share your knowledge. It is a way to achieve immortality.'"

Delaney was sure someone in the Reading Room had provided that. "Well said," she said. "Maybe you're right. We're walking to one of the prettiest waterfalls you'll ever see. Are you ready?"

"Do I need anything else?" Mae asked. She had the passenger door of her car open, and inside, Delaney glimpsed enough equipment and food to establish a small colony.

"Nothing," Delaney said. She pointed to the backpack at her own feet, which contained water and sunscreen and raisins, not much more. "It's an hour walk up, an hour back. We'll survive."

"One of us, anyway," Mae said. "I haven't hiked since I was about ten. Is it this way?" She walked ahead to the trailhead and then stopped. "Sorry. I'm so used to leading. You should."

"No, no. It's an easy trail," Delaney said. "You can lead. Or we can take turns."

"You know what?" Mae said, "Let's walk side by side. I'll walk in this grassy bit next to the trail. It's softer here."

There was a jagged rock in front of Mae, as big as a football, and just when Delaney was sure Mae would trip over it, she jumped over it as nimbly as a deer. In every way, Mae was far more able than Delaney had expected. Her social skills, her wit, her agility. On the first upward leg of the trail, she kept up with Delaney without difficulty, even while walking a tougher path. More than anything, she was shocked that Mae had come digitally naked. Delaney looked for any device and found nothing—no bodycam, no phone, no oval, no ear-buds, nothing. Twice now Mae had gone dark to spend time with her.

"So I wanted to run something by you," Delaney said.

"Okay," Mae said, and took a long stride over a fallen log.

"Can I speak freely?" Delaney asked.

"Of course," Mae said, though her mouth pinched just a bit. "We have consultants come in every month, Delaney. I can't be offended. And **you're** not charging me half a million dollars a day."

"Okay," Delaney said. "I've been kicking around an idea that might help the Every and its customers. But it's not just an app or a platform or a button. Not that there's anything wrong with those things," she added.

"Okay, I'm intrigued," Mae said.

"Well, I've spent six months rotating at the Every, and as organized as it is, I think it could be more so. There are so many departments and programs that aren't linked so much, but should be."

"Okay," Mae said, as if she'd been told that the Every campus was located on an island, and that much of the company's revenue came from advertising. Delaney knew she had to get beyond the obvious and into the world-saving.

"And I believe if they're linked," she continued, "and if you use the full power and reach of the Every's data, and of the real-world assets you acquired when you bought the jungle, and if you truly embraced the direction humanity is trending and where it desperately wants to go, you might just save the world and perfect the species."

"Now it's my time to stop," Mae said. Delaney stopped, too, and Mae gave her an agogged look. "You're good. You know that? I'm thinking you know that." She took a long sip of water. "Go on," Mae said when she was finished, and pressed ahead.

"Personal Carbon Impact," Delaney said.

"Wes Makazian's project? He was your old roommate, right?"

"He was."

"What was in the air out there in your old place? A lot of ideas from one trog shed."

Delaney skipped a breath. She assumed Mae might know they'd lived trog-style, but she knew about the Shed? But of course she knew. Even a trog shed could be photographed from the street, from above. In an instant she'd have access to photos, floor plans, building history, utility bills.

"Right now," Delaney said, "the PCI isn't public, but it's on its way to being public."

"And you object?"

"No. It must be public to have impact. There's the social opprobrium aspect, which is only half of it. When the PCI is public, people will feel shame if their number's high, but that doesn't necessarily change their behavior. That's the stick, but you need the carrot."

"And what would the carrot be?"

"Well, financial incentives are stronger than social opprobrium. We have the loyalty programs that motivate billions to buy through our portal. But we don't use them enough to shape better behavior."

"You were at AYS though, right?"

"Right. But that's more suggestive than coercive."

"That's what PrefCom's for."

"Yes, but we're still just managing an inherently chaotic system. We're helping people with their choices. We're trying to predict their movements and purchases. But what I'm suggesting is the control of choices in the first place."

Mae had stopped again, under a stand of Douglas firs. "Can we sit?" They found two opposing logs on a flat area off the trail. Mae flicked a few pieces of moss off the bark and sat down. "You were saying: control choice," she said.

"Right," Delaney said. "Gabriel Chu talks a lot about the paralysis of decision-making. We've had three generations now for whom the greatest stress in their lives is choice. And I'm convinced that people simply don't want it. It's not that they want fewer choices. It's that they want almost **no** choices. And more than anything, they want no bad choices. Think of mustard," Delaney said.

"Think of mustard, right," Mae said. "I did not see that coming."

Delaney laughed. "It's just a good representative product that proves the madness of the market.

Right now, there are more than two hundred types of mustard in the U.S. alone."

"That can't be true."

"Two hundred and twenty-eight. I researched this. And a lot of these manufacturers make terrible mustard. Even when the mustard's good, a huge percentage of it goes unsold. In general, these companies start up, they make their mustard, they fail, and then throw everything away. The cumulative waste for just this one industry boggles the mind. Now think of clothing. Tomorrow some designer will dream up a new kind of shirt, and this shirt will be hideous. But the designer, and his manufacturer, will think the shirt wonderful, and a half-million of these shirts will get made, go unsold and end up in landfills."

"Again," Mae said, "I think we're doing quite a lot to discourage these things. We steer people away from bad products. AYS and PrefCom—"

"Yes, but what if we didn't even make these things to begin with—millions of things every day, that used precious resources, only to be thrown away?"

"You were at Thoughts Not Things," Mae said.

"I was. So I incinerated thousands of unnecessary objects. Which was a start. But this was **after** they were made. But most of them never should have existed. What if we could control production and demand with surgical precision, and make only those things that we know would be used or consumed? What if we could include the consumers in the process of deciding what would and what wouldn't be manufactured?"

"Surveys?"

"Not just surveys. Ah look, an eagle." Delaney pointed to its silhouette, tracing an elliptical orbit above the treeline. Mae offered a perfunctory glance and turned back to Delaney.

"More," she said.

"Before that mustard is made, we test it with our own channels. Concensus, for example. We ask, Do you want a new mustard that tastes the same but has a new label? People say no, and we say we won't carry it. Or we find that it doesn't meet our environmental standards or whatever, so it's not made."

"Why wouldn't they just make it anyway?"

"Because we control 82 percent of ecommerce, which is 71 percent of all consumption," Delaney said. "If we stop them before they begin, none of those resources are wasted. All of those plants and spices and preservatives it would have taken to make that mustard, and all that glass and paper to package it, all those boxes and pallets, and all the trucks and gas and roads to transport it—all that would have gone into a failed product are spared, and humans have one less unnecessary choice."

"And **we** decide," Mae said.

"Right," Delaney said, "and then we stand at the gate. It's like the guards at the front of the Every who prevent the shitty gift baskets from entering.

Same principle. Bad stuff never gets through, and soon it's pointless to make it."

"And the things that do get made?"

"We give people what they want. Which is less. Three types of mustard. We vet all three, they all meet our standards for environmental responsibility, and we use AYS and PrefCom to help consumers make the right decision. Fewer choices. Everyone rejoices."

"You come up with that just now?"

"I did," Delaney said.

A long moment passed. Delaney thought Mae might have a note-book and pen on her person, but this was not the case.

"We can end all the things we don't like," Mae said.

"Exactly," Delaney said. "Think of wine. There are twelve thousand wineries in the U.S. They make about a hundred thousand types of wine. It's far too much."

"Just thinking about all those choices gives me hives," Mae said.

"So we eliminate most of them," Delaney said. "I'm sure most of that wine is bad. And all that water they use!"

"Manufacturers will kill us," Mae said. "Like what happened with the travel industry. The airlines were not happy with Stop+Lük."

"This will be the opposite," Delaney said.

"They'll love us. At least those we choose. If there are only three mustards, and demand remains stable, then the manufacturers have predictable revenue, and the prices drop. You agree to buy one jar of mustard a month, and the cost is less than half it is today."

"Wait. Why?"

"Because the manufacturers no longer have to factor in waste. Think about something even more regular. Breakfast," Delaney said. "A consumer has kids, and the kids eat the same two cereals ninety percent of the time. But right now, they pay retail for these two boxes once a week. But no one should pay so-called retail prices ever again."

"I've said this forever," Mae said. "But they continue to do so."

"You've convinced a lot of consumers," Delaney said. "But now you have to convince the manufacturers. Let's say a cereal producer makes 500,000 boxes of cereal a week. They're sent to 40,000 stores. Two-thirds of the boxes are sold, and the other third are eventually thrown away. The manufacturer's overall pricing has to account for all that waste. Everyone manufactures far more than what they sell. It's far worse for produce. That's a terrible and outdated way of doing business. And it destroys the world. Almost half the world's resource consumption is not even consumed."

Mae scoffed in grim recognition.

"So imagine this," Delaney continued. "Imagine

if that cereal manufacturer is simply sending most of their product direct to consumers—either through their own warehouses or ours. They manufacture to order, because the customers have committed to buy two boxes of cereal a week for a year, for five years. Now the company not only knows how many boxes of cereal to make, they know precisely where to send them. They save all the money they usually spend on making cereal, shipping it all to stores and throwing so much of it away. So consumers get cheaper goods, because the makers don't have to factor in the unsold products."

"Or retailers at all," Mae said. "**We're** the retailer."

"Basically, we're the **only** retailer," Delaney said. "Half the stores were killed by the pandemics anyway. Let the rest die."

Mae's eyes went wide. "Right. They become homes, parks. Let nature reclaim every mall and shop."

"Simpler this way," Delaney said.

"We're tracking consumer preferences already. Why wouldn't we be the conduit between all demand and all production? **We** decide."

"And we have the infrastructure to take everything from factory to front door," Delaney said. "When we bought the jungle, we got the logistics and distribution systems—the planes, the trucks, the warehouses, the vans. And I'm assuming that's why you've been buying the shipping companies."

"Right, right," Mae said, though the slightest

tremor in Mae's voice betrayed that perhaps there had been no grand design at all.

"You could scuttle half of those ships tomorrow," Delaney said. "The vans, too. Because you'd eliminate all the world's unneeded stuff. The clothing shipped from Myanmar only to be shipped back. The cheap toys from China that end up unsold and thrown away. Limitless choice is killing the world."

Mae looked up. "I like that. Did you come up with that?"

"It's actually hanging from the rafters at the AYS offices."

"And they're still involved?"

Delaney was sure Mae was doing cost-cutting in her head, eliminating this expensive department and many others.

"I think they'd still do some of the curation," Delaney said. "And then we eliminate all the cheap and poorly sourced products. We thin the herd. Fewer choices. Which alleviates Impact Anxiety."

"No one wants a shirt made in a sweatshop that pollutes the local water source. Or bananas in Boston in October," Mae said.

"Right. Those goods no longer have a marketplace. And the stress we all feel when faced with a hundred brands of socks, for example—that's gone."

"Because we decide," Mae said.

"Right," Delaney said, and took note: those words, **We decide,** were important to Mae. "We decide," Delaney said, "and then the companies are manufacturing only what they know will sell."

"It really works for both sides," Mae said.

"And it saves the planet," Delaney said. "And if anyone wants environmentally irresponsible goods, we hit them with their Personal Carbon Impact data. That's public, and instantly their Shame Agg jumps. They buy a four-pound steak made possible by the burning of the Brazilian rainforest, their PCI takes a beating."

"And if you have a high PCI, there are societal penalties. Hard to get a job maybe. Or housing. So companies stop making that stuff, and they get in line. And then when they do, and we're all in sync, they have certainty," Mae said.

"Right," Delaney said. "Stabilization of revenue, of profits. A factory that can predict two or three years of demand is infinitely more stable. Jobs are secure. Again, you're no longer guessing or hoping what consumers will do. They're making commitments."

"Almost out of duty."

"Well, the planet is collapsing," Delaney said. "This might be the only way to save it. We should only make what we need, right? Buy thoughtfully. Shop from home."

"And it all goes through us," Mae said.

"There's no one else that could do it," Delaney said. "This works with Stop+Lük. And StayStïl.

You're eliminating most of these unnecessary little trips. All of those car-miles eliminated. One delivery driver coming to the neighborhood as opposed to twenty-five people driving to a hundred different stores."

"Fewer cars, less pollution, accidents, fatalities."

Delaney looked up the trail. If they didn't get moving soon, they'd be hiking the steepest parts of the path during the hottest part of the day. "Should we keep going?"

They continued, passing through lupine and arrowleaf balsamroot, and Delaney had a terrible thought. It might have been the endorphins, but she was beginning to believe what she was saying. All through the trip home from Agarwal's, she'd struggled with the fact that her plan actually would reduce waste. Would create order. Would drastically limit the unnecessary exploitation of land, energy, animals. But it would also give the Every historically unprecedented power. It would make the Dutch East India Company look like a lemonade stand. What she had just described would surely mean the end of much of what makes a human free. It would be a doorway to far tighter restrictions on movement and choice. But it did have perhaps the best chance to slow the catastrophic warming of the planet. It would usher in a new, ever-more obedient era in the human procession, but our reckless freedoms and thoughtless whims were precisely what brought the planet to the brink. And with Wes on hand, she thought, with Agarwal in the fold, there seemed at least a passing chance that they could maintain some balance at the Every, carve out some space for idiosyncracy, for private thought. Maybe this was the only way—that only a monopoly could save the world.

"Do you have a name for it? Your whole system?" Mae asked.

"I'm toggling between Consensual Economic Order and Predictive Economy. PredEcon," Delaney said. "For a while I was just calling it Freedom from Choice."

"Ah. I like that, too. The liberation of it."

Then Delaney saw it—the waterfall. She pointed it out to Mae.

"See the little white feathers floating off the cliff?"

Mae squinted up at it. "I see it. We're climbing that far?"

"It's really just a dozen easy switchbacks. Easy," Delaney said. "And the view will get better all the while. We'll make it."

"So Consensual Economic Order," Mae said.

"Or benevolent monopoly," Delaney said.

"I like that. Benevolent," Mae said.

Delaney had another idea. She'd come to the trail with two, a double-helix, really, two systems that would work in concert to finally put the planet and its people in order. But she hesitated in explaining the second. Couldn't she leave it at this new economic paradigm? The second notion would complete the changing of the species, the hyperevolution that had begun at the cusp of the twentieth century. But it had stalled, and why? Because this final step hadn't been explained properly. What the hell, she thought. She'd be the one.

"I'll keep your mind occupied as we go," Delaney said.

"There's more?" Mae asked.

"There is," Delaney said. "I was just laying out the consumption part. But it's a piece of something far bigger."

They continued up, stepping over the occasional river of scree.

"I think a lot of what's driven the Every's growth is certainty," Delaney said. "We started with search, right? We answered the planet's questions. You have a question, you type it into our search engine, you get an answer. Then we helped map and measure the world, and we made it safer by illuminating every dim corner. We improved our understanding of books, paintings, and poetry, dance and film, by translating all that was ineffable into numbers. Then Friendy helped us improve our relationships with our loved ones. FaceIt helped us see ourselves more clearly. Concensus and OwnSelf help us do better in our daily lives. There are dozens of ways we provide assurances to people—so many ways we clarify their lives, snuff out doubt, and help them self-optimize."

Mae turned slightly, looking over her shoulder, her eyes amused.

"But it's still not enough," Delaney continued. "There's still uncertainty, and I'm convinced that it's because we're not being bold enough. We're leaving too much out there for people to wonder about, too much unsaid and unmeasured and, most importantly, unaggregated."

"Now I don't see it," Mae said. "The waterfall."

"It's there." The path had wound behind the cliff, Delaney explained. They'd soon climb the last few hundred feet and would come out where the stream began its final straightaway before the fall.

"So you're thinking of what? One number?" Mae asked.

"I know it was tried before. I know the Chinese had their social credit score, but it was never properly developed. I mean, the government developed it, so . . ." They shared a laugh about the inability of any government to do anything.

"We can do better," Delaney said. "We have ten times the data that the Chinese government had, and we're far more efficient. And remember, when the social credit score was introduced in China, there was almost no opposition. People want this."

"What, exactly?"

"One number that includes everything, cradle to grave. Grades in school, childhood behavioral issues, missed days, college records, test scores, any criminal behavior, workplace demerits, traffic tickets, suspicious travel, anomalous walk patterns, TruVoice dings, HereMe revelations, PrefCom adherence . . ."

"Your Shame Aggregate," Mae suggested.

"Right," Delaney said, loving this. Mae was already adding on. Delaney had to invite more. "Personal Carbon Impact score. AnonComs, KisKis grades . . ." She paused, hoping Mae would jump in.

"Demoxie numbers," Mae said. "Purchasing history, payment history, credit issues, zip code, tavs."

"Yup. Every message sent and received. Eyeshames. OwnSelf health and exercise assessments. Quantity and quality of friendships. Everything would get factored into one number."

"And the scale would be . . ."

"One to a thousand," Delaney said. "To better reflect all the subtleties of a person. At birth, you're in a pure state of nature—500. You misbehave in first grade, and you're at 499. Help an old lady across the street, you're at 502."

"People love credit scores," Mae noted.

"They've never fought them," Delaney said. "They've been around for decades and they've never met any pushback. Why? Because they provide **clarity.** There's never been any resistance, among any significant part of the human race, to attaching a number to any aspect of their existence. This one just . . ."

"Sums it up," Mae said.

"Right. People want order," Delaney said. "Above all things, they want order. And now we have the means to provide it. With a number, you always know where you stand. If you take an unnecessary trip to the Seychelles, you drop twenty points. Excessive meat-eating? Again, points are lost. Same with smoking, jaywalking, terseness of tone, looking somewhere you shouldn't—it all figures in."

"What about moving up?"

"If you're at 688 and want to get to 750, the steps are clear. Regular purchases, regular movement patterns and payments and participation. You inch up through predictable behavior, and by avoiding anything problematic. This is how it intersects with the Consensual Economic Order. And it's what PrefCom's been doing all along behind the scenes, but now it's more in keeping with the ethos of the Every: it's transparent. The number is the number."

"The number is the number," Mae repeated. "And it's **known.**"

"You start at 500, and if you act virtuously, then by the time you're 18 or 21, you're at 900. It incentivizes you . . ."

"To be your best self," Mae finished.

"Yes," Delaney said.

"Because it's public," Mae noted.

"Exactly. OwnSelf is great, but it's private."

"Even kids' scores would be known," Mae said.

"**Especially** kids," Delaney said. "Their numbers would be public—and tracked closely by parents and schools and local law enforcement."

"Right, right," Mae said, nodding vigorously. "Think about college admissions!"

"Adults and children, they'll all have to do the

right thing. Because the 900s will have access to things others don't. Access to medicine, housing, jobs. Who would employ someone under 900? Who would marry someone under 850? It won't be some mystery anymore why some succeed and others don't."

"It'll be **fair**," Mae said. "That's the difference. It'll finally be **fair**."

"Yes," Delaney said. "Because it's no longer subjective."

"And then we can aggregate social and professional networks."

"They'll urge each other to be better," Delaney agreed.

"Social engineering through network shame," Mae said. "It works the same for neighborhoods, cities, countries. For years we've measured the so-called happiness of each nation, but this will be far more accurate. This is, like, an all-encompassing virtue rating."

"And the high-scoring countries get rewarded."

"Naturally," Mae said. "Carrot and stick."

Delaney could see the bend of the trail up ahead, where it would rise for the last hundred vertical feet and meet the stream. It was time to sum up. "All through human history," she said, "people have wanted to know two things: **What should I do?** and **Am I good?** Religion has taken stabs at both, but their answers are never conclusive. Ask any question, and a dozen religious leaders will tell you a dozen different things."

"Or they won't have answers at all," Mae said. "**Mysterious ways.** Nothing quantitative."

"But now we have the ability to actually **answer** those questions. The first question is the easy one. We know people don't want to make decisions, and we're perfecting the tools to make them for people. Our tools already tell you when to exercise, what to eat, what to do and not do, what to buy and not buy, what to say and not say."

"And we help people live virtuously by controlling their choices," Mae said.

"Exactly," Delaney said. "This is how we improve the individual. But more importantly, if we eliminate bad choices—which are most choices—we save the world."

Mae ran her tongue over her teeth, as if tasting all of this, the power it would afford her and the Every.

"And **we** decide," Mae said again.

"And we decide," Delaney repeated, then amended: "The data does, yes. 'How do I live?' The data will tell you. 'What should I do?' The numbers will know. I was even thinking that you could see the effect on your aggregate ahead of time, before you act. Like if you wanted to say some problematic thing, or buy a certain not-vetted thing, or take some unnecessary trip, you could see its potential effect on your score."

"Like how they have to list calories on a menu," Mae said.

"Right. Again, we end uncertainty. We kill the subjective."

"Subjectivity is just objectivity waiting for data," Mae said. "You ever hear that phrase?"

"I have," Delaney said. "I'm pretty sure I have."

"And what were you thinking of calling the program?" Mae said.

"Well, my first thought was WeGood?, because it gets at the central question. But then I figured if we're preaching simplicity, the term needed to be simple, too. It's a number that summarizes all other numbers, and encompasses the utter complexity and majesty of the human experience. So I thought, SumNum."

"SumNum. I like it," Mae said. She walked on for a minute or two, then exhaled mournfully and stopped. She turned to Delaney. "You know, I've never been to church, but my parents used to go. And they told me that when my mom got pregnant, they were very young, and they went to their pastor—I think they were Episcopalian, or Presbyterian—anyway, they went in and wanted advice. Should they have me and keep me? Abort me? Put me up for adoption? They were twenty-one, twenty-two and just at sea."

"I'm sorry," Delaney said.

"It's not like they expected a pastor to

recommend an abortion, but he didn't recommend **anything.** He talked, he listened, he told them to trust their hearts, to count on each other and the advice of their families. I mean, it was utterly useless. Can you imagine occupying that seat, that place of so-called authority, and having no answers?"

"Criminal," Delaney said.

"Before my father died," Mae said, "he kept asking if he was good. We thought it was part of the delirium, but he kept asking the question, day and night. 'Was I good? Was I good?' We said, 'Of course, of course,' but it didn't assuage his doubts. He'd wake up in the middle of the night screaming the question."

"I'm so sorry," Delaney said.

"Now I can't help regretting that we didn't have this then. SumNum. He would have been in the 900s for sure."

"Of course," Delaney said.

"The number will tell you if your life has been lived right," Mae said. "The number will rise and fall on the merits of your actions and words. It's no longer subjective. You'll know every day where you stand. It won't be at the Gates of Heaven. It won't be one guy with a book open to your name. The number will be there, every day. There will be no more questions. You'll know it and control it, thank god."

"Thank **us,**" Delaney laughed.

"Right," Mae smiled. "Thank **us.**"

Delaney turned the corner and scurried up the last few yards. When she stood, as always, her stomach spun from the dizzy height. She steadied herself and took in the view. The sky was vermillion and she could see for a hundred miles, sagebrush and white pines and blue cliffs. The air was bracing and clean.

Mae followed her up to the summit, briefly scanned her surroundings, then sat down on the rocky boundary of the stream. "Just need to catch my breath."

"You did well," Delaney said. "I'm impressed."

"I'm impressed with **you,**" Mae said. "So have you told anyone about this idea of yours?"

"No one," Delaney said.

"Not Wes?" Mae asked.

"We've both been busy."

Mae smiled warmly. "You know what I'm going to say?"

"Sharing is caring?" Delaney said, and laughed. She looked over the waterfall's edge, as the spray lifted into the air and was refracted by the high sun.

"Anyway," Mae said, "I'm glad you shared it with **me.**"

"On that note, I wanted to mention," Delaney said, "I know Stenton is elbowing himself in. I know the pressure you must be under." She looked to Mae to gauge her reaction. Mae's face was stiff, her eyes narrowed ever so slightly. Delaney did not feel her intrusion particularly welcome, but she pressed on. She wanted to make it clear that she would be giving this idea, like all her ideas, to the Every, and asking for no credit.

"I just want to help," she said. "If these ideas help you maintain control, fend off his power-grab, they're yours." Delaney had a brief vision of the two of them enacting the plan, side by side. She saw it in a frantic montage of inspired work and global impact. The rise of Stenton would be thwarted as Mae and Delaney inspired the Every and the world with their plan. Mae and Delaney—and Wes! And Agarwal! And Joan—would bring clean air to Beijing and Mexico City, would bring about the resurrection of the Great Barrier Reef, the cleaning of the Venetian canals. The end of landfills, plastic, waste, chaos, degradation, the rising seas. Yes, yes, she saw Wes's way now. It was far better to be in the machine, with access to the levers, than outside, attempting juvenile sabotage. She looked over the landscape below, the white pines and sagebrush, all this irreplaceable splendor, and thought that with Mae's power and her vision, they might have the ability to save it. And couldn't there be room for them both in this world—the trogs and the techs? Certainly the Everyones could see their way to allowing humans to exist apart from their quest for order? Yes. There would be room to coexist. Delaney could work within the system, and if she failed, she'd return to this life apart. Surely that could be allowed.

"I guess I'm saying I'm here to help you," Delaney said.

Mae's mouth spread into a smile that her eyes did not immediately reflect. The effect was unsettling. As if knowing the dissonance, she squinted amiably at Delaney.

"Well, I think that's wonderful," she finally said.

No, Delaney thought. Just a coincidence. Such a common phrase. But there was the slightest edge in her voice, a sprinkle of acid in how she said **wonderful** that gave Delaney pause.

"How far down is it?" Mae asked.

Delaney peered over the edge again. The recklessness of the falling water gave her a shudder. "I don't know," she said, though she knew it was at least three hundred feet. "This trail was cut eighty years ago and isn't used much. I don't think anyone but me has been here in ages. I'm guessing the waterfall's never been measured."

As Mae watched Delaney's back, a slashing hatred grew within her. For months she'd known about Delaney's treachery; it was ludicrously obvious. How did this idiot think she could plot against the Every—**within** the Every? A spy within the global epicenter of surveillance? It was insulting. Gabriel had sniffed her out on day one. Observing the daily movements of a would-be saboteur on campus had yielded some insights, and they'd collected mountains of data about trogs, but more than anything it had been a pathetic demonstration—like watching a spider try to climb up from the downward swirl of a flushing toilet.

Delaney Wells had ideas, this was undeniable, and these new ones, this braided pair that might truly save the planet and perfect the species—they would give Mae a thousand-year reign. But it was time for Delaney to go. Gabriel had found Delaney's clumsy machinations vastly entertaining, even inventing an underground resistance within the Every, planting the idea that Mae was pregnant to see if Delaney would reveal it—he'd enjoyed toying with her while he could. But Mae was less amused. Delaney embodied everything she'd been trying to rid the world of—deceit, withholding, hidden agendas, lies. For months Mae had pictured a confrontation with Delaney, in some public forum, standing over her, finger wagging, thundering about betrayal, duplicity, and the pitiful hopelessness of Delaney's scheme. But now that they were out here, alone, there was no point. Who would hear such a diatribe? Who would remember it? Only Delaney Wells, and Delaney Wells was about to be pushed off a cliff.

XLV.

ON THE PLANE home from Idaho, Mae scrolled through RememberMe, a eulogy aggregator and template. She wouldn't be delivering any formal speech in Delaney's honor—she barely knew Delaney—but she had to have at least a few sentences at the ready. She scrolled through the suggested phrases. **A cherished colleague. A bright light.** What else? **Such limitless potential.** No, too much. Keep the praise muted. **Good worker. Valuable team member. A well-liked Everyone.** Mae looked at the template. **She touched the lives of so many.** That worked, but **so many** was too much, implying outsized impact and popularity—which might provoke too much curiosity. Better would be to say simply, "She touched the lives of many." That was the kind of faint praise that would end all intrigue.

When Mae returned to the Every, though, there was nothing like the outpouring of grief she had expected. Certainly nothing remotely approaching what there had been for Bailey or Soren and the others killed in the bombing. And why would there be? Very few people at the Every knew Delaney well, or at all. Most of her social media interactions had been faked; that really was a new low, Mae thought. What about Delaney was authentic, after all? No wonder she had few friends. She was close with Wes Makazian and distantly connected with someone named Winnie Ochoa in Thoughts Not Things. She'd spent a month or so at AYS and seemed to be chummy with Joan Pham, who'd tried to parlay the bombing into some sickening settlement; like a small tumor, she would need to be excised. Otherwise, no one seemed to know Delaney Wells or would miss her. A memorial was unnecessary. Mae monitored the campus mood with a hundred metrics and found no reason to make a fuss.

Such a shame, Mae told her followers. She decided her eulogy would be brief, twenty seconds, in between other, more glittering announcements. An Everyone has fallen to her death in a remote Idaho canyon, she said. She'd gone off the known path—had gone into the wilderness without a phone, untracked and unknown and unseen. Mae had been careful to create a second set of tracks, heavy and male, in case the police investigated, but they didn't. Anything unfilmed was not pursued, and because there were no journalists, Delaney's death was abstract and incomprehensible—yet more evidence that there were parts of the world that were unmapped and perilous; the unseen were putting themselves in perpetual danger. These unknown places must be brought to heel, and the people that go there, that scurry around in the shadows, must be brought to their senses.

Yes, her followers said. Of course, they said. What drives these meaningless deviations from safety? they wondered. What kind of nihilism? What unnecessary recklessness? Delaney's parents, too, shook their heads in dismay. She'd been willful for so long, they said. She'd left without her phone! Mae reached out to them directly, sending them a yellow digital emoji-face crying sky-blue tears. They were moved by this personal gesture, and sent her back two grateful smiles and an oversized thumbs up.

Soon it was Dream Friday and Mae was finished thinking about Delaney. This would be Mae's first Dream Friday presentation in years, and she had no bandwidth for saboteurs. From the wings of the stage, she looked out on the audience, and wondered if there could be any other insurrectionists in her midst. She saw a few thousand people in lycra using the same phones, the same tablets, their hearts and health measured by the same devices fastened tightly to their wrists. And Wes Makazian in the front row! Gabriel and Stenton, Mae's stalwart partners, had been watching him and determined that he was no danger; he wanted to improve the future, not prevent it. The rest of the Everyones assembled were wonderfully compliant. As Mae waited for her cue, they sent each other smiles and frowns, rainbows and Popeyes and pictures of their lunches. She laughed. Rebellion, here or anywhere, was not likely.

The applause as she stepped onto the stage was rapturous, adoring. She basked a bit longer than she should have, but it had been a hard year, and she needed it—they all needed it, this unalloyed joy, this sense of shared mission.

"Revolutions do not come on schedule," she said, knowing her audience would feast on those words, **revolution** and **schedule.** "But they come if you're listening." The applause crackled then roared. The Everyones were primed; this would be so easy. She would outline SumNum and the Consensual Economic Order, the seamless way they would work together, and the world's last bits of chaos and uncertainty would evaporate like dew in sunlight. Where there had been din and disorder there would be the quiet hum of a machine that saw all, knew all, and knew best—that was committed to the perfection of people and salvation of the planet. The applause continued until she raised her hands and clasped them together in gratitude.

"Thank you," she said. "Now, let me tell you about my idea."

ACKNOWLEDGMENTS

Thanks to these friends for crucial assistance at pivotal times: Kitania Folk, Thom Unterburger, Frank Uhle, Zach London, Kathy Senello, John Warner, Amy Schmitz, Campbell Campbell (courageous human), Cameron Finch, Felicia Wong (most incisive of forest rangers), Mokhtar Alkhanshali, Hannah Rose Neuhauser, Jenny Traig, Davis Mendez, Anne McPeak, John McMurtrie, Lindsay Williams, Deb Klein, Duncan at Freisens, Em-J Staples, Jessica Hische (yes logo), Sarah Stewart Taylor, Tom Barbash, Nancy and John Cassidy, all of our cover-artist co-conspirators, and Eve Weinsheimer.

The McSweeney's staff, we happy few: Sunra Thompson, Claire Boyle, Eric Cromie, Dan Weiss, Annie Dills, Alvaro Villanueva, and Chris Monks. Thank you. And thank you Lucy Huber and Brian Christian for your timely expertise.

Thank you as always to Andrew Wylie, for twenty years my partner. Thank you to Luke Ingram,

Jeff Posternak, and all at the Wylie Agency. My friends at Knopf and Penguin Random House have been so patient and tolerant and flexible. Thank you to the forthright and bold Reagan Arthur, and to John Freeman, champion of this book and all books. Thanks also to Maya Mavjee, James Meader, Jenny Jackson and Julie Ertl. At the very brave and mischievous Baker & Taylor Publisher Services, gratitude goes to Jeff Tegge, Mark Hillesheim, Dan Verdick, Matthew Warner, and Claire Holloway.

A big salute to all the independent bookstores who fight every day to stay alive in a world that loves monopolies. And to the people who keep these independent entities alive by never forgetting the dim dystopian specter of a world without actual bookstores inhabited by actual humans who actually read books.

Speaking of: this book would not have made it into the world without the care and faith and editing and unflagging enthusiasm of Amanda Uhle, courageous publisher, and Amy Sumerton, unparalleled editor. Thank you, dear friends.

And with limitless love to my family.

ABOUT THE AUTHOR

Dave Eggers is the author of many books, among them **The Circle**—the companion to the book you are holding—and also **The Monk of Mokha, A Hologram for the King, What Is the What,** and **The Museum of Rain.** He is a cofounder of 826 National, a network of youth writing centers, and Voice of Witness, an oral history book series that illuminates the stories of those impacted by human rights crises. He has been a finalist for the Pulitzer Prize, the National Book Award, and the National Book Critics Circle Award, and is the recipient of the Dayton Literary Peace Prize and the American Book Award. He has attended the JetPack Aviation academy in Moorpark, California, but is not yet certified to fly off-tether. Born in Boston and raised in Illinois, he has now lived in the San Francisco Bay Area for three decades. He and his family often consider leaving, but they do not leave.

www.daveeggers.net